WARRIORS OF THE APOCALYPSE

BOOK ONE

ANTHONY GIANGREGORIO

Copyright © 2012 Anthony Giangregorio
ISBN Softcover ISBN 13: 978-1-61199-048-5   ISBN 10: 1-611990-48-3
All rights reserved.
Open Casket Press is an imprint of Living Dead Press
ww.livingdeadpress.com

This book was printed in the United States of America.
For more info on obtaining additional copies of this book, contact:
www.opencasketpress.com
Visit the author on Facebook

PRELUDE

The day of World War 3 began as any other day. That is until bombs began falling from the sky.

In the blink of an eye, the world we knew was gone, replaced by vast sections of radiation and nuclear fire. EMP pulses knocked out all radio and television frequencies in seconds, thus preventing further communications. The population of the world found itself blind, deaf and burning.

Major cities in the United States had been decimated, leaving behind massive craters of twisted metal, smoldering steel, and charred corpses. Even places that served no purpose in destroying were hit, thanks to faulty weapon's guidance.

But despite this, the entire planet was not laid waste to become nothing but barren landscape as scientists once assumed.

Pockets of refugees still existed, and due to the shifting winds, the radioactive fallout wasn't as bad as predicted.

But the civilized world was gone, in that there was no doubt.

After the initial confusion of that first day, the survivors that had escaped the worst of the bombs began to crawl out of their holes, to face a new world. In shock and overwhelmed, many simply fell to their knees and cried.

But others saw opportunity, and began to prey on their fellow survivors.

There were no longer local authorities to keep the peace, and though some tried to maintain order, it was soon clear this would be impossible.

In too short a time, the things every human relied on began to run out: food, water, electrical power, medicines to treat the sick and dying, all gone—all exhausted.

Slowly and inexorably, the survivors came to the realization that these items were gone and there would not be any more for the foreseeable future, well, not for their future anyway. There would be no international relief, for other countries were suffering just as bad, or worse.

As each man and woman came to grips with their new reality, some went mad while others simply killed themselves…and then there were the ones that turned opportunistic.

They became the worst of all, capturing men and women and making them slaves to help them rebuild their small but growing empires or to use the survivors as cattle to practice cannibalism, which began to rise thanks to a lack of food.

The thin veneer of civilization had finally been peeled away, to show the true face of humanity: that of a greedy, selfish, and uncaring animal that was both malicious and cruel.

America had gone insane, where the law of the land was ruled with a gun, and kill or be killed was the mantra sung over campfires.

Out of the ashes of this decimated country, came a man who refused to accept this reality, who still believed in honor and kindness. Though not afraid to kill, he would show mercy when necessary and still believed in the America of old.

Together, Hank Summers, with his three companions, Laurie, Carl and Stewart, traveled the blighted nukescape in search of a home, for a place where the acid rains didn't fall or the radiation lepers didn't exist, where slavery and cannibalism was abhorred.

In a world gone to hell, only a special breed of human could survive—a new warrior for a new age.

The age of the apocalypse.

BRAVE NEW WORLD

"What do you think?"

"Looks empty."

"We goin' in?"

"Don't think we have much of a choice."

"No, not really. We're almost out of food and water."

"Tell me somthin' I don't know."

"So when do you want to go?"

"No time like the present." After putting down the binoculars, Hank Summers picked up his two-way radio. He clicked it twice, alerting the other three team members he was calling them.

"Go for Stewart," a voice crackled through the radio in response to the click.

"We're goin' in," Hank said curtly. "Get ready."

"Got it," Stewart Matheson said and signed off.

"Laurie here, I heard that, ready when you are, Hank," Laurie Collins said through the radio.

Hank nodded slightly to himself, then said, "Take it slow, Laurie, we don't know if it's really empty."

"Will do, out."

Hank turned to the man beside him as they lay on the outcropping of debris, the man nodding back. "Ready when you are, Hank. Let's go see what's in there."

Hank said nothing to his second-in-command. Carl Rivers had traveled with him for more than two years now, ever since the bombs first fell and wiped humanity back to the dark ages, only this time mankind had firearms.

"No heroics, Carl. We get in, check it out, then go, you hear me?"

Carl put on his best smile, his yellow teeth flashing in the harsh sun. "Hey, man, it's me!"

"Yeah, that's what I'm afraid of," Hank grunted in response. He clicked the radio three times, paused, then twice more; the signal to begin the approach to the building two hundred feet away.

Hank and Carl crawled down the debris, ignoring the charred remains of bodies long dead, of corpses fried in the blasts. As he descended, his foot kicked free a doll's head, the plastic face scorched and melted. The head rolled down the hill and came to a stop at the bottom.

Hank finished his descent, and when he came down on the ground, his right boot crushed the head, the plastic now brittle after being exposed to the intense heat of two years of sun damage thanks to not having a decent ozone layer.

He checked the radiation badge on his lapel, making sure it was still in the green. The small needle hovered on the edge of green to yellow, which meant the area was hot, but not so hot his team couldn't stay for an hour and see what they could scavenge. Red would have meant death.

Carl dropped down next to him, landing with the grace of an ox. Hank smiled at his friend but said nothing. Hank quickly checked his weapons as he slowly made his way around the debris pile, Carl right behind him.

Hank was a walking arsenal of death. His hand went down to the butt of his handgun, a SIG-Sauer P-226 9mm pistol. On his left hip he carried a panga with a sixteen inch blade. To round out his armaments, a Heckler & Koch G-12 automatic rifle and fifty caseless rounds of 4.7mm was slung over his left shoulder. A web belt adorned his powerful chest, three grenades remaining. Two were flash and one was frag, meaning fragmentation.

In the new world of fire and death, you could never have enough firepower.

Even without the guns, Hank was a formidable man. As if he was bred for the new world, he was tall, strong and hard, his skin bronzed from exposure to the sun. He had adapted quickly when the world turned into fire, and when he and others like him emerged from bomb shelters, a new world awaited them, one of lawlessness and murder, where only the strength of man's will and the strength of his hand would decide his fate. And of course, the size of his gun.

Carl walked behind Hank while checking his own weapons. Draped over his shoulder, the Mini-Uzi swung back and forth, and holstered on his right hip was a big Steyr AUG 5.6 mm pistol. He carried one flash grenade on his web belt, the rest used more than a week ago when they had been ambushed by raiders. The raiders had come to regret their decision to attack the four warriors.

Where Hank was over six feet with broad shoulders and skin the color of a setting sun, Carl was small, barely over five feet with skin as white as a sheet, despite his constant exposure to the sun. He was thin and wiry and wore a battered Yankees baseball cap on his thirty-five year old head. But what he didn't have in muscle and strength, he made up for with his skill as a marksman and his ingenuity. Many men had died finding this out after underestimating the small warrior.

Across the street was a high school. The west side of the school was nothing but rubble, both the first and second floors blown in. But the rest of the structure looked intact. To the left of the building was the school parking lot. It was full of cars and trucks, each one now covered with inches of dust and dirt, the paint fading after two years of being exposed to the harsh sun.

Overhead, the sky was the color of brass, a burnt orange with a few shifting purple clouds, now tainted due to the radiation. When the sun set, the sky became a kaleidoscope of color, and when the sun was finally down for the night, the darkness was so complete it was like crawling into a closet and making sure no light could enter. Absolute darkness, as the moon and starlight were prevented from reaching Earth thanks to the cloud cover that never left and only occasionally allowed the moonlight to peek through.

Hank caught movement out of the corner of his eye and his hand went for his SIG, but he slowed when he saw it was Laurie making her way towards him.

She was tall and statuesque, looking more like a model than a modern day warrior. She wore all black leather, and her cowboy boots were tipped with silver points—weapons in their own right—and a slim dagger road her hip. In her right hand, she carried a small, pearl-handled PPK .22 pistol. Though the gun didn't have much stopping power, it was all she had ever needed. She was an excellent shot and could put out a man's eye easily, the .22 killing the target instantly as the small round sliced the target's brain to mush.

Hank let his eyes roam over her luscious body as she approached, his arousal growing despite the danger they were in. He couldn't help it. Laurie was his lover and just thinking about touching her soft flesh and kissing her warm lips made him wish it was night and they had made camp.

It had been more than a week since the last time they made love. To be so vulnerable, they needed to be someplace safe, and have some alone time, and for the past two weeks the four warriors had been moving, sleeping light and making a cold camp.

As she joined Carl and Hank, she smiled slightly, then moved to his side, her eyes always scanning her surroundings. "Hey, lover, we goin' in or what?" she asked.

"Yeah, where's Stewart? Once he gets here we go in," Hank replied.

"I'm here, I'm here," came a voice tinted with age. Hank knew the voice instantly and he didn't draw his gun. Turning to the side, he saw Stewart walking up to them. He had been covering the south side, and when given the signal to return, he had done so, only he was a little slower due to his age.

Stewart was a large contrast to Hank.

Where Hank was in his late forties, Stewart was in his late sixties with long white hair and a wooden cane. But the cane wasn't just for walking. Inside its handle was a small sword, which could be used in a pinch.

Stewart carried a gray Heckler & Koch submachine gun with a drum mag of fifty rounds of 9mm with a built in silencer, and a .45 pistol on his hip.

While not the most skilled warrior, Stewart Matheson was highly intelligent and had been an engineer in his former life. His intelligence more than made up for his lack of strength and he was a valuable part of the team.

"These old bones don't move as fast as they used to," Stewart said as he hobbled over the debris to reach the others.

Hank let a slight grin crease his lips as the old man rushed to reach them. Then it was washed away and only the hardened warrior remained. "All right, so it looks deserted, as we all know, but the odds of the only building in the area that's still standing not being inhabited is slim to none," Hank said.

"But you want to go in, right?" Carl asked.

Hank nodded. "Yeah, a school has a cafeteria. There may be some canned goods inside. It's a long shot, I know, but if we don't find some food and water soon, we'll be eatin' dirt for dinner tonight and drinkin' our own piss." He studied the school one more time. "Let's move out. I don't want to be out here in the open any longer than necessary, it's asking for trouble."

The four warriors spread out so as not to make an easy target if someone tried to take a shot at them, and they made their way across the street and into the school parking lot.

As they walked, detritus of a fallen society blew about their feet. Newspaper brittle and yellow, paper cups and McDonalds wrappers, along with Styrofoam coffee cups and food containers. All of it would be around long after man was wiped from the Earth.

Halfway to the school, Laurie slowed to inspect a wrecked car sitting at an odd angle to the white parking lines.

It was a Toyota, the once blue finish now pitted and scarred by wind and acid rain. All the windows were shattered, the tires flat, and as she peered inside the interior, she found a dried up corpse behind the steering wheel.

By the long straggly hair stuck to the skull and the purse on the seat next to the body, it was apparent the desiccated skeleton was a woman. Laurie reached inside the car and pulled out the purse, dumping its contents onto the hood of the car. As she did this, the others kept a close watch on the school and anywhere an attacker might hide. So far, all was quiet, which was the way Hank liked it.

A few of the items in the purse rolled off the hood of the car to land in the dust. Laurie ignored them. As she picked through the items with the muzzle of her .22, she found a wallet. Laying her gun on the hood, she picked up the wallet and examined it. Inside was a faded picture of a beautiful blonde woman with a man and two children. All wore smiles and the photo looked as if it had been taken at an amusement park. The sky was a deep blue and the sun was bright and cheerful behind the four smiling people, the family unaware of the coming future when the picture was snapped.

Laurie tossed the wallet away, wondering if the sky would ever be that blue again; at least in her lifetime. She looked back at the corpse, trying to imagine how the grinning skull had once been the pretty woman in the photo. As she watched the corpse, a cockroach slid out of the eye socket and crawled down the face and slipped into the gaping mouth.

Laurie had to look away then. She was a hardened warrior of the new world but even a sight such as the one she saw was sometimes too hard to take.

Hank moved up next to her. "You done sightseeing?" he asked curtly.

She picked up her .22 and nodded.

"Good," he said, "let's keep moving."

Carl and Stewart slid to the side some more to keep distance from the others as the four warriors approached the double doors to the school.

They were made of thick safety glass, and though pitted by blowing sand from all the wild storms Mother Nature now heaped upon the Earth, and the surface becoming frosted in places from the constant blasting, the glass was in good condition.

Carl was first to reach the doors and he pulled on the handle to the right one. His left eyebrow went up when the door opened easily.

"Now that ain't right," Carl said under his breath.

"Why's that?" Stewart asked.

Carl gestured to the intact doors. "Simple. I can't believe that no one's found this place and that the doors would just be open like this."

"Shit, Carl, we watched this place for almost half a day and there's been no sign of movement inside or outside," Stewart said. "The building sure as hell seems empty."

"Looks can be deceiving," Laurie added as she joined them at the doors. "People don't need to leave every day when they got a good place to hide."

Hank was behind her, his eyes on their back trail. If someone tried to sneak up on them, he would see them before they made three steps in their direction.

He was about to turn around and follow the others inside when he caught movement on his left.

Turning to face the threat, his eyes immediately took in the five shapes scurrying across the ground like marsupials. Each figure was so bent over that they had to use their arms as well as their legs to propel them across the ground. From a distance, the shapes looked like animals, but Hank knew what they were immediately.

The closest word to use as a description would be mutant, but the word still didn't fully explain what the figures were exactly.

For they weren't mutants in the sense of the word that they had been born disfigured. Instead, the mutants of the new world were simply men and women who had stayed in the hot zones, despite the deadly radiation.

While most died, rotting from the inside out, many continued a tortured existence, and some had managed to thrive, despite losing all their hair, boils and pus now covering their bodies from head to toe as the radiation ate them from within. They all had the look of terminal burn victims, or lepers, their hands scarred and cracked with deep fissures, their faces blistered, tongues swollen and black as they poked through cracked lips.

The radiation had played hell with their bodies and peeling skin wasn't uncommon and many had withered, dried limbs, some cut off when they had turned gangrenous. Other limbs hung by their sides, useless, as well as legs were dragged behind them as they hobbled using old canes or wooden clubs for crutches. Scalps were covered with odd tufts of hair, bald spots prevalent from where hair had fallen out. Their eyes were twisted and warped, most looking as if they had severe cataracts.

It was rare for a mutant to carry a gun, the most sophisticated weapons they used were usually knives, spears or swords. The main reason was the same radiation that was changing and slowly killing them, also fried their brains so that they only had a rudimentary intelligence. Like a pack of wild animals, they hunted their prey and fed once it was taken down, usually not bothering to cook it, becoming cannibals.

The Heckler & Koch G-12 rifle had many features that made it an excellent weapon to have. The laser sight made the weapon extremely accurate over a significant distance by day as well as by night thanks to the infrared laser nightscope.

Hank had read once before the world burned why the three round burst, a main feature on the G-12, had been added to the rifle. The article had said that on full automatic, most rifles, such as the M-16, tended to begin to rise after the first four or five rounds were fired, making the rifle difficult to control as well as keep the gun aimed at the target. But as in the case of the G-12, by firing short, three round bursts, the cycle was broken before the muzzle would rise and the weapon was easier to control.

As Hank spun to face his attackers, his hand was already wrapping around the pistol-grip trigger, firing from the hip, though it wasn't recommended by any of the manuals for the weapon. Though he had owned the weapon for more than a year, he still found it odd not to be surrounded by spent brass as it dropped by his feet when he fired. The nitrocellulose caseless cartridges were used up instantly as the rifle discharged the 4.7mm rounds.

Sounding like a single report, the first, three-round burst sprayed concrete a foot from the first mutant, spraying the figure's legs with shrapnel. The creature that was once human let out a yelp in pain, but continued forward, ignoring the small flecks of blood adorning its legs.

The second tri-burst stitched a mutant from groin to chest, blowing large holes out the back of its body. The deformed human took three more running steps before falling flat on its burnt face. Swiveling to the left, Hank sent another barrage of death into another attacking shape. The burst was high, the first round striking a misshapen woman in the neck, the other two bullets impacting directly in her face. The back of her skull blew out in a glorious spray of bone and brain matter. Tripping on her feet, she tumbled to the pavement, her limbs twitching as her nervous system shut down.

By now the other warriors were joining in the slaughter. Carl was shooting before he had fully turned to face the mutants, his Mini-Uzi spitting death and taking down a radiation leper that had tried to go wide and come at them from the side. The bullets stitched the deformed man from groin to neck, then back again, Carl making a figure eight in blood and gore. The man danced a jig as his chest was torn to ribbons and he fell heavily to the ground, his insides spilling onto the warm pavement.

Laurie was slower on the draw but it was a purposeful act. When she spun to see the attackers, she raised her .22, took careful aim on a bearded mutant with only one eye, and shot the man in his remaining orb. The round wasn't strong enough to blow out the rear of his skull, but it bounced around for a few seconds, mashing the brain into porridge. The man took on a look of confusion, as if he was trying to understand why his brain wasn't functioning, before he fell face first into the dust and dirt covering the ground.

That left two more to go and neither mutant was so much as the slightest bit intimidated by the warriors' superior firepower.

Both charged forward, each waving a wicked looking blade before them.

Hank shot the closest one in the face with another tri-burst, the high velocity fire disintegrating the scarred visage and turning it to mush, practically blowing the head clean off the shoulders. The body made a few more running steps in Hank's direction, but the battle-hardened man sidestepped the body as it bounced off the doors to the school and flopped on the ground.

There was only one mutant remaining and this was the one Hank had shot at but missed, only peppering its legs with shrapnel. The mutant was charging at Stewart, a mad gleam in its eyes as the stained blade of dried blood prepared to split Stewart's head in two.

But Stewart was ready for the assault, and as the attacker came within five feet of him, the old warrior sprayed the man with his Heckler & Koch submachine gun, a dozen rounds chewing into the torso and making it resemble hamburger more than a man. The body twisted sideways in death and fell to the ground, the man screaming in pain. Though peppered with bullets, none were killing shots.

Laurie silenced the man's screams with a well placed bullet directly in his open mouth. The .22 round bounced off a rear molar and was deflected up into his brain. The bullet punctured the brain stem, killing the man instantly. Like a light switch, the screams ceased and with the exception of the gunshots echoing on the wind, the parking lot grew quiet.

"Status check!" Hank yelled as he scanned the area for more attackers. It looked quiet, nothing moving, except the first of the flies that were attracted to the spilt blood.

"I'm fine," Laurie said as she holstered her gun.

"Me too," Carl answered, as he took a step closer to one of the deformed attackers to examine his handiwork.

"I'm fine, too, Hank. No injuries," Stewart said. "And how could I when we never let the filthy bastards get that close?"

"True enough, Stewart, but still, one might have gotten off a throwing knife before getting taken down." Hank repositioned his rifle so he could open the glass doors to the school. "All right, the excitement's over. Let's get inside and see what we can find."

The others nodded in agreement and Hank pulled open the doors, peering into the gloom of a long hallway. The wind swirled inside, blowing the dust on the floor to the side, making small sand dunes. With the rifle leading the way, Hank entered the building, the others right behind him.

The air smelled old, musty, but there was no sign of living humans. The fragrance of unwashed bodies, cooking meat or feces was nowhere to be detected.

With Hank in the lead, the four warriors entered the first corridor and fanned out, slowly moving from one door to the next, a series of them staggered on both sides of the hallway. Each door had a number and residue of where tape had been holding a picture or paper on the door. But now they had disappeared, perhaps part of the scattered paper and debris littering the hallway like dried leaves on an autumn day.

"Spread out and search the classrooms and we'll meet up at the far end," Hank said as he went to a door and opened it, the doorknob turning easily.

The others did as ordered, each moving to another door that led to an adjoining classroom.

Hank normally kept them together, but as the school seemed abandoned, the dust on the floor undisturbed by fresh footprints, he felt it would save time to split up. Better they looked separately to speed up the search.

Hank stepped into a classroom, his SIG- Sauer leading the way. The room was empty but there was telltale evidence of at least one killing, perhaps two within.

On the chalkboard on the far corner, the last day's math still etched in white chalk, were the dried remains of brain and bone matter. The streaks and bits of gristle were old and now a dull brown. Death had visited this room, but the bodies were long gone now, nothing but a few dried puddles on the floor below the chalkboard.

He checked the rest of the room quickly, and with one last glimpse at the brain matter, left the room to search the next.

When Hank entered the hallway, he spotted Laurie coming out of another room at the far end. Her face was bleach white and he was about to call out to her and ask if she was all right when she looked up and waved for him to join her.

As Hank strolled down the hallway, Stewart and Carl exited their classrooms, informing Hank they had found nothing of use. Laurie called to them as well.

"I found something," she said. "But I think it would be easier to show you than tell you."

A few seconds later, the group was together once more.

"Go 'head, Hank, just go inside, there's no danger, just…" she trailed off and Hank couldn't remember the last time he'd seen her so upset.

"Carl, you and Stewart stay out here with her," he said. "I'll call you when it's clear." He opened the door and stepped inside, his SIG leading the way out of habit.

The room was small for a classroom, all the chairs and desks piled into a corner— some upside down, others sideways—to make more room. The far corner of the room, near the three windows, was covered with soot and a smoke-encrusted ceiling from the residue of the fire that had burned for weeks by the amount of soot collected. Charred remnants of Math and History books littered the extinct fire and small animal bones could be seen scattered around the perimeter.

But that wasn't what had caused Laurie distress, Hank knew, as his eyes scanned the rest of the room. As he looked into the farthest corner, he knew immediately what he was seeing and his arm went to his nose and mouth, covering them so as not to breathe what might be deadly, foul air.

After the bombs dropped, for the next six months, nuclear winter had wrapped the Earth in darkness. But contrary to what scientists had predicted, the ash and soot burned off quicker than expected and the sun touched the Earth once more a half year later.

But when man crawled out from his hiding places, he found disease had run rampant; mostly due to the millions of corpses not buried. Now, simple ailments once cured by penicillin were now on the loose again. Hank had seen an entire town wiped out by symptoms harking back to the Black Plague. Cholera and a hundred more diseases were now finishing off what the bombs left of the population.

Hank had come upon small campsites with a dozen or more people. But they had all been dead, most looking as if they had died hard through vomiting and bleeding of the orifices.

That was what Hank now saw in the corner of the school room.

There had to be twenty corpses, more than half under fifteen years of age. There appeared to be more men than women but some were so desiccated it was hard to tell what gender the body once was.

The bodies were laid out in rows, the feet pointed to the far wall, their arms flat out along the sides of them, legs pressed together.

One corpse was lying in the opposite corner, its right leg separated near the hip, its head detached and resting on its lap. Another was in a kneeling position, as if the person was about to pray and had then become tired and had fallen asleep with its forehead on the floor.

The charnel-house smell of death was barely noticeable, and after another few seconds of taking in the scene, Hank lowered his arm from his face, deciding whatever had killed these people had long since departed. As long as none of the warriors touched the bodies and risked contamination, they should be fine.

With his heartbeat slowing a little now that the initial danger was over, Hank stepped a little closer and studied the bodies some more. By the look of the old clothing, the people had been poor, scrabbling to live day to day. There were a few knives scattered about the corpses but they were of poor quality.

The flesh had all but melted off the bones, leaving it taut and leathery. A few wore a grinning rictus of death, their teeth large and yellowed from exposure. The eyes were gone from the faces, the first to go along with the insides of the nose and mouth, then the lobes of the ears. After that any of the remaining juicy parts of the bodies would have begun to rot away. In a few places, the skin had stretched to the point of cracking, allowing the cracked bone to be exposed.

Hank saw one of the corpses begin to move and he shifted his stance, his SIG-Sauer ready to send the creature to Hell. He had a vision of the corpse rising, standing on skeletal legs, its death mask glaring at him. It would open its mouth and the smell of rot and decay would pour forth, and before the creature could so much as step forward, Hank would put a bullet in its bleached white skull, blowing it into a thousand shards of bone.

As all this flitted through his mind, he saw a rat poke its head out of the corpse's chest and run off into the corner where the desk and chairs were stacked. A dried piece of muscle, now similar to beef jerky, was in its mouth.

Hank held his fire, not wanting to waste a bullet on the filthy rodent.

He went back to studying the corpses.

He could see they had died close together, probably within hours or days of one another. He knew this because if only one or two had died, the others would have moved on, but here, they had all stayed together and had laid each body out after death.

Hank was able to take in what had happened in an instant. When whatever plague had run through these people, they had died off fast and it had been the two bodies off to the side that had been the last to go. The one with its skull detached had died second to the last and had arranged the bodies after each victim died, and the one kneeling over in prayer had been the last to go, perhaps praying he would join his friends and family in the afterlife.

With no more to see, Hank exited the room, then let Carl and Stewart examine the room as well. When they were through, and with everyone shaking their heads at the futility of it all, Carl closed the door behind him—the last to exit the room—and they moved down the hallway, leaving the corpses alone once more.

The school was big, bigger than it looked from the outside, and it took another half hour for them to search the rest of the hallways.

That left only the cafeteria and the gym to be searched. The obvious place to go first was the cafeteria, so they followed the signs on the walls and soon were on the lowest level of the building.

As they entered the cafeteria, their footsteps caused small insects and rats to scurry away.

Hank was on point, with Laurie and Stewart in the middle, and Carl bringing up the rear, each watching the shadows for signs of danger.

"Looks empty," Stewart said as he pushed a lunch tray to the side where it sat on one of the tables in the center of the large room. Spiderwebs were everywhere, draping the rafters in white gossamer.

"Just 'cause no one can be seen doesn't mean it's empty in here," Hank replied. He gestured to the lunch line with empty steam tables, the kitchen beyond wreathed in darkness. "Over there, watch it, triple red, people."

They skirted the rest of the tables and moved to the lunch line. Here, the red tiles of the kitchen took over from the white linoleum of the cafeteria. Hank had holstered his SIG-Sauer and had his Heckler & Koch G-12 automatic rifle at waist level. If there was something in the shadows, the 4.7mm rounds would blow it back to the Hell it came from.

The four friends stopped at the entrance to the kitchen and peered into the shadows. It was all but pitch dark, and all knew before they could go further there would have to be some light added to the situation. It was Laurie who provided the illumination. Reaching into the small rucksack on her hip, she pulled out a small, hand crank flashlight. Turning the lever a few times, a dim beam began to push back the darkness, and after a few more cranks, a steady beam filled the kitchen.

"And the Lord said let there be light," Stewart said as he watched from the side.

Hank spit and shrugged at Stewart. "Can't say I care too much what the Lord says these days, Stewart, not after the shit he let us get into."

Stewart smiled slightly. "Ah, but Hank, it's not God who dropped the bombs, but man who did it. But if it makes it easier for you to accept our reality, then blame away. He's a tough Lord, he can take it."

"Don't matter what you do, ain't no God, it's all horseshit," Carl said silently to no one in particular as he lifted his baseball cap and wiped his forehead with his sleeve.

"Ah, Carl," Stewart said. "Even if you don't believe in Him, He believes in you."

Carl replied by hawking up a loogie and letting it fly.

"Over there, the freezer and walk-in," Hank said, making Laurie point to the corner of the kitchen. The light beam went up to the wall and the four friends walked closer, the beam bouncing with each step Laurie took. The heels of her boots clicked on the tile floor, the silver points reflecting what little light touched them.

"Carl, check out those cabinets over there, and Stewart, go see if there's a back room for canned goods," Hank told them as he ushered Laurie to follow him to the freezer and walk-in chambers. "We'll check these out."

Carl and Stewart mumbled acknowledgments and headed off, their footsteps fading into the darkness. Each man drew a small penlight and used it to search deeper into the kitchen.

Laurie stopped at the tall, stainless steel doors of the freezer and walk-in. "What do you think?"

"Go 'head and open the walk-in," he said as he pulled his SIG from its holster. "Probably nothin' but rottin' food in there anyway."

She nodded curtly, turned, and gazed down at the handle. There was no padlock on it and as she wrapped her hand around it, she used the tip of the flashlight to tap on the door. She waited for ten seconds, pressing her ear to the cool surface. Finally, she looked back at Hank and said, "Nothing, all quiet."

He nodded for her to continue, expecting as much.

She pulled on the handle and the door popped open. A horrendous smell erupted, causing both warriors to fall back. But after a few seconds they were able to peer inside the walk-in with watery eyes.

Laurie played the beam over the mold-covered mush that had once been vegetables and eggs, as well as cheese and containers of leftovers. Flies buzzed and flew into the kitchen, escaping the walk-in, and maggots could be seen along with cockroaches, but there weren't very many as the walk-in was a sealed room—a sealed habitat—and over time most had died out only to be followed by the next generation of vermin.

"Close it, quick," Hank gasped through gritted teeth as Laurie slammed the door closed, sealing off the foulness.

"Well, what did you expect to find? Caviar and quails eggs, all in perfect condition and ready to be eaten?" Laurie asked as she wiped the tears from her eyes.

"Yeah, I know, but we had to look," Hank said.

Carl and Stewart returned empty handed and Carl waved his hand in front of his face at the miasma hanging in the air. "Damn, who farted?"

"Not funny, Carl," Hank frowned. "All right, fine, the walk-in's a bust. Any luck with the cabinets or a back room?"

Carl shook his head. "Nah, all empty."

"Nothing in the back room, either. It's been picked clean," Stewart said. "Though I did find this." He tossed Hank a small can of sardines.

The warrior chuckled and tossed it back. "Any port in a storm I guess. It's better than nothing," Hank said.

Stewart caught the small can and slid it into his backpack while Hank turned to the freezer, the padlock still attached to the pull handle of the door.

With a smooth motion, he pulled his SIG-Sauer and shot the lock off, the pieces of metal falling away to slide under a nearby table. "All right, let's check in there, and if it's a loss we can move on. We've wasted too much damn time in here as it is."

Laurie went to the door and placed her ear against it, her left hand on the handle, ready to pull it open. Carl, Stewart and Hank stood behind her, their weapons drawn in ready. Though this might seem foolish to some, after all, the freezer had been locked, only a cautious man lived to see the next sunrise.

"I can hear something in there, Hank. Sounds like scratching," Laurie said with her ear pressed against the door.

"Probably rats," Carl stated. "That doesn't sound too good."

"Yeah, probably just rotting meat like the food in the walk-in was, but we have to check for sure. For all we know, it's full to the ceiling with canned goods. We can't walk away without knowing for sure," Hank said as he looked at Carl.

Carl nodded, knowing exactly what Hank meant.

A few weeks ago, the four warriors had been checking through the rubble of a bank. They had come up with nothing worth keeping and were about to leave when Carl had spotted a small door at the back of the teller's stations. When he went to it, figuring it was nothing more than a small closet filled with stationary, he found a stockpile of junk food. Chips, candy bars and crackers, piled high to the ceiling. It had been the find of a lifetime and they had taken every morsel with them.

So they all now knew the value of checking under every rock and searching every piece of rubble.

"Shall we get this over with?" Stewart asked as he shifted his HK in his hands. He was an odd sight, looking more like a frazzled professor than a soldier, and the submachine gun in his hands only added to the strange picture.

"Yeah, Stewart, we will," Hank said and then nodded to Laurie and said, "Open it, baby."

Laurie flashed acknowledgement with her eyes, stepped back from the door, and pulled on the handle. There was a soft snap as the lock disengaged after more than two years of being sealed, and there was a hiss of the air inside escaping as it was sucked into the kitchen like oxygen into the vacuum of space.

Though all four warriors had their weapons drawn, in truth none were ready to use them. They knew it was impossible for anything to have existed inside the locked freezer for almost two years since the bombs fell.

And in a way they were right.

Nothing large enough to threaten them that a bullet couldn't stop was inside the freezer, but there was life.

As Laurie cracked the door, it was quickly forced open by an unimaginable wave of cockroaches and beetles. A living sea of insects poured out of the freezer, swarming around the warriors' combat boots to begin burrowing under their pants.

"What the fuck!" Hank yelled as he fell back at the onslaught of the creatures, his eyes trying to take in the awesome sight.

"Jesus Christ, look at 'em all!" Carl yelled as he jumped away from the tide, spraying the insects with rounds from his Uzi that did nothing but become lost in the quagmire of glistening shells.

"Oh, God, they're everywhere!" Laurie screamed as she began brushing them off her legs. They were swarming up her body so fast it was like she wore a living second set of clothing. She brushed at them with her hands, a few sticking to her arms and to her knuckles.

On top of the onslaught of cockroaches, there was an over-whelming smell of rotting meat mixed with mold and mildew. Hank was able to see into the gloom of the freezer and what he saw made his stomach roil within him.

The lumps of meat that were once steak, lamb and pork that had sat on the shelves of the freezer had long been devoured, leaving bubbling piles of feces that fed more cockroaches. Unknown to the warriors, a small hole in the ventilation allowed the cockroaches to come and go and they had made the freezer a massive hive, thousands of generations living and dying inside while others went out for food and to grow the colony.

Before Laurie had opened the freezer door, the cockroaches had filled the small room to the height of three feet, a swirling mass of antennae and shells, seething and roiling as they fought to survive.

And now the colony was free to continue into the kitchen and to envelop the four hapless warriors. Stewart was spraying the wave with his submachine gun, ripping hundreds of the roaches to shreds, but there were so many it was like spitting into the ocean.

"What do we do?" Carl yelled as he slapped at his pants, the little bumps under the material showing where the insects were crawling on his flesh.

Hank slapped at a dozen on his left arm and spun around, his eyes going to the nearby stainless steel tables. Already the cockroaches were more than ankle deep with even more spilling forth. It was a black tide of undulating life that threatened to take them all down if one was unlucky enough to slip and fall.

"The tables! Get on the tables!" Hank yelled as he turned and lunged for the nearest one. As soon as he took a step, he felt himself falling, his boots slipping on the slick shells. But at the last second he recovered and continued forward, glancing over his right shoulder to see the others following him.

No one fired their weapons, as it was a hopeless action. No amount of bullets could ever slow the unrelenting sea of life that shifted in the shadows, only Laurie's flashlight illuminating the floor of the kitchen.

Carl cried out and almost fell but Stewart shoved the man in the back with his cane, halting Carl's descent. Carl righted himself and moved forward, reaching a table and climbing onto it. As soon as he was on it, he slapped at a few more cockroaches and beetles on his legs and reached out for Stewart. The older man let his cane be his lifeline, and with Carl holding the end, Stewart was pulled onto the table. As the two men stood on the steel surface, each man began slapping the other's shoulders, then spinning around so the other could brush off the cockroaches.

Carl was dancing a jig as the insects slid under his clothing and he looked like a madman, punching himself repeatedly. But each blow silenced a small intruder and the wetness of the crushed carapaces was proof he was stopping them cold.

Hank had climbed onto another table and he turned and grabbed Laurie who was behind him. She, too, almost fell but at the last second, as she went tumbling head first, Hank managed to lean over and grab her by her flowing hair. She yelled as the hair was all but ripped out by the roots but it stopped her forward fall. Hank gently pulled her up and only her slight frame allowed her hair to support her. Once she was up, he grabbed her right hand and pulled her to him. The two lovers quickly went to work wiping, slapping and brushing the vile insects off them, Laurie's face one of utter revulsion as she felt them slide under her outfit. She had a vision of them getting between her legs, crawling deep inside her to lay their eggs. The shiver she felt was one that would be hard to shake, and she gritted her perfect teeth, squeezed her legs tightly together, and continued to kill as many of them that were still on her.

"What the hell are we going to do?" Stewart yelled as he slapped more of the insects off his body, as well as off Carl's shoulders and back. "They're everywhere! We try and make a run for it and they'll be all over us!"

Hank knew the older man was right. They had just barely managed to reach the stainless steel tables and even then they were becoming covered. The second they stepped onto the floor, the cockroaches would swarm them. A crackling sound, similar to dry leaves being crushed by heavy feet filled the kitchen, the sound of a million carapaces rubbing together. He knew they were in trouble.

"I'd kill for a flame thrower right about now," Laurie cried out as she slapped a particularly large roach off her cheek. The insect had crawled up her like a small tiny Sherman tank, its legs sticking to her clothing.

Carl heard her comments and reached into his backpack, an idea forming. He pulled out a bottle of lighter fluid, one they used for campfires, and after brushing off a few roaches stuck to the container, he held it up so the others could see, only Laurie's flashlight illuminating him to the others.

"This might be what we need to clear a path!" Carl yelled as he popped the top off the plastic bottle.

"Do it, and hurry!" Hank yelled. The cockroaches were crawling up the legs of the tables and it was all the warriors could do to kick them back off. But with more rounding the tables' edges each second, in less than a minute there would be too many to stop.

Carl turned the bottle upside down and began to squeeze it, spraying the flammable fluid onto the floor. But the floor never saw a drop, just the roiling sea of miniscule bodies. When the bottle was empty, he tossed it into the wave and pulled out a book of matches. He lit one, then set the rest of the book alight; dropping it without fanfare into what he hoped was a saturated point in the cockroach sea.

Then luck or fate intervened and the flaming matches found a wet spot, immediately catching and spreading from one drop to another. Soon, the sea of roaches was burning quite well, the heat making the shells pop as the air inside the insects expanded.

At the same time, everywhere Laurie aimed her flashlight beam, the roaches shied away, not used to the bright light. Like an electric sweeper, each time she aimed it at a spot, the insects dispersed.

As more of the roaches exploded, it sounded like small squeals of pain, though Hank may have imagined it. With the crackling of the fire, soon other flammable parts of the kitchen began to catch, such as old rags and trash left to rot for more than twenty months. Rubber trash barrels melted and menus and recipes boxes burst into flames that then fell onto the floor to be lost among the insects.

Hank could see there wasn't enough flammable material in the kitchen to make the area a kill zone and they needed to move fast before the fires went out and the roaches regrouped.

They had a minute at most to make their play of escape before it closed like a steel trap. There were more stainless steel tables leading to the exit at the far end of the kitchen and Hank saw this as their best chance of escape. Gathering Laurie to him, he pointed to the next table a few feet away. "Jump!" he yelled at her and shoved her in the table's direction. She didn't argue, knowing from past experience to just go with whatever idea Hank had. There had been times when if she had taken a second to question his judgment, it would have ended her life and possibly the others' lives as well.

She made the leap easily, landing and sliding to the edge, but she didn't fall off. Hank was right behind her and he landed hard, the sound of his heavy military boots striking the table loud enough to override the simulated screams of the burning bugs.

Carl and Stewart saw what Hank was doing and they followed suit, each leapfrogging to another table.

Soon, the four warriors were making their way across the kitchen while the moving floor of insects burned and twisted in what seemed like human agony. In the light of the fire, the roaches seemed to take on one life, as if a hive mind had taken control of them. Hank saw this and tried not to think about it. Since the bombs had dropped, soaking radiation into the ground like a sponge, he had seen some unusual things. Insects and small animals lived short life spans so it wasn't unusual to have multiple generations come and go over the course of a two year period. In that time, mutations were occurring, changing once basic creatures into something only seen in horror movies of the past.

In less than two minutes the four friends reached the end of the kitchen. As Hank dropped down to the floor, he glanced over his shoulder one last time at the kitchen behind him, his eyes going to the area around the freezer.

The cockroaches and beetles were still massing, and there was already a small amount near where the four warriors stood. In seconds, where they stood would also be covered. Hank watched as the wave moved towards them, as if sensing they were there. He had no doubt if one of them had fallen and been consumed, they would have been suffocated and quickly devoured, miniscule bite by miniscule bite.

Crossing the room, Laurie opened the door at the end of the cafeteria and checked the gloom-filled hallway. Other than a few stripes of light filtering in through some cracks in the foundation, the hallway was lost in shadows.

She pulled her head back inside and nodded to the others that it was safe.

One at a time, they moved into the hallway, and when Hank was last, he slammed the door, thus closing off the kitchen and cafeteria from the rest of the school. As soon as the door sealed closed, he heard small scratching, as if seeds were being tossed at the door. A few of the smaller cockroaches crawled out from beneath the door and he stepped on them out of instinct.

"Come on, let's get the hell out of here," Hank said to the others as they turned and headed deeper into the school. "This entire place is turning into nothing but a waste of time."

"Unless you love bugs," Stewart said idly. "Then it's a cornucopia of finds."

"Christ, I hate it when you talk like that, Stewart," Carl sneered. He was scratching where the roaches had bitten him, plus the cracked shells and small bodies under his clothing were uncomfortable. "I need to take a break and clean this crap out of my pants and shirt, Hank," he said. "And I swear to God the little fuckers were biting me under my clothes."

Hank nodded at that. "Yeah, me too. I have a feeling if one of us fell into that shit we would have been eaten like they were little piranhas."

"Land piranhas, great," Laurie said. "More new species to add to the list." She meant the other interesting and deadly mutated creatures they had found on their journey north.

"Well, they're behind us now. Best to focus on what's ahead," Hank said. "But Carl's right. Let's find a classroom that looks empty and get cleaned up. Then we'll finish up and get out of here. It'll be dark in a few hours and I don't want to make camp in here. Too many exits and entrances and way too many windows. There's no way to defend this place from attackers."

"Yeah," Carl added, "but if we needed to retreat there's plenty of ways to do that. We're not backed into a corner in here."

Hank shook his head. "No, Carl, too risky. We search another hour and then we leave, no matter what." His tone was firm and Carl knew not to argue. Hank had been the leader of their group since they had all come together and all had agreed at that time that only one could lead. There was no time for a vote when the bullets were flying or some rad-blasted mutant that had once been human was trying to stick a blade in your chest.

They quickly found a classroom that would serve their purposes and in no time had stripped and shaken their clothing clean of insect carapaces. By the time Carl was finished, a small pile of shells and legs was at his feet. Laurie produced a small container of Clorox cloth wipes from her pack. It was a lucky find and she doled them out sparingly; each of them took a few and washed up with them. Water was too precious to waste on bathing and they had a limited supply, so no matter how dirty they might be it wouldn't be wasted on cleanliness.

Soon, they were dressed and taking stock of their situation. The windows in the classroom were gone, the shattered glass littering the floor and Hank went to one of them and peered out at the open landscape. There was nothing but rubble and debris for over a mile in each direction, the windows allowing light into the room so the corners were in shadows but the rest was illuminated.

"So, Hank, what's next on the agenda?" Stewart asked as he shrugged into his pants after shaking them carefully. A few live roaches dropped out and scuttled into the darkness of a nearby, dust-covered desk. He ignored them, just glad to be free of the small insects.

"We check our weapons, take a small rest, and then finish searching this dump. Nothing's changed. There can't be much left to check around here."

"What about the locker rooms?" Laurie suggested.

"Locker rooms?" Carl asked. "What could be there we could use?"

Laurie was dressed once more, and was using a comb to brush her hair free of legs and other minutiae. Though all she used was a few wet wipes to wash, her complexion seemed to glow. "Well, there are lockers there. Kids leave candy and snacks in their lockers. We might get lucky and find some junk food. Not to mention toothpaste, hair products and the like."

"That's good, Laurie, very good. I didn't think of that," Hank said.

Items like toilet paper and toothpaste were a valuable trading commodity. If they found a good supply, they could use it to trade with others along their travels. Though civilization had ground to a halt, the survivors remembered their former lives and missed many of the luxuries if not all of them. Brushing one's teeth was a way to stay in touch with a past blown away in nuclear fire, plus there weren't many dentists around if you needed a tooth pulled or a cavity filled.

Stewart was looking at a map on the far wall. It was a map of the school, with all the exits marked in red and a *You Are Here* in a circle, stating which classroom the warriors were in, in relation to the rest of the school.

"Says here the gym is on the east side of the school," Stewart said as he broke the plexiglass over the map with the butt of his Uzi and ripped the map from the wall. "Shouldn't take more than a few minutes to get there with the help of this."

Hank turned away from the window and nodded. "Good job, Stewart, anything to get us out of here faster." He looked to the others. "Okay then, if everyone has gotten the roaches out of their ass cracks, let's eat and move out."

They opened their packs and pulled out what rations they had. Beef jerky, a few Power Bars and a bag of potato chips was the main course, washed down by a few bags of dried nuts. It wasn't much, but it gave them the energy to keep going. A month ago their packs had been overflowing with food. They had come upon a small vending machine van filled to overflowing with every conceivable candy and snack. They had piled in anything they could carry and their pockets had been filled to bursting along with their packs, Twinkies being one of their favorites. They had hated to leave so much behind, but there was only so much they could carry. To carry more than was possible would be as bad as none at all. If raiders or outlaws got the drop on them and they were too weighed down with food to get their guns out, they would be on the last train west long before the first shot was ever fired in defense.

Ten minutes later and they were fed, repacked and moving out.

Hank was on point as always with Laurie right behind him. Stewart was next and Carl took up the rear, his Uzi ready if so much as a wayward bug looked at him the wrong way.

They reached a part of the school that was half rubble and half debris. Picking their way through the detritus, they ignored the hands and feet of crushed humanity, the dissociated bodies scattered across the floor. The flesh was long rotted off, only a few dried patches of skin remaining. A few hands still held notebooks, some pens and pencils, a few broken cell phones. Hank imagined the hallway had been full of school children when the shockwave hit, sending tons of ceiling struts and cement onto the frightened kids.

The place in his heart that should feel sympathy for the long dead was locked up tight. It had to be, for if he let each death he found affect him, there would be no way to continue onward each day. Survivor's guilt had taken many men and women to Hell and he refused to succumb to it. He was glad he was still alive and he knew he should feel no guilt for being that way. Though many times, when the sky was dark and it was after he and Laurie had made love and she was curled up next to him, both their bodies tired and sweaty, he wondered if the dead weren't the lucky ones.

As if Stewart sensed Hank's musings, he said, "Poor souls. What terror they must have felt in their last moments as the sky turned to fire and the sun seemed to be blotted out, the air sucked from their lungs."

"That how you think it happened?" Hank asked the older man.

Stewart nodded sagely. "Perhaps. Or maybe they simply were buried in rubble and suffocated and bled out. One is the same as the other in the end, I suppose."

"Fuck yeah," Carl said plainly as he adjusted his baseball cap. "Dead is dead. Don't matter how you get there, the finish line is the same no matter what."

Stewart tipped his cane to Carl. "Very true, dear boy, very true."

"Enough chit chat," Hank snapped, louder than he had wanted to. The truth was the hallway filled with dead children was getting to him though he was loathe to admit it. He glanced at Laurie to see her staring at the corpse of a young girl and he could see the sadness etched on her face. "Let's keep moving, there's nothing we can do for these kids. Their pain's over."

Hank led them out of the hallway and back to a part of the school in better shape. Other than two inches of dust covering the floor, the hallway was as pristine as the day the last bell rang.

Stewart used the map to lead them in the right direction and soon they were at the swinging doors leading to the boys' locker rooms.

Hank glanced at his friends who glared back at him. His eyes said what he didn't say, which was 'get hard and get ready for anything'. With a curt nod to Carl by his side, Hank kicked in the left swinging door and Carl kicked in the right one. As the two men lunged into the room, rolling a few feet to come up in a shooter's crouch, Stewart and Laurie stepped a foot past the doors with only half their bodies visible, their guns aimed at the shadows, their eyes looking for a target.

There were only a few small but dirty windows near the ceiling of the locker room and they let in a suffuse amount of light. In the gloom of the room, small bits of dust swirled on the thin rays of light where the dirt on the windows wasn't complete.

Nothing moved and it was blatantly obvious there was no threat. Hank and Carl came to their feet as Stewart and Laurie joined them. Before them stood the steel lockers and each one was wide open, their contents strewn about the floor like trash. Anything of value had long ago been picked clean and now there were only a few rags, only good for use as toilet paper or for kindling in a fire; that is if the material was flammable.

"It's been gone through," Hank said as he kicked a football jersey covered in dried blood out of his way. "Shit, this entire recce has been for nothing. Come on, I've had enough of this for one day. Let's get moving, maybe we'll get lucky down the road."

No one could argue with his logic, and as they turned and prepared to leave, the muffled sound of a woman crying out in pain filtered into the locker room. All four warriors raised their weapons as they looked around for the source of the cry.

"Carl, go right, see what you can find, Laurie, recce left. Stewart, you're with me. We'll go back into the hallway and circle around. We all meet back in five minutes or less. Got it?"

Each of them nodded and they slipped off into the shadows to investigate the disturbance. Hank and Stewart stepped through the double doors and back into the hallway. Looking left and right, he saw the large door that led to the actual gym at the far end. Gesturing with the muzzle of his pistol, the two men moved out.

Seconds later, they were at the door and Hank opened it slowly as he directed Stewart to continue down the hall and check it for the source of the scream. With Stewart's boot steps echoing away, Hank moved to the door. No sooner did the door separate from its jam then the smell of roasting meat came to him. But where normally his mouth would have salivated at the hefty fragrance, this particular aroma made him gag. It was sweet, like pork, but he knew for an absolute fact there were no pigs in a hundred miles of his position. That led only one other option and it bode badly for some poor soul.

Pressing his eye to the door crack, he peered into the gym of the high school. This had once been a place for basketball games, rallies, team spirit and bake sales, but now it was a charnel house of death, a debauchery of horrors any normal man would witness and turn away screaming.

But not Hank, nor his allies. Since the sky had grown dark and the nuclear flames had devastated the world, he had been fighting the good fight, trying to save as many as he could from the debasement that humanity had fallen into while struggling to eke out another day. Though not afraid to kill a man if he was attacked or threatened, Hank was also a man who couldn't turn away from someone in need of aid.

As he peered through the doorway at the center of the gym, he indeed saw people in need of his help.

From a quick count, there had to be over two dozen people in the gym, but these weren't the ones that were in dire need. The ones who needed mercy were off to the side, locked in makeshift cages of wood tied with heavy rope.

In the center of the gym, a dozen men and women were working, carving up a large hunk of meat. But Hank knew this was no meat that walked on four legs.

Off to the left was a small fire, the smoke rising to the ceiling where it hung like black clouds before finding the small windows along the top of the walls, where the ceiling met at a right angle.

Over the fire was a spit and on this was the torso of a human being. A small man with one eye was standing to the side of the spit as he slowly spun the meat so it wouldn't burn on any one side. But no matter how well he turned it, this couldn't be stopped. The meat looked burnt on the outside and no doubt was bloody and raw in the middle. Every now and then he would spray something onto the meat and Hank guessed it was either water or some kind of flavoring. Sometimes the man would reach out and let his finger become covered in juices as he rubbed it over the meat, then he would lick the digit dry like it was the best ribs he had tasted.

At the opposite end of the gym, Hank saw five dogs tied up. One of the cannies hacking at the large hunk of meat pulled something from inside it. Hank knew immediately it was a hunk of intestine. Casually, the cannie tossed the dripping rope to the dogs, and they instantly began fighting over it. Their growls overrode all noise in the gym as they battled for their supper.

Off to the side, ten feet from the fire, was a fifty gallon metal barrel, and beside the barrel were three faded white propane tanks. Hank watched one of the men go over to the barrel, scoop out the liquid inside it with a coffee cup and carry the cup over to a small lawnmower engine mounted to a wooden butcher block table. After pouring the contents of the cup into the plastic fuel reservoir of the engine, he pulled the cord and the mower raged to life. The engine was connected to a grinding wheel and the man got to work sharpening a few long blades.

Doing an inspection for weapons, Hank saw that most of the cannies were armed. He saw a few handguns, an old muzzle loader, a few shotguns and a couple of rifles. There was nothing particularly awe-inspiring, but more than enough to give the warriors a good fight.

Hank and his friends carried above-grade firearms. The reason for this was more luck than design. On their travels after becoming a unit, they had come upon a gun store. It had been ransacked, picked clean, but just as they were about to leave, Carl had stepped on a trap door. When they had opened it, they found the secret stash of the store owner and had taken everything they could use and had used the rest they could carry for trade and barter. It had fed them for months afterward, but eventually their surplus had dried up. But it had been wonderful while it lasted.

Hank watched the tableaux for a few more seconds before ducking back into the hallway. He knew if he wanted to be selfish, he should gather his friends and depart the school now, before the cannies knew they were around. But his conscience wouldn't let him. Since the world went to Hell, he had seen many depraved things and there had been times he hadn't lifted a finger to stop it. Later, those actions had haunted him, and right or wrong, he knew someone needed to stand up for what was right, even in the hellscape that was the new world.

There were innocent people in the gym that would be slaughtered like cattle, gutted and cooked over an open flame if he and his friends didn't help them. Their only crime was that they hadn't been strong enough to prevent from being captured.

If he left them to their fates, it was the same as if he killed them himself. And if that was the case, then it would be merciful to put a bullet in each of their heads rather than let them watch as one of them was slaughtered each day to feed the cannibals' appetites for human flesh.

It hadn't taken long for mankind to devolve into cannibalistic tendencies. With no food supplies being trucked in to the inner cities and across highways, and no way to grow it with the weak sun and radiation storms, there was only one plausible way to gather sustenance—by eating each other. While some people turned up their nose to the idea, many more embraced it, almost as if they had always wanted to do it and the hellstorm that had come was their excuse.

After checking his wristwatch and seeing it was time to go, Hank crept back to the locker room to rejoin the others. Hank was already formulating a plan in his head on how to save the prisoners by taking out the cannies, and once that was done, the warriors could scavenge what ammo the cannies had laying around. A few of the calibers would work in the warriors' guns and those that didn't could still be traded for ammunition that did. But first he would need to go over his ideas with the others and finalize the battle plan.

As another scream echoed from the gym and into the hallway, he knew there wasn't much time if he wanted to save as many lives as possible.

Hank was the last to arrive at the locker room. By the looks of the others' faces, he could tell they had seen what he had.

"So how are we gonna do this?" Carl asked flatly. His knuckles were white from squeezing his Mini-Uzi too tight and Hank knew it must have been a monstrous act of will for the man not to charge into the gym with weapons blazing.

"We hit 'em from a different door and lay down suppressing fire," Hank said. "I spotted a barrel filled with fuel and a few propane tanks." He touched his last frag grenade. "I'll use this on their fuel supply and when it goes up it'll take out more than half of them. The rest we can mop up easily in the ensuing fire and smoke."

"What about the prisoners?" Laurie asked.

Hank nodded to her. "You come up on them from the back of the gym and once you free them, get them out and back here. Then we can lead them to safety."

"And after that?" Stewart asked.

Hank shrugged. "After that they're on their own. I'm not looking to form a clan, Stewart. We save 'em and get the cannies ammo for ourselves plus whatever else they might have we can use. The prisoners get saved 'cause there's no reason not to. But our priority is each of us. Don't risk your life for one of those prisoners."

He looked each of them in the eyes. "You got it?"

"Got it," Carl said, speaking for the rest.

With the map of the school Stewart carried, Hank quickly assigned each of the other three warriors an entrance to the gym. Hank would use the one he had been to and Laurie and Stewart would come in from the back, through the locker rooms. Carl would loop around the school and enter the gym from the opposite side of where Hank would be. The two men could then lay down an angled fire that would take the cannies entirely off guard. After reminding his friends to be on the lookout for guards on watch and anything else that could put a wrench into their plan, they prepared to head to the gym

"Okay, let's move out," Hank said as he kissed Laurie and patted her backside. She smiled at him and winked, the gesture speaking volumes to the two lovers.

The plan was set and it should go off like clockwork, but Hank had learned a long time ago that nothing was set in stone and one simple mistake could ruin even the best laid plans.

Again in the hallway, Hank opened the door to the gym once more, peering through the crack to study the occupants for the second time in under an hour.

As he watched, he saw the time it had taken to prepare the others for the raid had caused another prisoner his life.

A man in his early twenties, with a scraggly beard and his ribs poking through his chest, was supine on the killing table. The man's shoulders and arms were tan from exposure to the sun but his legs, chest, and stomach were a pale white.

The man was seconds from death and it made even Hank's hardened stomach roil inside him. The cannies had placed the man spread-eagled on the table and had used a machete to split him from neck to groin. The man screamed in agony but with the gag in his mouth his cries were muffled. Blood spilt out of the open wound to splatter onto the floor and buckets had been set up under the table to catch most of the drippings. A large cannie with rings in his nose and ears was gleefully hacking at the man like the body was a giant chicken being chopped up for the grill. The dying man's head was shaking back and forth, his eyes wide in agony as the machete carved his insides and bloody hands pulled out his organs. The man stared in pain and astonishment as his own heart was carved from his chest and held before him. The hapless man had only seconds of life remaining as he stared at his heart and then, mercifully, lack of oxygen shut down his brain and he finally died. The cannie laughed as he held the heart aloft for them to see, and as others began to clean up the blood and pull out the rest of the organs, the large cannie walked to the open fire, stuck the heart on a long skewer, and propped it over the flames so it would begin to cook. Blood sizzled and fat bubbled as the flames licked at the organ.

Hank's grip on his Heckler & Koch G-12 automatic rifle grew so tight the stock began to creak and he ached to send a 4.7mm slug through the evil bastard's head.

As the cannies clapped and laughed as they prepared their meal, and the prisoners sobbed and prayed for help in their cells, Hank waited for Carl to appear at the far end of the gym so he could move. The far door was the same as the one he stood at and he had a perfect line of sight to it. He knew he had to wait for at least three minutes while Carl ran around the far side of the school.

The seconds turned to minutes and Hank was growing nervous, and for the thousandth time he wished they could have used the comms to talk to one another, but the stone and steel of the school blocked the weak signals, the batteries almost to the point the signal strength would be useless.

He was about to consider leaving and going around to check on Carl when the door he was standing at was suddenly pulled open and a filthy woman with sagging breasts and scraggly hair looked up at him, as shocked to see him as Hank was to see her. For some reason, the woman had picked the worst time to go for a walk or whatever errand she was going on, for now Hank was discovered.

So much for a well-oiled plan.

Before Hank could stop her, she let out a piercing scream that had every cannie turning their heads in her direction. Hank knew the jig was up and there were only two options. One was to retreat and the other was to go in full force and take the bastards by surprise. For though the woman's piercing scream filled the gym, none of the cannies quite knew what was wrong.

Hank filled them in as he shoved the muzzle of his automatic rifle under the woman's chin and squeezed the trigger. The 4.7mm round went through the bottom of her mouth, through the upper palate and then into her brain. But the round was so powerful it continued onward, blowing off a large chunk of her scalp and sending a pink mist of brain matter into the air. With the scream still on her tongue, she fell over, twitching as death claimed her.

Hank barely noticed her as he stepped over the spasming corpse and charged into the gym.

At the same time he did this, Carl opened the far door and ran inside, too. He had heard the yell and the gunshot and had recognized Hank's weapon immediately.

As he entered the gym, his Mini-Uzi began spraying hot death in all directions, though the man was careful to keep his field of fire from getting anywhere near Hank's position.

Hank fired on full auto, spraying cannies from groin to neck as the bodies danced a jig of death. As they fell to the floor, bleeding out, the rest quickly came to their senses, picked up their weapons, and dived for cover. Hank dropped down by a table, tipped it over, sending the chopped pieces of human meat across the floor, and used the blood-covered table as a shield. No sooner did he get under cover then he heard the impact of slugs on the table top. A few penetrated the table enough to splinter it, but none had the power to go all the way through the thick wood.

Hank waited for the shooting to lull and he popped up, spraying the cannies in three round bursts. The weapon shook in his hand as he sprayed body after body.

One cannie, thinking he was clever, tried to sneak around Hank on his right. As he got close enough to shoot, Hank spun on his knees and sent a round into the man's head. The top half of his head simply disappeared, and as the man fell over, the lower half of his brain popped out of his head. But it didn't go far thanks to its attachment to the spinal cord.

Carl was hiding behind a pile of canvas bags holding rice, flour and wheat. The bullets aimed at him sank into the bags like they were filled with sand and for the moment he was safe from harm. He called out to Hank to see if the warrior was unhurt and Hank waved that he was.

Peering around his protective table, Hank saw the far door at the back of the gym open and spotted Laurie and Stewart as they peeked past the jamb. He knew this was the time for the main distraction, so they could save the prisoners.

Pulling the frag grenade from his web belt, Hank pulled the pin and turned to the left, where the gas and propane was stored.

Without so much as a deep breath, he let go of the handle and tossed the grenade. It bounced once and then rolled until coming up directly at the base of the barrel of gas. Hank lowered himself down and waited for the inevitable boom.

But once more a simple plan went awry as one of the cannies, who had seen the grenade, lunged for it, wanting to save the fuel reserves.

It was Carl who prevented the plan from going too far off course. As the cannie ran for the grenade and picked it up, Carl popped up and sprayed the rest of his clip at the man's arm and hand that now held the grenade. The first three bullets hit the wrist of the cannie and the rest of the rounds chipped bone until the hand was blown off the limb. The severed hand with the grenade still in its grip fell on the floor, the fingers still twitching like live worms. As for the cannie, he yelled in pain and shock as he stared at his severed stump now spouting blood in thick gouts of red.

But the man's agony was short-lived when the frag grenade finally went off. The cannie was enveloped in fire a second later and his shrieks of death were lost in the massive explosion as the gas and propane ignited, blowing the body into a hundred pieces that slapped wetly onto the floor and walls. The explosion was so loud and powerful the entire gym shook, knocking men and women alike to the floor. The massive fireball that rolled onward consumed another half dozen cannies, scorching them to charcoal and leaving behind emaciated figures with grinning white smiles, a rictus of death if there ever was one.

Hank stayed low as the heat wave rolled over his hiding spot, and as the vacuum sucked in all air and sound, he waited, his mouth open and his hands on his ears.

He counted to five, then with the blast still echoing in his ears, he jumped up and began firing once more.

The cannies were shell-shocked and he and Carl made a quick sweep of the remaining ones still alive and able to fight. One of the cannies managed to free the dogs and sent them at the two warriors. Hank and Carl had to swivel to the side and waste precious ammo on the mongrels. Bullets smacked into fur-covered torsos as each of the dogs whined in death, a few not dead but mortally wounded.

Meanwhile, after the initial blast, Stewart and Laurie ran to the cages at the back of the gym as fire and smoke began to fill the front part. Screams and pleadings for help came to their ears as they began hacking at the locks of the cages.

When Laurie had the lock off the first cage, she opened the door, quickly ushering the prisoners out and to the back door that led to the locker rooms.

As one man came out, Laurie didn't see the madness in his eyes. The man had witnessed his wife being killed and slaughtered like a turkey days before and the vision still haunted him. He was completely mad; the other prisoners having pushed him in a corner of the cage, making him stay there.

Now free, he didn't see Laurie as his savior, but as another of his captors, come once more to take him and gut him like a fish.

An attack was the last thing Laurie would have expected from the weak, hopeless people she was saving. Before she realized what was happening, the man had jumped on her and was punching her, spittle flying from his mouth as he screamed at her and cursed her for killing his wife.

Laurie was so overwhelmed by the man's ferocity she couldn't go on the offense, but merely kept her hands up to protect herself from being pummeled. Even so, a few blows struck her chin and cheek, causing her to see stars.

The man might well have killed her if not for Stewart, who upon seeing what was happening, ran to her aid. As he reached the raving man, he didn't bother trying to drag the man off her. Times of compassion for a lost soul were a thing of the past. You either pay your way or get left behind.

Stewart raised his Heckler & Koch submachine gun and sent a 9mm round through the man's left ear, his brains and other ear, along with a good size portion of his head, spurting into the air to splatter the floor red.

Laurie bucked her hips and knocked the already dead man off her. As she rolled to her feet, she sucked in a breath, fighting the panic that had taken hold of her. The madman had been like an animal, his fury knowing no relatable bounds. All he had wanted to do was kill Laurie and his own survival, his own existence, was irrelevant.

Breathing heavily, Laurie reached out and touched Stewart's arm. "Thank you," she said simply.

Stewart nodded, not replying. There was no need. Next time it would be she who saved him and then it would be him who saved her. The four warriors held each others' lives in their hands and would die for one another if necessary. They were more than friends; they had become a family, a family forged in the fires of nuclear hell and ash.

A cannie from across the gym began shooting at Stewart and Laurie and both dropped to the floor as bullets flew over their heads. The gym was filling with black smoke fast and in another few minutes there would be no way to avoid sucking in the deadly fumes.

Hank and Carl were working their way to the prisoner cages and taking out any cannies still trying to fight. Carl felt a tug on his backpack and when he spun around, an old woman with a handgun was staring at him, her eyes wide with hate, the gun she had just used still aimed at him. Carl lunged to the side as she fired again, the bullet missing him by inches. His finger was already squeezing the trigger and the fresh clip he had slapped in a second ago was quickly exhausted as he sprayed the woman from legs to neck. She looked like a sputtering pincushion by the time he was finished firing, the body all but a mangled mess of meat. He had shot her once in the face and the round had pulverized her nose and the sinus cavity beneath. She hit the floor hard, bleeding from a dozen bullet holes, her eyes now glazed over in death.

Carl rolled to his knees and pulled on his backpack. He felt something wet and he reached inside it, wondering if his hand would come out red. But instead, he smelled a fishy odor and the wetness was a clear fluid, like oil. Reaching deeper into the pack, he pulled out the can of sardines, now with a bullet hole in the upper half.

"Well, I'll be," he said as he tossed the can to Hank who looked at it, grunted and tossed it away.

"You're one lucky bastard, Carl," Hank said simply.

Carl was about to reply when another shot rang out and both men dropped to the floor. Hank felt the bullet buzz by his hair, reminding him of an angry hornet. He was lucky, and if his reflexes had been a tad slower, he might have ended up with a new hole in his head.

Searching for the shooter, the smoke burning his eyes, Hank breathed through his nose to avoid coughing. Mucus dropped down his lip and chin as he fought not to cough.

There he was! The cannie was hiding behind a pile of bodies. Hank didn't wait for the man to shoot again.

"Cover me!" he yelled to Carl, and as the skinny man began to lay down covering fire, Hank jumped up, lunged to the right and fired two, tri-bursts at the cannie. The first burst went wide, the bullets impacting the dead flesh of nearby corpses, but the second burst found its target. The cannie cried out as all three rounds blew his chest apart, killing him instantly.

"Come on, Carl, it's time to go!" Hank yelled as he headed to Laurie and Stewart's position. On his way, he picked up a few guns and loose ammo scattered on the floor. The cannies wouldn't need it any more and Hank knew they needed to take something for the expenditure of ammunition they had used on this action.

Carl was doing the same, shoving as much as he could into his backpack.

By the time Hank and Carl reached Laurie and Stewart, the two warriors had gathered what they could and wrapped it in a blood-stained sheet.

"Where are the prisoners?" Hank asked Laurie.

"I sent them to the door leading to the locker rooms like you said. Other than that your guess is as good as mine."

"Okay, they're not our problem any more." Hank began coughing. "We need to go before this smoke kills us all."

Laurie nodded, and began coughing uncontrollably, her eyes rolling up into her head. She went slack and was about to fall when Hank caught her in his arms. He carried her out of the gym as the others followed.

A few gunshots followed their departure but they were wild. In the thick smoke filling the gym, visibility was down to a few feet, and the cannies that had survived would soon be dead by smoke inhalation or burned by the fire which was growing with each passing second.

As the four warriors stumbled into the locker room, they saw a few prisoners were still there, while others had taken their chance for freedom and had used it, running as far from the school as possible.

"Go, you're free," Hank said to them as he set Laurie down on a bench where students used to sit and change for dodge ball and basketball.

"But where do we go?" one woman asked. She was skinny from malnourishment and her body was covered in grime and sweat.

"I don't care," Hank replied. "We saved you and that's more than most people would have done. You're on your own now." He pulled his canteen from his hip and let Laurie drink from it. A few prisoners saw he had water and began to moan but he told them to get away. The water he had was precious and he wasn't about to waste it on some random stranger. Laurie drank deeply and her coughing resided. After a few seconds her eyes opened and focused on him.

"What happened?" she asked in a hoarse whisper.

"Smoke got you. How're you feeling?"

"Been better, but I'll live," she replied.

Behind them, the door from the gym burst open and a cannie staggered inside the locker room. The man was empty handed other than a knife and for a brief second the warriors were caught off guard. Stewart was the one to act first. Drawing his sword from his cane, he lunged with it and pierced the cannie's throat. As the long blade pierced flesh, Stewart twisted his wrist, the blade slicing tendons and the carotid artery in tandem, then he withdrew the blade.

The cannie reached for his neck, feeling the blood spurting between his fingers. As he gasped for air, he dropped the knife and slumped to his knees. Evidently, he was taking too long to die for

Stewart's taste so the older man used the sword again, piecing the cannie's right eye. The tip of the sword went in deep, and as the blade was removed, the cannie dropped face first to the floor, dead. Hank knew Stewart had given the man a merciful death after the first wound. Instead of bleeding out and gasping for air, he had been put down quickly.

Grimly, Stewart wiped the sword clean on the back of the dead man's pants, then resheathed it. "I think we should take our leave of this place," he said as if he was asking for the time of day.

"That's a damn good idea, Stewart," Carl added as he moved to Laurie's side. "You want some help there?"

She shook her head. "I'm fine, all of you, quit fussing over me. I sucked in some smoke, I'll live. I'm not a weak little woman who needs you to care for me."

"No one said you were," Hank said. "We're just worried about you, that's all."

She patted Hank's cheek. "You're sweet, but like I said, I'm fine."

A rumbling explosion shook the locker room and the doors to the gym rattled in their frame.

"That's our cue to get the fuck out of Dodge," Carl said as he shouldered his backpack.

No one argued. The four warriors turned and headed into the hallway that would lead them back outside. A few of the prisoners came with them and a few stayed behind. Hank didn't look back at the ones who remained in the locker room. He had done all he could for them, what came next would be up to them. At least he had put their fates back into their own hands.

By the time they reached the glass double doors leading outside, the sky was growing dark, the reds and oranges fading as night claimed the horizon.

All of the prisoners but one had wandered deeper into the school, not knowing where else to go and not in any condition to face the outside world just yet. Hank knew soon they would have no choice. If the fire in the gym continued raging, soon the entire structure would be one massive conflagration.

With the one remaining prisoner by Hank's side—a woman in her early twenties—he was in the lead as they exited the school and stepped back into the open air.

Though his hand was on his SIG-Sauer in case there was trouble, he would later admit to his shame that he wasn't paying as good attention of his surroundings as he should have been. Though he knew one moment of lax attention could get him or one of the others killed, after the battle in the school he wasn't up to peak performance. It had been a long day, and dealing with the cockroaches in the kitchen and then the battle in the gym had taken him to the point of total exhaustion, the adrenaline rush, now faded, leaving him drained, and only his insurmountable will keeping him going, as well as the others with him. All were looking forward to making camp and getting some much needed rest.

As he stepped out of the double doors of the school, he didn't see the deeper shadow off to his side, one that blended in with the darker, natural shadows lining the school.

His first sign of an attack was when he heard a low growling and turned his head to see two glowing red eyes.

The creature was partly silhouetted in the fading light, the rest of its form lost in darkness. The face was composed of thick hair and muscle, and it seemed as if the flesh covering the skull didn't quite fit right. A long mouth filled with razor sharp teeth opened slightly and a long, low hissing emerged.

All this Hank picked up in an instant before the creature lunged for him.

With hind legs made of solid muscle, the creature shot from a sitting position like a rocket, its mouth open wide, its tongue lolling outward. Hank was already raising his pistol but even as he did this, he knew he was going to be too late to stop the beast from reaching him.

But at the last second, the woman prisoner beside him jumped in front of him and instead of the creature attacking Hank, it went after the woman. Its teeth sank into her soft throat, tearing it out as it reared back its head on powerful neck muscles and the woman had time for one soft squeak before her head was practically severed from her shoulders.

The creature landed hard and spun round, hissing and growling at Hank as the others came out of the building, each with weapons raised and ready.

As the clouds broke for a few moments and the moonlight slid through, casting the parking lot of the school in its pallid glow, Hank got his first good look at the beast. It was a dog, a Mastiff by the looks of it and it was large even for the gigantic breed. Living on the run, it had turned feral, feeding on whatever it could catch. And human was just as good as deer, cat or rabbit if that was what it came upon. It had been in a few hot zones too, the radiation burns apparent on its hide, a fresh covering of blood now on its muzzle and lower face.

As the woman's corpse cooled at Hank's feet, he leveled the SIG-Sauer at the dog's head, and with a slight nod to the other warriors behind him, they each began firing at the giant canine.

The Mastiff charged at Hank, seeming to shrug off the barrage of lead as each bullet found a home in its thick hide. But with each step it took, another pound of lead was added to its massive frame, and by the time it reached Hank, it was crawling.

Hank raised his left hand for the others to stop firing and he looked down at the animal as it seemed to lick his combat boot.

Hank stared at the dog, at the corpse of the woman, and then back to the dog again. Bringing the muzzle of the SIG to the Mastiff's head, right between its large glowing eyes, he squeezed the trigger once more, sending a 9mm round into the dog's skull and blowing its brains onto the back of its body. The canine huffed once and its head dropped to the bloody ground, the chest heaving one last time, then it was still.

Hank knelt down by the woman, and with his free hand, he closed her still open eyes. He carefully arranged her head, fixing her tattered neck stump so that she looked almost normal. Tearing off some of her shirt, he used it like a scarf to cover where her neck had been torn. Then he stepped away from her. That was as good as it got for someone when they died. The time and energy to bury the body wasn't worth it.

"She saved your life, Hank," Laurie said as she placed a hand on his arm.

"Yeah, and I didn't even know her name," he said.

"It was karma," Carl said. "You saved her from the cannies and she returned the favor. 'Sides, what chance did she have now that she was free?"

No one said anything. Without a team to travel with, one that was armed, most survivors wound up as either slaves, dead, or if you were female, working in one of the brothels that were in every town that had survived the bombs. Even some men wound up in one, but not too often.

In many ways the world had been blasted back to the 1800s, where the law of the gun owned the land and rules varied from township to township.

"It's gettin' dark, we need to go. I want to make camp before it's too dark to travel," Hank said in a low voice.

They headed out, leaving the school behind. Hank slowed and glanced over his shoulder once when they were a few hundred feet away. He could see where the gym was located at the back of the school, and also the dull red glow as the fire continued to burn, quickly getting into the walls and ceiling. Eventually it would burn out, leaving the only useable structure in the area nothing but charred remains, much like the rest of the world.

Laurie slid her hand into Hank's and squeezed it gently. "Is it wrong of me to say I'm glad it was that woman who was killed by that dog and not you?"

Hank shrugged. "Don't know. Can't say that I'm complaining about it, though," he said as he turned to look at her. Carl and Stewart were still walking and were now twenty feet away, so he and Laurie were alone for a few seconds before the other two men realized they weren't being followed.

"I don't know what I'd do without you," she said while hugging him.

He wrapped his arms around her. "Me too, baby. You're one of the few things that still make it worth living in this damn world. If I didn't have you, I don't know what I'd do."

"And you never'll have to. We're in this together. Until we find someplace safe."

"Sounds good to me." He leaned closer and they shared a kiss, tongues mingling gently, then pulling away.

"Mmm, play your cards right and maybe you'll get lucky tonight when the other two are both asleep and on watch." One of them always stood watch while the others slept; a rotating shift throughout the night.

He chuckled. "Oh, I have a feeling luck will have nothing to do with it."

She made a face and slapped him playfully on the arm and he laughed, a full-bodied laugh that said it was good to be alive, no matter what their surroundings.

"Hey, you two love birds done making out or what!" Carl called from further down the road. It was almost full night and his and Stewart's shapes were lost in the gloom.

"We're coming, were coming," Hank called.

Laurie slid her right hand into his left hand and they began walking down the road side by side, the illusion of two lovers going for a moonlight walk almost perfect.

The only thing to break the image of a young couple out for a stroll was that Hank had his right hand resting on the butt of his SIG-Sauer, ready for a quick draw if necessary, and Laurie's left hand held her .22, her trigger finger outside the guard, but ready in a second's notice if warranted.

CONVOY

The sky was a burnt orange, resembling a fire that would never cease burning; a remnant of the nuclear war that had thrown the Earth into chaos more than two years ago, leaving mankind fighting to survive in a lawless land. Slashes of red pierced the low hanging clouds, making the horizon look as if it was bleeding.

A few crows flew overhead, eyeing the small convoy as it made its way through what was once the heart of Kansas.

Hank Summers checked the radiation badge on his shirt, pleased to see it was still in the green, though the needle was close to touching the yellow. If it had been in the red, he knew he would be dead, puking his guts out days later, a sign the rad sickness had gotten him. It was a hard way to die, as your insides melted and your hair fell out. By the time you finally succumbed, every orifice was leaking fluids and a man would beg for a bullet in the head to end his suffering.

His hands went to his weapons on instinct, but as always, his SIG-Sauer 226 9mm pistol was in its holster and his sixteen inch panga rode his hip, ready to be used at a moment's notice.

His Heckler and Koch G-12 automatic rifle was on his shoulder and his web belt held three grenades, all fragmentation. He was lucky at the last town he'd been in; a merchant had allowed him to trade for a few of the precious explosives.

He sat in the back of a redesigned fire truck, his three friends sitting next to him, and he looked at them one at a time.

Stewart Matheson, an old man in his sixties, was as smart as a whip and carried a cane with a hidden sword in it. He once said if he ever had to pull it from its sheath, as a matter of honor, the blade must taste blood before being resheathed. In the past, the blade had tasted blood countless times. His Heckler & Koch submachine gun lay across his lap and his .45 was secured to his hip. His white hair blew out around him as the truck drove down the deserted highway.

Beside him was Carl Rivers, a thirty-five year old with a pasty complexion and a Yankees ball cap on his head. The man was almost never seen without it, even going to sleep with it on. His Mini-Uzi was in his left hand and his right rested on the butt of his AUG 5.6 mm pistol.

Carl noticed Hank looking at him and he nodded back, grinning from ear to ear.

Hank let his gaze move to the last member of his team. Laurie Collins was a stunning blonde wearing all black, her pearl-handled PPK .22 on her hip. She was a crack shot and the small caliber weapon was more than she needed to put down any attacker. Her boots were tipped with pointed steel, a deadly weapon she used well in a close-up brawl.

When she saw Hank looking at her she blew him a kiss and he smiled. The two were lovers and had been since the day they met. He would do anything for her, and she for him, and both had done so on many occasions.

After the bombs fell, the world was changed forever. Society had collapsed and only the strong survived, usually by killing the weak. Man lived hand to mouth, doing what he had to do to survive, and Hank had done many things he regretted as he traveled the nukescape, searching for a better home.

He looked out over the plains of uncut wheat, unharvested and falling over on itself. Sometimes, if he looked hard enough, he spotted a lone soul out cutting the wheat near the edge of the land, but they were few and far between.

This area of Kansas had been hit hard by the bombs, though no one knew why. Most guessed that the missiles had been knocked off course to fall in no man's land. Either way, the damage was done and anyone living in the area had to deal with it. The only positive was that most of the bombs that pummeled Kansas didn't do as much damage as possible and many hadn't been nuclear.

The four warriors each sat straighter as the fire truck slowed, the other engines of the vehicles in the small convoy revving louder as the drivers downshifted.

The convoy was transporting canned goods and bottled water—the treasure trove found in a warehouse—to a town about a hundred miles due west. In exchange for the food and water, the town would pay in fuel and ammunition.

Hank and his fellow warriors had applied for work in the last town when the convoy had let word out they needed security to protect the convoy. As the four friends had their own weapons and ammunition, it was pretty much a guarantee they would be hired.

And they were, the leader of the convoy taking to Hank almost immediately as a kindred soul.

Tyrell Tisdale was a grizzled black man in his late fifties with short cropped hair and a shock of white through the middle, resembling a lightning bolt.

He carried a .357 Colt Magnum and a nine inch Bowie knife on each of his hips, and when he smiled, a friend would feel welcomed and an enemy would know he was as good as dead. The trader had once been a carpenter, but as with most people who survived the end of the word, he made due with what he could find.

What he found was the fire truck and a few other vehicles, all tucked away in a garage, untouched and safe. Knowing the roads well from his youth, he became a trader, moving much needed supplies from town to town.

There was a reserve of fuel found as well, and after siphoning all he could carry, he began using the vehicles. The nearby towns that were trying to get back on their feet welcomed him with open arms.

But wherever man tried to rise above the muck, there were always lowlife scum and cold hearts, eager to take what wasn't theirs and feed on the weak.

After being hit twice in less than a month by raiders, Tyrell had decided it was time to fight back.

This time, if the convoy was attacked, he had the manpower and weapons to fight them off, or at least make the raiders pay dearly for what they took.

The convoy came to a full stop and Hank looked to the road ahead. In front of the lead vehicle in the convoy, a battered station wagon with steel plates welded to it, making the car resemble something out of an apocalyptic movie, there was a blockade of two cars on the road.

Both cars had missing windows and the tires were all but bald, the finishes on both of them scratched and peeling, rust showing around the tire wells. But that wasn't what Hank was concerned about.

It was the five men standing behind the two junk cars, all with firearms raised in his direction.

Hank crawled forward until he was leaning over the cab of the fire truck. From there he could hear Tyrell, who was sitting in the passenger seat of the front cab.

"What's going on?" Hank called down.

Tyrell's voice came back, sharp and quick. "We got ourselves a roadblock. One of my men is gonna go talk to them, see if we can work this out without anyone gettin' killed."

"That would be a nice change for once," Carl said from behind Hank.

Hank turned to face his second-in-command. "You're right about that one, Carl, guess we'll just have to see how the dice falls. All of you, stay sharp and be ready for anything."

Laurie and Stewart nodded and pulled their guns, each checking to make sure safeties were off and a round was chambered. Hank did the same, then he hunkered down and watched the tableaux play out on the road before him.

The passenger in the armored station wagon climbed out and slowly walked toward the blockade. His hands were at his sides and he knew if one of the raiders wanted to, they could wipe him from the face of the Earth with a squeeze of a trigger.

On top of the fire truck, the four warriors watched with baited breath, knowing there were only two ways the scenario would end.

The man Tyrell sent to talk to the raiders walked casually towards the blockade, his arms out to his sides.

Hank watched the man reach within ten feet of the blockade and begin to speak. A few times the man turned halfway around, pointing back at the convoy. Then his hands went out before him, as if he was pleading for something.

Hank gripped his Heckler & Koch G-12 automatic rifle tighter as he rested the stock on the cab of the fire truck. Using the tip of the muzzle, he drew a bead on the raider who seemed to be the one in charge. With the cross hairs centered, he calmed and waited for what would come next.

Inside the cab of the fire truck, Tyrell was busy talking to the rest of the convoy on a two-way radio. Every vehicle had one and though the radiation wouldn't allow for much distance, the vehicles were so close it worked fine.

"So far so good," Laurie said from behind Hank as she looked over his shoulder at the blockade.

"Perhaps diplomacy will win the day," Stewart added.

Before Hank could respond, a shot rang out, followed by two more. As he looked to where the envoy should have been standing, Hank saw him now prone and lying in the road with half his head blown off.

"Shit, I fucking knew it!" Tyrell screamed from within the cab. "Smith, get out of the fucking way and let us go first! We're crashing that goddamn road block!"

The driver of the station wagon, Smith, swung out of the way as the fire truck began to move, slowly picking up speed.

"Hold on back there, it's gonna get rough!" Tyrell screamed back to Hank and friends. "This is where you earn your pay!"

The fire truck picked up speed, and just before it hit the center of the two junk cars, Tyrell sounded the horn, blasting the road with screeching noise. The front bumper of the fire truck connected with the two cars and pushed them aside like they were made of paper. Screeching metal and torn steel still resulted, and as the two vehicles were literally thrown to the sides of the road, the front bumper of the fire truck sustained limited damage as it was made for plowing through traffic if the need arose. Reaching a fire was tantamount to saving lives and the fire truck was made to batter its way through any obstacle if necessary.

Carl almost fell off the roof but Stewart reached out and grabbed him by his left arm, the material of Carl's jacket stretching to the point of ripping. Then the younger man was back on the truck, safe.

He nodded thanks to Stewart who flashed him a smile in reply.

"Hank, we got company!" Laurie yelled as she pointed to the right of the fire truck where four dune buggies were coming directly for them.

"Over here, too," Carl added from the left as he looked over the side to see dune buggies outfitted with sheet metal bearing down on them as well as four motorcycles.

The second the dune buggies were spotted, the passengers in each one began shooting at the convoy.

"Take those bastards out!" Tyrell screamed into his two-way radio.

"Shit, they were lying in wait for us!" Hank yelled as he sent a spray of caseless rounds at the closet dune buggy. The rounds bounced off the sheet metal harmlessly as the driver swerved to the right. As the small vehicles approached, a plume of dust bellowed out from behind them, and when they reversed course, they became lost in the cloud of dust.

"The damn things are armored. Go for the tires!" Hank yelled as he fired a tri-burst at the next oncoming buggy. Beside him, the others began sending a barrage of fire at the attackers, causing the buggies to spread out to avoid the deadly hail of lead. A dune buggy came up on the left side of the fire truck and a man climbed out, wanting to get aboard the fire truck. Carl leaned over the side and sent a dozen rounds into the raider's chest with his Mini-Uzi.

The raider's chest seemed to explode as his ribcage was pulverized along with his heart and lungs. Letting out one scream of pain, he fell off the side of the fire truck and landed on the hood of the dune buggy. The driver of the buggy hit the brakes and the body slid forward to land in the dirt on the shoulder of the road. No sooner did the corpse land on the ground, then the dune buggy was racing forward, bouncing over the body as it trundled onward.

The armored station wagon was behind the fire truck, Smith shooting and steering the car at the same time. Two dune buggies came up on the station wagon together, and as the one on the right distracted Smith, the one on the left pulled up close and the driver tossed a live grenade into the passenger seat of the station wagon.

Smith saw the grenade land on the seat and tried to reach out and grab it, but as he did, he was shot in the head, which was perhaps a mercy killing. As his head slumped forward with the side of his skull missing, the grenade went off, sending the station wagon three feet into the air before it came crashing down. On the fire truck, Hank ducked to avoid shrapnel as it was propelled away from the flaming hulk of metal.

The dune buggies swerved around the debris, driving through the oily black smoke cloud to soar out the other end, still hot on the convoy's tail. One of the motorcycles miscalculated and the front tire hit debris. The rider flipped over the handlebars and fell face first onto the ground, snapping his neck instantly. A second later, his motorcycle landed on him, breaking his legs.

"Damn it, we lost Smith!" Hank yelled down to Tyrell.

"I know. Just keep the bastards off our back for a little longer. Once we reach the junction to Interstate 135, the road opens up. Those dune buggies will never be able to keep up with us!"

"Got it!" Hank yelled back.

Laurie shot a man in one of the dune buggies as he leaned out to shoot at her. Even with the two vehicles bouncing madly, she only missed his left eye by two inches. The .22 round penetrated the man's skull where it rebounded around, slicing his brain to mush. The man slumped out of the buggy's window and when it hit a bump, the body fell out to flop in the dirt. No sooner did she fire then her arm was swinging around. A motorcycle was coming up on her right and she shot the rider in the mouth, the bullet smashing through the man's front teeth and ricocheting into the upper palate. Dead or not, the man toppled off his bike to roll in the dirt. A moment after he landed, a dune buggy drove over him, leaving the twisted remains of flesh to lie in the bloodied soil.

"Keep the pressure on!" Hank yelled. "Maybe if we take enough of 'em out, they'll give up. We need it to not be worth continuing!"

"Easier said than done," Carl quipped back as he sprayed another dune buggy with bullets. They all missed hitting anything vital until the last one slid between two metal plates and hit the front tire. There was a loud pop and the tire exploded, the dune buggy flipping over to land upside down. The top was crushed instantly, the men inside crushed into a bloody paste.

The convoy sped onward as the raging gun battle continued.

There were only two vehicles in the convoy left besides the fire truck and Tyrell was yelling into his two-way radio for both vehicles to pull in together, so Hank and his fellow warriors could protect them better.

On the roof, Hank shot at a dune buggy that had reached the rear bumper, and as the bullets whined off the sheet metal, a man climbed out of the passenger seat and latched on to the rear of the fire truck.

Meanwhile, the same thing was happening on the opposite side. Stewart saw it happen and went to handle the situation. As the raider jumped onto the side of the fire truck and began to climb up, Stewart shot at him. But the fire truck bounced over a bad spot in the road and Stewart missed. The raider raised a revolver and shot at Stewart who dived for cover, his H&K falling from his hand to clatter around on the roof. Looking over his shoulder, Stewart saw that the raider had almost reached the roof, and thinking fast, he reached out and grabbed his sword stick where it lay on the roof. Lightning fast, Stewart pulled the sword from the cane and rolled onto his side just as the raider reached the edge and was about to fire at him. The tip of the sword slid into the raider's right eye like a hot knife through butter. For good measure, Stewart twisted the sword, slicing the raider's brains and scraping the interior of the eye socket.

The raider fell away where he was promptly run over by one of the convoy's vehicles.

Hank barely saw Stewart's fight as he had his own raider to deal with. The man was heavily tattooed with a mohawk and a brown leather jacket. Hank thought he looked like a reject from a Mad Max movie but no sooner did the thought enter his head, then he had to duck as the raider shot at him.

Hank dropped to the roof and drew his SIG-Sauer. As the tattooed man climbed higher on the side of the fire truck, Hank began crawling towards him. Behind him, he heard Carl spray a dune buggy with bullets. The buggy exploded, rolling three times before finally coming to a halt in a spray of dust and flames.

There were still four more dune buggies and two motorcycles trailing them, more than enough to finish the job. Three men in each buggy, the convoy was outnumbered after the losses they'd suffered. The only way they would come out of this in one piece, was if they made it to the Interstate and used the speed of their vehicles to outdistance the raiders.

Tyrell was hanging out his window in the cab, shooting at any dune buggy that moved too close. More often than not, his shots went wide, but when he managed to hit something, a large hole would be the result. A motorcycle pulled up alongside and the rider tried to shoot the front tire of the fire truck. Tyrell rewarded the rider for his enthusiasm with a bullet to the back. The rider splayed his hands out as he let go of the handlebars, the bike flipping over to land heavily in a cloud of dust. Tyrell never saw if the man was still alive, the wreckage already behind him as the fire truck roared down the road.

The fire truck swerved as a dune buggy pulled out in front of it, the driver trying to slow the large red truck down. Tyrell ordered them to go faster and the driver of the fire truck floored it, hitting the dune buggy right behind the rear right corner of its bumper. The hit caused the buggy to swerve wildly back and forth, and as it turned to the left, the fire truck broadsided it, sending it flipping through the air. It came down in the center of the highway, and to add insult to injury, the fire truck plowed into it, killing all three passengers and sending the twisted remains of metal and flesh to the side of the road.

Hank had been about to shoot the tattooed raider just as the fire truck struck the dune buggy for the second time. The jarring of the roof beneath his feet sent Hank rolling to the side, where he reached out to stop himself from falling off. He had to let go of his pistol as he needed both hands, and it clattered away to become jammed under a cross beam. As for Hank, he grabbed the only thing available to him, the long, hundred foot ladder that ran down the center of the roof.

As he wrapped his hands around it, the fire truck jumped under him as it ran over a body lying in the road and the ladder broke free of the roof, swiveling to the right.

Hank, holding on for dear life, felt like he was flying over the road as the pavement zipped by beneath him. As he struggled to hold on, a dune buggy pulled up close to him. Hank could do nothing but stare at the driver and passenger, both men laughing as the passenger leaned out the window and prepared to shoot Hank.

As the raider leveled his handgun, a small gunshot rang out and the raider's head snapped back before he slumped over the door as if he had fallen asleep. Hank looked back to the roof of the fire truck to see Laurie lowering her .22. Then he had to focus on holding on as the ladder swung out even further, the tip of it clipping trees, shrubs and road signs, each time jarring him to the bone.

As he looked to his right, he saw the tattooed raider was also holding on to the ladder. He had slipped off the side of the vehicle and had barely managed to catch the ladder before falling to his death.

The only way back to the safety of the roof was past the tattooed raider, so with no other options other than to hang in the air like a sitting duck until he was either shot or the swinging ladder snapped off when it struck something too heavy to knock over, or deal with the raider. Hank decided the raider was the lesser of the choices.

Hand over hand, Hank began to move down the ladder as the raider did the same, heading towards him. The man had an evil grin on his face and he was looking forward to reaching Hank.

All the while, the fire truck swerved and drove at breakneck speed down the highway as Tyrell and the other three warriors shot at the dune buggies.

An agonizing two minutes later, Hank was only a few feet from the tattooed man. The raider laughed, spittle flying from his mouth, and now that he was closer, Hank could see his opponent's eyes. They looked glazed and wild at the same time and Hank knew the man was on something, a mind-altering drug, no doubt.

Hank tried to let go with his left hand but as he did so, the ladder bounced and he almost fell off. With nothing but his legs, he kicked out, connecting with the raider's stomach. The tattooed man grunted but barely acknowledged the blow, his pain receptors dulled by the drugs in his system.

Hank knew he had to act fast, for exposed as he was, he would soon run out of luck, either by a bullet finding him or the ladder snapping off.

Acting fast, he swung his legs up and over one of the metal rungs on the ladder, letting himself now hang upside down. The tattooed man laughed at this and swung closer. Hank smiled too, but for a different reason.

As the tattooed man lunged for him, Hank pulled his panga. With the blade free of its sheath, he slashed at the tattooed man's left arm. The blade bit deep and sliced through muscle and bone, a spray of blood shooting forth to become lost in the wind as the hand fell away, sheared off at the wrist.

The raider screamed as he hung by one arm, the other still locked on the ladder.

But Hank wasn't done. As the raider screamed in agony, Hank used the panga to slice off the man's remaining arm, severing his connection to the ladder. With blood shooting from both arms like a fire hose, the raider fell to the pavement where he was promptly run over by one of the dune buggies. Hank looked and saw the hand was still wrapped around the ladder, the severed appendage looking as out of place as a football player wearing full gear at a tea party.

A shot rang out and the bullet was so close to him that he felt the air hum with its passing, and he moved, knowing he needed to get back on the roof and its relative safety.

Wiping the panga clean on his pant leg, he resheathed it. Dropping back down so he was hanging by his hands again, his legs swinging back and forth as the fire truck fought to stay on the road, he swung hand over hand until he was once more at the side of the fire truck. When he reached up, Carl was there and he helped Hank back onto the jouncing roof.

"Shit, Hank, thought we lost you for a second there," Carl said quickly.

"You're not getting rid of me that easily, Carl," Hank gasped as he dropped to the roof. His eyes met Laurie's and he saw the relief in them.

"You all right?" Stewart called from behind him.

Hank rolled over and said, "I'll live."

"Well, then get the hell up and help us, these bastards don't know how to take no for an answer."

With a grunt, Hank rolled to his knees, surveyed the situation and frowned. It was time to get serious. Though he hated to waste one of his grenades, they wouldn't do him any good if he or one of the others were killed.

"Fire in the hole!" he yelled as he pulled a frag grenade from his web belt, plucked the pin, counted to three, and dropped it off the rear of the fire truck.

At the exact moment the grenade landed, a dune buggy drove over it. The driver never had a chance to swerve. The grenade went off instantly, sending shrapnel up and into the undercarriage of the dune buggy, killing all three men in less than a second. The buggy swerved and drove off the road, as clouds of black smoke poured out of every opening.

Tyrell got lucky with a shot and he took out the driver of a dune buggy. The vehicle began to swerve back and forth until it hit the shoulder and flipped onto its side. With wheels still spinning, it remained motionless. No one crawled out of the wreck. Carl took out the last motorcycle, hitting the rider in the shoulder. The bike went down, the rider still alive, but he wasn't following them and that was what mattered. Out of the fight was good enough and better than nothing.

Carl took out the last dune buggy, spraying the front end with a full clip from his Uzi. Only a few bullets managed to sneak in past the sheet metal armor, but once inside the metal cab, the bullets ricocheted wildly, destroying the human bodies within.

The buggy didn't crash, it just lost momentum, slowed to a crawl, then gently bumped into a tree on the shoulder of the road. If anyone had been around to inspect it, they would have seen a steady dripping of blood from the underside.

"That's the last of them!" Stewart yelled as he let out a cheer. Laurie moved over to Hank and he took her in his arms. The two kissed briefly, the embrace speaking volumes for how they felt for one another.

Ten minutes later, at the junction to the Interstate, the fire truck slowed to a stop along with the two remaining vehicles. Tyrell jumped out of the cab as the four warriors climbed down off the roof. As soon as the fire truck stopped, two of Tyrell's men ran over to it and began working on getting the ladder back onto the roof and locked down. The top six feet of the ladder was a mangled mess, thanks to the abuse of it crashing into every sign and tree on the road.

"Goddamn, if that wasn't the shit," Tyrell said as he walked over to Hank and the others. "Without you four, I truly doubt if I'd still be alive, let alone have a cargo to deliver."

"When you get paid for your cargo, just make sure to give us our salary and we'll call it even," Hank said while he shook the trader's hand.

Most of that pay would be used to replenish their depleted ammunition reserves. What was left would be used for food and lodging. In most towns that had a sense of law and order, there were two ways to acquire services or supplies. Barter was one and a chit system had been set up in most towns to keep an economy running.

"That I will, Hank," Tyrell said. "I said it before when I took you four on, I'm an honest man. Treat me right and I'll do the same. Today, you four saved my ass. I won't forget that anytime soon."

One of Tyrell's men walked up to them and said, "Sir, we should get moving. We don't know if there's more raiders out there."

"That's true. You're right about that. We should get going. Tell everyone we leave in three minutes," Tyrell told the man who jogged away to inform the rest of the now, much smaller, convoy.

Tyrell turned back to look at the four warriors. "Seems we're at the Interstate, we should be there by dusk, as long as we don't run into anymore trouble."

"If we do, I have a few more rounds to greet the bastards with," Carl laughed as he held up his Mini-Uzi

Everyone chuckled at his jibe, not because it was particularly funny, but after the attack, and adrenaline waning, each just wanted a release.

Tyrell clapped his hands together and grinned, his teeth flashing in the sun, his smile far too white for a collapsed world. Evidently toothpaste was high on the man's list of items he used every morning. With a struggle each day to survive, something simple like brushing teeth wasn't high on the list of things to do for most people.

"Tell you what," Tyrell said. "When we get to town, the first rounds on me at the bar. What do you say?"

"I say, let's go already, I'm thirsty now," Stewart said with a grin that rivaled Tyrell's.

A few more chuckles slipped out and the four warriors climbed back onto the roof of the fire truck, the two workers having just finished moving the ladder back.

It had to be tied down with rope as the clamps once holding it had snapped off. Hank tried not to think about his time hanging from the ladder as he sped down the road, seconds away from death.

Hank picked up his SIG-Sauer, glad to see it was fine, as well as his G-12 automatic rifle.

Tyrell waved to his men and climbed into the cab of the fire truck, the driver starting the engine and sounding the horn. Black smoke belched out the back and with a quick order from Tyrell over the two-way radio, the convoy began to move once more.

On the roof of the fire truck, the four warriors sat together, each licking their wounds and taking stock of their weapons. All their armaments would need a good cleaning once they arrived in town, but for now they could take a few moments to relax, knowing that though the next threat could be just over the hill, hopefully it wasn't.

Laurie curled up next to Hank, and he had his arm around her. Stewart and Carl sat side by side, talking softly. As the fire truck swung onto the Interstate and began the final leg of its journey, Carl stopped talking to Stewart and looked right at Hank, as if he wanted to tell him something.

At first, Hank ignored his friend but finally he glared at him and asked, "What? Why are you looking at me like that?"

Carl merely shrugged before he said, "Me and Stewart were talking it over and the next time you want us to get a job as security on a convoy, we've decide to make sure you change your mind."

"Oh, why's that?"

"Why? 'Cause after the shit we just went through, we've both decided that next time we'd rather walk." He said it so matter-of-factly that at first Hank thought he was serious. But as Carl tried to keep a straight face, his facade broke and he began to grin.

Hank did the same, as did Laurie. Stewart let out a healthy laugh that soon had them all joining in.

Whatever had happened was in the past. The future wasn't here yet and all that mattered was the present. They were all together, a family forged in battle and blood, four against the world, and if push came to shove, the world would lose.

CAVERN OF THE RATS

After staring into the slavering jaws of a giant rat, with a nose to tail length of over four feet, even the most hardened man may well find himself saying a silent prayer for salvation.

Even a man like Hank Summers, who was now flat on his back with a giant rat on his chest, its blood-red saliva dripping from its jaws to splash the ground around him. The blood was residual leftovers from the last man the rat had fed on, a man now lying in the corner of the cave with half his throat torn out.

All around Hank, dozens of scrambling, giant rodents were about, each one trying to find the tasty meat that was Hank and his small group of travelers.

The rats came out of holes in the cavern walls and ceiling, a few coming out of holes dug deep into the earth itself—thanks to their razor-sharp claws—all with feral eyes and a hunger that could only be satiated in one way—human flesh.

With two years passing after the bombs had fallen and blasted civilization from the Earth in one fell swoop, plus residual radiation in the air in many places, and the rats' capacity to breed so fast, the end result was genetic misfits, giant rodents with a hunger for human meat.

The rat on top of Hank bent over and tried to bite his face off, but as it leaned down, Hank shoved the muzzle of his SIG-Sauer 226 9mm pistol into its slavering mouth and squeezed the trigger.

The initial gunshot was muffled by the rat's throat, but the explosion of bone and brain matter out the back of its head bounced off the cavern wall behind it, mixing with the screams of humans and rodents alike.

Hank bucked his hips and the rodent fell off to land in the dirt, its remaining brains spilling out of its skull, as Hank jumped to his feet.

Looking to the right, he saw one of the people he was traveling with, a middle-aged woman named Lisa, go down under three rats, each the size of a small child. Nearby, another man named George Smith was already dead and being fed upon.

The screaming woman's face and her upper body disappeared behind the black fur of the rats, and her yells of agony only stopped when one of the rats bit her head off, a loud *snap* cutting through the din filling the cavern.

Lisa's legs began to dance spastically and then they stopped forever, her limbs still, as she died a hard death.

Another rat came for Hank and he jumped to the side, tripping over another one that had been behind him. The rat snapped its fangs at him, and Hank rolled out of the way, then continued to roll as the rat came for him, teeth snapping again and again, each one inches from his arms. His arms were scraped and cut as he rolled across the jagged, mica-flecked floor of the cavern, but he ignored it, knowing to stop for an instant would cause him to lose a limb.

Another rat landed where he'd been a moment ago, and its teeth snapped down on a stone outcropping. Its right fang snapped off and the rat screeched in either pain from its wound or anger for the loss of its prey. Its eyes turned inward for a second and then refocused on Hank, before it came at him, joining the other one in fast pursuit.

In the back of Hank's mind, he had to wonder what was the bad luck that had allowed him and his team to pick this cave to hide in, when the acid rain began to fall.

Not that he or his group had much choice. To stay in the acid rain without protection was a death sentence, and if they hadn't found the cave, even now they would all be nothing but puddles of black and red goo and pieces of bone. And their deaths would have been hard, even harder than dying by killer rat.

When the acid rain touched flesh, it sizzled like hydrochloric acid, and enough of a coating would sizzle and hiss as it slowly melted the skin from your bones and ate at the muscles beneath. As the victim screamed in absolute agony, vapor in the air from the acid rain would be sucked into their lungs, where the acid would begin working, thus eating the hapless bastard from the inside out until organs began to liquefy and fall out of the body in gallons of dark brown sludge.

Hank and his team had found themselves trapped out in the middle of nowhere as the clouds rolled in, and with his three companions by his side, along with the seven other travelers they had joined up with, he knew they had minutes before the clouds opened up and dropped liquid death on their heads.

He had given the order to run as fast as their legs could carry them. They had traveled a mile in six minutes flat, an excellent feat even if they hadn't been carrying their gear on their backs. Just as the first drops of rain sizzled in the dirt at his feet, Hank spotted the cave opening, its mouth hidden by some waist high scrub brush and overgrown trees.

He had given the order to double-time it, and as they reached the mouth of the cave and plunged into the Stygian darkness, the clouds had opened up, a deluge of moisture falling like God Himself was trying to wash the world clean, perhaps trying again after the bombs had failed to wipe mankind from the planet.

"Wait, we're missing Martin," Hank said as he stopped at the mouth of the cave. "The rest of you go inside, I'll wait for him," he ordered the others.

No one argued, each of them exhausted from the hard dash to the cave entrance. With the footsteps of the others receding into the tunnel leading deeper into the earth, Hank squinted his eyes in the hope of seeing Martin.

The man was in his late sixties and wasn't in the best of health. Though Hank felt bad that the man had been left behind, he also knew if one of the group had attempted to help him to the cave, then there would now be two people left behind and exposed to the acid rain due to the old man's slowness.

The rain was now coming down in sheets and Hank began to cough as he breathed in the caustic vapor. He was about to retreat into the tunnel when he saw a lone figure through the driving rain.

It was Martin, the old man stumbling as he tried to make it to Hank.

"Come on, Martin, you can do it!" Hank yelled, coaxing the old man on, but it was all for nothing. As Hank stared in horror, he saw Martin's clothes begin to wash away as they dissolved in the acid rain. Next came the flesh, and as Martin began to scream in agony, he fell to his knees and collapsed into a puddle, his face melting off in seconds. Hank could only stand silently and witness the old man's demise, and though he felt terrible, deep in his heart he thought only one thing, *Better you than me, pal.*

Then, as the storm grew heavier, Hank stepped back a few feet, his eyes never leaving the pool of sludge that was once a man. As the vapor became worse, he turned and entered the tunnel, knowing he would have to be the bearer of the bad news of Martin's death. He knew the one who would take it the hardest would be Stacey. She was Martin's daughter, the two only having each other.

He had entered the tunnel, seeing the others had gone deeper already. He had walked a couple hundred feet, the voices of the others floating back to him as they echoed off the cave walls.

Deeper into the earth he went, until he wondered just how far he'd gone.

Slowly the walls began to take on a luminescent quality and he found a thin layer of moss coating the rocks, giving off a dull green glow. He continued walking towards the sound of the voices, his boots splashing in the muddy brown water that pooled on the floor, thanks to it dripping down the walls in thin rivulets. Luckily it was fresh water from an underground spring no doubt.

He was almost to the others when the first screams of anger and fear, followed by gunshots, filled the tunnel and he began to run.

When he reached the main cavern, a good two hundred feet with a ceiling so high it was lost in shadow, he found his fellow companions surrounded on all sides by giant rats, the smallest still measuring a good three feet, minus the tail.

Hank snapped back to reality as teeth clacked a mere inch from his face. He decided how he and his group arrived in the cavern was irrelevant. Now, all that mattered was how they were going to escape alive.

Rolling to his feet, he pulled his panga for some in-close fighting, and as a rat came at him, he brought the sixteen inches of razor-sharp steel down and sliced the head clean off the attacking rat. Blood geysered from the exposed wound and the rat's legs twitched, the mouth of the severed head still opening and closing as nerve receptors shut down.

A second rat lunged at him and he spun, shooting it with his SIG-Sauer in a quick draw that would have made any Wild West fan envious. A double tap was all it took to put the giant rodent down, its tail curling up tight against its furry body as it died.

Hank found himself in the corner of the cavern, for the briefest of moments alone and unthreatened. Only the dimly glowing moss on the cavern walls and the few torches that had been lit and now littered the cave floor gave off any light to see by, and by this wan illumination, Hank took stock of the battle between human and rodent.

Directly in front of him stood his lover and a warrior in her own right. Laurie Collins waved her pearl-handled PPK .22 and used it with deadly accuracy each time she fired. In her left hand was a small hunting knife which she hacked and slashed at the attacking rats.

Hank let his gaze swing to his right where Stewart Matheson battled three rodents single-handedly. In his right hand was a sword, one he had pulled from its sheath, which was a disguised walking stick. Though in his sixties, the old man fought like a man half his age. On his shoulder hanging by its sling, he still had his Heckler and Koch submachine gun, but now in his left hand he held his .45, only using it when he felt he had no choice. They were all low on ammunition and he used his sword as much as possible as it didn't need to be reloaded, and as long as his arm was strong it would deal death.

Hank saw Stewart was holding his own so he looked to his left, where Carl Rivers did battle with half a dozen of the feral rats. With his Mini-Uzi in hand, the thirty-five-year-old sprayed the rats from legs to neck, sending more than half rolling away while bleeding from a dozen bullet holes. Hank noticed the man still had his Yankees baseball cap firmly affixed to his head.

Hank watched as Carl pulled a grenade from his web belt, let out a, "Fire in the hole!" and threw the grenade into a dozen of the rats. The bodies swarmed over the small object and a second later, the muffled explosion filled the cavern, sending rat chunks flying in all directions.

Hank was far enough across the cavern that the bloody chunks of rat meat didn't reach him, but he saw that a sizable amount did hit the last of the four travelers in his group.

First was Stacey, the daughter of Martin, her fiery red hair splayed out behind her as she fought like a banshee to live past the next few minutes. She was strong and beautiful and if Hank hadn't been deeply in love with Laurie, he would have been attracted to the woman as more than a friend. Standing to her side and back-to-back with her, were three other men. None of the men were particularly special looking, all of average size and weight, with average faces and builds. One was named Roger, another Bill and the other was Tim. Hank had learned their last names upon meeting them a week ago, but truth be told, he didn't remember them now. There really was no need anymore. A first name was pretty much all a person needed to get by nowadays.

The four of them were doing their best to fend off the attacking rats and each had hopes of being the victor, that is until a giant rat with boils of pus under its fur used its claws to scale the wall and jump onto Roger, forcing the man to the floor as its claws tore open its victim's chest.

Roger managed one blood-curdling yell before his throat was torn out. Bloody froth spewed from his mouth as the rat drove its head into his torso and began to burrow, eating the man from the inside out. Mercifully, Roger was already dead.

Hank had no time to see more of the man's grisly demise, thanks to five rodents coming at him from his left.

Firing his SIG-Sauer, he took out three of the rats before they could take their first step at him, but the other two continued their attack, heedless of their dying brethren.

As the first one in line leaped, Hank swung the bloody panga with all his might, taking off the head in one swipe. The head fell to the left and the body to the right of him, the head rolling for a few feet before coming to a halt.

Hank stood his ground and glared at the last rodent. The rat's eyes seemed to glow in the gloom and its mouth opened and closed as the tongue flicked back and forth. Bits of gristle still clung to its teeth, dripping blood on the cavern floor, and Hank realized he'd seen prettier things in his time on Earth.

Hank held the rat's gaze with no fear in his mind, for to even show an ounce of it would spell his doom. The two beings from different worlds stared at each other, as if sizing the other up.

Then the rat charged, its breath coming out in short gasps as its claws clacked on the rocks below its feet. It saw Hank as nothing but food, to be torn apart and rendered inert.

Like it was some miniature armored truck, it came straight at Hank, its eyes going wide as it prepared to sink its teeth into the warrior and taste his blood.

Hank spread his legs and waited for the exact moment to attack, and when the rat was only a few feet from him, he lowered his panga and used it like a spear, throwing it directly at the open mouth of the rodent. The tip seamed to gleam in the wan light as it sailed through the air and pierced the rat directly in the back of the throat, slicing into bone and cartilage and then into the small brain.

The rat tripped on its feet and fell heavily to the ground, its eyes popping from its skull from the blood filling its head thanks to the blade now wedged within.

With eyes hanging from bloody sockets and the handle of the panga jutting out of its mouth, Hank ran over and pulled it free, a bloody froth of crimson filling the air. The rat's back legs twitched and its tail flicked one last time before the rodent ceased to move.

Hank heard more screams around him and he spun about, knowing there was no time to gloat over his kill. He spotted Tim on the ground with three rats feeding on his corpse, the rodents happily slurping down his organs and viscera. As Hank watched, one of the rodents tore off his head and galloped into the shadows to feed on its prize without being bothered by its brethren. A glance to his left showed him there wasn't much left of Roger's body either, the rodents making short work of the meat and bones.

Hank holstered his pistol, wiped the blade clean on his leg and resheathed the panga, then unslung his Heckler and Koch G-12 automatic rifle from off his shoulder. He let loose a continuous blast of death from his rifle, sending round after round into the gaping maws of the feeding rats.

The rodents' heads exploded and the ones not mortally wounded, squealed in anger and pain, retreating, not wanting to be hit again by the bullets that flew through the air and hit them, causing pain and death as if by magic.

The giant rats had fed on humans before, but it had never been so difficult to kill them. Those times it had been easy to wait in the darkness and then fall on the hapless humans as they entered the cavern to seek shelter from the frequent acid rainstorms. But this group was something else. They had guns and blades and fought with a ferocity equal to the killer pack itself.

Already, many of the pack lay dead and dying but still, the rest fought on, for now there would be more food for the remaining ones. And though their numbers had been whittled down this day, there would be more as the rats bred quickly, and after two years of breeding uncontrollably, many generations had come to pass, each one slightly larger. Human bones littered the cavern from past kills, some only the size of small children.

At the far side of the cavern, Carl was giving a group of rats a run for their money as they surrounded the man with teeth bared. Taking another grenade from his web belt, he pulled the pin, waited a heartbeat, then tossed it into the center of the pack and ducked down as a moment later shrapnel ripped through the furry bodies, severing heads, tails and limbs as if they were made of soft butter.

With some breathing room, he used his Mini-Uzi like a broom, sweeping the rats away from him as more climbed over their fallen brethren. Hank nodded briefly, knowing that Carl was handling himself well and that at least Hank wouldn't have to worry about him.

He turned to his right at the sound of an ear-piercing scream. Bill was on the ground and a rat was chewing on his right arm, the bloody limb deep inside the rodent's maw. The rat's teeth were grinding back and forth as it slowly sawed off the man's limb.

Hank ran at Bill, hoping he could save the man, the rat barely noticing the arriving human, so caught up in its feeding as it chewed on the flesh of Bill's arm and swallowed each chunk.

Hank ran right up to the rodent's head and placed the muzzle of his rifle against its ear, pulling the trigger and holding it there.

The beast was suddenly knocked off the ground, as if it was a puppet lifted by its operator, and it released Bill's half-chewed arm, the man falling away with blood shooting from the ruined stump.

The rat's head disappeared in a glorious spray of blood and bone and Hank leaned over and grabbed Bill's good arm, dragging the man free of the headless rat as blood shot out of the neck stump to spray the ground red.

Hank managed to get Bill to a low outcropping of rocks and he placed him down, the man barely conscious. He could tell the hapless man was already going into shock. He knew the symptoms well: trembling lips, his face had gone white, and his eyes were staring off into nothing, as if he was preparing to meet his maker at any second.

Bill's arm was badly mangled to the point of being useless. Bits of bone and tendon were exposed and hanging out, making the man's limb look like the torn arm of a child's ragdoll after the family dog had finished playing with it from a game of tug of war.

Though Hank wanted to help the man, at least apply a tourniquet, there was no time to tend to him. Leaving the man and turning back to the battle, he jumped into the fray, his Heckler and Koch spraying bullets as he ran.

More rats were pouring out of the holes in the walls and cavern floor, and Hank had to wonder how many could there possibly be?

He heard movement above him and he looked up to see more coming out of holes in the ceiling, each one dropping out to fall to the ground with its legs already scrabbling for purchase. He raised his rifle and began spraying the ceiling, hoping to take out as many as possible before they landed and joined the fray.

A sixth sense told him to turn around, and as he did, the maw of a rat clamped down on the fabric of his jacket, missing the flesh on his arm by less than half an inch. One of the rodent's incisors had snagged Hank good and the beast began to tug, trying to drag Hank into the shadows of the cavern.

He fought to free his arm but the material of his jacket was made out of heavy leather and it wouldn't rip. The damn thing had him! For all the strength of his two hundred plus frame of muscle, he couldn't get free and he was continually dragged into the shadows where he caught a glimpse of a small nest of baby rats, these only a foot in length, their low pitched squeals filling the air as they saw their lunch coming right for them. There had to be two dozen at least. With their squirming pink bodies always moving, it was difficult to count them.

Hank wasn't able to use the rifle due to the fact that was the arm the rat had locked on to, so he reached down and pulled his panga free of its sheath and swung it at the rodent's back. The razor-sharp edge bit in deep and the rat squealed in pain, but still it dragged Hank closer to the baby rats. He looked deep into the rat's eyes and he saw a determination there that rivaled his own.

This beast would feed him to its young even if it was the last thing it did.

"Hank!" Carl yelled when he saw what was happening and tried to help. The only problem was there were almost a dozen rats blocking the path between Hank and him.

Hank turned his head and spotted Carl and he waved, while yelling, "Toss me a grenade!"

Carl didn't say anything more, but pulled a grenade from his web belt and threw it to Hank. The small orb arced over the heads of the rats and for a moment, it looked like it might miss Hank altogether, but at the last second, Hank managed to reach up and catch it. As soon as he stretched and plucked the grenade out of the air, he was yanked back down by the rat as it dragged him along. Hank used his teeth and pulled the pin on the grenade, then casually lobbed it into the nest of baby rats with a, "Eat this!"

The grenade bounced off the head of one of the babies and then rolled to a stop almost directly in the center mass of squirming pink bodies. Seconds ticked by and then another *whump* filled the cavern as baby rat parts went flying, splattering everything in a ten foot radius. Gore and viscera struck the walls and slid down in dark red globs, while small legs twitched, minus the bodies they were once attached to.

The rat holding on to Hank turned back at the sound of its babies exploding and its eyes went wide in what seemed to Hank to resemble genuine horror in its truest form.

It let out a muffled screech around the leather of Hank's jacket and then the rodent went completely crazy, its gaze swiveling back to Hank, as if it knew he was the reason for the destruction of its babies.

Like it wanted to avenge its dead, the rat let go of Hank's arm and lunged for his face. Hank raised the panga up after he pulled free of the rat's back, and the blade slid into its mouth, the teeth clacking down an eighth of an inch from his nose, so close that spittle hit him in the face and he felt the warm breath of the beast. With his arms shaking from the weight of the rat, he was knocked to the ground where the rodent climbed on top of him. He felt its rear claws dig into his thighs, only the thick material of his jeans saving him from real damage, and he let out a yell, his arms straining to keep the large head at bay. Saliva dripped from the rat's maw and it looked like a hundred, finger-sized teeth were inside there, each one glistening in the gloom.

The panga slid into the back of the rat's mouth but the teeth stopped it from going in enough to do the rodent serious damage. Meanwhile, the rat's back legs were tensing as it prepared to claw Hank's legs to shredded meat.

Hank knew his time was numbered to mere seconds, but still he fought on, knowing if he was going to go down, then he would go down fighting.

As he grappled with the rat, he waited for the inevitable pain as claws dug into the flesh of his legs, no doubt severing his femoral artery where he would then bleed out.

The sound of gunshots and screams around him faded into the distance as his ears filled with blood at the strain he put on his upper body, the rat still trying to bite off his face.

He barely heard the report of Laurie's .22 when she walked up to the rat, pressed the muzzle of her PPK against its right eye, and fired, sending the small caliber bullet into its skull, where it then bounced around, ricocheting and chewing up the small brain until finally exiting out the back of the head, barely having enough energy to escape.

The rat stopped cold, blinked once with its good eye, as if not quite understanding what was rattling around in its head, then it spasmed once and released its bowels, collapsing on top of Hank.

The warrior then found himself suffocating under the fur, the foul smelling beast causing him to gag.

He bucked his hips, trying to shift his weight and knock the rat off him but it was very dead and very heavy. With a surge of strength, he pushed up on the carcass and began to drag himself free of the rodent.

All around him was the sound of yells, gunshots and screams as the remaining travelers did battle with the giant rats. A full scale battle was going on between human and rodent and who would win was still anyone's guess.

Laurie came to him and he nodded to her in thanks. That was all that was needed between the two of them. He had also saved her life countless times before this day, and he knew, if they lived through this battle, there would be more times as well.

He did a quick scan of the cavern, his eyes taking in the dozens of dead rats littering the ground, sometimes the bodies piled so high he couldn't see over the still forms. He saw Bill out of the corner of his eye, but the man was very dead, four rats having torn him apart. As they fed on his insides, two began to fight over his lower intestine.

Hank spotted Carl and Stuart battling together, and near them, Stacey fought like a wild banshee, a pile of bloody carcasses at her feet.

Carl tossed another grenade—a fragmentation one this time— into a group of rats and a second later a muffled boom filled the cavern as more rat parts flew threw the air to splatter every surface.

With Laurie by his side, Hank made a run for his friends, knowing the best way to win the day was to stay together and guard each others' backs. As he took his first step, a rat blocked his path. Before the rodent could so much as make an attempt at an attack, Hank pulled his pistol and shot it in the left eye. The orb disappeared in a splatter of pink goo and the rat snapped its head back in pain.

Blinded in one eye and suffering horribly, it turned and attacked another rat. Hank briefly wondered if the rodent was so filled with pain it was blind to what it was attacking and was merely lashing out. Still, his bullet caused two more rats to become occupied with something else other than trying to kill the humans.

Hank and Laurie reached Carl, Stuart and Stacey, and the five humans made a circle with their backs facing one another. All around them, the rats seemed to pause and take stock of the situation. Hank stared in amazement, not understanding what was happening. It was like the rats were thinking, like they knew it was time to re-evaluate the situation.

Though merely rodents with limited intelligence—despite being giant—he had to wonder if they realized their brethren were lying dead at their feet and it was time for a new plan. Carl tossed one of his last grenades into a thick crowd as the rats gathered, though the rest remained still as nearby, seven rodents were turned into bloody mush.

For a few seconds it went deathly quiet in the cavern, the rats ceasing their movement and only the heavy breathing of the humans broke the silence.

Hank was trying to understand what was happening when he heard a loud clicking come from the far side of the cavern. His eyes went to follow the noise and he spotted a darker shadow amongst the normal shadows lining the cavern wall.

And then, from out of the darkness, something appeared and Hank felt his chest go tight.

"You've got to be fucking kidding me," Carl said from Hank's side as the man spotted what Hank saw.

"It can't be real," Laurie said as, she too, spotted what the others had seen.

"Surely this is all a nightmare and we're somehow suffering the same fevered dream," Stuart said. He took a step back from the sight before him.

"What the hell is it?" Stacey asked.

Hank used the cessation in the battle to change the clip on his SIG-Sauer and make sure his rifle had a full load, then he said in as calm a voice as he could manage given the circumstances, "That's the biggest fucking rat I've ever seen."

Before the companions, half its body poking out of the hole in the far wall of the cavern, was a rat that had to be at least five feet wide and seven feet long, and that wasn't including the tail which was hidden behind the massive rodent. The rat was fat, real fat, and Hank took a wild guess it was pregnant.

As he stared at the queen mother's two tea cup-sized eyes, and in the dull gloom, he saw something different in this one's gaze. There was an intelligence he hadn't seen in the smaller ones.

The queen rat lifted its head and began to chitter, the high-pitched squeaks reminding Hank of fingernails on a chalkboard.

No sooner did the rat 'speak,' then the rest of the rodents formed up closer ranks, closing any holes in their line that the companions might have tried to escape through.

"Holy shit," Hank said, his voice as low as he could manage but still be heard by the others. "I think that big mother over there is somehow communicating with the others. It's controlling them somehow."

No one deigned to disagree as the proof was before them. Though only two years since the bombs fell, the leftover radiation had already begun to play havoc with the smaller life forms on the planet, the ones that had a shorter lifespan and so more genera-tions passed in the same time as one human life.

Flies lived mere days and dozens of generations could come and go in the space of a few months. So far, the flies hadn't mutated but there had been talk of Africanized bees that were the size of humming birds with stingers as long as a man's finger.

The rats swarmed at the group of humans banded together in the corner of the cavern, the rodent's claws clicking on the rock floor, dozens of them surging forward. The air was thick with the odor of burnt meat, offal and cordite from fired guns and exploding grenades. Everyone had to breathe through their nose or risk succumbing to a coughing fit.

Hank and the others raised their weapons, preparing for the final battle, and then Hank looked up and had an idea, one that would be their only chance to survive the oncoming attack.

As the army of rats began to surge forward, Hank grabbed Carl and pulled the man close, asking, "We need to take out that big bastard over there, you have any more grenades?" He had to yell over the rats' claws striking stone, it was so loud.

Carl reached down and checked his web belt, finding two more, one a fragmentation grenade, the other a standard explosive.

"I've got two, but I don't know how much good they'll do against something so big."

"They don't have to. Look," he said and pointed at the shadowed ceiling. "If you can time it right and have the grenade go off close to the ceiling, it should stop that thing by bringing down the roof. The question is, can you get it that high? It's our only chance of making it through this in one piece!"

"Try and stop me!" Carl replied as he pulled a pin on the explosive grenade, released the handle and counted quickly to run down the timer in the grenade.

The seconds went by and Hank was about to yell at Carl to throw the damn thing, when the Yankees fan finally pulled back his arm and let it fly.

At the same time, Hank quickly warned the others of what was about to go down and to back up. He had everyone move to the wall behind them as fast as they could run. There was a rocky overhang protruding from the wall about eight feet up and he had all of them get under it for cover.

The rats were getting closer as they prepared to swarm over the humans, but still not charging, and Hank wondered if perhaps even rats could sense the dead of their brethren around them and they were hesitating, despite the orders from the queen mother.

The grenade soared through the air and was soon lost from sight as it went high into the shadows of the ceiling. But a second later, a bright flash filled the cavern, making it seem as if the sun had somehow pierced through the ceiling.

There was a low rumble at first, but it soon grew louder in pitch, and as Hank and the others watched, the ceiling of the cavern near where the grenade went off began to break apart and crumble to the ground below, shaking the cavern floor as if an earthquake had struck.

The rat queen began to screech loudly as the first boulders struck it, then more and more pummeled its body. It tried to back up into its hole, but with the ground shaking, it wasn't able to move fast enough. A large stalactite cracked off and fell to impale the queen mother just behind its head. The squeal of pain it let loose caused the humans in the cavern to place their hands over their ears.

And then the keening began as all the other rats stopped moving and began to wail at the loss of their mother.

Hank was the first to recover, and as he saw the rats all raising their heads to the ceiling and wailing, he knew the time to win the battle was at hand.

"Now, everyone, concentrate your fire on the remaining rats while they're distracted!" Hank yelled.

The five humans did just that, sending bullet after bullet into the dark furry bodies. Some were practically pulverized and more than half were dismembered as the hot lead dissected their bodies in the most painful way possible.

A rat made it right up to Hank and it lunged for him, but this time he was ready. Firing into the beast's stomach as it came for him, he then dropped his gun and grabbed the rat by its head, a hand on each side. Like a discus thrower of old, he began to turn, swinging his entire body around with the rat flying out until Hank let go and it soared across the cavern. It struck the wall hard and a wet splash was the result. The bloody carcass dropped to the ground where it remained still.

Carl let fly his last grenade, one that struck the wall five feet above the queen mother. The explosion blew out three feet of rock and sent even more cascading down. Dust filled the cavern, making it hard to see and breathe, but through the swirling clouds of grit, Hank saw the large pile of boulders where the rat queen was buried.

A small rivulet of blood seeped out of a crack in the rocks, meandering its way along the ground, telling of the fate of the queen mother.

There was only a score of rats left alive at most and these seemed slow to act, as if they didn't know what to do. Hank wondered how long he and the others had been inside the cavern. Ten minutes? An hour? He realized time had been standing still since he'd entered the cave mouth to escape the acid rain.

Hank pointed to the tunnel leading out of the cave. "Fall back to the opening, now's our chance!"

The others did as he said and began to make a withdrawal from the cavern.

A rat went for Stuart as the old man made his escape and the man swung his sword at the rodent's head. The blade sliced through its nose and the rat fell back, squealing in pain.

Another dove for Stacey, and before she could reach the tunnel, the rat was on top of her, its claws raking her back, the tips slicing into her warm flesh. In less than a second her spine was exposed to glisten in the gloom, the woman screaming in agony. Hank saw the attack but was too slow to stop it, though he did manage to put half a dozen rounds into the right side of the rat on her. The bullets blew out the left side, entrails and blood spewing forth as the rodent fell off the woman to twitch and spasm in death.

Hank ran to Stacey and scooped her up in his arms, careful of the exposed wound. The mortal wound ran down her back from the top of her neck to just above her butt, and she moaned loudly in pain, half-in and half-out of consciousness.

Carl covered Hank's retreat, shooting a few rats to make them stay back.

The group made their way through the smoky tunnel, the shadows of the remaining giant rats following them.

When they reached the cave entrance, Hank and the entire group let out a collective sigh—the acid rain had stopped and the sun was out, the red sky clear of clouds.

Hank motioned to Carl. "Here, take her," he said.

After the man took the bleeding woman, Hank reentered the tunnel, running fifteen feet inside. The rats had just rounded a bend and they stopped at the sight of him, their noses twitching, their beady eyes glowing in the light coming in from the entrance. Hank saw they were ready to attack en masse. But before the rodents could take a single step, he unslung his rifle and aimed it at the ceiling.

Spraying a dozen rounds, the bullets knocked rocks loose and a small avalanche of granite and mica began. He stepped back, his arm over his face for protection. Shards of rock sprayed out and more dust rolled across the tunnel. The rats were visible for one brief second before the entire ceiling collapsed, sealing off the cavern for good. Or so he hoped. He had no idea if there was another way into the cavern, but for now, the rats were stopped and his group was safe…well, most of them were.

He turned and jogged back to the others, who were still standing with guns aimed at the tunnel interior.

Hank held his hands up for them to relax. "I collapsed the tunnel. They can't get to us anymore, we're safe."

"Oh thank God," Laurie said as she went to Hank and fell into his arms. He hugged her and brushed her blonde hair off her face. Her flawless skin was covered in a thick layer of blood, soot and dirt and a few scratches were on her forehead from flying debris, but to him, she'd never looked more beautiful.

"Ah, guys, a little help here?" Cal asked as he leaned over Stacey. The woman was lying on her left side, a puddle of blood pooling at her back as she bled out. Hank studied the wound more closely now that they were in the sunlight and he knew immediately it was fatal. The fact the woman was still alive even now was a miracle.

He knelt down beside her, cradling her head in his hands.

"My father," she whispered. "Where is he? Is he all right?"

Hank weighed his answer. He looked out of the cave opening to the scorched earth that was the remnants of the acid rain. For as far as the eye could see, there was nothing but melted bits of nature. To the right was a pair of squirrel skeletons, the bones so white they looked bleached. Only if you got closer would you see the marks where the acid had been eating at them. Trees everywhere were dead husks, the leaves and bark burned off by the deadly rain. Whether the land would ever recover would be a mystery.

Directly across from the cave opening, Hank saw the skeleton of Martin, the skull bleached as clean as one found in a medical school. The jaw was askew, the eye sockets gaping holes. Not so much as a fly was about, no ants either.

The entire area was dead. Hank thought it all looked like a deadlands, blighted to the point of resembling some strange alien planet. The sky was its now normal red thanks to the radiation in the atmosphere, for the once clear blue sky of the past was long gone.

Scorched earth in its truest form.

Hank turned away from the ravaged land and sighed as he gently wiped a tear from Stacey's cheek.

"Your father's fine, honey. He couldn't make it into the cave with us, but I saw him seek cover before the rain was too bad. He's fine. In fact, he's probably on his way here now. You can see him when he gets here."

Stacey managed a wisp of a smile and then she choked, spitting blood as her entire body was wracked with pain.

'That's good," she whispered. "He's an old man and he couldn't survive long without me." She made a quizzical face. "My legs are numb, am I okay."

Hank only nodded. "Sure you are, honey, you're just tired. Rest now, everything's gonna be fine, you just need to rest."

She sucked in a breath filled with wheezing and she blinked once. "That's a good idea, I am really tired. We had a hell of a time in there with those rats. Wow, they were so big, it's hard to imagine…" Her head sagged and Hank realized she had died in mid-sentence. Gently, he laid her head down and stood up.

Stuart came over to him and patted his arm. "That was kind of you to tell her that her father was still alive."

Hank shrugged. "The truth didn't seem to matter much. At least she died thinking he was still alive, not filled with sorrow for his loss."

A few stones began to shift near the tunnel collapse and all eyes went to it, guns raised and weapons cocked. Each of them tracked the small, baseball-sized rock as it rolled off the pile and came to a stop a few feet near them.

False alarm.

"Come on, let's get out of here, I don't think I want to trust that blockage to stop those bastards." Hank leaned down and picked up Stacey's body, ignoring the blood. "We'll bury her a little ways from here. I want to put some distance between us and this damn cave."

"Amen to that," Carl said, the others agreeing wholeheartedly.

The four warriors set off, careful to avoid stepping in any puddles, the small rain pools still smoking as the acid dissolved the dirt beneath.

Eventually, another rain storm would arrive, hopefully this time with clean rain, and it would dilute and wash the acid away.

Half an hour later, the four companions stood around a shallow grave. Nothing was said.

They had only known Stacey for a few days and so anything said would have been a lie. She was dead and they were alive. In the end, that was the only thing that mattered.

Together, they turned and walked off, the blood red sky looking down on them, not knowing what awaited them, but knowing they would face it together.

As any family would.

DEATH RIDE

Hank Summers fought to stay upright as the motorcycle crested another incline of the dry lakebed, the engine roaring beneath him.

Before the bombs fell there had been a massive lake here, but after a bomb had landed directly in the lake, it had all burned off, leaving nothing but dirt, rocks, and a massive crater where the middle had been.

The terrain was rough and a walking man would have had difficulty, so to say the driving was hard with the motorcycle would be an understatement.

The Honda 750cc engine ticked softly as Hank slowed to a stop, the motor coming down to a dull idle, the heat from the overworked engine baking him from below while the sun did it from above.

It was hot, really hot.

It had to be over a hundred easy and Hank did his best to ignore his discomfort. The shirt he wore was sleeveless; his arms tanned a dark brown from the harsh rays. On his collar he wore a radiation badge, the arrow safely in the green, any radiation from the bomb long dissipated.

As he scanned the austere landscape bordered by mountains, he wondered if he would ever reach his friends.

The four of them had been driving through a narrow pass between two massive cliff faces at the edge of the Rocky Mountains, each of them riding their own motorcycle, when a rock slide had blocked the pass. Hank had been the last one in line and had been cut off from the others. Only his quick reflexes had saved him from being crushed by tons of stone and gravel. When the rock slide began, he looked up, saw what was happening, and knew he couldn't get through in time. So he locked the brakes, spun around, and retreated, a massive boulder landing where he'd been only a second ago.

Such an occurrence had been planned for already, and he knew the others would have gone on and he would have to backtrack and find another way through the mountains.

If all went well, he would rendezvous with the rest of his team in a day at a predestined point they had picked on a map.

Unfortunately, finding another way through the mountains had become more difficult, and each time he found a possible route, it either dead-ended in another rock slide, was washed out by flooding, or went in the wrong direction.

Putting the motorcycle in neutral, he wiped his brow and reached for his canteen. He only took a few sips, knowing he needed to conserve what he had. After putting the cap back on the canteen, he let it go, the container falling to his side where it hung on its strap. His hand went to his weapons out of instinct, he didn't even know he was doing it.

His right hand went to his side arm, holstered to his hip. The SIG-Sauer 226 9mm pistol had a full clip and the clasp on the holster was off for an easy draw. Slung on his shoulder was a Heckler and Koch G-12 automatic rifle, and on his left hip rode a sixteen inch panga, the edge honed to razor sharpness. A web belt covered his chest and there were two hand grenades remaining, both fragmentation grenades. He'd had others but they had been used. He would only use them when the situation was desperate to the point of no return, as they were hard to come by.

Hank gazed up at the sun to get his bearings, and when he was confident he was going the right way, he drove onward. The bike bounced under him like a bucking bull and more than once he almost lost it. With the rocks and scrub that consisted of the land, he knew his fall wouldn't be without injury.

He traveled for almost an hour until he found himself in an even more desolate area—if that was possible—nothing but smooth ground in all directions. The mountains were off to his right and he continued on, knowing when he reached the edge of the mountains, he could cut back in, then swing around to meet up with his friends.

He was halfway across the lakebed when he saw another dust cloud on the horizon. He didn't have to wonder if it was friend of foe. Everyone was considered a foe until proven different nowadays.

Since the bombs fell nearly two years ago, any trace of civilization had been wiped clean from the face of the Earth. Now it was man versus man. Only the strong survived and radiation-mutated humans and the slave-trade abounded, as well as cannibals and coldhearts that would slit your throat if you looked at them wrong. With no real medical care, diseases such at typhoid, cholera, and small pox had slowly been making a resurgence.

It was the Dark Ages all over again.

Hank slowed his bike and weighed his options. He could turn and go back the way he came, he could try to go parallel to the approaching vehicle, or he could wait for them to reach him.

From the way the vehicle changed direction, he knew the driver had seen him.

Deciding he wasn't going to retreat, and there was no way to avoid the oncoming vehicle, he chose to meet it head on. Gripping the throttle and gunning the engine to the motorcycle, he took off, spraying gravel and dirt behind him.

As he got closer to the vehicle, he could see it was a mid-sized truck, and was the kind used to transport livestock. As the dust cleared, he frowned deeply at what the vehicle was transporting.

People, more than a dozen, were packed into the back like sheep being brought to the market.

Hank slowed his motorcycle and pulled his Heckler and Koch rifle from off his shoulder. He made sure the weapon was loaded and ready, then waited for the truck to reach him.

When the vehicle was less than a hundred yards away, his eyes took in every detail of the truck and its occupants. There were three men in the cab, each looking scraggly and unkempt, with long hair and hard faces.

Slavers, by the looks of them.

Hank knew the surrounding area in a fifty mile radius had become a booming slave trade and slavers were more common than not. A lone traveler with no one to watch his back was easy prey for their kind.

The people in the rear bed were tied together so if one was stupid enough to try to escape, they would only end up hanging by their arms to the others.

As if someone in the back of the truck had been thinking that very same thing, or perhaps it was just clumsiness, when the truck hit a small bump, one of the people in back toppled over and fell off.

The body tumbled over the waist-high railing and fell straight down, but when it had fallen no more than six feet, it was yanked back by the arm of the next slave it was attached to. But the body managed to fall enough to have one of its feet catch a rear tire. Like steak pulled into a tenderizer, the body of the screaming man was pulled under the tire and pulped to mush, the screams falling short a second later.

It was possible the entire group of slaves could have been dragged off the rear bed if not for the simple fact that the second slave connected to the corpse had his arm snapped off at the wrist from the yanking of the corpse under the truck's wheels. The man began to scream as the jagged stump sprayed blood in all directions. The truck slammed to a halt and two of the three men jumped out. One man ran around to the left while another went to the right, and as the slave shrieked in agony and bled out, he was mercifully shot in the face, thus solving the problem of his wound and silencing his screams.

Hank watched all this impassively. Though he would have liked to help the slaves, there were three slavers and only one of him.

He considered driving away while the men were distracted, but as he began to roll, he saw both slavers turn in his direction, their guns aimed at him. He knew if he tried to run, there was a good chance he would be shot, and he couldn't shoot back and drive the motorcycle at the same time.

Not wanting to take the chance, he slowed the bike as he steered towards the truck and stopped fifty feet away. He turned off the motorcycle and climbed off it. With rifle in hand, he began to walk another ten feet towards the truck.

The driver climbed out of the cab and watched Hank move closer while the other two men took a moment to calm the slaves before returning to the front of the truck.

Each man held their guns pointed to the ground, but Hank could see it would take less than half a second for them to raise them.

Hank evaluated the firearms of the slavers. The driver, a heavy-set man with a bald pate and two chins, carried a shotgun, while his two partners, both thin men with long hair, carried hunting rifles. Two of them also had side arms strapped to their hips, and one had a large blade that appeared to be a machete, the knife as big as Hank's panga.

The three slavers began to walk closer as Hank stood and waited. The fat man glanced over his shoulder at the rear of the truck, but the slaves were still there and silent. Even if they escaped their bonds, there was nowhere to run to in the wide-open plain. It would be child's play to retrieve any slave who ran and no doubt they would suffer gravely for the inconvenience to the slavers.

When the men were within twenty feet, Hank raised his hand and called out, "That's far enough."

"Who are you?" the fat man asked. He was sweating like a pig, large pools of sweat under his arms.

"Just a traveler," Hank said. "I see you're slavers."

"Yeah, asshole, so fucking what?" one of the other men said. "You got a fucking problem with that?"

Hank did have a problem with it, but three-to-one odds made him know when his chances were bad. "I'd watch your mouth if I were you, pal, I'm not one of those slaves in the back of your truck," he hissed as he gripped his rifle tighter. "I can fight back."

The man snarled, his upper lip coming up and he raised his rifle, but the fat man stopped him before he could raise the gun halfway. "Take it easy there, Jake, we don't want no trouble with this man," the fat man said.

Hank saw the fat man eyeing his weapons and Hank could read his mind. The fat man knew if he tried anything, more than just Hank's blood would be spilled onto the dry ground.

The automatic rifle in Hank's hands could spray the three slavers with bullets before they could get off their first shot. Not to mention, they would need Hank alive to be a slave, and if they killed him, all they would get for their trouble would be his weapons.

Not a bad deal if they could manage it without getting themselves shot, but still, capturing him alive would be better.

"Where you headed?" the fat man asked.

"My business, not yours," Hank replied. The wind was warm and it dried the perspiration on his face as fast as it appeared.

"That's some firepower you got there," the fat man said as he licked his cracked lips. "Mind telling me where you got it?"

"Like I said, that's my business." Hank shifted his stance, the other men also doing the same. "Look, are we gonna stand here all day? Or are you gonna move on and so will I," Hank scowled. "We both know if you try and take me you won't live to see it happen. So what's it gonna be? Leave and continue on, or die here in the middle of nowhere."

"That's tough talk considering you're all alone, asshole!" the thin man yelled, the one who had addressed Hank before.

Hank smiled, a wide one that said he knew something the slaver didn't. "But I'm not alone. I have my friends with me." He raised his rifle and patted his SIG-Sauer.

"Let him go, it's not worth it," the fat man said to the other two.

"But, Larry, we can…" the first man began but was cut off.

"I said fucking leave him be. We got enough slaves and we're runnin' late as it is. We don't need to take on someone with his kind of firepower." He turned and began walking back to the truck, the second man, the one who had said nothing, right behind him.

The thin man growled low in his throat. "Next time, fucker."

"Yeah, next time," Hank replied as he stared the man down.

The thin man turned and walked back to the truck, the other two already climbing inside the cab.

The truck's engine started and drove away in a spray of dust, and as it passed Hank, the eyes of the slaves bore into him. Some cried out for help, some begged for him to kill them, while others said nothing, merely stared at him with dead eyes as they passed him.

Hank watched the truck go, and when he was sure it wasn't going to turn around, that it was no trick, he climbed onto his motorcycle, started the engine, and sped off. He felt guilty for not being able to help the slaves, but he was only one man.

He knew he couldn't save the world and today it had been an absolute fact.

Trying to put the faces of the slaves behind him, he drove on.

If he saw the truck come to a jarring halt in his rearview mirror, he gave no indication.

The truck slowed to a stop and the fat man studied his side mirror, watching Hank disappear into a depression in the lakebed.

"What's wrong? Why're you stopping?" the thin man asked.

"I'm waiting."

"For what?"

"For that guy to feel he's safe, then we can turn around and come up on him from behind."

The thin man grinned slyly. "Why you old dog, you do want to take him."

"Sure I do," the fat man said. "We just needed to make sure there's no way we can lose. There's three of us and only one of him, he can't beat those odds."

He spun the truck around and began to head back the way he'd come, his foot pressed flat on the gas pedal, the truck bouncing over the uneven terrain. "We'll come up on him from behind and there's nothin' he can do to stop us."

The thin man laughed. "All-fucking-right! And if that asshole so much as tries to fight back, I'm gonna put one right in his heart. Fuck the cash we'll get if we take him alive."

The fat man looked at his partner and nodded. "All right, but only if there's no choice. A guy like him will be worth three times what the other slaves are worth." He stepped on the gas pedal harder, the truck surging forward.

Any second now he would see the dust cloud from the motorcycle. And when he did, the fun would begin.

In the basin of the depression, Hank waited.

He had seen the truck turn around and he knew the only way to deal with the slavers was head on. He unslung his rifle and rested the barrel on the seat of his bike. The engine was hot and the heat wafted up to cook the underside of his arms, but he ignored it.

The sound of the truck's engine grew louder and seconds later it appeared at the top of the depression. Hank waited until there was no way the truck could avoid his fire and he let loose, spraying a line of bullets up the sand and into the grille of the truck. There was a loud rattling as the bullets tore into the fan and radiator, and a second later there was a loud bang as something under the hood exploded.

The hood popped off to spin in the air, landing end up in the dirt fifteen feet away. Smoke billowed forth and the slaves in the rear screamed as the three men in the cab jumped out and began to return fire.

Bullets impacted the dirt inches from where Hank was, but he never flinched.

He continued to fire, catching one of the slavers in the shoulder. It was the man who had never spoken. The man spun on his feet and fell to the ground, but was up a second later, firing again.

A bullet ricocheted off the motorcycle's gas tank, only denting the metal, and Hank let out a breath of relief at what might have happened if the bullet had been an inch lower.

Another round zipped past his head, so close he felt the wind shift, and he concentrated his fire on the wounded man. Four bullets hit the slaver, one in the groin, one in the waist, one in the neck, and finally one in the nose. The last round blew out the back of his skull and caused the body to flip over in the air from the impact, a fine pink mist wafting away on the light breeze. The dead man dropped to the dirt and remained still, his blood seeping into the arid land.

A round caught Hank on the right arm, but as soon as he felt the hit, he looked down to see it was a flesh wound. Ignoring the blood seeping down his arm, he fired at the fat man.

The fat man was prone in the dirt and he was a hard target to hit. Hank waited patiently, knowing the man had to poke his head up to shoot.

And then that was exactly what the fat man did. As he rose off the ground a few inches to fire at Hank, the warrior was ready and he sent two rounds into the fat man's head. The head exploded outward, spraying bone and brains in all directions. The fat man's legs kicked a jig as neurons began to cease and the body slumped to the ground, from the neck down looking as if he was taking a nap.

Hank shifted his aim to find the last slaver, and he saw the thin man was running back to the truck. Hank jumped up and ran as well, wanting to get to the man before he could do whatever he was planning. Then he realized it would be quicker to ride, so he spun around and dashed back to the motorcycle, slung his rifle on his shoulder, hopped on the bike, and gunned the engine.

The thin man went back to the cab and reached inside, coming out with a small duffel bag. He reached into it and pulled out a hand grenade.

He pulled the pin and threw it into the basin, right where Hank would have been.

But Hank wasn't running, he was riding, the bike flying across the ground, his tires churning sand and dirt behind them, moving faster than the thin man accounted for.

As the grenade arced through the air, Hank drove right underneath it. As he looked up, he saw the black orb pass overhead, then he was out of the basin and heading directly at the truck.

Behind him, the grenade went off, spraying shrapnel in all directions. Hank had managed to clear the blast radius, but even though he was out of range, he still picked up some minor flesh wounds to his shoulders and lower back, his backpack protecting him from serious harm.

He roared over the edge of the basin and skidded to a halt, letting the motorcycle fall to the ground as he jumped off it. He came up in a crouch, his SIG-Sauer in his hands and the thin man was caught completely off guard.

"No, please, don't kill me," he begged, the man showing himself for the coward he truly was. "For Chrissakes, let me go…please!"

Hank replied by firing a double-burst into the man's chest, sending his internal organs blowing out his back in fist-sized chunks. The man slumped to the ground, his mouth spitting blood as his eyes rolled up into the back of his head. Hank walked over to the thin man and looked down at him. The man was somehow still alive, though he was bleeding out fast. Hank watched as he tried to reach for his gun which had fallen a foot from his body. The hand was weak and it began to inch across the sand, while Hank stood over him, his shadow blocking out the sun. The man actually managed to reach his gun, but just as his fingers caressed the grip, they went limp, the man succumbing to his wounds.

Hank leaned down and picked up the handgun, sliding it into the waistband of his pants. It wasn't his caliber gun but it would be a good item to use in trade at the next recovering town or refugee camp he and his friends came across once he met up with them again. He left the other firearms where they'd fallen, not caring about them and not wanting to be burdened with carrying them. If a man carried too much, it was just as deadly as carrying too little. Besides, let the slaves have them, they would need them for protection and they'd earned it.

He looked up at the sounds of the slaves calling out to him.

"Please help us!" one called.

"Save us!" another cried out.

"Don't leave us!" another said.

Hank bent down and took the hunting knife strapped to the dead man's belt. He threw it at the slaves with the blade still in its sheath. A filthy man with long hair and a scraggly beard caught it and waved, then began quickly cutting his and the other slaves bonds.

Hank went back to his motorcycle. It had stalled and he started it, glad to hear it roar to life. He was worried it might have been flooded when he dropped it.

As he was about to turn away and ride off, one of the slaves, a woman, called out, "What about us? What are we supposed to do now?"

Hank turned to look at her and the other faces behind her, and he shrugged, then pointed west. "Start walking, fifteen miles that way will get you to the end of the plain."

Without waiting for a reply, he gunned the throttle and tore off, back into the basin, around the blast crater from the grenade, and up the other side. He was gone from sight minutes later, even the dust cloud left in his wake lost on the breeze.

With nothing to do but what Hank said, the slavers quickly stripped the dead men and the truck of anything of value, scavenged the guns, and began to walk.

Hank reached the end of the lakebed without issue, and after finding a path into the mountains, he began to wind his way to where he hoped his friends would be waiting. He thought of them as he rode, a smile coming to his lips. First there was Laurie Collins. She was a statuesque blonde with the body of a supermodel and the fighting prowess of a warrior. She wore all black and her boots had silver tips, sharpened to a razor's edge. If needed, she could do some serious damage with them in a fight.

Next was Carl Rivers. A thirty-five year old man with a balding pate and a pasty complexion. He was never seen without his Yankees ball cap or his Mini-Uzi.

And last was Stewart Matheson, a crotchety old man in his sixties with white hair, a cane that had a hidden sword in its frame, and a Heckler and Koch submachine gun.

The four of them had been surviving since the bombs first fell, scavenging for food and ammunition and traveling from place to place, hoping to find somewhere safe. So far that hadn't happened but there was always hope that over the next hill, past the next horizon, there would be someplace that was normal, like the world was before the bombs fell.

Hank had become their leader, his years spent in the US Army now an asset to him and his friends' survival. His knowledge of weapons and combat had kept them alive and he hoped it would continue to do so.

Hank slowed his motorcycle to only a few miles an hour. He could smell smoke hanging in the air. It wasn't the odor of trees burning, this smell was acrid, like when insulation is burning or a house is on fire.

He shifted in his seat and made sure his SIG-Sauer was within reach, and after shifting the bike into second gear, he sped up, his eyes darting every which way.

He was on what had once been a road. There was no pavement beneath his tires but the road was easily discernable beneath the vegetation that was creeping from both sides. Within another two years the entire road would be lost under a thick carpet of vegetation.

Every now and then he spotted a sign within the overgrowth. They were all unreadable now, lost in the myriad of branches and kudzu that now grew unchecked.

He continued on, the smell of smoke growing stronger.

He rounded a bend in the road and came upon what was once a rest stop. Like the road, the area was a fraction of its original size thanks to the growth of trees, shrubs and weeds.

Pulling into the rest stop, Hank wished the motorcycle would be more silent but knew it was a wish that wouldn't be fulfilled. The muffler on the bike had been damaged during the firefight when it had fallen over and it sputtered and coughed like an old Harley Davidson.

At the far end of the rest stop was the origin of the smoke. An old Winnebago was burning, the flames licking out of the shattered windows, the roof all but melted in. It was bad, a raging fire that very possibly would spread to the surrounding area.

Hank stopped the bike and turned off the engine. Slipping off his backpack, he unslung his rifle as he began to inspect the carnage before him. If the flames were that hot, then whoever had done this couldn't be that far ahead of him. They hadn't passed him on his way to the rest stop so they had to be ahead of him.

If he continued up the pass, it was possible he would come upon them.

Next to the Winnebago was the charred body of what was once a man. There was a massive hole where the man's chest should have been and already flies and crawling insects were feeding, even the smoke of the fire not enough of a deterrent to stop them.

Ten feet away was the body of another man, this one leaning against a tree. It was hard to know what the man looked like as his face had been blown off, leaving only from the lower jaw down.

From a cursory glance, it looked to Hank like it had been by a shotgun at almost point-blank range.

A crow sat in the bowl of the head, feeding on the tongue. It pulled and ripped at it and when it saw Hank, it cawed once, tore the tongue free, and flapped away. No sooner did it rise into the air then another crow darted from a nearby tree. The two black shapes raced through the air, the second one trying to steal the tongue from the first. Hank watched them for a few moments, then the crows disappeared over the tree tops, only their cawing as they fought one another floating back.

He let his eyes rove over the rest of the area and his gaze came to a stop at what looked like a campfire. The fire was still burning in the circle of rocks and what looked like dinner was hanging over a spit in the center. As he stepped closer, he also saw the body of a woman, naked from the waist down, lying on the far side. With his rifle ready in case it was a trap, he walked closer to the campfire. Behind him, the walls of the Winnebago fell in on themselves, more smoke and ash rising into the sky.

When he was halfway there, Hank stopped, slung the rifle and pulled his SIG-Sauer. He needed the handgun in case there was any close-in fighting to be had. The rifle was better for long distance targets.

He walked the remaining distance from the woman, and as his eyes studied her back, he couldn't see any blood. But that didn't mean her front was fine, and in fact, it could be nothing but a bloody mess.

His imagination got the better of him and he cringed slightly. If the two men were so damaged, he could only imagine what the woman looked like.

He was only a few feet away when he stopped walking and studied the surrounding treeline.

His instincts kicked in and he could now see there was something wrong with what was before him.

For one thing, with all the overgrown brush surrounding the rest stop, a small army could be hiding within, waiting for the right chance to take him down.

For all he knew, it was a trap, set up by cannies or slavers. They would lay a few bodies in a camp area, light an old wreck on fire, then wait for some travelers to come by and investigate.

Despite the world being a cold and hard place, most people still had good hearts and would try to help a stranger, some even risking their lives to do so.

But not Hank.

A warrior from the first day the world ended, he wasn't about to take a chance, especially over a corpse. He turned and walked back to his motorcycle, this time walking twice as fast.

It was as he was about to start the engine and drive away that he glanced back one final time at the dead woman…and saw her leg twitch slightly.

At first he thought it was his imagination, or worse, a rat or some other creature had burrowed into her corpse and was now feeding, causing her limbs to move. But when it happened again, he knew the woman was alive.

"Damn it," he muttered under his breath, knowing he couldn't leave her like that. What if it had been Laurie lying there? Wouldn't he want someone to help her?

Climbing off the bike, he moved back to the woman to see what he could do to either help her, or if she was too far gone, at least he could show her mercy and kill her quick.

He hated how she was in the open like that, and his eyes scanned the surrounding bushes, his ears straining to hear anything that shouldn't be there. The woman let out a small moan, reminding Hank she needed help.

With his hand on his SIG, he crossed the few remaining feet separating her from him.

Though on guard, he couldn't help but shake the feeling there was someone or something in the bushes. He imagined a gun going off and then feeling the impact of the round to the chest. He would fall down, his insides spilling out of him as he began to bleed out. He imagined raiders coming out of the bushes and jumping on him, slowly stripping him of his gear as his vision began to fade.

But that didn't happen and the brush remained silent.

If there were people waiting to attack, for some reason they were holding their ground. Hank wondered if it was his weapons, and if he had more grenades to spare, he would have used one now, pulling the pin and tossing it into the treeline. That would sure as hell spook anything in there. But with only two left it wasn't worth it, especially for just a hunch.

He knelt down near the woman's head and touched her shoulder with his left hand…

And nearly had his head blown off when she rolled over and fired a revolver at his face.

If he hadn't been so alert, so wary of a trap, she might have succeeded, but his reflexes were snapping into action before the report of the gun had faded. He bent his back to the side and snapped his head back, the bullet coming so close to his nose he felt it graze the tip.

As for the woman, she was yelling loudly, a maniacal laughter mixed in with her cries. Her eyes were wide with fury and hate as spittle rolled down her chin. Hank didn't give her time for a second shot. As he jumped back to avoid a new hole in his head, he brought the SIG around and used it as a club. The butt of the grip smashed into the woman's nose, crushing it and sending shards of cartilage into her brain. She was dead before she realized her trap had failed, her eyes rolling up into the back of her head and her body going limp. In her death throes, she managed to squeeze the trigger of her gun and it fired once more, the round going wide to end up digging into the dirt ten feet away.

It was hard to hear, thanks to the gunshot so close to his head, but even over the ringing, Hank heard the three filthy men bound out of the nearby foliage, weapons in hand, howling like wild animals.

The first man, a stubby bald man with a thin mustache, was firing wildly in Hank's direction but none of the bullets even came close. It was as if the man was in a world of his own, or perhaps he hoped that as long as he kept shooting, sooner or later one of the bullets would find a target. One did, but it was the wrong body. The bullet hit the woman in the throat, exploding out the back of her neck to end up in the ground beneath her. The woman didn't even twitch, she was already dead.

Hank returned fire immediately, sending a double-tap into the man's chest. Both bullets found their mark and the man tripped on his feet and fell face first into the dirt, sliding a foot before stopping. His feet kicked up and down as he died, a pool of blood seeping out from under him to soak the earth a dark red.

Hank had to make up his mind who to take out next.

The second man had a shotgun and was having a bit of trouble with the breach. The third man, well over six feet with a huge gut and a machete, was just leaving the treeline and Hank decided the man with the shotgun was the greater threat.

Just as the man with the gun fixed what was wrong and raised the weapon, Hank fired another double-tap into his face. The back of the raider's head disappeared in a spray of blood, skull bits and brain matter, and he flopped back into the brush, his legs kicking into the air comically as he fell.

He didn't get back up.

Hank quickly realized his choice of targets may have been wrong when he suddenly found the large man with the machete looming over him, the man moving faster than Hank would have guessed possible given his huge bulk.

As the machete came down to take off his head, Hank used the SIG to deflect it and knock it away, the blade falling to the ground to slide three feet away. Hank brought up his left knee into the raider's groin. Other than a slight grunt, the huge man didn't flinch. Before Hank saw the fist coming at his head, he felt a roundhouse that sent him to his knees, stars and flashes of light dancing across his vision. In the scuffle, he dropped the SIG and tried desperately to shake the cobwebs from his addled brain.

He heard the big man coming in for the attack and Hank rolled away, just doing his best to stay out of reach of those large hands and heavy fists.

Seconds was all he needed, and as his vision cleared, he opened his eyes to see another fist coming at his face. This time he managed to duck it, and as he raised his arm to deflect the blow, he kicked out with his right boot, the sound of a cracking knee filling him with pride.

Howling and yelling, the big man limped forward, his hands open, fingers flexing as they prepared to wrap around Hank's neck.

And then Hank spotted a fourth man coming out of the brush. This man was small, barely over five feet with a scraggly beard, and he held a hunting rifle in his hands.

With one eye on the big man and one eye on the small one, Hank saw the new arrival raise his rifle to shoot him.

There was nowhere to hide, nowhere to run, so Hank took the only option available to him. He jumped onto the back of the big man and held on for dear life. He hoped that as long as he was connected to the large brute, the small man wouldn't shoot.

It was like riding a bull only bigger and Hank felt the air leave his lungs as the big man tried to throw him off his back. Even the man's crushed knee didn't slow his fury.

Hank was pummeled on both sides as the brute tried to get him off. Then, the big man wrapped a meaty hand around Hank's right wrist and pulled Hank's hand off his neck. Hank slid off and the big man began to swing him, like when a father swings his boy in a circle for fun, the two holding hands.

When he let go, Hank knew he was in trouble as he flew through the air. He knew that as soon as he landed, the small man would shoot and that would be it. He would be on the last train west with a one way ticket to Hell.

The air whistled through his ears and then he was on the ground, rolling. His rifle had been with him the entire time but he wasn't able to get it and there was still no time as he kept rolling, the rifle's strap sliding off and the gun sliding away. Then Hank was flat on his back, staring up at the sky, and he heard the big man laughing. He sounded like a retard and Hank wondered if the man was slow in the head.

The small man jumped into the air and kicked his legs happily as he prepared to shoot, but overconfidence had taken over and the man was taking his sweet time.

As Hank lay there, he felt something under the small of his back. When he reached under his body to see what it was, his eyes went wide when he felt the solid grip of his SIG-Sauer. By luck or fate, he had landed on it.

Wrapping his hand around the grip, he snapped it up and aimed it at the small man, squeezing the trigger without hesitation.

Both men fired at the same time, but Hank was just a fraction of a second faster. The round caught the small man in the shoulder and he spun and fell. The man's bullet went over Hank's head, but ended up in the groin of the big man behind Hank. With blood seeping from between his legs, the brute went to his knees, screaming as his shattered knee took his weight and blood dripped down his pant leg.

Hank was on his feet in a second, his head filled with fog and dizziness. He fought it down, knowing he needed to stay focused if he was going to see his way clear of the trap.

The small man was getting to his feet again. One arm was useless and hung limp by his side, the entire limb covered in bright arterial blood. More blood ran down his chin from where he'd bitten his lip at being shot. He hissed angrily, scarlet spittle running down his chin to splash in the dirt.

He was trying to raise the rifle again.

Hank fired one shot, directly at the man's head. The bullet impacted the man's left eye, slicing into it like a hot knife into warm butter. The back of his head blew out, spraying the ground with red gore and brain matter. The man was thrown backward where he landed with splayed limbs.

Hank heard a roar come from behind him and he turned to see the brute of a man was on his feet once more. He had his machete as well, and though limping heavily, he began an awkward charge at Hank, his eyes filled with rage.

Hank didn't hesitate nor did he let the man get any closer. As the brute roared another challenge, Hank shot him in the chest.

The big man seemed to falter as the bullet pulverized his heart. He stopped his forward momentum and stood perfectly still. His eyes blinked once at Hank, as if he wanted to ask a question.

Then he tipped over like a fallen tree, bouncing once when he hit the ground. As a dust cloud dissipated over him and the smoke from the Winnebago drifted into the sky, Hank went to a knee and sighed.

All around him was death, and he cast a glance at the man with half a head, one of the corpses he'd found when first arriving.

The trap laid by the woman and her partners had worked on the owners of the Winnebago and would have probably worked on him as well if not for a few lucky breaks and quick reflexes.

Still, a flip of the coin could have had him lying in the dirt with half his head blown off and all his weapons and belongings stripped from his body.

As he took stock of himself and sucked in a deep breath, glad not to feel any sharp pains in his ribs, he stood up. He had made it through the battle intact, and though a little sore, he suddenly felt an overwhelming hunger fill him.

He was starving.

Nothing worked up an appetite more than a fight to the death.

He looked back at the campfire and the spit with meat still roasting over the open flame. By some miracle of good fortune, the meat was untouched by the fight and other than some charring on the bottom part facing the flame, was more than edible.

After reloading the SIG and retrieving his rifle, he dragged the woman's corpse away from the fire and sat down next to it. Pulling his panga from its sheath, he cut himself a healthy piece of meat. At the first bite he knew it was rabbit, and he chewed happily while grease ran down his chin to drip between his legs and land in the dirt.

Surrounded by death and flames, Hank dined alone, the dead woman only a few feet away, now nothing more to him than carrion.

Hank glanced down at the speedometer and did some quick calculations on how many miles he'd traversed. By his count, the gas tank on the bike should be just about empty. The bike did have a fuel gauge but it was broken, the needle permanently stuck on the E.

The road he was on had once been used as the scenic route through the mountains, but now it was just a little bigger than a footpath. Fallen trees, overgrown foliage and rock falls had turned the road into a narrow trail sometimes only a few feet wide, while other times it was as large as before the bombs.

Wildlife was prevalent; Hank had seen everything from deer, a family of bears, to roaming packs of what were once simple housecats but were now feral and wild animals.

When the world collapsed, dogs and cats survived along with people, but in a world where every day was hand to mouth, unless you were going to eat your pet, there was no use for it. Thousands upon thousands of pets had been, eaten, abandoned or set free to fend for themselves. The end result were the animals returning to what they were before domestication—wild animals that hunted in packs.

The sun was low in the sky as Hank pulled over to refuel in a small clearing just off the road. There was a small luggage rack on the back of the motorcycle, and inside his sleeping bag was a two liter soda bottle filled with scavenged gasoline.

As he pulled the bottle out of its hiding place, he briefly thought what would have happened if a stray bullet had found it during his shootout with the slavers, but he quickly brushed the image away. To think about what might have happened served no purpose.

Since traveling the hellscape of the new world, Hank had learned not to worry about the past or future, to only live in the here and now.

Opening the gas cap on the bike's fuel tank, he filled it up, using his remaining supply. Without putting the cap back on the bottle, he tossed it to the side where it rolled a few feet and stopped.

Reaching into a side bag on the bike, he pulled out a candy bar and ate it greedily, then washed it down with water from his canteen. With more room on the luggage rack, he strapped his backpack to it so he wouldn't have to carry it.

Studying the sky, he knew it would be night soon, but he hoped to be with his friends before it was completely dark. The headlight did work on the motorcycle, though it was never wise to travel at night, but he was so close he wanted to end his lonely journey.

Before he headed out, he decided to empty his bladder. He walked a few feet from the bike, picked a good tree, and unzipped his fly. He sighed softly as the pressure was released and then quickly zipped up, careful not to have an 'accident' with his zipper.

When he was zipped up and ready to leave, and was about to turn around and go back to his bike, he suddenly froze. He'd heard a low growl come from directly behind him.

He immediately stopped moving and realized he had dropped his guard while urinating and had opened himself up to an attack.

Slowly, careful not to make any sudden moves, both his hands went down to his weapons as he slowly began to turn around. His right hand wrapped around the grip of the SIG and his left found the worn handle of his panga. He didn't pull either, not wanting to spook his attacker.

The growling grew in pitch and he could only pray he would have time to at least face his foe before he was jumped. He knew what the growl meant, and that if he didn't stay calm and act when necessary, he wouldn't live to see the sun rise the next day.

As he slowly finished turning around, his eyes went wide when he saw one attacker was the furthest thing from the truth.

When he heard the low growl, he knew instantly it was a wild dog, but he didn't expect to see an entire pack, or he'd hoped there wasn't an entire pack. One dog would be child's play to take down by an armed man, but an entire pack was a new challenge altogether. Sure, he could shoot the first one or two, but while those were being taken down, the others would overwhelm him.

His eyes played over the feral pack before him. Each dog was dirty and malnourished, and more than one had its ribs clearly defined on its matted fur. More than half of the pack had legions and weeping sores covering their bodies, remnants from the bombs. Radiation or biological fallout was Hank's guess.

There were six in all, one German shepherd, two Dobermans, one Collie, a Mastiff that wasn't yet full grown, a Bulldog, and one that was a mix of the others with a few more breeds thrown in; a pure mutt if there ever was one. The mutt was as large as the Doberman and seemed to be the lead dog, the alpha male. This was the animal that had growled.

As Hank studied his adversaries, he saw that three of the dogs still wore dog collars with tags on them. Though they may have been man's best friend at one time, he knew they were now nothing but natural born killers.

"Okay, fellas, let's not do anything we'll regret," he said as he tried to take a step to the side so he had more room to maneuver.

His main fear was if the dogs carried rabies. One bite from one of them and he would be in a world of hurt. He tried to see if any of the dogs showed signs of the disease, but it was hard to tell. As far as he could see, none were foaming at the mouth, and there was no water nearby to test the rabies theory either and he wasn't about to waste his canteen supply.

When he shifted to the side, the alpha dog growled again, followed by the Doberman who lowered its head and raised its haunches.

"Good doggies, nice doggies," he said with a wide smile. "You don't want to eat me, I'm old and stringy. I'll give you the runs."

The German shepherd lowered its head and its ears went tight against its skull at the same time as the mutt's did. Hank knew this would only end one way and that was with blood spilt on the ground. Whether it was canine or human was yet to be seen.

His knuckles were white on his weapons and it took all he had not to pull them, but he knew the instant he moved, the dogs would attack, seeing his motion.

It was difficult trying to watch all seven dogs at the same time, but he did his best, wondering which one would attack first.

And as soon as the thought crossed his mind, he had his answer.

It came from the dog he would have least expected—the Collie.

One second the dog was growling like the others, and then it was a blur of fur as it jumped from a crouched position.

No sooner did the dog attack, then the others followed suit, all barking and growling as their teeth flashed in the waning light. Hank pulled his weapons and lunged to the left, the Collie missing his left arm by inches, its teeth clacking on empty air.

Rolling across the ground, he came up shooting, sending a round into the side of the Collie. The bullet went in one side, leaving a small red hole, but when it exited on the opposite side, it took a large portion of intestine and meat with it. The dog yelped in pain as it fell to the ground, its teeth snapping at the wound, not understanding why it was in pain.

The German shepherd turned away from the pack and attacked the Collie, tasting the blood in the air, and began to fight with the Collie. Hank saw this in a glance and realized the dogs were so hungry they would turn on each another at the first smell of spilled blood.

Using this to his advantage, he swung the panga low near his knees and slashed at the bulldog as it tried to bite his thigh. The blade bit in more than an inch before hitting bone, and the dog let out a yelp that sounded hauntingly like a human scream. It rolled away and growled, but was quickly attacked from behind by the mastiff. The larger dog sank its teeth into the side of the bulldog and the smaller dog yelped yet again.

Hank shot the mixed breed mutt as it lunged for him and hit it squarely in the chest. The bullet went deep into the body, pulverizing organs, and the dog landed at Hank's feet, dead.

As he stepped away, one of the Dobermans charged in and began tearing at the carcass, its sharp teeth gouging out furrows of fur and flesh. Hank shot the Doberman as it began feeding, hitting it in the shoulder. As the dog yelped and began to bleed out, it never stopped eating, so strong was the urge to feed. Then the second Doberman tasted blood in the air, and it attacked the first one, both soon fighting one another, the carcass of the mixed breed forgotten.

Hank saw that all the dogs were now either fighting one another or feeding, and he took his chance to escape. Dashing across the glade, he holstered his weapons, jumped onto the motorcycle, turned the key in the ignition, and drove off, the rear tire spraying dirt behind it.

The dogs looked up as the bike roared away, but quickly discarded it as not worth their time and went about fighting amongst themselves.

Hank glanced in his side mirror one time to see that the German shepherd was under siege by two other dogs, its intestines hanging out of its side as the other dogs pulled on them like it was a game of tug-of-war, then he turned down a bend in the road and the pack was lost from sight.

Concentrating on the road ahead as the light faded to black, he left the carnage behind him and continued onward.

Hank was only a few miles from his rendezvous with his friends. But unfortunately, night had fallen more than an hour ago and he was struggling to keep his eyes open. He had wanted to stop and rest, but after barely escaping the dog pack, he decided to keep moving, knowing a moving target was harder to find.

He hadn't felt so alone in a long time. Though the nukescape of the world was filled with danger at every turn, he had always felt he could handle it thanks to his three friends. But now, alone on the road, with no one to watch his back…well, the feeling of vulnerability was one he just couldn't shake.

The road had shrunk in size, the trees and shrubs encroaching on both sides. In the last mile or so the kudzu had been like a living creature, growing six feet tall in some places. Its vines were mingled with everything, choking the life out of the other plant life. Hank could only imagine what this part of the road would be like in another year, hell even six months.

The road dog-legged sharply to the right and Hank leaned into the turn, weeds slapping at his legs as he drove. His headlight was the only source of illumination; even the stars and moon were hiding behind heavy cloud cover.

It was as he was going into the turn, that he didn't see the zip line stretched across the road until he connected with it. There was no time to duck, stop or do anything but brace himself as he felt the line go taut and he was lifted off the bike and thrown backwards. The motorcycle continued on for another twenty feet before veering off to the left. It went into the treeline and was stopped cold, the tires catching the kudzu and the vines holding it fast. It toppled over, the lush foliage like a massive green pillow. The rear tire still spun, the engine still running; it was still in gear.

Hank saw none of this. Flying backwards, he landed hard on his back in the middle of the road, the air in his lungs leaving him like a giant foot had stepped on his chest. His rifle was under him and he could feel where the gun now pressed into his back.

He lay still, dazed, for a few seconds not knowing where he was. The back of his head had struck the road and only the thin layer of plant life had saved him from a cracked skull. But still, he was so confused that he didn't do anything but lay immobile, as if he was dead.

From his right, out of the treeline, four human figures emerged. If it wasn't for the headlight of the motorcycle—which though facing the wrong way, still let a dim backlight of a glow suffuse the road, as well as the rear red taillight—Hank wouldn't have been able to make out the four figures.

In the dull gloom, through cracked eyelids, he saw that the four people weren't normal. They were mutants, or as close to what a mutant was in the hellscape of the new world.

When the bombs fell, the closest to the blast were incinerated in a split second, but those miles away from the blast were dosed with high counts of radiation. Now, two years later, the result of being bombarded by those rads was evident. Though still the shape of a human being, that was where the resemblance ended. By some curse of God, the exposed people hadn't died from radiation poisoning, but had instead morphed, changed, into something only seen in nightmares.

Their skin was bright red and peeling, the exposed tendons glistening in the wan light. Some had missing eyes and ears, one had a missing nose, and all had faces covered in blisters, the bubbles looking as if they were ready to pop at any second.

They wore the barest of clothing, due to the fact that anything touching their flesh was pure torture. They lived in constant agony, as if they had received the worst possible burns and then had to live with it forever with no hope of ever recovering.

Their faces were set in a perpetual rictus of pain, their eyes—those that had them—glowing from the rads they'd absorbed. They grunted and moaned as they came out of the treeline, a few words spoken curtly.

They quickly surrounded Hank, each leering over his still body, their swollen tongues licking cracked and split lips. They were hungry and Hank would become a feast fit for a king.

Each of them carried a weapon. There were three men and one woman. Two of the mutated men held knives, and the other man carried a gun, but by the way he held it, the gun didn't appear loaded or the man didn't consider Hank a threat. The woman carried a simple wooden club carved from a tree branch. There were a few nails embedded on the tip, making it a deadly weapon despite its simplicity.

Hank controlled his breathing as he regained his faculties, showing no signs he was awake. Surrounded and outnumbered, the only advantage he had was surprise. His enemies thought him either dead or unconscious which he was neither, but he had to wait for the right time to act. If he just jumped up and attacked, he might manage to take out two, even three of his adversaries, but the odds of the fourth one getting the drop on him was over-whelming.

No, he needed to wait for the right moment and pray it came.

Two of the men reached down and picked him up under the arms. The third man stood to the side and gestured for the woman to take Hank's weapons. She nodded, and with a low grunt, went to Hank and slid off the automatic rifle, having to make one of the men let Hank go so she could slide it off his shoulder.

She turned and handed it to the third man, and as she did, the third man's view of Hank was blocked when she stepped in front of him.

Hank, his head hanging low as he played possum, realized his chance to act was now or never, especially while he was still armed with his SIG and panga.

As the woman handed the gun to the man, Hank's head suddenly snapped up, causing the two mutants holding him to gasp in surprise.

For one instant in time they were flatfooted, caught completely off guard.

Hank flexed his right arm and yanked the man to him, then swung him into the other one. The two men slapped together and both went down in a clump of arms and legs.

Meanwhile, the woman had turned around at the sound of the scuffle, and with a throaty yell, she lunged at Hank, while behind her the man who had taken Hank's rifle tried to bring the gun up to shoot Hank and end the conflict before it began.

Hank saw this and made an oath to himself that he'd be damned if he would be killed by his own gun.

As the woman came for him, her club raised high to crack his head open, Hank ducked under her blow and punched her in the face. As she went to the side, he grabbed her arm and pulled her to him to use as a shield. He did this just as the man fired the rifle, the bullet hitting the woman in the stomach.

Hank felt the bullet pass through her and hit him, too, but by luck it hit his belt buckle. Even though, he still felt the force of the expired round. Letting the woman drop, he pulled his SIG and panga at the same time. As the man tried to fire the rifle again, Hank shot him right between the eyes, sending his brains and the back of his head spraying out behind him. The man dropped like a sack of potatoes that had fallen off a truck, his legs twitching as nerve endings shut down forever.

Hank saw none of this as he turned to deal with the last two men.

The mutant he had used to swing into the second one was on his knees, ready to jump at Hank, but before he could get to his feet, Hank swung the panga in a horizontal swipe that sheered the mutant's head from his shoulders as if he was a stalk of wheat. Blood geysered up like a fountain as the arms flayed about, then the decapitated corpse toppled over.

The last attacker was on his feet and with his knife in hand, he came at Hank.

But the warrior was ready and Hank shot him in the chest, missing the heart by less than an inch. The man stumbled forward, his mouth open in shock, as he looked down to see blood spurting from the new hole in his chest.

When he looked up, he saw Hank coming at him.

Hank had the panga low and he brought it up and under the mutant's chin. The tip of the blade went straight up, slicing through jaw bone, through the mouth, and into the brain, killing him instantly. As he shit his pants in death, the body dropped to the ground, blood spurting from its mouth in great gurgles and bubbles.

The panga was jammed into the skull so tight that Hank had to let it go as he turned to face the next threat.

He saw all the mutated humans were down.

And then the woman moved.

She began to crawl across the ground, her hand reaching out for the club she'd dropped. Hank walked over to her and stepped on her hand, the bones breaking as he slowly swiveled the heel of his boot back and forth. She gasped in pain and slowly, like a child, turned her face to look up at Hank.

Her gaze was greeted by the open barrel of the SIG-Sauer. She only had time to blink before her head exploded as a round was fired point blank into her forehead.

As blood shot out of the massive head wound, Hank stepped away, not wanting to get any more blood on him.

He went to his Heckler and Koch rifle and picked it up, studying the barrel and stock to make sure it wasn't damaged. Slinging it over his shoulder, he went to one of the fallen mutants and used the scrap of clothing on the corpse to wipe his panga clean.

He gave the scene of carnage one last look, then walked over to his fallen motorcycle. After turning it off, he picked it up and dragged it out of the trees. After inspecting and securing his weapons, he started the engine and was relieved when it turned over on the first try.

He headed off, the illumination from the bike's head-and-taillight fading as he drove further down the road, the four corpses soon swallowed by the darkness.

It was still an hour before dawn when Hank slowed the motorcycle and finally stopped it.

Though he wanted to keep going, his eyes were so heavy he knew if he didn't rest he would end up falling asleep and driving off the road.

He pushed the bike into the dense foliage lining the road and went to a nearby tree with lush leaves and thick branches. He stood silently at its base, listening.

After stopping and standing immobile for more than five minutes, he was confident he was alone. All around him the background noise of the area came to him: crickets chirping softly, night birds calling to one another, and a few rodents scurrying about. The engine on the motorcycle ticked softly, but that soon passed.

Using the shoulder strap of the H&K, he swung it up and over the lowest limb of the tree—which was about eight feet off the ground—and began to climb. He ascended more than fifteen feet, then found a place where two limbs grew out from the trunk to make a tight V shape.

After hanging his pack on a head-level branch, he took his rifle and began cleaning it, careful not to place his gear on a branch where it might fall off. Under the starlight that managed to filter through the thick canopy of leaves above him, he worked quickly. When the Heckler and Koch G-12 rifle was clean and oiled, he pulled out his SIG-Sauer 226 and quickly disassembled it and began oiling and greasing it as well.

Lastly, he pulled his panga from its sheath, and with some of the gun oil, he gave the blade a thick coat, doing his best to clean any blood that might have gotten into the grip.

When all his weapons were clean and loaded, he ate a light meal of what he still had in his pack. Then, after climbing to the side, away from his perch and urinating while standing, the stream falling to the leaves and ground below on the opposite side of him, he got as comfortable as was possible given he was going to sleep in a tree.

He closed his eyes, secure in the knowledge that as high as he was, even the most determined predator couldn't get him.

As the sun broke through the horizon of burnt sky, Hank slowly came awake to the sound of barking and growling.

For one brief instant, he didn't know where he was and almost rolled clear out of the tree. But then his instincts kicked in and his memory of where he was came flooding back to him. The barking grew louder and he looked down at the base of the tree to see another dog pack there. It looked like they had followed him. It didn't really surprise him when he thought about it for a moment.

He had been on the road for more than a day and between the sweating and the blood splatter he no doubt had on him, the sensitive sniffer on many dogs would make him easy to track.

The pack was smaller than when he had last tangled with it and only a few of the dogs were from the original one. As he studied the pack, he saw the remaining Doberman and the mastiff. Both were covered in blood and had wounds on them, but had evidently escaped the dog fight in one piece.

There were three new dogs with the original two, all three looking half-starved and ravenous. At least two of them looked as if they might have rabies.

Out of the three new dogs, Hank could only recognize one by its breed.

It was a Labrador retriever, with a large head and its ribs poking out of its ratty fur. Its once lush dark coat was now a matted black, and even from where Hank sat, he could see that the animal was feral, as were the rest of the pack. It snarled and slavered as its front paws scratched at the tree trunk, the dog wanting to climb the tree and pull Hank down.

Hank weighed his options, trying to decide on the best tactic. In the end, he decided to wait the dogs out. Sooner or later, they would grow tired and hungrier, then would move on for easier prey.

He felt like a cat chased up a tree, and though frustrated with his situation, he took heart in knowing that if he had camped on the ground, it was very likely the dogs would have attacked him easily and would even now be feeding on his corpse.

But as the hours passed and the dogs showed no signs of leaving, Hank realized he had no choice but to shoot them one by one.

He hadn't wanted to do this for the simple reason that if there were any human enemies in the area, the gunshots would have alerted them to his location, and with his ammunition dwindling, he didn't want to take that chance.

It was noon when he shot the first dog, the bullet going through its head and blasting the ground with gore. As the dog crumpled to the dirt, the others turned on it and began to feed.

With the automatic rifle set to single shot, Hank shot the mastiff next. The round from the H&K struck the animal in the upper right shoulder and then went down into the torso. The dog yelped and its head swung back to bite at the wound, not understanding why it was in pain. As the blood seeped from the bullet hole, the other dogs smelled the fresh blood, and before the mastiff knew what was happening, the Doberman and another of the dogs were attacking it. Hank watched from above as the dogs fought amongst themselves, teeth and claws tearing into one another.

He shot two more dogs, each time only wounding them, but the spilt blood did plenty to keep the frenzy going.

It took almost an hour for the final two dogs to square off and for the loser to succumb to its wounds. As the last dog fed on the carcasses of its brethren, Hank shimmied down the tree with his rifle now shouldered and his SIG aimed at the animal.

Reaching the ground, he carefully crept to his motorcycle, wary for the dog to turn and attack him. But it did no such thing, its muzzle buried in the stomach of its fresh kill, chomping and tearing at the meat.

Making it to the motorcycle, Hank climbed on, checked one last time to make sure the dog was still occupied, and lifted his right leg to kick start the engine.

It was as his leg was raised that he heard the sound of one or more car engines over the noise of the feeding dog.

He hesitated for a brief second as he listened and the distinct sound of the engines and people yelling floated on the wind. With each passing moment, the noise became louder.

"Damn it," he snarled as he kick-started the motor. It was just as he'd feared. When he'd shot the dogs, he'd called attention to himself. He didn't know who was coming down the road, but by the way they were yelling and laughing, he doubted they were the Welcome Wagon.

Spraying dirt behind the rear tire, he swung the bike around and gunned the throttle at the same time two four-by-four Jeeps erupted from the brush off to the side and behind him, both vehicles filled with men.

A flurry of gunshots rang out and Hank felt one pass so close to his head that he felt the wind displace in its passing. More shots rang out and the ground behind the motorcycle was chewed up as someone with an automatic rifle began walking bullets to their target.

But as the bullets landed where Hank's rear tire should have been, the area was empty, the motorcycle shooting down the road at a breakneck speed.

The feeding dog, finally disturbed by all the commotion, looked up and snarled at the oncoming Jeeps. But that's all the animal had time for before a stray bullet found its brain and pulverized it. With half a head, the animal dropped to the ground, very dead.

The Jeeps roared past in pursuit of Hank.

Branches slapped Hank's face, and from behind him, as they gave chase, the men whooped and hollered even louder. They continued to shoot at him and Hank swerved back and forth, hoping that as long as he stayed a moving target, the men couldn't hit him.

On a straightaway before he swerved yet again, Hank glanced in his side mirror to try and get a better look at his pursuers and by doing so, hopefully would know how good his chances were of escaping alive.

On his brief glimpse, he saw four men in each Jeep, all looking filthy, with hard faces and long, unkempt hair. More than half had scraggly beards.

Slavers or cannies probably, Hank figured, but either way he didn't want to find out which—both were bad news.

Overgrown branches reached out onto the road and slapped Hank's face again as he gunned the throttle, shooting ahead of the leading Jeep. Sounds of anger floated back to him over the whining motor and he could hear the report of gunshots. He swerved as best he could, the hairs on the back of his neck standing at attention as he anticipated getting a bullet in the back. He imagined it would be a moment of shock and pain before he was knocked off the bike by the impact. He was going well over forty miles an hour, and if the bullet didn't kill him, it was possible the fall to the ground would.

With nothing to lose, he engaged the throttle all the way, redlining the engine as he shot forward.

He almost lost control as he rounded a sharp bend, the front tire slipping on the lush greenery covering the pavement, but at the last possible second he pulled the bike up, wobbled for a second, then burst onward.

The lead Jeep made the corner as well, but the second one took the corner too fast and too wide. Its front bumper banged off the moss-covered guardrail and almost flipped over, but the driver was either incredibly skilled or incredibly lucky. At the last possible moment, he brought the Jeep under control and continued on, a few car lengths back but still in one piece.

The chase went on for more than an hour and Hank knew his luck had to run out sooner or later. He was about to pick a spot that would give him cover, pull over, then draw his weapons, hoping to at least take as many of the coldhearts with him as he could before he was gunned down.

His blood surged in his ears as he concentrated on holding his ground, the engine roaring beneath him. Time seemed to stand still, and after the second hour, he was in a daze, staring at the road ahead—nothing else mattered.

He was so focused on escape that he didn't notice when he came around a bend in the road, took an onramp, and the new road opened up to a two lane highway.

A state highway sign was on his right as he drove past it, and he realized he was close to the rendezvous with the rest of his group.

With a smile on his lips, he gunned the throttle yet again, seeing the two Jeeps pull onto the highway behind him.

Hank had an advantage now that the Jeeps didn't have. Abandoned cars and trucks littered the highway, and though the motorcycle could weave its way through the vehicles, the Jeeps had a tougher time, sometimes having to drive onto the mud-filled shoulder of the road, their thick tires churning the wet earth and long grass into a dark brown slurry.

Hank began to make headway and put more distance between himself and the Jeeps.

Ten minutes later and he spotted the off ramp he knew he needed to take, and he drove onto it, a glance in his side mirror telling him the Jeeps were still there and that the men knew he had exited the highway.

At the bottom of the ramp, he took a right, and as he moved around the derelict cars and trucks here as well, he soon came upon another rest stop with a burned out husk of what had been a small convenience store.

As he turned into it, he found there were three people with their guns aimed at him, but the owners all held their fire.

Hank didn't stop the bike to get off it, but merely slowed down and jumped off, letting the motorcycle continue another fifteen feet before it crashed into the thick foliage bordering the forest surrounding the area.

There was no time to stop properly, as every second mattered, and at any moment the two Jeeps would be upon him and the three new people.

Standing before Hank with weapons now lowered, Stewart, Carl and Laurie all waited for an explanation for Hank's strange behavior.

Stewart had enough time to say, "Hank, what the hell is the matter with you?" Before Hank began talking, fast and curt, explaining that he was being followed, the engines of the two Jeeps came to them as the sound floated on the wind, signaling their approach.

The instant Hank was done filling in his companions, they went into action, each taking up a firing position across the rest stop.

Carl went to the far right, his Mini-Uzi aimed at the road, his Yankees baseball cap pulled down tightly on his head, covering his bald pate.

Stewart took the far left, his Heckler and Koch submachine gun leveled at the open road, his white hair blowing in the gentle breeze. For all of his sixty years, he still looked formidable, and his cane with the hidden sword was now hanging from his belt if it was needed.

Standing in the middle of the rest stop was Hank, his SIG-Sauer pistol in his hand, and beside him was his lover Laurie. Her long blond hair blew off her shoulders and swayed in the wind and her all black leather outfit made her pop out from the surrounding green foliage. On the tips of her boots, the pointed steel flashed in the sunlight. In her hand she held her PPK .22. The small caliber gun was wielded with exceptional skill and each shot fired by her was deadly. She had once told Hank she could shoot the ass off a fly and he knew on more than one occasion she'd proven it.

Together, the four warriors of the apocalypse stood their ground, ready to kill or be killed, when the two Jeeps arrived.

In the new world of carnage and death, retreat wasn't an option…only victory was.

Sirus Miller laughed and hooted louder as the Jeep he was in crested the road and gained on the man on the motorcycle. The three men with him also yelled and screamed, shooting at shadows as the Jeep roared around the bend.

Behind him, the second Jeep followed, the four men in it also yelling up a storm.

The eight men were slavers and they had been on the hunt for prey when they had heard the echoes of Hank shooting the dogs.

Quick to act, they had doused their campfire, climbed into their vehicles, and within two minutes were on the road again, following the sounds of the gunshots.

The Jeeps were four wheel drives and did a great job of blazing their own trail through the thick forest.

Sirus was the leader of the slavers and had reached that position by strength alone. Though not the brightest man in the world, he was strong, stood well over six feet, and had no conscience. He would kill a man for looking at him funny and had done so on multiple occasions.

He had been a farmer before the bombs fell but when the world collapsed in on itself, he'd found a different calling. Never a decent man before the world ended, now with only the law of the gun ruling a devastated land, he was able to let his inner demons loose. He felt no guilt for making his fellow male survivors slaves, damning them to a life of back-breaking work, little food, and eventually death. Or for damning the females to a life of working in a brothel, to have countless filthy men lay with them, violate them, and sometimes beat them to within an inch of their life.

Nope, he figured it was either them or him and he knew he wasn't about to be anyone's slave. So he become the master and did it to them before they could do it to him, or so he told himself.

When his Jeep burst out of the treeline and he saw the man on the motorcycle climb on it and drive off, he knew he wanted him alive. Even from the back, Sirus could see the man was strong, with powerful arms and a strong back. He would fetch good cash at the slave market fifty miles away.

And the motorcycle and the man's weapons would be a nice bonus as well.

He was already counting the money—or what went for money these days—he would get for the man, as he knew there was nowhere for the rider to escape to.

Sirus knew the road he was on well, and there was nothing but a deserted highway further on and off ramps covered with over-grown weeds and kudzu. Sooner or later, either the man would have an accident, be blocked by wrecked vehicles, or one of his men would get in a shot that would take him or the motorcycle down.

That would be unfortunate, but though he wanted the rider alive, if it came down to killing him, well, it was better than letting him escape.

He patted the driver of the Jeep — a thin man with a long beard and a scar on his forehead — on the top of the head and urged him to drive faster. Once they reached the highway, the road opened up and he knew he or one of his men would get in a good shot of the rider.

It was all so simple, he thought as he licked his lips in anticipation of the capture. Sometimes it was so easy he almost felt guilty.

The four companions were ready when the two Jeeps appeared around the bend in the road, each vehicle racing at them at well over fifty miles an hour.

Hank knew he didn't have to say a thing, as each of his friends would know the right time to fire.

As the Jeeps sped up, the first of the gunshots began to pepper the area and that was the signal for the warrior group to return fire. With bullets slamming into the ground inches from his feet, Hank began firing at the lead Jeep, Laurie doing the same by his side.

Carl and Stewart concentrated their fire on the second Jeep, though their target was harder to hit as the first vehicle blocked it. Still, they knew in a matter of seconds that would change, one way or the other.

The first Jeep revved its engine and surged forward, the three men holding guns firing at them while the driver grinned from ear to ear. But no sooner did the men begin to laugh and whoop at the sight of their prey, then they realized that the one man they were chasing had turned into four, and that all were armed to the teeth.

Sirus was the quickest to figure out that things weren't going as planned, and he stopped shooting long enough to yell at the driver to seek cover. They still outnumbered the four people two to one, and as long as they went to ground, sooner or later their extra numbers could outflank them and then Sirus would be capturing four slaves instead of one.

It was as Sirus looked down at the driver of the Jeep and began yelling at the man that he quickly learned that the man couldn't hear him. The reason for this was simple. He now only had half a head, a round taking him center mass in the face and blowing off the top of his skull.

No sooner did the top of the driver's head disintegrate into a collection of brains and bone fragments, then the man to Sirus' right was shot in the neck, blood spraying out to blow back into his face as the wind caught it.

Trying to act fast, Sirus reached down for the steering wheel, the Jeep veering fast to the right and out of control.

But the dead driver had slumped over the steering wheel, and try as he might, Sirus couldn't get the body off it.

The Jeep plowed into the vine-covered guardrail and went airborne, the wind whistling in his ears. He heard his other man scream as he was tossed out of the Jeep, and even over the rustling wind he heard the loud crack of the man's neck when he landed upside down on the road.

Sirus' world was upside down, and when he looked up, which now faced the road, he saw the pavement coming at him way too fast, as if he was hanging out of the bottom of a plane as it came in for a landing.

He felt only one sudden flash of pain when his head connected with the pavement and began to scrape off as if he had been pressed into a cheese grater. Then, with half his head grinded off, the Jeep landed and snapped his neck, pulverizing his arms with its weight.

The Jeep rolled once and came to a stop, antifreeze and oil leaking out of the cracked engine block, as the second Jeep shot past it, the four slavers still hell-bent on taking the companions down.

Their goal was cut short when a flurry of rounds peppered their bodies from chest to neck, all four men receiving a simultaneous blast from Carl's Mini-Uzi and Stewart's submachine gun.

The driver went limp in his seat and his foot left the gas pedal, the vehicle swerving to the left to plow into a copse of trees and shrubs. The bodies were jolted forward and two went flying over the hood to land in a heap of dead limbs.

The engine rattled for a few seconds and then stalled.

"Fan out, check for survivors," Hank said, though he was fairly sure there were none. Still, a lazy man was a dead man.

Hank and Laurie took the Jeep that had flipped over while Carl and Stewart walked over to the other one.

Hank and Laurie approached the Jeep cautiously, and when they were no more than ten feet away, the odor of shit and urine mixed with oil and antifreeze assaulted them from the crushed and pulverized bodies.

Laurie took the left side and Hank the right, and a second later Laurie called out, "All clear, they're road kill."

"Yeah, same on this side," Hank said as he went to inspect the man who had fallen out of the Jeep. One look was all it took to see the man was very dead. When his neck had snapped, it had been forced around so the man's face was now looking over his shoulder. If he bent over backward he would be looking at his own ass.

Flies were already beginning to gather, the insects not wasting time, and Hank walked back to Laurie who was waiting at the back of the overturned Jeep. In her free hand was the gun of one of the slavers as well as a small bandolier of ammunition.

"Let's go see how Carl and Stewart are making out," Hank said as he walked side by side with Laurie.

Carl was just coming out of the woods on the right side of the Jeep and a big smile was on his face. "The Jeep looks fine. None of our bullets hit the engine. Other than a shitload of blood on the seats, it's useable."

Stewart joined him and nodded. "That's good, 'cause my bike's had it. I think the clutch went. I barely got it here in one piece. It's done for."

"Really?" Hank asked. "Well, I suppose we could just have you ride with one of us."

Stewart shook his head. "No thanks, Hank. I can't stand those damn things. It looks like we got ourselves four wheels and I for one vote we take it. We can transfer all our gear into it, empty the gas from the bikes, and ride in style for a while."

"Yeah, once we clean up the seats," Carl said.

"Of course, Carl, after we clean the seats," Stewart agreed.

Hank looked to Laurie to see what her answer was and she smiled. "I'm with them, Hank, my rear is killing me from riding on that thing all day. I can't say motorcycles are my favorite form of transportation."

"Okay, fine, I have to say that I'm with you guys. I've been on my bike for more than a day straight and if I never see another one it'll be too soon." He pointed to Carl, then the Jeep. "Hey, Carl, give me a hand getting this thing out of the trees." He turned and gestured to Laurie and Stewart. "Why don't you two get our gear and whatever else we're taking with us. Then we'll siphon what fuel we can and transfer it into the Jeep's tank. Oh, and gather as many of their guns as you can find, we can use them as trade at the next outpost we come across."

With a wave, Laurie and Stewart headed off to where the motorcycles were hidden.

Hank and Carl had to clear the Jeep's wheels of branches and brush that had become entangled in them, and chop at a small sapling that was wedged in the front right wheel well. Then they were ready to back it out of the trees. Carl climbed behind the driver's seat after yanking the corpse out of it. He used a rag he found on the floor to wipe most of the blood clean. It was still sticky as he slid behind the wheel, but he knew beggars couldn't be choosers.

The engine turned over on the third try, and with Hank pushing from the front grille, the Jeep backed out of the woods and onto the road. Hank jumped into the passenger seat and Carl drove it to where the others were waiting.

Stewart had begun draining the tanks of the motorcycles. He did this by removing them from the bikes and then tipping them into a plastic funnel stuck in a bottle, which he had five of. He had already finished one tank by the time the Jeep pulled alongside him.

Laurie tossed their gear into the back of the Jeep and cleaned more of the blood from it. She knew in the hot sun the blood would dry and then it would simply flake off the leather material.

Soon, all four of them were in the Jeep and driving away, leaving the four motorcycles in pieces behind them. Hank hadn't given them much fuel from his motorcycle, as he had gone so far out of his way to reach the others, but no one cared, they were just glad to have their leader back in one piece.

As the Jeep drove down the road at a speed that would equal a man running, their eyes sharp for possible danger, Laurie slid up next to Hank and hugged him. He turned and kissed her softly, feeling her reciprocate. If they could find a safe place to camp later that day he was hoping they would be able to make love that night. It had been a while and he knew they both needed it, but sometimes there was no safe place for them to spend a few minutes alone and it would have to be put off till later.

With the wind blowing through his hair and drying the sweat on his brow, Hank sighed, finally able to take a second to relax.

"So, Hank," Laurie asked, "how was it getting back to us? You had to travel all the way around the mountains to reach us."

Hank shrugged. "It was pretty quiet actually. Other than picking up my followers near the end, it was smooth sailing."

She could see where he had been shot by the slavers and the small wounds on his back, the shrapnel from the grenade, and she knew none of those wounds had been there before they had split up the previous day and a half. She cocked her head to the side as she looked at his face, trying to tell if he was being truthful and knowing he wasn't. Her long blonde hair waved out behind her in the wind and her blue eyes flashed in the sun like two crystals. "Oh, really? Nothing else of interest happened other than the two Jeeps chasing you?"

"Yup, it was nice and quiet."

"Hmm, I don't know, Hank Summers, something tells me you're not being entirely truthful here."

He laughed. "Laurie, you know me way too well."

From the driver's seat, Carl called back to them as he slowed the Jeep. The road forked and they had to decide which way to go. "Which way, Hank, left or right?"

Hank's eyes took in the fork in the road and a second later he patted Carl on the shoulder, pointing left. "Go that way."

Carl stepped on the gas and the Jeep jerked forward. When they had taken the left fork, Stewart looked up from the passenger seat and asked Hank, "So, why'd you pick left?"

"No reason."

"No reason? But for all we know there's a gang of cutthroats just waiting for us and the right side is nothing but clear skies and friendly people."

Hank looked at Stewart and gave him a sly grin. "Then I picked the right way," he said.

"Really, how's that?" Stewart asked.

"Because if you're right, then at least the way we're going will be interesting."

Stewart laughed. "I swear Hank, it's like you've been asleep all your life and only woke up when the world was bombed to shit. It's like your home now."

"I never gave it much thought, Stewart, but you may be right." He kissed Laurie again and laughed long and loud. "All I know is right now, at this exact second, I'm happy. And whatever tomorrow brings, I'll deal with it when it gets here."

"Amen, brother," Carl said. "But I still miss cable TV."

Stewart moaned loudly. "What? Reality TV, spoiled sixteen-year-old's and their birthday parties, and cooking shows? To hell with it, maybe the bombs were the best thing to happen to the world."

Hank laughed again at the two men's banter and gazed up at the blood-red sky. "Only time will tell, Stewart. Only time will tell."

REVENGE OR JUSTICE

The harsh Kansas sun beat down on the heads of the four weary travelers, as they made their way down the middle of the lonely highway ten miles outside of Wichita. Behind them, their shadows were short and stunted, as if those, too, were hiding from the noonday sun.

Hank Summers was in the lead, his broad shoulders almost wide enough to be hidden behind, to be used for shade, blocking out the harsh sunlight.

Laurie Collins did just that, following Hank's footsteps perfectly, trying her best to stay out of the sun, her leather boots tipped with pointed steel stepping exactly where Hank stepped. Her long blonde hair blew in the wind, resembling a golden halo. She carried a pearl-handled PPK .22 on her hip and though the caliber was small, she was a crack shot and did more damage with the small handgun than an average man could do with twice the caliber.

Every now and then, Hank would glance over his shoulder at her, wanting to admire her long legs and her shapely bosom. The two were lovers, and even more than that, they were partners in life…and death. The two had fought side by side and had killed so many evil men and women that a bond had been forged in blood that could never be broken.

Behind the couple were two men, one almost double the age of the other. The older of the two walked behind Laurie.

Stewart Matheson was a little over sixty-years-old, his hair so gray it looked white. He carried a walking stick, one that held within it a long, thin sword of Toledo steel. The hidden weapon was only used if the situation was dire, for to pull a sword, it must taste blood before being resheathed. At least, that's what Stewart believed. His sword-cane wasn't his only weapon. Slung over his left shoulder was a Heckler and Koch submachine gun; a .45 pistol rode his hip.

Behind Stewart, and the last in the group, was Carl Rivers, a thirty-five-year old man who wore a Yankees ball cap and refused to take it off, no matter what. Perhaps the cap was kept on to hide his balding pate or to protect his pasty complexion from the harsh sun. Not a tall man, his made up for his lack of stature with the shear amount of weapons he carried. A Mini-Uzi hung on his chest in a holster and an AUG 5.6mm pistol rode his hip, along with an eight inch hunting knife. A web belt filled with extra clips adorned his chest. He carried a black satchel, and inside it was a treasure of explosives raided from a National Guard truck found off the beaten path. Grenades and C-4 were some of the goodies looted from the abandoned facility, and next to food and water, the explosives were priceless.

In the distance, purple clouds rolled with thunder and heat lightning flashed across the sky, signifying the possibility of a rainstorm. At least there was no smell of sulfur, which would signify the coming of acid rain. Ever since the bombs fell over two years ago, destroying the world in thermonuclear fire, the sky had been the color of burnt orange. New York was gone, as well as Washington and most once great cities, all blasted into a radiation pit of Hell. Anyone that passed too close to the hell zone in their travels, said they could still see the area glowing when night fell.

Hank reached down and did an automatic check of his weapons. Over his shoulder by a sling, he carried a Heckler and Koch G-12 automatic rifle. On his right hip rode a SIG-Sauer 226 9mm pistol, and on his left, in a leather sheath, was a sixteen inch panga honed to razor sharpness. If the cut was at the right angle, and he had enough strength behind it, he could sever a man's head from the shoulders in one fluid swipe.

After checking his weapons, he glanced down at his radiation badge. All four of the companions wore one. He was pleased to see it was still in the orange. Yellow would have meant a hot zone was close and red would mean get the hell out of there or prepare to have his organs melted out slowly as he began to rot from the inside out.

"Hank," Stewart called out. "I was wondering if you'd planned where we might be making camp tonight."

Hank shrugged his powerful shoulders. "It's hours to sundown, Stewart, so I hadn't given it much thought yet. Why, you tired?"

"I'm fine, but it's hot as hell."

"Tell me about it," Laurie said as she lifted her hair off the nape of her neck with one of her hands. "Try having all this hair and then tell me how hot it is."

Carl chuckled at her. "You could always cut it off?"

She shot him a glare that would have melted him if she'd had the power. "That's not funny." She quickly tied her hair into a ponytail. "Don't even joke about that."

Carl took off his baseball cap and wiped his brow with his arm, then placed it back on his head, adjusting the brim so it was even over his forehead. "I get it. Laurie cutting her hair would be like you cutting off your wiener, Stewart. It's not gonna happen," Carl joked.

"Oh really?" Stewart said. "Then I have to agree with Laurie about keeping it."

Carl called up to her, as she was still in front of him. "Forget what I said, your hair is fine."

"Heads up, people, we got cars," Hank said as they walked over a rise in the highway. Before the four travelers, more than two dozen cars and trucks sat empty with hanging doors and their trunks popped open. As they moved closer, it could be seen clearly that all the tires were flat, and many of them were missing wheels altogether. Any glass not shattered was missing as well, and the closer Hank got, he could see that almost everything that might be of value from the vehicles had been stripped clean and taken away, including the seats, and in many cases even the engines. As long as a person had gasoline, the engines could be jury-rigged to become generators to run anything from washing machines to electric ovens for cooking.

An eighteen wheeler was lying on its side at the front of the pile-up, and had been the cause of it. The long silver trailer had been filled with milk, though now it had all evaporated after years in the hot sun, leaving behind a hard-crusted sludge. All the tires were missing on the semi, as were the attachments to the trailer to drain and load the milk.

Hank walked past the trailer, with the others directly behind him, but not too close that they would make an easy target for snipers, though unlikely. They had three feet between each person, the length done instinctually and without thought. The four had survived for so long after the bombs fell because they were smart, and had quickly adapted to the warrior's way of life.

Hank stopped by a faded-red Toyota to peer into the interior. Two bleached skeletons were in the front seat, and even in death the two figures held hands.

"Poor bastards," Hank whispered as he passed the car to check on another one.

Laurie followed, and as she peered into the Toyota, a large cockroach slid out of the left eye socket to disappear into the sagging jaw. Making a disgusted face, she continued walking.

Carl moved off to the side to explore on his own. He came across a Lincoln Towncar, the blue paint now scratched and faded from exposure to the harsh sun. Peeking into the backseat of the car, he spotted a backpack on the floor, something that other looters had somehow missed. Reaching in, he pulled it out and plopped it down on the hood. Opening it, he found an Ipod and a handheld gaming system. As he looked back into the car, he also spotted an Xbox lying on its side. He couldn't help but chuckle at this. Of all the things people had thought to bring with them when they escaped the bombed cities, these people had thought of video games and music, not food and water and other life-giving essentials. Shaking his head, he wondered if the world didn't deserve what it had gotten. Leaving the backpack on the hood of the car, he continued searching the wrecks.

"Hey, look what I found," Laurie called as she searched the glove box of a Ford pickup. The others turned to see when she held up a AAA map.

"Good job, baby," Hank called, then returned to inspect the SUV before him. There wasn't much to find. A baby's car seat was in the backseat, some brown flakes on it that looked like paint but was no doubt old blood. A rattle lay beside the baby seat, more dark-brown splatter on it. He studied the interior, seeing more dried blood on the ceiling and the remaining, unbroken windows. The people in this SUV had died hard a long time ago. There was no sign of the occupants; no bones or dried flesh. Nothing to mark their passing but some blood splatter.

A few small items were also found by Stewart: a pencil, a small notepad and some old batteries that Hank wanted tossed away when shown to him. The odds the batteries were useable was slim and to carry them and risk them leaking or exploding wasn't worth the trouble.

"Then I'll carry them in my jacket pocket," Stewart said adamantly, wanting to keep the batteries.

"Fine, do what you want," Hank said, the matter closed.

They left the vehicles behind and continued walking, picking up their pace to beat the storm.

"This area doesn't seem so bad," Laurie said, walking beside Hank. "Almost makes you believe the war never happened."

Hank nodded, understanding what she meant. There may have been a war, or maybe not. No one left alive knew what really happened, other than missiles had fallen out of the sky from out of nowhere. A few missiles had struck the heartland of Kansas, but whether it was to take out America's heartland or simply warheads that had gone off course due to their systems failing, was unknown. Hell, there was far too much that was unknown about what had happened. Seconds after the first missiles struck, the massive EMP pulses had knocked out power. Television and radio had gone out soon after, so there was no way for the population to get any useable information. Not long after, nuclear reactors across the United States had gone into meltdown, either from flooding or earthquake damage from the earthshaker bombs. Alabama, Nebraska and Virginia were only a few reactors that had suffered massive radiation leaks. Not that it really mattered in the end. The 'who' was irrelevant, so was the 'why.' All that mattered was the here and now.

As they crested a rise in the highway, an old, dilapidated structure came into view on the left-hand side of the road. Hank stopped and pulled out a small pair of powerful binoculars from a pocket in his camo jacket. Zooming in on the one-story building, he watched silently while counting to thirty. "Looks quiet," he said finally and lowered the binoculars.

Carl squinted as he stood by Hank's side. "An old gas station maybe? Or a farm stand?"

Hank grunted. "Way out here, probably one or the other."

"A good place to stay for the night, yes?" Stewart said as he stepped up to Hank's other side.

Overhead, the clouds rumbled louder and a few stray drops of rain fell to sizzle on the ground by Hank's feet. It was acid rain, the deadly storm sneaking in right behind the normal one.

"Shit," Hank hissed and grabbed Laurie's hand as he took off running. "We don't have a choice now, come on!"

Lightning flashed overhead and the wind picked up, blowing anything not rooted to the ground into the air. Everything from old coffee cups to bits of paper began to swirl around, some if it slapping the companions in the face.

Carl picked up speed and ran past Hank, wanting to get to the structure first and take a few seconds to inspect the interior before the others arrived. Hank glanced over his shoulder to see Stewart hobbling along, his cane flying around him as he ran. "Come on, Stewart, move your ass!"

"Or it'll get melted off!" Laurie added when she saw the older man having a hard time.

The rain began to fall heavier but the drops were widely spaced. The four warriors took advantage of this and ran for their lives. A drop landed on Hank's head and he felt the sting as it bit into his scalp, then stopped. He cringed at the thought of what a hundred more, or worse still, a thousand more would do to him.

As the old structure came within sight of the naked eye more easily, Hank took in the details. There had been a place for gas pumps in the front but now all that was there was a ragged hole in the ground. As he scanned the building, he could see there was fire damage to the north side he hadn't been able to see with the binoculars. Half of the structure had collapsed, but the other half seemed intact, though all the windows were shattered and whether the roof was sound would be something he would find out in a few seconds.

Carl reached an opening in the side of the building. The hole was about five feet high and two feet wide. Someone or something had carved an entryway into the still-standing side of the structure. He was about to go inside when Hank and Laurie reached him, all set to enter as well.

"Wait," Carl said, "I haven't done a recce yet."

Hank shook his head. More drops of acid rain had landed on him and his scalp and hands felt like a dozen bees had stung him. "Doesn't matter. We stay out here, we're dead." As he finished, Stewart joined them, breathing heavily, his face red from the exertion of the mad dash.

"Good point," Carl agreed. "So we check the place out together."

"Right," Hank nodded. "Okay, people, get sharp until we know if it's safe in there. Me and Laurie are on point, then Stewart." He glanced at Carl and said, "Carl, you take the rear."

Thunder rattled overhead so loud that the entire building shook, then the clouds released their payload of boiling death. That was the cue for the companions to get inside the building, no matter what waited within.

As the clouds outside swallowed the sun whole, the interior of the structure was one of pervasive gloom. Refuse cluttered the floor as the four warriors slowly moved deeper inside. As Hank moved with Laurie by his side, more signs of the structure's previous purchase could be seen. Faded posters of sparkplugs and air filters covered the walls, and in the corner there was a set of shelves lined with oil filters and alternator belts, though most of the shelves had been picked clean. There was a ten by six foot hole in the floor, where a mechanic would crawl into and then easily change the oil of a vehicle.

Hank peered into the darkness of the grease pit, his G-12 automatic leading the way, but all he could see was a scum of water at the very bottom. Whether the water was an inch deep or two feet was unknown. The top of the liquid was slick with float-ing oil and a few rats that had fallen in and become trapped.

Far above the roof, in the sky overhead, thunder boomed, shak-ing the very foundation of the building. A few places inside were becoming wet as small holes in the roof allowed the rainwater in, but lucky for the four companions, the roof seemed relatively intact and it was easy to avoid the few drips of water. The cement floor sizzled as the acid rain ate into the cement.

It was as the group looked left and right, their eyes desperately trying to penetrate the shadows, so far nothing of danger being discovered, that Hank was about to tell them to relax, that it looked like the building was empty, when a dozen screaming, radiation-burned humans popped up or out of every conceivable place there was to hide in the garage. From inside cabinets, behind oil-stained boxes, from within the very walls itself, they appeared and attacked. Some had hidden in the shadows of the ceiling rafters and dropped down onto the backs of the companions, their teeth open wide to bite, hands curled into claws to scrape and gouge out the flesh of the norms.

The radiation lepers shrieked in hatred at the four normals within their midst, their fever-rattled minds only wanting to kill, and then consume, the four companions, who for the briefest of seconds were caught completely off guard.

But like candle smoke in the wind, that second of alarm was quickly gone and all four warriors went into action, knowing to hesitate was instant death.

Though the mutants rarely used guns, the companions knew to stay clumped together would make them an easy target for any-one carrying one, so they moved a few feet apart. Hank swung the G-12 around and fired, sending a tri-burst of death into the first attacker, at the same time heaving his shoulders and tossing off the creature that had landed on his back.

The first and second bullets went wild, but the third impacted the burned attacker directly in the throat. Both gnarled hands reached up to staunch the flow of blood, but the carotid had been hit and the attacker was already dropping to the dirt-covered floor, dead.

Carl threw off his attacker, which in the gloom of the garage, he saw she was a woman, though she was now missing her left breast, and shot her in the face with his Mini-Uzi. Her head didn't so much as explode, but instead seemed to disappear in a glorious spray of blood, brains and bone matter. The headless corpse flopped to the floor, the arms and legs still twitching in final spasms.

Laurie was tackled as the weight of a full grown man landed on her after dropping from the rafters. Keeping her grip on her PPK, she jammed the muzzle tight against the screaming man's temple and fired. The bullet wasn't powerful enough to exit the skull but it bounced around, mulching the brain to mush. The man's eyes rolled into the back of his head and Laurie pushed him off, her eyes already searching for a new target.

Stewart had been a little off to the side during the first seconds of the attack and he had a little more time to gather himself. As the others were besieged from above, he was free to spin around and take out four attackers in one burst of his submachine gun. The Heckler and Koch roared steel-jacketed death, stitching the attackers from side to side, and allowing him even more time to defend himself. Then he was grabbed from behind and all bets were off.

Hank heard Laurie cry out as she was forced to the floor but he was too busy dealing with three more attackers of his own. As he shot one—only hitting the man in the arm—the other two came at him, wrapping him in their burned and peeling arms and pushing him backwards, his HK going flying into a corner of the room, lost to him. Before he knew what was happening, he was falling into the grease pit. The attacker Hank shot in the arm shrugged off the injury and jumped in after them, not wanting to miss out on the fun of killing the normal.

Hank landed on the bottom of the pile, oily water spraying out on all sides of him. He felt the air leave his chest as three people landed on him. All three had massive burns from being too long in a hot zone, and as Hank struggled to escape their clutches, he reached out and grabbed them, only to have their burned and bubbling flesh slide off their bodies as if it wasn't attached. Sagging skin came off like wet paper to expose muscle and tendons, and though hardened to even the most visceral sight, Hank tasted bile from touching his disgusting assailants. One time, over a campfire, he and Stewart had talked about the rad-blasted mutants and why they went on living. Hank had told Stewart that if he was ever in the same predicament of radiation poisoning, he would eat a bullet instead of suffering such a horrible fate. Stewart had simply said that he believed when it came right down to it, most men would go on living, no matter what their state, as if by some hand of fate they would get better.

Fists began to pummel Hank as he fought for his life. Throwing a wild punch, he felt his fist sink into the solar plexus of one of his attackers. Grabbing the man by the neck, he yanked him off and slammed his palm up and into the chin of another one. The attacker's head snapped back, the crack of bone coming to Hank's ears, even over the cacophony of battle going on above him on the main floor.

With only one more assailant to deal with, Hank reached down and tried to grab his panga, but couldn't grasp the handle due to the oil coating pretty much everything. As his attacker jumped on him, he reached up and began to grapple with the man, ignoring each time the skin sloughed off the man's bones. The man had no eyelids or eyebrows, the orbs white with flecks of red in them.

Opening his mouth, the man screamed, the tongue swollen and purple. Hank punched him in the face and tried to grab his panga again. As his hand slid down his thigh, he missed the handle once more but ended up touching something on his attacker's waist. Wrapping his hand around the orb, he pulled it to him and realized it was a grenade.

Most of the rad-blasted mutants never used anything to fight with other than wooden tools and knives, so to have one carrying a grenade wasn't par for the course. Not that Hank was complaining. Kicking the attacker off him, he jumped to his feet, only to slip and fall back onto his butt in a spray of oily water. The burned man laughed and came at Hank again, but received a punch in the spleen for his trouble.

As the man fell back, Hank ran at the man, then used the man's shoulder as a stepping stool. Jumping up, he slapped his arms on the floor at the edge of the grease pit and pulled himself up and over the edge with a low groan. Pulling the pin of the grenade still in his hand, he yelled, "Fire in the hole!" as he rolled away from the opening.

Seconds later an enormous explosion ripped through the grease pit, sending a geyser of oily water, blood and body parts straight up, thanks to the channeling of the explosion from the walls of the pit. Dark liquid splashed the rafters in the ceiling before raining back down into the pit, the edges quickly covered in gore. A few body parts bounced off the ceiling to land on the floor, rolling this way and that. A head bounced like a warped soccer ball and ended up in a dark corner, the open eyes staring blindly at nothing.

One of the last attackers came at Carl, who had run out of ammunition. Pulling a hunting knife from the sheath on his waist, he avoided the club his attacker wielded and kicked the man in the chest, sending him flying back to hit the wall hard. Coming up on him, Carl brought the blade around in a sideways swing and jammed it into the man's neck so that it looked as if the man would live. Though the knife was in his neck from left to right, Carl had avoided killing him…yet.

As the man's mouth opened and closed, sputtering, Carl yanked his arm straight back so that the blade came out of the neck from the front, thus slicing the man's throat open and severing jugular and trachea. With the neck now partially severed, the head flopped back and forth as the man drowned in his own blood, the scarlet fluid cascading outward in a strong spray. Slumping to the floor, the man exhaled his last breaths in frothy red bubbles as Carl stepped back to avoid getting doused in hot sticky blood.

The last attacker, a woman with no hair and missing both breasts, turned and tried to run away after popping out of a metal cabinet once used for tools, knowing she was now outnumbered. As she began to run, Laurie shot her in the back of the head, directly over her spine, from across the garage. In the gloom inside the building and shadows everywhere, and only the lightning outside illuminating anything for the briefest of seconds, the shot was incredible. The woman went flying forward to fall face down on the floor, her arms splayed out in front of her, her legs crossed. A small hole in the back of her head seeped blood.

"Everyone all right? Anyone hurt?" Hank called out.

"I'm fine," Stewart said, kicking one of the radiation lepers in the head to make sure the man was truly dead.

"All good over here," Carl said, stepping over a severed arm and leg, more refuse from the grenade going off in the grease pit.

"I'm okay, too," Laurie stated and went to join Hank. "What about you, lover? You hurt?"

Hank quickly patted himself down, ignoring the grease, oil and blood on his clothes and skin. "I'm good. Damn lucky, too, I'll tell you that."

"Amen," Stewart added. He looked around the garage, shaking his head in disgust. "If we're still planning on staying here for the night, we have some cleaning up to do."

Outside, the storm grew worse, pummeling the small building. A dead body lay directly under one of the holes in the roof, and the dripping acid rain was slowly eating into the corpse's torso, the stench of burned meat permeating the air, adding to the stench of death and offal.

"That hasn't changed Stewart," Hank said. "The storm isn't stopping anytime soon so we might as well get comfortable. For all we know, we could be here for days."

Carl bent over and grabbed a dead woman by her hair and began to drag her to the grease pit to dispose of the body, but Hank stopped him, having a better idea. He quickly explained his thoughts.

"You sure?" Carl asked after hearing the idea. "It would be easier to simply dump them in the hole. It's closer and all."

"No, let's do it my way. Trust me, when it's done, you'll thank me," Hank said.

As Hank was the defacto leader, Carl didn't see a reason to protest, so with the others joining in, they got to work cleaning the garage of bodies.

An hour later, the storm still raged outside but at least the garage was clear of bodies, if not spilt blood. The corpses of the dozen radiation lepers were now dissolving a few feet from the building, the acid rain slowly eating away at the flesh. Like melting candle wax, faces sloughed off skulls and internal organs bubbled into puddles.

In no time, all that would be left would be a pile of bones in a pool of viscous sludge and then even that would be gone as it soaked into the sodden earth.

The four warriors could finally relax, for with the rain so deadly, there was nothing living that could sneak up on them. And if a vehicle arrived, it would be seen easily from the cracks in the facade of the structure.

Carl and Stewart got to work making a fire for two main reasons. One was to keep back the cold that had permeated the air since the storm began and the other was to fill the garage with the odor of wood smoke, which hopefully would override the smell of blood and gore, which was still hanging in the air, and would continue to do so. After the bodies had been tossed outside through the hole the warriors had first used to enter the gas station, Hank had called it quits on cleaning. If he knew for a fact they were holing up in the place for days then he might had thought different, but if all went well they would be on their way in the morning.

While the two men made a fire in an old oil drum, making sure there was a hole in the roof overhead to allow the smoke to vent, Hank stood by a crack in the wall facing the highway, peering out into the storm and the road they had recently traveled.

After making sure the perimeter was secure, Laurie joined him. Walking up to him, she placed her hand on his shoulder, ignoring the blood splatter there.

"That was some fight," she said with a smile.

Turning, Hank looked at her, and when she hugged him, he returned the embrace, wrapping his arms around her. The two looked into one another's eyes for a brief moment, then kissed, their tongues dancing together, lips caressing the other.

"Hey, you two, you want me and Stewart to step out for a bit? I mean, we'll end up melting in a pool of blood but hey, if it'll give you guys some privacy," Carl joked.

Hank and Laurie separated and both smiled at each other, then Hank turned to Carl. "You're just jealous you don't have a woman with you."

Carl laughed. "Hell yes, I'm jealous. We need to find a town soon so I can find me a good-lookin' hooker to have some fun with."

"Oh, Carl," Laurie said. "Why not find someone to love and then you won't have to pay for it?"

"No thanks," he barked. "I don't want some woman hanging all over me, telling me what to do all the time. Just let me get laid every now and then and I'll be happy."

Laurie laughed as she hugged Hank. "Our Carl, such a hopeless romantic."

"Damn straight, that's me. I love the idea of love." He waved his hand at Laurie. "Turn around, will you? I need to piss, and the pit here will do the job just fine."

Normally, they would have gone outside but with the acid rain that wasn't possible so for the time being, the toilet had to be something close at hand. Laurie did as she was asked and a second later the sound of Carl urinating filled the garage. When four people spent as much time together as they did, fighting and traveling as a group, modesty wasn't that much of a concern, though proper etiquette was still performed when possible. The world may have been full of men that had turned into animals, but that didn't mean the companions had to deteriorate to that level as well.

"Okay, I'm done," Carl said and walked away from the grease pit. Later, when he felt nature call again, he wasn't looking forward to taking a dump over the pit, that was for sure. One slip and he would be covered in oil, blood and gore, not to mention whatever bodily wastes had been put there from his friends over the course of the night. Maybe finding something else to use as a chamber pot might be a better course of action.

"I'm starving. What say we crack open what we have to eat," Stewart suggested.

"Now that's a good idea," Hank agreed, and the four warriors joined up in the center of the garage around the fire and quickly began to unpack their supplies.

Gathering the few bottles of purified water they had and canned goods, they ate in silence, each of them comfortable enough with one another not to feel they had to fill every second of silence with chatter.

After setting up a rotating watch, Hank took the first shift, the others bedding down for the night wherever they could find a clean dry spot.

Having someone stand guard probably wasn't needed because of the acid rain, but it only took one mistake to end up dead. There were no second chances in life.

Hank found a wooden crate and used it as a chair, then made himself a table out of spare wood scattered in a corner. With his weapons placed on the table, he set out gun oil and rags he used for just this purpose. As Carl and Stewart began to snore almost immediately due to the exertion and adrenaline rush of the battle, and now a full stomach, and Laurie drifted off into a light sleep, Hank began stripping and cleaning his weapons. When he was done, he planned on cleaning Laurie's .22 as well. She'd laid it beside her with the knowledge that he would take it and replace it to its position when he was finished. Stewart and Carl could clean their own weapons when it was their turn to go on watch.

With the acid rain pattering the roof, and the wind howling, thunder and lightning filling the sky, the four weary warriors rested.

The next morning, the sun was out once more, and though the sky was its typical burnt orange tinged with red, the purple clouds were gone. It was the best anyone could hope for in a world filled with radiation and death.

After having a quick breakfast of dried jerky, canned fruit and instant cereal, the companions gathered their gear and headed out into the world once more.

Stepping over the cleaned bones that had been the radiation lepers, they walked single file onto the highway and continued their journey, making sure to avoid the puddles scattered here and there. Though diluted, the puddles could still cause a problem if someone was foolish enough to splash or fall into one.

As Laurie walked, the steel tips of her boots reflected the light, though her all-leather attire consumed it. Her blonde hair flowed behind her with the gentle wind and Hank admired his woman for what had to be the thousandth time. Despite danger and death looming around ever turn in the road, she had been the one good thing he'd found since the world had gone to shit. Though he longed for the world he once knew, on many ways he cast it off, for if the planet hadn't succumbed to almost total nuclear annihilation, he would have never met Laurie and that to him was a fate worse than death.

Sensing he was watching her, Laurie cast a glance over her shoulder and flashed him a smile with a sly wink. Hank retuned her gesture, knowing what the wink truly meant: *If we get a chance to be alone, I'm going to fuck your brains out.*

The highway was for the most part deserted, only the occasional abandoned vehicle left on the shoulder of the road. One such vehicle looked untouched, as if the driver had run out of gas, locked it, and had gone to the nearest filling station to get a gallon of fuel. But looks could be deceiving. When Hank reached the car and peered within its enclosed interior, he saw the putrid remains of a human body after it had dried to the consistency of leather. Similar to if it had been placed in a hot oven, the enclosed car had done a good job of mummifying the corpse. There was a small pistol on the seat next to the body, which was still propped behind the steering wheel. On closer inspection, the top of the skull had a large hole and there were dried bits of brain matter on the head-liner. Hank's jaw was taut as he stared at the corpse of the man, who still wore a shirt and tie, and a pair of once tan slacks cover-ing the skeleton's lower torso. The driver had taken the easy way out, as many had done before him. Perhaps he had been a sales-man, his family back in New York. Upon finding out New York was gone, as was his family, the man had decided he didn't want to go on without them. Or maybe the man had been a coward, too civilized to live in a lawless world, one where such necessities as running water were a thing of the past.

Truthfully, Hank didn't give a damn. Using the butt of his panga, he shattered one of the windows and stood back to let it air out for a few seconds, not wanting to breathe in the dust of the corpse. He'd heard of men becoming sick after breathing air from closed bomb shelters filled with corpses or bank vaults with old air. With no air circulation and bodies degrading, it was a concoc-tion of death in a bottle.

When he was satisfied the car was aired out, he reached in and unlocked the door, then rummaged through the glove box and took the pistol. The clip was empty. The dead man had used his last round to escape this world. But the pistol was still valuable and he quickly stuffed it into his pack to use as trade in the next town or enclave he came across. In the backseat was an Amazon kindle, the battery long expired when he tried to turn it on. He picked it up and looked at it for a second, chuckling lightly to himself at the worthless piece of technology. Leaning out of the car, he threw it like a Frisbee. The square disc spun off to be lost in the grass thirty feet away. That was all the damn thing was good for nowadays. There was a beat-up paperback book in the back seat, and that he took and pocketed. At least the book he could read and was still valuable.

"Find anything good?" Carl asked as he sat on the closed trunk, his feet on the bumper. Stewart and Laurie sat beside him, all resting for a few minutes while Hank explored. None were interested as to what was inside the car, having seen more than their fill over the years.

"A pistol, but it's empty," Hank said. "And an old paperback. Nothing else is worth taking." The skeleton wore a watch but it was battery powered and not worth anything. Even the metal was cheap. He almost reached in and took the wedding ring on the corpse's finger, but decided to leave it. Let the dead man rest in peace. At least until the next scavenger came by without a conscience.

"Okay, let's go. I'm done here," Hank said and joined the others at the rear of the car.

They began walking again, Carl and Hank in front talking together, while Laurie and Stewart were right behind them, the two also chatting about life before the bombs fell.

Twice they took bathroom breaks on the shoulder of the highway, when an area containing a few shrubs appeared, and both times all involved wished for a world where toilet paper was made on a daily basis and could be purchased at just about any store. Something once taken for granted was now worth more than gold…at least that's how it felt when a person had to wipe their ass with a handful of leaves on a daily basis.

It was late afternoon, and after taking a break to eat a light lunch from their supplies, they were once more back on the road. That was when Laurie spotted smoke coming from over the next hill to the west of their present position. When she turned to tell Hank, he was already nodding and looking off in the same direction. "Yeah, I see it, too. Something's burning and I don't think it's from a campfire."

Stewart stepped up beside Hank. "If it is, they're the stupidest people in the world. That smoke can be seen for more than a mile. Any coldhearts in that radius will be on them in no time."

Suddenly, gunshots floated on the wind, followed by a faint scream due to the distance.

"Sounds like someone's already found them," Hank stated.

"We need to go help them, whoever it is," Laurie said. She took a few steps forward but stopped when she realized the others weren't following her. "Come on, someone needs help."

"It's really none of our business," Carl said. "If we go running to a firefight every time we come across one, we'll either be dead or out of ammo in no time."

"That's bullshit, Carl," Laurie snapped. "People need help; it's the right thing to do."

"What do you want to do, Hank?" Carl asked. "It's your call."

Hank glanced at Stewart, wanting the old man's opinion as well. Though Hank might be the defacto leader, he still liked to know what the others thought of any given situation if there was time to ask.

"Whatever you want to do is fine with me, Hank," the older man said. "If someone I knew was in trouble, I know I'd want someone to help them, and if it was all of us in danger, I'd certainly welcome support from outsiders."

More gunshots could be heard, followed by more screams. Whatever was going on over that hill, people were dying in a hard way.

"Stewart's got a point, but so does Carl," Hank said.

"But, lover," Laurie began but Hank held his hand up to stop her.

"But I gotta go with what Stewart said," Hank continued. "Let's go do a recce and see if we can help. But if I don't like what I see, we back off and keep moving."

Laurie wasn't entirely pleased with the decision but she nodded, knowing what Hank agreed upon wasn't that bad. Besides, once they got closer and saw what was going on and if people needed help, she knew she could change his mind. She had in the past and no doubt would again in the future.

"Fine, but let's get going," she said and began walking again, then started to jog. Her .22 was already in her hand, her finger on the trigger.

"There goes one tough woman with a big heart," Carl said. "She doesn't even know what's going on over there and she wants to help."

"Tell me about it," Hank agreed. "Only sometimes I worry her altruistic nature is gonna get her killed. She sometimes forgets things have changed. Good Samaritans are a thing of the past." He was walking now, as were Stewart and Carl. As Laurie got further away from them, the three men began to jog, too.

"So, you got a plan once we get to the top of that hill?" Carl asked.

Hank shook his head as he jogged, his pack bouncing lightly on his back. "Nope. We'll take it as it comes. We'll know more once we see who is trying to kill who and for what reason." He picked up his pace, wanting to reach Laurie and rein her in before she did something foolish, such as charging over the hill like the cavalry.

As Stewart and Carl were left behind, both men looked at each other, and with a knowing nod, began to pick up their pace as well.

As the four companions stood on the top of the hill, gazing down into a small reservoir of water filled with trees and grass lining the shore, seeming untouched by the world around it, the origin of the gunshots and screams became apparent…to their equal disgust.

On the shore of the reservoir, a camp had been set up. Two cars with peeling paint, broken windows, and a hundred dents each, were parked off to the side in the bushes of the small dirt road that led into the area. Four tents had been set up, though now they were pulled down, torn apart, and most were covered in blood—human blood.

The smoke came from a campfire that had been set up in the middle of the camp, only now the flames were out of control, in part thanks to the human body that lay in the fire. As the body fluids seeped out and the fat of the corpse dripped into the flames, it created the smoke wafting into the air.

There had been ten travelers at the beginning, but only five remained alive at the moment and they were being killed fast. The raiding party of half a dozen cannies had been proficient in their kills after creeping up on the camp and attacking, the element of surprise more than enough to win the day.

Off to the side, a few feet away from the general melee, a woman was on her stomach with a cannie on top of her. The cannie was a large man with a thick black beard, his entire body covered in soot and grime. All he wore was a ragged pair of shorts, and a pair of leather sandals on his dirty feet.

Though the man held a large knife to the woman's throat, she still struggled to escape. He backhanded her and she ceased fighting for a few seconds, as her mind tried to clear itself of the haze from the blow. As the woman lay stunned, the cannie pulled out his dick and ripped off the woman's pants in one powerful yank. His dick already hard from the excitement, he slid it into her without lubrication, sodomizing her, pumping manically as drool slid from the corner of his mouth to drop onto the top of the woman's head. The woman's eyes opened from the assault, and she began to scream, then tried to bite him. Fed up at her not submitting, he sliced her throat and began to lap at the blood while still pumping away. The woman's kicking slowed and finally stopped as she died while being raped. When the cannie was done, he planned on cutting her up and having her for dinner as well. Unlike some of the other cannies he traveled with, he loved to fuck his meat before eating it later.

"Bastards," Laurie hissed and began running down the hill, her PPK already coming up to shoot the cannie raping the now dead woman. Laurie was within fifty feet when she fired her first shot. The .22 caliber round zipped through the air to impact the cannie at the back of the neck. Slicing into the fat roll of flesh, it continued onward and out the front of the man's throat, taking out the cannie's prominent Adam's apple as it exited. The man stopped fucking the corpse beneath him and began to gag, then spit up a clot of dark blood mixed with saliva, the glob flying out of his mouth to splash on the dead woman's head—she didn't seem to mind.

The cannie reached up and grasped his neck with both hands as blood shot through his fingers, then he slumped limply on top of the corpse. It looked like the two were lovers and the man had just orgasmed and was too spent to climb off his mate.

The other cannibals looked up from slaughtering the rest of the campers at the sound of the gunshot, and for a few seconds silence filled the air. Then Hank, Carl and Stewart, who had followed Laurie into the fray, began shooting as well and all hell broke loose, as any cannie with a firearm began shooting at the companions.

Hank followed Laurie to the left while Carl and Stewart went to the right, to take cover behind a group of waist-high boulders. Bullets began to fly through the air like angry bees, but none of the companions were hit.

However, the cannies weren't as lucky on that account.

Hank lined up a big cannie with rolls of fat and muscle, who looked to be in his late thirties, give or take a few years. The man had long hair and was missing an eye, the eyelid sealed shut with thread or glue.

When the cannie saw Hank shooting at him, Hank quickly figured that the man would drop to the ground when danger appeared, the man's mind screaming at him to get down, that someone was shooting at him. Before the cannie would even realize what he was doing, he would be ducking for cover. Hank was ready for this, and he fired his SIG-Sauer not where the man was, but where Hank believed the cannie's head would be a second later.

The first 9mm slug impacted the man in the mouth, destroying his jawbone and leaving nothing behind but a mush of bone, flesh and teeth. But the bullet didn't stop there, and continued into the man's brain, making a home for itself before ricocheting out of the skull via the cannie's left ear canal. More bone and brain matter erupted from the side of the man's head as the body began to twitch in death, sliding to the ground where it remained still, blood pumping out of the head wound and shattered jaw.

Another cannie tried to draw down on Laurie as she moved through the camp, and Hank spun to the side to make himself a smaller target and shot the cannie in the chest, destroying the man's heart and killing him instantly.

Moving through the war zone, Hank searched for anyone worth saving but found only death. Seeing they were under attack, the cannies had killed each of their hostages before turning to face the new threat of the companions. As Hank ran through the camp, he saw men and women, as well as a few children, all with throats slashed or stab wounds.

Hank was near the shore of the reservoir when a cannie jumped up from playing possum and tackled him, both Hank and the man falling into the water. The SIG-Sauer fell from Hank's grip to land on the shore and his HK was slung over his shoulder and out of reach. As the two men went into the water, Hank found himself on the bottom, his head under the surface. As he fought to rise, his lungs began to burn; he was using up oxygen quickly due to his exertions. Stars swam before his eyes as the cannie wrapped his large hands around Hank's throat and began to squeeze.

A lesser man no doubt would have drowned there and then, but Hank was anything but. Drawing on his iron willpower, he forced himself to calm down and assess his situation. The man holding him down was almost twice as big as Hank was, with meaty hands that almost wrapped entirely around Hank's already formidable neck. The man was straddling him and Hank realized his legs were between the cannie's legs. The instant that thought came to him, Hank went into action, bringing his right knee up and into the cannie's groin. No matter how big the cannie might be, his testicles were still as vulnerable to attack as a man half his size.

Hank felt his knee fit into the V of the man's pelvis and immediately the iron grip on his throat lessened. Taking full advantage,

Hank twisted his legs to the side and knocked the wounded man off balance, thus freeing himself from the iron grip.

As his head broke the surface of the lake, Hank sputtered, sucking in air in great gulps. His head began to clear immediately and he spun his head around to see where the cannie was. It was as he turned his head to the left that the cannie came charging at him again, grappling like a wrestler and knocking Hank back into the water.

The two struggled, rolling one over the other like two human alligators battling over a kill. Each time Hank tried to punch the man, his blows were slowed by the water to be all but ineffectual. If only it had been the same for the cannie's blows, which though slowed, still packed the power of two men.

Knowing he would never be able to win this fight on brute strength alone, Hank reached down with his left hand and felt along the bottom of the lake, his hand finally sliding over a fist-sized rock. Grabbing it, he swung his arm in a wide blow, the rock leading the charge.

His swing was good, though later Hank would wonder if it had been more luck than skill, and the rock connected with the cannie's left temple, dazing the giant cannie and causing the man to fall back as he tried to regain his composure.

That few seconds was all Hank needed to even the match.

Reaching down, Hank wrapped his right palm around the handle of his panga and drew the sixteen inch blade, the sunlight reflecting off the wet knife like it was a mirror.

As the cannie recovered and came at Hank for the third time, Hank planted his feet in the rocky bed of the lake and lowered his head. If the giant cannie cared that Hank held a large blade, he didn't show it, no doubt because the man was lost in a haze of battle, only wanting to kill Hank and later feed on his flesh.

Hank flexed his right arm, his muscles tightening, the veins bulging as the cannie splashed through the water, screaming loudly in the hope of scaring Hank.

Once more, a lesser man would have been cowed to see this sodden behemoth roaring his rage as he came forward. But Hank was a warrior of the new world, and no matter how overwhelming the odds, he would face it to the death on his feet, with weapons in hand and hopefully his friends by his side.

The cannie swung a meaty fist at Hank's head, only the warrior ducked and then popped back up, the panga coming out of the water like a steel fish to slice point first in the cannie's large belly. As the blade sank in six inches, the cannie stopped cold, the pain holding him fast. But Hank wasn't finished with the man, not by a long shot. Gripping the handle of the panga with both hands, Hank began to pull up on the knife, slicing deep and upward. When he had gone seven inches, he twisted the blade and then yanked it to the right, then spun it around and yanked it to the left. All this was done in the space of three seconds, the cannie standing stupefied as the blade carved him up like a Thanksgiving turkey.

As Hank yanked to the left, the jagged wound spilled open, spilling forth blood and viscera, which splattered on Hank's arms. The warrior ignored the hot, sticky feeling as organs splashed over him, and he stepped back, taking the blade with him.

The cannie had a wound that if closed, would resemble one from an autopsy and he looked down and tried to prevent his insides from spilling out.

Gutted, he fell to his knees, still not dead but close.

That wasn't good enough for Hank, who knew a man could be gutted and still go on living for hours. As the cannie dropped to his knees—the water washing the blood and viscera away—Hank brought the panga back up and sliced it sideways, the razor-sharp blade biting into the spine and then continuing into the tendons and muscles that supported the cannie's neck.

Only Hank's raw strength was enough to chop through muscle and bone and sever the head cleanly from the massive shoulders. As blood spurt upward and then pattered into the water like scarlet rain, the body toppled sideways and remained still, floating silently.

Falling to his knees, the water up to his chest, Hank let out a weary breath and realized he was the victor.

He got all of five seconds to rest before he heard Carl call out, "If you're done playing in the water with your new friend, we could use your help on land."

Hank turned to look back to see Carl, Stewart and Laurie watching him. Laurie looked relieved to see Hank was okay, and Carl had a wide grin on his face. From the looks of their body language, the battle on land was over and the companions had survived intact and unhurt. As Hank stood up, he winced slightly, his neck muscles spasming. It hurt to swallow, too. The large cannie had almost done him in.

"If you guys were watching," Hank breathed heavily, "then why the hell didn't one of you shoot the bastard?" He began sloshing to shore.

"You were too close to him," Laurie said. "I could have just as easily hit you if you went left instead of right." She helped him out of the water as he splashed onto land, dropping to his knees as he gathered himself. Carl handed him his SIG-Sauer, which he'd found on the shore.

"Thanks. My HK is in the water," Hank said, realizing it was no longer on his shoulder.

"I found it," Stewart said after going in a few feet and peering down into the clear water. Luckily, the dead cannie floated ten feet away and his blood was flowing in the opposite direction, away from the shore, so it wasn't clouding the water where Stewart had been searching.

Hank dropped down on the shore to rest, his knees bent, his arms resting on them. He looked up at Laurie who stood beside him, brushing his wet hair away from his face.

"Well, you should have tried to shoot the guy anyway," Hank said. "That big bastard almost had me."

"I wanted to, Hank, believe me," Laurie said with concern. "But it was too risky."

He let the matter drop, knowing there was no more reason to discuss it. Besides, what was done was done. Coming to his feet with a groan, he scanned the campsite. Nothing but prone bodies. The one that had been in the fire was now nothing but charcoal, only the legs from the knees down untouched, the pink skin a stark contrast to the burnt corpse.

Carl joined him. "We took down all the cannies but not before they slaughtered everyone."

Hank nodded, understanding. They had tried to help. There was nothing else anyone could have asked them to do. Hell, most people wouldn't have bothered to help at all, but would have waited until the cannies left and then seen what they could take. "Okay, let's see if there's anything around we can salvage. We need to make up for the ammo we wasted." Hank gave Laurie a brief glimpse which she caught but didn't reply to. She knew he meant that they had risked their lives and wasted precious brass, and it had all been for nothing.

The four warriors got to work, searching bodies and gear bags of anything worth taking. They found many items, that though weren't overly valuable, would still be worthy of trade with others they came across. The few guns they found were of poor quality and most were left where they'd fallen. The companions could only carry so much before becoming weighed down.

Carl inspected the two cars but both had been shot up badly by stray rounds. Each one had two flat tires with no spares and one had a hole in the radiator, antifreeze seeping out to pool on the ground like green blood. Both cars had different size rims so swapping out the good tires and making one whole car wasn't an option.

Fifteen minutes later, the companions gathered in the center of the camp to discuss what they'd found. After evenly dividing the wares amongst themselves for easy carrying, Carl said, "What do you want to do about the bodies?"

Hank considered the question for a few moments. It would take far too much time and energy to dig graves for the slaughtered. Then his eyes rested on the smoking fire again. "Well, fuck the cannies, they can rot where they lay, but the others…let's take a few minutes and put them by the fire. We'll burn them, give 'em a burial by fire."

"Good idea," Stewart agreed. They got to work once more, dragging the bodies of the cannies' victims into the fire. Soon, they were tossing them one on top of the other. Carl siphoned fuel from one of the cars and doused the bodies with it, then lit a branch with his lighter and tossed the flaming stick onto the pile. Immediately there was a loud *whoosh* and the funeral pyre began to burn, smoke drifting into the sky once more.

The companions stood quietly and watched the flames but then the wind shifted and the odor of cooking flesh hit them and they walked off.

Before they left, Stewart called, "Wait a second, guys, I need to take a leak. When you reach my age, things don't work as good as they used to."

"Okay, but make it quick, will ya?" Hank said. "That smoke and all the gunshots means we're sure to have company any second."

"I won't be a minute." Stewart turned and hobbled away, avoiding stepping on the bodies of the cannies. He walked a few feet away from where the two cars were parked, then stood before a large bush. As he unzipped and began to urinate, he stared straight ahead. As he did, he realized the bush didn't look like a bush, that it was far too dense. Finishing up, he shook himself three times and zipped up. Wiping his hands on his pants, he stepped forward and began pulling at the branches. He was surprised when they came away easily, and after checking their ends, he saw that they had been cut. The branches weren't attached to anything.

After a full minute of digging, he gasped in surprise when he saw steel, then a headlight appeared.

"You okay over there?" Carl called. The others were watching the area for signs of new attackers, impatiently waiting for Stewart to return so they could get moving.

"I found something," Stewart called out. "It's some sort of truck."

The others went to investigate while Stewart continued to pull branches off the hidden vehicle. When they joined him, all four of them began clearing off the large vehicle.

"What is it?" Hank asked. "It looks military."

"Shit, I know what this is," Carl said, tipping his Yankees ball cap and wiping his forehead. "It's an APC. An M113A1 by the looks of it. Though it could be an A2."

"A what?" Laurie asked.

"An armored personnel carrier. An APC for short. Ground forces used them in wars. This one was from the late 60's if I'm right. My grandfather was assigned to one during WW2. He told me all about them."

"No shit? I wonder if it runs," Hank said as he stared at the large vehicle. It didn't have wheels but instead had fifteen inch wide metal tracks, like a bulldozer. There were two hatches on top and a door in the back that was held together with two large hinges, as well as rectangular ports on both sides about four inches wide and six inches long for shooting through; it was painted green, black and brown, the paintjob looking more homemade than professional. Hank turned to face Laurie. "You go back to the edge of the camp and keep an eye out for anyone," he directed. "We need a few minutes to check this thing out. If it works, we'll be riding in style for a while."

"Got it." She leaned over and kissed Hank, who was already drying now that he was out of the water. He patted her behind and then she was off, keeping guard while the others inspected the APC.

Carl climbed onto the front of the APC and crawled over it till he was on top of it. Then he opened one of the hatches set on the top, and after peering inside to make sure it was empty, climbed down into it.

Hank and Stewart talked about his find, Stewart proud about what he'd spotted. "And to think, Hank, if I hadn't had to piss, we never would have known it was here."

"Lucky for us you have a weak, bladder, Stu," Hank chuckled. "Still, I wonder why it was hidden here."

"I bet I can figure out that one. As valuable as this thing is? Shit, of course they hid it. Too bad they couldn't have gotten to it when they were attacked. Even if it doesn't run, once they were inside they could have waited the cannies out. The cannies might have given up and left after a while."

Suddenly, there was a loud pop and a belch of smoke and the 212hp, two-stroke, six cylinder diesel engine came to life, rumbling softly. A second later, the APC lurched forward, causing Hank and Stewart to jump out of the way. The metal tracks began to move and the vehicle drove out of the thicket it had been hidden in. It crossed twenty feet of terrain and came to a stop, crushing the body of a dead cannie under its twenty-one thousand pound frame. The body punctured like a balloon, spraying viscera and blood in all directions.

The hatch popped open and Carl's head was there, smiling widely. "Man, this machine is fantastic. And get this…the ninety-five gallon fuel tank is half full!"

Stewart nodded. "These things get around three hundred miles a tank on open road, so if we have half a tank…"

"Yeah, Carl, I get it. I know math, too," Hank said with a grin.

"And it keeps getting better," Carl added, his voice high, his face animated like a kid on Christmas morning. "This baby is loaded for bear. It's got an armory with grenades of different types, like Willy Pete's, hi-ex and frags, a dozen M-16s, and enough clips to last for a while. There's even some 9mm rounds for my Mini-Uzi and a gallon of gun oil to clean them. Plus there's a Browning .50-caliber and a .30-cal inside and stanchions on the roof to connect them. All we have to do is hook them up and we're in business. We hit the fucking jackpot here!"

"Then let's do it later, once we're gone from here," Hank said as he looked up at Carl's grinning face. "You say you can drive this thing?"

"Sure, it's not hard. If you can drive a car you can drive this. Plus, I read about them years ago."

"Then let's do this." Hank slapped Stewart on the back again, his face beaming. "Stewart, my friend, the next time I get mad when you want to stop for an unscheduled bathroom break, just remind me of today and it'll be fine."

"I'll hold you to that," Stewart laughed.

The APC revved as Carl engaged the accelerator, then it rolled to the side a few feet, the metal tracks churning up both bodies and dirt. His head popped back up. "Come on, guys, let's roll.

Like you said, Hank, we can go through it more later once we're out of here." Carl's head disappeared again as he dropped down into the armored carrier.

"Okay, let's gather everything we're taking with us, pick up Laurie and get out of here," Hank said.

"You know, Hank," Stewart mused. "We really don't have to rush now. If more raiders or whoever show up, we now have the firepower and armor to take them down."

"Yeah, maybe so, but there's no reason to fight and waste ammo if we don't have to. God knows we'll get into more scrapes sooner or later."

Stewart nodded, knowing what Hank meant. In a world with no law and order, people took what they wanted, and usually killed you when they had what they needed. Civilization was such a tenuous string. It bodes the question of back when civilization was still around, and if a man knew he could kill another man or rape a woman with no repercussions, no law to seek vengeance, then would that man truly care whether he committed murder or rape? Hank believed he already knew the answer and it chilled him to think about it.

Hank called Laurie back and together they quickly loaded all their gear and were soon locked inside the APC. There was plenty of room for the four people as the machine held a crew of thirteen; eleven passengers, one driver and one on the hull center. With a wide smile, Carl began rolling forward. "You know," Carl said over the noise of the engine and metal tracks as they churned up dirt, enjoying telling the others what he knew about the machine. "This baby can go into the water, too. Streams, rivers, hell, even lakes. It's made of lightweight aluminum so it floats." He drove back onto the highway they'd been traveling on before their detour.

Hank nodded in reply. He was studying a manual found inside the APC, while Stewart inspected the Browning .50 and .30 calibers machine guns. The guns looked clean and in working order, though no doubt Hank would want them broken down and inspected before use. The manual had all sorts of useful information. The APC had a top speed of forty mph, was manufactured by FMC corp., which stood for Ford & Kaiser Aluminum & Chemical Co. Items such as the weight, width and height were also listed, as well as the engine size. Hank tossed the manual aside. Carl knew how to drive it and Hank doubted there would be much use for the manual if there was nothing in it about how to fix the APC should it breakdown.

"Where do you think this thing came from?" Hank asked Carl. "I mean, how do you think those people back there got a hold of it?"

Carl shrugged. "Who knows? From the paint job on this baby, I'd guess it came from someone's private collection."

"Well, it's ours now," Laurie said with a smile as she looked around the interior, then stretched her lithe body like a cat relaxing. "This sure beats walking."

"I hear that," Stewart agreed. "So, Hank, now that we have transportation again, where are we going?"

"Don't know. But I'll tell you when we get there," Hank joked. He walked over to Carl and patted him on the shoulder. "Just stay on this road. Sooner or later we should come upon something of interest."

"Got it, boss," Carl said and leaned back in his chair. He took off his cap again and wiped his sweaty head, then put it on again.

Hank got Stewart's attention. "Let's get that .50-cal checked out."

Stewart nodded and went to it, then with a groan dragged it across the metal floor so it was in the center. He laid a towel down so that no small pieces would roll away and get lost.

"What about me?" Laurie asked.

"You can clean my HK. It was in the water, remember?" Hank said.

"Sure, no problem," she replied and began laying out what she'd need to field strip the weapon.

As everyone began their chosen tasks, the APC rolled onward.

As the armored APC drove off, insects had already begun feeding on the corpses of the cannies, only the smoke from the fire keeping them at bay for so long. But food within reach was too much temptation to stop them.

With the engine of the APC fading away, the corpses were quickly attacked from the air and the ground. Crows flew down from trees, where they had been watching warily, anxiously waiting for the four humans to depart.

Ants arrived and began crawling over the bodies, first just a few and then thousands more. Marching in lines, they swarmed over the bodies and began feeding, one micro-bite at a time. Soon, the bodies were covered in moving blankets of insects as blowflies joined in, all the insects and birds fighting to get a piece of the pie. The crows went right for the soft meat, plucking out eyes and tongues with their sharp beaks.

It was a feast the creatures hadn't known in a while and they relished it happily. Even in death, the cycle of life continued.

"Jesus, this thing is noisy," Hank said as the APC rolled down the center of the highway. A few times pile-ups blocked the road but the APC simply pushed through it, sending cars and skeletons flying over the shoulder of the road to land in a spray of dust. One time, they came across a downed AH-64 Apache helicopter forty feet from the road in a green field of tall grass. One of the stub wings was gone, having been blown off in the crash landing. The same went for the rocket pods, Hellfire missiles, and the 30mm chain guns the chopper had carried.

The large rotors were missing, no doubt having sheared off to now lie in a ditch somewhere. The wreckage was blackened from fire but the area around the downed bird was lush and green. After laying there for two years, the burned area had regrown, shoots of green foliage coming up through the ashes from the initial fire. Anything worth taking was long gone, including the ruined engine, no doubt by some ambitious salvage team.

"What do you expect?" Carl said. "We're pretty much in a tank right now."

Hank only grunted in reply, and that was lost in the noise of the growling diesel engine. He glanced at his radiation badge on his jacket and was pleased to see it was well into the green. At least the area was safe. Though armored, the APC wasn't airtight and radiation was still a factor.

After traveling a mile from where they'd found the APC, Carl had pulled over and gone through the vehicle better. Once the Fifty and the .30-cal had been inspected and were found operational, they were hooked up to the top of the APC. The group felt better when that happened, knowing they had some serious firepower to protect themselves. The Fifty had over two thousand rounds of ammunition for it and the thirty had half that. The Fifty could be used in a 360 degree arc so nothing could sneak up on them.

With the armor of the APC, they were about as safe as someone could be in the new world. After having a brief meal, they drove on.

They had covered more than thirty miles without incident. A few times raiders or slavers had taken potshots at the APC from somewhere off the highway but the bullets had bounced off the hull, doing nothing. The shooters had quickly decided there were easier picking elsewhere and had let the APC be.

When Carl slowed the armored carrier and then stopped in the center of the deserted highway, the engine cycling down to idle, Hank jumped up from his seat and moved to join him, peering out the slim front windshield. All his weapons had been cleaned and greased and he was ready for action if needed. The other guns had been serviced as well.

"What's wrong? Why'd you stop?" Hank asked, his eyes darting back and forth. Was it raiders? Slavers or more cannies? With food scarce and manpower scarcer, many coldhearts had become the lowest forms of life, preying on their fellow humans to survive instead of working together.

"There," Carl said simply, pointing.

Hank followed where his friend was gesturing and spotted the plywood sign that had been propped up in front of a mile marker. It had been one of the green and white signs that dotted every highway in America but it had been painted over white with black letters. After reading it, Hank said, "I'll tell the others."

"How far do you think Overland Park is from here?" Laurie asked from the back of the APC as she chewed on a piece of jerky.

Stewart leaned forward so he didn't have to shout over the engine. "Fifty miles, give or take, I believe. Why?"

Laurie shrugged, as if it was no serious matter. "I knew some people that lived there. Couldn't help but wonder if they're still alive or dead."

"Let's pray they're still alive and doing fine," Stewart said, a slight smile on his lips.

"Yeah, Stu, it's a good thought, but no doubt they're dead, like everyone else I knew."

Hank's voice broke through their conversation, causing both Stewart and Laurie to look to the front of the vehicle. "Hey, guys, we got a sign for a town," he said simply. Stewart and Laurie joined him and Carl, all four warriors peering out the bulletproof front windshield to read the sign.

Arcadia, five miles, the black letters declared, standing out starkly against the white background. *Only good, God-fearing people welcome. All others will get a bullet or the noose.* In smaller writing were the directions to find the town after taking the next exit off the highway.

"They're not fucking around, are they?" Carl said as he glanced at the others.

Hank rubbed his chin, feeling the sandpaper feeling on his face. He hadn't shaved in days. "Can't say I blame them."

"Then why put that sign there at all?" Laurie asked. "If you don't want to risk being attacked, then don't advertise."

"Maybe they have plenty of manpower and weapons to protect themselves from attack," Stewart mused. "But they still need to get traders and new blood into the town to survive."

"Sounds plausible," Hank agreed. "Either way we need to go somewhere and that town sounds as good as any. You guys agree?"

Everyone nodded, Laurie the most eager. "If they have a running town, maybe they have hot showers. Hell, even a cold one would be fine."

"Makes sense, this far off the beaten path they should have been fine," Carl said.

"True," Stewart added, "but as you know, most cities and towns that weren't destroyed by the bombs ended up suffering a similar fate by their own residents. Fires, looting and murder to name a few. Many places have burnt to the ground simply because of man's greed and cruelty to one another."

"Well said, Stu," Hank smiled. "Very poetic."

Stewart grinned with pride. "Thanks, Hank, I do have my moments, you know."

"Okay, Carl." Hank slapped Carl on the back. "We have a destination. Onward."

Revving the engine, Carl put the transmission into drive and the APC began moving again. The air was different inside the APC now, each of the warriors inwardly excited to reach a functioning town. Perhaps civilization wasn't dead after all and in time, America would grow out of the ashes to become an even stronger nation.

The lookout sitting on the hill a hundred yards off the highway watched the APC begin to move again after stopping before the sign. Using his binoculars, the man watched the APC take the exit that would lead the vehicle onto the urban roads that would bring it right to Arcadia.

When the APC was gone from sight, the rumbling of the engine and metal tracks having faded, he picked up a two-way radio on the ground by his side to call it in.

"We'll be ready for them," a voice on the other end of the radio replied. "Did you see how many?"

"No, they're in some kind of personnel carrier from the army or something," the lookout said.

"Is it armed?"

"I think so. I saw two large machine guns on the roof."

"Did they look hostile?"

"Couldn't tell, they stayed inside the machine. But they were driving an armored truck so…" He trailed off.

"No matter," the voice said. "We'll do what we've done to everyone else who comes to us."

The lookout chuckled at that, knowing the saying that was used to jack new arrivals. "Kill them with kindness?"

"You got it, brother. Kill them with kindness. Over and out."

The lookout put the radio down and began scanning the area again with a wide smile, seeing nothing but a few birds. He didn't know who was in that machine, but he knew they were in for a surprise once they were welcomed into Arcadia and they let their guard down. Some who had arrived before them had been wary, too, but sooner or later all had been trapped. After all, no man could stay sharp twenty-four hours a day indefinitely.

The ride to the town was quick, mainly because anything blocking the APC's path had been cleared long ago. Wrecked and abandoned cars once sitting in the middle of the skinny roads had been pushed aside to the shoulders to clear a path. Signs had been posted at regular intervals so that Carl always knew which way to go when approaching an intersection.

It was obvious they had arrived when the APC reached a twelve foot wall that had been made of anything the builders could find back when it was created.

Old tires, pieces of cars, trailers beds, as well as old washing machines and refrigerators were packed together, welded to one another in most places.

Rats could be seen scurrying between the pieces, the warren of hiding places perfect for them to make their nests. The road leading up to the gate was more of a suggestion now, the sidewalks and front yards now all one giant passageway.

The curbs had been taken out and there were one and two-foot high boulders scattered everywhere, with the exception of a winding path through them for any approaching vehicle. Hank studied this from inside the APC and nodded in approval. The small boulders would prevent an attacking force on wheels from simply coming in hard and ramming the gate.

He also saw there was nothing higher than the boulders so an approaching force on foot would have no decent cover when laying siege. Whoever the leaders of the town were, they had done a good job of fortifying their home.

Men stood in two guardhouses set on either side of the gate, which was made of sheet metal and old signs that used to be used for advertising. As the APC drove down the winding path and the gate came before them, the painted, smiling face of a boy eating oatmeal looked back at the vehicle. Below the face were the words:

...Lowers your cholesterol if eaten with
a healthy diet and exercise...

As the APC slowed to a stop to idle, Hank couldn't help but wonder why the vehicle had been allowed to get so close to the town before being stopped, but then he peered down at the ground and saw Claymore mines on both sides of the APC.

Looking straight down over the nose of the vehicle, he also saw landmines; only these had been set to go off remotely when one of the guards pressed a button.

The APC approached slowly so the guards never felt threatened, knowing they could destroy the vehicle with the touch of a button. Though armored, the APC wasn't invulnerable, and the personnel carrier would have been severely damaged, or at least one of the metal tracks used for propulsion could have been ruined.

The APC couldn't operate well if one of the tracks was severely damaged and there was even the chance of a roll-over if the APC was still driven, the machine pulling into the good track and fighting the driver the entire time.

A man stood on the wall of refuse, holding a LAW in his hands, as well. So the town hadn't been worried at the companions' arrival. One wrong move and the APC would have been blown to hell. An impressive showing of firepower, Hank had to admit, and he hoped it wasn't a mistake coming here.

A man walked out of a small opening to the side of the gate made for pedestrians, and stopped in front of the APC. He was heavy set with a thick black beard, bushy eyebrows that gave him a unibrow look and a scar going down the right side of his face, from below his eye to his upper lip. Back when he'd gotten the wound, it must have looked nasty. He wore the uniform of a police officer, though nowadays it seemed out of place, but Hank figured if these people had a running town, then the old ways would still be in effect. The man wore a name tag over his silver badge: *A. Marshall.* He gestured for Carl to turn off the engine and yelled, "I want to talk to your leader!"

It was unspoken who that was inside the APC and Hank went to the left hatch on the top of the APC and climbed out so that he was visible from the waist up. He felt vulnerable, and hoped there wasn't a sniper with an itchy trigger finger who even now had Hank in his sights.

"Hi there," Hank said with a wide grin, trying to look as friendly as possible, despite being in an armored transport. "Me and my friends saw your sign on the highway and thought we'd come and see you. I was hoping we could do some trading."

Marshall smiled widely as he studied Hank. "Oh yeah? And what makes you think we won't just kill you and take your shit anyway?"

Hank blinked in surprise, not sure how to react to the man's question. It wasn't that he was shocked to hear the man say it, it's just that no one had ever been so blunt.

Hank patted the Fifty to his left and smiled as he gestured at the APC. "This baby is armored to the gills and we have the firepower to defend ourselves if need be. We came in friendship, but that can change. Seems like a waste though."

Marshall's face went hard, and Hank was beginning to tense, when Marshall began to laugh, as did the other uniformed men behind him who were watching. "Relax, friend, just having a bit of fun with you. It gets boring out here on guard duty and I like to entertain the men whenever possible."

Hank smiled but he didn't relax. He knew better. His right hand slid down into the hatch and he signed to the others to stay sharp. Stewart patted Hank's leg to assure him he, Carl and Laurie were ready if things went haywire.

"The name's Marshall, I'm the police chief, the mayor, and the city treasurer, too. Welcome to Arcadia. Who might you be and how many you got in there?"

Hank decided he had to disclose the truth or else there would be no real trust between him and the town, so he said, "There's four of us all together."

"You guys mercenaries? Where'd you get this baby?" Marshall gestured to the APC, clearly envious of the powerful machine.

Hank ignored the second question. "No, we're not mercies. Just travelers and sometimes traders."

"What you got to trade?"

"Guns mostly," Hank said. "M-16's with ammo for them. Some other weapons we took off a cannie raiding party we came upon."

Marshall spit in the dirt at his feet. "Fucking cannies, scum of the earth. You kill them?"

Hank nodded. "Every fucking one of them."

That seemed to seal the deal and Marshall's facial muscles relaxed, and so did Hank.

"You folks are welcome in our town. Follow the rules and there won't be any trouble. But step out of line and…" He trailed off, hoping Hank's imagination would be enough. It was.

"I hear you, loud and clear," Hank said. "We've been to this dance before if you get my meaning."

Marshall only grunted in response and nodded and waved a hand in the air. "Open the gate, these people are traders, they can pass." He turned back to Hank. "Go through the gate and bear to the left. There's a parking lot where you can put your machine. From there you have to walk into the main part of town."

"Sounds good," Hank nodded curtly.

"After you've checked in at the police station and given all the information we need from you, stop by the tavern on the corner of Main and First Street tonight. It's a good place to eat, drink, get laid and relax. The homebrewed beer is fantastic, but keep away from the stew. Just don't tell Fran I said that, she'd kill me."

"What's wrong with the stew?"

"You ever heard the saying 'mystery meat'?"

Hank nodded.

"Well, it's become a running gag around here as to what the meat is each day. It could be anything from dog to road kill to rabbit to skunk, even rat I heard once, though we stopped that shit fast. Whatever Fran manages to get that day."

"I'll keep that in mind," Hank said.

"You do that. Like I said, just don't tell Fran I told ya. She's got a mean temper. I'm there every night, keeping the peace and having a good time if I can. Maybe you and me can talk some more. I always like hearing how things are going out there in the rest of the state, hell, the country." He smiled, this time the gesture going to his eyes. "The first round's on me."

"Sure, sounds like a plan."

"Ah, I was wondering, you're all going to be there, right?"

Hank shook his head. "No, one of us will remain with our vehicle to keep an eye on it."

"Ah, that's not necessary. You're safe here with us."

"Maybe so, but you can never be too careful," Hank rebutted, his eyes creasing slightly.

Marshall's face seemed to scrunch for a second but it was gone before Hank realized it was there. "Fine then, but it's not needed. You're safe here with us behind these walls."

Hank didn't answer, but instead slapped the roof of the APC and the engine started. Carl shifted the transmission into drive and the vehicle began to move. Imposing, the APC rolled through the gates. It was a tight fit but the APC managed to roll through without damaging the fence. Every man on duty watched the armored personnel carrier. After all, it wasn't every day a tank—or close to it—rolled into town.

There was a wide open area of asphalt that held a few cars and trucks so Carl drove there. Off to the side was a garage, the sounds of hammering and the sparks of welding coming through the open bay doors.

Next to that was another building, the use unknown, but a group of old timers sat in plastic chairs, watching the APC roll in, talking about it happily. A woman in her late forties walked by pushing a baby stroller. She took a quick glance at the APC and then hurried on her way.

Finding a good spot, Carl turned the APC so that it would be facing outward and parked the vehicle, turning off the engine with a belch of black smoke.

Carl stayed behind on guard duty, while Hank, Laurie and Stewart climbed out the rear door and stretched.

Looking back at Carl through the opened door, Hank called, "If you have any trouble, just fire off the Fifty. That'll tell us to come running."

"Will do. But I don't see anything happening. With me locked up in here, no one would be stupid enough to try anything."

"You hope," Hank said.

"I suppose. I'm gonna catch up on some much needed sleep. Just bring me back some grub will ya?"

"Sure, buddy, you can count on it." Hank closed the door and heard Carl locking it from within, then he joined the others, who were standing a few feet away talking.

"Carl's happy. He said he's planning on taking a nap," Hank informed the others.

"I don't blame him," Stewart agreed. "I have to admit, it's been a long day. I could use some shuteye myself."

"And that's exactly what we'll do," Hank said. "But first let's do what that cop said. We'll check in, then get some hot food for ourselves, bring Carl back some and bed down for the night."

"In the APC?" Laurie asked.

"Maybe. But I suppose we could have one of us stand guard for four hours while the rest of us stayed in a hotel or whatever they have here for visitors."

"Well, I don't care where we sleep, just as long as it's safe," Laurie said. She moved closer to Hank. "But if we get a room, then maybe we don't have to go right to sleep, if you know what I mean." She winked slyly.

"Baby," Hank whispered into her ear. "I want that more than you know, but only if it's safe."

"Are you two love birds ready?" Stewart asked. He'd been standing to the side quietly, letting them have a moment together.

"Sure, Stu. Let's go see what this place has for us," Hank said and began walking, his weapons hanging from his person. He was surprised Marshall hadn't tried to make them give up their weapons, but then again, if Marshall had enough of a police force, a few visitors with guns certainly couldn't do much. It's not like they could take over the town or anything.

As the three warriors walked into town, behind them, Carl's snores already floated through the armored plating of the APC.

Just before the companions reached the town proper, there was a hangman's gallows with one body swinging gently in the wind, the arms tied behind its back. It was clear why the body had been left there.

It was a warning to all in the town to behave. The leader of the town had gone back to medieval times as a way to keep order.

The corpse's eyes were gone, leaving behind nothing but gaping sockets. The skin was like dried leather, telling of how long it had been hanging there. The clothes were nothing but rags, the stray ends flapping in the wind.

"Looks like Marshall runs a tight ship," Hank stated.

"Poor bastard," Stewart said under his breath.

"Maybe," Hank added. "But we don't know what that guy did. He may have been guilty as sin."

Laurie wrapped her left arm around Hank's right arm. "I think we need to be careful around here, lover. This place gives me the chills."

"It's your imagination, baby," Hank replied. "So far, I haven't seen anything different from any of the other places we've visited. New world, new rules, I guess."

The trio kept walking. Before they reached Main Street, they began to detect the odors of people living their lives. Wood smoke was prevalent, and so was the aroma of cooking meat. Any building in sight had an extra layer of material on the roof to help protect from the acid rains. Floor mats, sheet metal, plastic sheeting, rubber raincoats, anything that wouldn't be easily eaten away by the rains.

It was overcast and a building half a block down was fully lit with neon signs in the windows and the sound of laughter and music came from the open door. It was cool out but not cold, and many of the buildings stood with doors open wide and windows open to let in the light breeze. Night was still a few hours away.

Next to the building with laughter and music was a brothel, the two buildings connected by a second story, enclosed walkway. In front and in the windows, women dressed in sexy nightgowns, some exposing their breasts, while they waved to Stewart and Hank, cajoling them to come in for a drink and a lay in the sack. One woman even called out to Laurie and licked her lips seductively. A few men were coming and going, all with wide smiles on their faces, more than one looking drunk.

Dogs ran by, barking at the companions, then racing off to be lost in alleyways.

From somewhere wafted the odor of a barbecue, the charcoal taking the three friends back to a better time, before death fell from the skies and wiped out civilization. The humming of a generator could be heard coming from an enclosed alley near the brothel.

"You can almost close your eyes and pretend everything's fine," Laurie said as she took in the aroma of the cooking meat.

"I know what you mean, but still..." Hank paused. "Don't get lazy and let your guard down. This place looks nice but we don't know anything about it."

"You don't think the townsfolk mean us harm, do you?" Stewart asked.

Hank shrugged. "Sure hope not but a lazy fool is a dead one."

"Amen," Stewart added.

They walked the length of Main Street and Hank read the street signs and saw that the tavern with the laughter and music was the one Marshall had said to meet him at. Hank pointed to it.

"This is the place. Let's get something to eat." He was starving, though he knew he wasn't hungry enough to want the stew.

Upon entering the tavern, the smells of unwashed men, stale beer, old sweat and spicy food greeted the three warriors.

In the far corner, four men were playing cards, an oil lantern in the center of the table. Other lanterns were hung around the tavern, and candles were spread out along the bar under coasters to catch the dripping wax. A few electric lights were on as well, but they were few.

A jukebox played a country song in the far corner, three men and a woman standing around it talking. All had drinks in their hands. Cigarette and cigar smoke hung heavy in the air, and now that the companions were inside the tavern, the noise level increased another twenty decibels. Someone played a piano in the back, that and the jukebox fighting for dominance, but too many people were in the way for Hank to see the piano or its player.

A few other tables were full with men and women. The women sat on laps or leaned forward so their cleavage would show, making sure they were seen in the most flattering position.

The companions crossed the floor and sat at a table in a far corner, so they could keep an eye on the front door, their backs to the wall. The floor was sticky from old food and spilled liquor. Placing their guns on the table for easy access, a few men and women glanced at the three warriors, eyeing the weapons, then each one in kind went back to what they were doing.

A heavy set woman in her late fifties with a perpetual scowl, wearing a dirty apron, approached them. She leaned over and slapped a filthy rag on the table, then began to wipe around the companions' guns. The dirty rag spread more germs than ever could have been on the table previously.

"We don't get visitors much anymore, nice to see some fresh faces around here." She scratched her plump belly with a dirty fingernail. "What're you folks doing here?"

"We're here to trade with your town. Marshall sent us here," Laurie said.

"Really? Good, we can always use some more stuff. No more trucks coming in with deliveries like before, huh? I'm Fran. What can I get ya?" she asked in a voice that clearly said she'd been smoking for more than half her life.

"Food," Hank said flatly.

"The house special is stew and I just finished making a fresh batch," she said, wiping with the rag some more. She stopped and leaned forward, her prominent, though sagging breasts, jutting forward. "How 'bout three bowls?"

"My, that sounds good," Stewart said, not knowing about the warning from Marshall.

"What else do you have?" Hank asked.

Fran seemed taken aback. Strangers never said no to her stew and usually asked for seconds. "Well, I can offer you oatmeal with sugar and fresh milk or something from my canned goods, but that'll cost ya."

One more look at the filthy rag and the disheveled cook was all Hank needed to make up his mind. He reached into a pocket and pulled out a full clip for an M-16. The black metal was shiny with fresh oil. "What will this get me?" He said it like he knew exactly what it would buy him and Fran saw it in his eyes.

"Well, mister, that can get you anything you want. And if you give me the whole thing, I can probably set you up at Merle's Hotel for the next three nights, on me."

"Sounds like a fair deal," Hank said, sliding the clip across the table. "Bring us food from your canned goods and a pitcher of beer. You have beer, right?"

Fran nodded energetically. "Sure do, make it ourselves." She turned and yelled at the bartender, a mouse-like man with thinning hair and a bushy mustache to make up for what was missing on top. "Hey, Frank, a pitcher of beer over here for these strangers!"

The bartender nodded and turned away.

"Be right back with a list of what we got," Fran said and moved away.

While she was gone, the companions watched the people in the bar. For the most part, no one paid the three strangers any attention and that was how Hank liked it. Fran returned a few minutes later with a short list of available food. Hank picked baked beans and cocktail wieners for himself and a can of Progresso minestrone to bring back to Carl. Stewart chose a can of Chef Boyardee pasta and Laurie decided on LaChoy chicken chow mein and a side of crackers.

Fran took their orders and left, only to return a minute later with a basket of cans, some plates, silverware and a can opener. Placing the basket on the table, she smiled halfheartedly. "Enjoy your meal. I'll be right back with your beer."

"Only the finest dining for us, it seems," Stewart said as he reached in and took his can of pasta.

Laurie did the same, and with the can opener, took off the lid to her meal. "It does the job," she said as she took a fork, cleaned it on her shirt as best she could, and began to eat.

"Food is food," Hank said as he dug into his beans. They had a hint of maple flavor and he was ashamed to say they tasted wonderful. It was funny what a man could come to appreciate when other things had been taken away.

Fran arrived and plopped down the pitcher of beer and three mugs, the foamy head slopping over the rim to splash onto the table. She was gone before anyone could complain or ask for a napkin.

"The service is sorely wanting here, no?" Stewart said as he ate.

"Just eat it and be grateful," Hank said and poured each of them a glass of beer. It was close to lukewarm and had a strange aftertaste but he assumed it was from the fermenting process. Homemade beer was a far cry from what used to come in bottles and cans from Budweiser and Coors, to name a few.

The three ate in silence, one eye always on the patrons of the tavern.

They were just about finished and were relaxing with full bellies, half of the pitcher of beer gone, when a raucous began in the far corner of the tavern. A woman wearing heavy makeup, a short skirt, and high heels—obviously a hooker—was fighting with a man who had grabbed her and forced her to sit on his lap.

"Get off me, Dave! Let me go!" the hooker yelled as she struggled to free herself. All around her, the other men laughed at her predicament, though the other women watching all had disapproving glares.

"Ah, come on, Brenda, how 'bout a freebee for old times sake!"

"No, let me go!"

Dave slapped her, the crack of flesh meeting flesh was loud enough to break through the din. Brenda's head rocked to the side and she would have fallen off the man's lap if he hadn't been holding onto her with his other hand.

"What makes you think I was askin'?" Dave hissed as he yanked Brenda to her feet, standing up, as well. He was twice her size and held on to her like she was a child. She tried to bite him and he slapped her again, harder this time, the *crack* of flesh on flesh filling the air. A red mark was left on her cheek from the blow and she was dazed for a few seconds.

Across the room, Hank was growing angry at the scene before him. He didn't have patience for bullies, and a man that liked to pick on women was the worst of them all. He made fists of both his hands as he watched.

Laurie reached out and touched his arm. "Leave it alone, Hank. It's none of our business."

He seemed to calm a little and he looked into her eyes. "Yeah, I know it's just…"

"I know. I don't like it either, but we're new in town. We don't want to call attention to ourselves."

Hank nodded and went back to his meal, but as soon as he began to eat, Brenda cried out again. Hank turned to see she was on the floor now, Dave standing over her with a clenched fist. Once more, all the men watching were laughing and joking.

Dave wrapped a fist in Brenda's dark black hair and began dragging her across the floor to the stairs that led to the second floor. Hank knew there could only be one thing on the second floor that would make Dave take Brenda with him — rooms to fuck in.

Brenda kicked her legs up and down as tears rolled down her cheeks from the pain of being dragged by her hair. Small dots of blood appeared on her scalp. Dave was only using one hand and his other grabbed his crotch as he made lascivious sounds to make the other men laugh, which they did.

Dave had reached the stairs and was about to begin dragging Brenda up them when Hank stood up. "That's it! I can't just sit here why that jerk rapes that woman." He looked at Laurie. "What if that was you over there? Sorry, but I can't watch and do nothing."

She had never looked so proud of him as right then. "Lover, if you could leave it alone, then you wouldn't be the man I fell in love with. Go get that bastard and kick his ass."

"I agree with Laurie," Stewart said, angry also. "Someone needs to teach that asshole a lesson. Feel free to let me know if you need my help."

"Will do, Stewart, but keep an eye on Laurie for me and we'll call it even."

"Of course," Stewart said, wrapping his left hand around his sword-cane.

Hank left his G-12 rifle on the table and Laurie placed a hand on it to guard it. Then he was off and across the room in seconds.

Dave was on the fourth step and was having a hard time as Brenda held onto the railing to keep from being pulled up the steps. Dave had his right fist raised, and was about to bring it down onto Brenda's face, when Hank lunged at the man, blocking the blow and punching Dave square in the face, breaking his nose.

Blood shot out of the damaged nose and Dave fell back to land heavily on his butt. Letting go of Brenda's hair, she crawled away, some of the other women going to her aid.

"Who the fuck are you?" Dave spat, the words garbled from his broken nose.

"I'm the guy whose gonna teach you some manners about women," Hank hissed.

"Fuck you!" Dave screamed and jumped off the steps, tackling Hank, both men falling to the floor with Dave on top. Immediately, a crowd gathered around them, a few making bets on who would be the winner.

Hank felt a blow to his right side and he grunted, ignoring the pain. He jammed his elbow into Dave's ribs, the man letting out his breath in a wheezing gasp. He quickly followed this with a chop to the man's Adam's apple.

Dave's eyes rolled up into the back of his head and his face turned beet red. Hank bucked his hips and threw the man off him,

Dave falling to the side. Hank came to his knees, then staggered to his feet, Dave doing the same.

Before Hank could attack again, Dave jumped back and reached out for a crying Brenda, who was standing nearby with some other women. He pulled her to him and drew a six inch hunting knife from his back, then placed it at her throat. He pressed just hard enough that a thin trickle of blood seeped from beneath the blade.

"Don't you fucking move, stranger, or the slut gets a new mouth." Blood covered his mouth and chin, his nose bent to the left. If it wasn't set correctly it would be crooked for the rest of his life.

Brenda whimpered, the blade pressed to her neck digging in a fraction more, allowing more blood to drip into her ample cleavage.

"Put the knife down and you can walk away, free and clear," Hank said, his hands out before him. "You don't want to hurt her."

"What do you know about what I want?" Dave growled. "This is my fucking town. You don't come in here and tell me what to do." He was talking more to himself than to Hank. Trying to get closer and disarm the man, Hank took a step forward and Dave added pressure to the knife, Brenda gasping with pain.

"I said don't move!" Dave licked Brenda's cheek, tasting her tears. "This slut mean something to you? She kin or somethin'?"

"No," Hank said calmly, while all around him the patrons of the tavern stood quiet. You could have heard a pin drop if someone had been so inclined.

"Then why do you give a shit about her?" Dave asked.

Hank remained silent. How do you explain to a coldhearted bastard what it means to care about another human being? Even if it's one you don't know? It would be like explaining color to a blind man.

"Please let me go," Brenda sniffed.

"Shut the fuck up, slut," Dave hissed. "This is all your fault. If you'd given me what I wanted in the first place you wouldn't be in this fucking predicament."

"I still can, Dave," she begged. "I can give you want you want. We can go upstairs right now."

"No we can't, this asshole won't let us."

"Sure he will," Brenda said, almost nodding her head, but realizing it wasn't a good idea. "You'll let us go. Right, mister?"

"Sure," Hank said. "It's fine with me."

Hank lowered his hands a little, seeing that Dave was calming down, that the situation was about over. And it would have been if not for one of the patron's, who barked out laughter and called Dave a pussy for letting a slut tell him what to do.

The second the man yelled out his quip, Hank saw Dave's eyes gloss over in anger. He saw Dave's arm flex as he prepared to open Brenda's throat and kill the object of his humiliation.

But before Dave could drag the blade across Brenda's throat, Hank was already moving. Reaching down to his SIG-Sauer, his hand wrapped around the grip and he pulled it out so fast his draw was nothing but a blur. Knowing there was no time to raise it, he shot from the hip the second it was out of the holster and leveled. The 9mm round hit Dave in his open mouth, the bullet ricocheting upward to exit out the back of his skull. A piece of scalp on the back of his head flipped up and bone and clots of brain's shot out to hit the wall behind him.

The crowd was deathly silent as Dave's legs wobbled and the knife fell away from Brenda's neck to clatter on the floor. Dave fell back to hit the wall, then slumped to the floor, dead.

Stewart and Laurie joined Hank a second later, their eyes scanning the crowd for anyone who might want revenge for Dave's death. One man in the corner looked like he was going to try something, but when he made eye contact with Stewart and Laurie, both with guns drawn and aimed at him, the man quickly changed his mind.

"Now, the way I see it!" Stewart yelled so all could hear. "This was self-defense. That man tried to kill that woman but Hank was quicker and he saved her life." He eyed each man in succession as he scanned the room. "Anyone have a problem with that?"

Silence.

"Good, then this matter is closed."

Hank walked over to the bar and placed five 9mm rounds on the counter. "This should cover the mess and disposal of the body," he said flatly. The bartender merely stared at Hank, as if the man was some kind of God. Hank returned to Laurie and Stewart.

From the door of the tavern, the sound of stomping feet came; Marshall had arrived with more men in police uniforms. The officers leveled their pistols with the safeties off, not knowing who was an enemy and who was a friend. One cop held a shotgun.

Marshall's eyes scanned the room quickly and then settled on Hank, Stewart and Laurie, who stood in the middle of the room still holding their weapons. "Just what the fuck is going on in here? I got a report of a disturbance."

Two men went to Marshall's side and began talking to him, both patrons pointing at Hank as they talked. Marshall stared at Hank, too, as he listened, his grimace turning into a deep frown. When the men were done talking, they took a step back and Marshall pointed to the companions, the officers now aiming their guns on the three warriors.

Marshall walked up to Hank. "Those two said you shot and killed Dave, and by the looks of it...." He cast a glanced at Dave's body still lying on the floor, a pool of blood under it. "That's exactly what you did."

Hank nodded slowly as he holstered his pistol, but kept his hand on the butt of the SIG-Sauer. His G-12 was on his shoulder again, after Laurie had handed it to him upon getting up from the table. "He was gonna kill that woman there." Hank pointed at a still crying Brenda. "I couldn't let him do that."

Marshall walked over to Brenda while the other officers kept their guns leveled at the companions. "Is that true Brenda? Did Dave really try that?"

Brenda sniffed and nodded, then stood up straighter.

Hank could see she was a fighter.

"It's true," she said. "The bastard wanted me to fuck him for free and when I said no, he tried to drag me upstairs to rape me. No one would have stopped him either, shit they all laughed." She pointed to Hank. "But that man tried to stop him and Dave got pissed and put a knife to my throat. He would have killed me if this man hadn't shot him." The other women began talking, telling their side of what they'd seen, yelling at Marshall to leave Hank alone, that he'd done right and where the hell was Marshall when the shit had hit the fan? Marshall listened for almost a minute before raising his hands to silence the women.

"All right, enough. I said enough!" he roared when the women wouldn't be silent. "It seems to me there were enough witnesses to what happened that it was clearly self-defense. This man killed Dave to save Brenda. This isn't the old world, there's no need for a trial and all that shit. I rule in cases like this and I say it's settled. Dave bit off more than he could chew and he got what he deserved." He glanced at Dave's corpse. "The dumb bastard was always a little slow in the head, if you ask me." Marshall pointed to two cops. "You two, get Dave's body out of here. Call the coroner and tell him we got another one for the ground." The two men went to the body, picked it up, and carried it out of the bar, a trail of blood drops left behind them.

"As far as I'm concerned, this matter is closed, but you better watch yourself," Marshall told Hank, his warning clear. "I think you and your friends better leave in the morning. But to let you know there's no hard feelings, how 'bout I have a couple of pitchers of beer sent over to where you're sleeping tonight."

"We're gonna sleep in the truck we came in on," Hank said. After what had occurred, he didn't want to have to deal with any of Dave's friends who might be looking for revenge. Better to sleep in the APC with its metal hull protecting him and the others.

"Really? But the hotel is a hell of a lot more comfortable, running water and everything. Tell you what, I'll have some of my men take you there."

Hank could tell when he was being coerced to do something and his hand slowly gripped the butt of his SIG-Sauer, Laurie and Stewart doing the same with their weapons, albeit casually, as if the gesture was simply a place to rest their hands. "I said we're sleeping in our truck. With the man I left back there," Hank said, referring to Carl.

Marshall held up his hands in surrender, seeing to push the matter more would only get Hank angry. "Okay, that's fine with me. I'll have the beer sent over to your truck later tonight."

"Much appreciated," Hank said.

"I know I said I'd have a drink with you here, too, but given the circumstances, I think it would be better if you left."

Marshall nodded, gesturing to his men to leave, and then left first, though two officers were left behind to make sure it stayed quiet in the tavern. As soon as Marshall and his men left, the music began again and people started talking. The two cops left behind on guard detail picked a table in the corner with their backs to the wall and simply watched quietly.

The bartender left the bar with a rag and a mop and a bucket of dirty water and began cleaning the blood off the wall and floor. He didn't care about what was on the floor other than sopping up the worst of it, as the hardwood floor was filthy beyond comparison anyway.

"What was that about?" Laurie asked. "He sure wanted us to stay at the hotel."

"Don't know, but I don't like it," Hank said as he looked at Laurie and Stewart. "I think it's time to go. Stewart, grab that can of soup on the table to bring back to Carl."

Stewart did as asked, went to the table, and was back a moment later with the food. The companions began to leave the tavern with all eyes on them, when Brenda came up to Hank and wrapped her arms around him. "I wanted to thank you," she said and kissed him smack dab on the lips.

Hank's eyes went wide as the woman kissed him and out of the corner of his eye he saw Laurie cross her arms over her chest in annoyance.

Hank tried to push Brenda off him but she wouldn't budge.

"It's fine, really. I did what any man in the bar should have done."

She nuzzled his face. "But they didn't. They would have let him rape me and laughed about it later, the pigs. You're a good man, and so are your friends. That's why you need to know something. Be careful of the beer, it's drugged." She kissed him again and Hank realized she was doing it so that no one would know she was talking to him.

He returned the kiss this time, and mumbled softly, "What are you talking about?"

"The beer," she said, whispering through the kiss. "It's drugged. This town isn't what it seems. Be careful. Don't trust anyone." She stepped away before Hank could ask anything else. She smiled to the crowd, which was now catcalling and laughing, then she disappeared into a group of women that she'd been with earlier.

Hank began to walk out of the tavern again when Laurie said, "What the hell was that all about? You seemed like you were getting into it." The jealousy in her voice was apparent to a deaf man.

Hank waited until the three of them were outside before he replied. Stewart also had a questioning look on his face. Laurie seemed like she wanted to shoot Hank at any moment.

"It's not what you think," Hank told Laurie. "She said something to me while she was kissing me. Come on, let's get back to Carl and I'll fill you all in at the same time." He began walking fast, Stewart and Laurie following.

"You better, lover," Laurie said angrily. "Or I can tell you without question that you're going to be sleeping alone for the next month."

Carl had just woken up and was going through more of the APC when the others arrived and knocked on the side of the hull, alerting him they were back. After letting them inside and taking the can of soup from Stewart, Carl sat in the driver's chair and ate quietly while Hank told the group what Brenda had whispered to him. When he was done, he looked at the faces of the others, waiting for their opinions.

Stewart was first. "You know, I do feel a little lightheaded, but I just assumed it was because it had been a hard ride to get here. Then we got to eat a meal, and with a full stomach, I was simply tired."

Laurie nodded, agreeing. "I feel the same way. I feel like I could sleep for a week."

Hank reached out and took her hand, squeezing it. "I feel like that, too, but I don't think I'm going to pass out. Do any of you?"

Stewart and Laurie shook their heads.

"No," Laurie said, "just really tired."

Hank rubbed his unshaved jaw. "Seems to me that whatever they put in the beer must be slow-working. It's probably supposed to put us in a deep sleep when we finally bed down for the night. Then, with us all out of it, anyone could just come right up to us, slit our throats, and they have a brand new APC and weapons, all without spending a dime."

"But why would they do that?" Laurie asked. "It makes no sense. We're willing to trade with them."

Stewart chuckled. "Why trade for a few seeds or a few bullets when you can have the entire bag and clip?" He turned to face Hank. "It seems we've come across some real dirtbags here, Hank. This isn't something they just happened to decide to do to us only. No doubt they've been doing it for a long time. Who knows how many good people have come through here, only to be drugged, killed, and their belongings taken as booty."

"What do you suggest?" Hank asked. "Other than simply driving out of here right now. There's no way they could stop us."

"We hope," Carl said. "But the road leading out of here was mined, you said. And who knows, if they've done this before, they probably have contingences for people who try to run."

"Good point," Hank agreed.

Stewart smiled. "Sure, but what stops them from doing harm to the people who come along behind us? Even we might find ourselves back here one day, but next time we won't have an armored vehicle to protect us. Who knows if they wouldn't have simply taken us down if not for Carl being inside here safe, where he could exact vengeance for us if we were killed. What I suggest is that we give these evil bastards some payback for all the misery they've been spreading across this land, as if there isn't enough already. Teach them a lesson they'll never forget."

"I'm in, spill it," Hank said

"Me too," Laurie agreed. "These assholes need to pay for what they've done and what they were going to do to us."

All eyes went to Carl, who merely smiled as he repositioned his Yankees cap. "Hey, I'm all in. Let's teach these fuckers a lesson they'll never forget."

Gathering together, Stewart ran his idea past the others.

An hour later, the beer arrived, sent by Marshall. Hank had accepted it with a smile and had even taken a sip. He and Marshall had chatted for a few more minutes about how things were outside the walls of Arcadia and then the man had left, taking the three cops he had with him.

Hank held the three pitchers of beer and had waited a full minute after Marshall and his men had left, then he'd gone to the rear of the APC and poured out the pitchers. After making sure no one saw him do this, he carried the empty pitchers back into the APC. An hour later an old woman knocked on the door. She said she had come to retrieve the empty pitchers, but Hank knew she had been sent to confirm that the companions had indeed consumed the laced beer.

The old woman did her best to make it seem like this was no big thing, but Hank and the others knew better. Hank had done his best to act like he was exhausted, that he could barely keep his eyes open, even to the point of slurring his words. The old woman never commented if Hank was all right, which further solidified the companions' belief that the beer had been laced with some kind of drug.

"You should sleep with the rear door open," the old woman had said. "It's a nice night out. And you're safe within Arcadia's walls."

"That sounds like a good idea," Hank had slurred. "My friends are already asleep, and when you leave I think I'm gonna bunk down for the night, too."

The woman had nodded and then left, the pitchers in her hand, clinking together as she walked. Hank had watched her, his face losing the drugged visage as soon as she'd turned around.

He had to agree that leaving the rear door unlocked was a good idea. If it wasn't, and the men that came couldn't get in, who was to say they wouldn't try placing explosives under the APC or disabling the tracks and then try to burn the companions out?

Once the old woman was gone, everyone talked a little more, then made sure their knives were in hand and their weapons were by their sides. As night fell, the town became quieter, with the exception of the rowdiness coming from the tavern at the end of the street. Inside the APC, all was dark as the companions lay silently, waiting for what would come next.

Hours later, with the sun long set over the town of Arcadia, the streets gradually emptied of revelers and Marshall's police force. There was a full moon, and as it peered through the clouds, it cast the town in a pallid glow. On top of this, candles were lit and gas lamps ignited. A gas generator hummed somewhere far off, the steady throb like a cat's purring.

On the wind was the odor of cooking meat. Pig or goat would be the first guess, though even dog might not be too far off.

"Think we're being watched?" Stewart asked as he lay prone inside the APC beside the others.

"Probably," Hank said and shifted position on the steel floor, only a thin blanket between him and the deck plates. He held his panga in one hand and his SIG-Sauer in the other. "Once they know we're good and out of it, that's when they'll make their move."

The rear door to the APC was ajar a few inches, but still closed. Hank had considered leaving it wide open, but he didn't want the attacking men of Arcadia to think he and his friends were too trusting. Better to leave the door slightly ajar, as if he'd wanted the protection of it being closed but still wanted to let some air in.

Down the street, a fire burned in a rusty barrel, having been started hours ago by a few old men who had gathered and talked for a while. Now the flames were dwindling, the shadows of night encroaching once more.

Laurie shifted in her bedroll, her hand wrapped tightly around her hunting knife. "I wish they'd get on with it already."

"Yeah," Carl agreed. "It's the waiting that gets to you." He was sitting in the driver's seat, and his head was tilted back as if he was sleeping. From anyone peering in through the front windshield, it would look as if he he'd fallen asleep in the seat. On his lap, he held a knife of his own, the Mini-Uzi slung over his shoulder so that it sat on his lap. He was tense and he willed himself to calm down. There was no point in wasting energy on worrying what would come next. When it came, it came, and then all bets were off. Only instinct and perseverance would win out.

Minutes passed in silence, and then, as he peered out the windshield through half-closed eyelids, he spotted shadows moving towards the APC. He remained motionless, watching the shadows as they hopped from obstacle to obstacle. Then he saw a head, followed by another.

"They're here," Carl whispered as he tried to count the shadows. "I got at least six heading our way, maybe more."

The crunch of footsteps on gravel came through the partially-opened rear door. Hank heard them first. "I got a couple back here, too. Get sharp, people, it's go time," he hissed softly.

At the front of the APC, the shadows transformed into men, their faces covered with soot to help them blend into the night. They carried knives and hammers, and more than one carried a gun, .45s and .38s. The metal was coated with black shoe polish to prevent the moonlight from reflecting off the polished steel and giving the men's position away.

Inside the APC, Hank began to snore softly, hoping the act would be enough to fool the attackers. As the six men crept along the APC, and three more joined them at the rear of the vehicle, Hank had to admit that Marshall knew what he was doing.

Make sure the prey was knocked out with drugged beer, and when they were good and unconscious, simply do a nightcreep and slash the prey's throats, taking everyone out at the same time, and thereby keeping the booty intact with not so much as one bullet expended.

The odor of oil came to Hank's nostrils and then the rear door slowly began to open. Smart bastards, Hank thought. They oiled the hinges on the door before opening it, making sure there would be no noise to give them away. Doing something as small as that meant that this town had done this before, that the men about to enter the APC had made killing something that was done by the numbers.

In the back of his mind, Hank wondered if maybe this had been a bad idea, that leaving the rear door open and letting these coldhearts into the APC was a grave mistake. But hindsight was easy when there was no way of knowing other outcomes. The town could have placed a bomb under the APC and simply blew it up, then sifted through the wreckage when the flames had died down.

Like wraiths, four men entered the APC while one man waited at the rear opening, and the other three stood guard to make sure there were no problems outside. Each one wanted to be in on the killing but knew only four could enter the APC, one for each of the companions. The men had drawn straws before heading out.

Hank's right fist was wrapped tightly around the hilt of his panga as he waited for the men to get fully inside the APC. His heartbeat was so loud he couldn't understand why the killers didn't hear it, but in truth the pounding was only inside his head.

Knowing he had to time it perfectly, Hank waited for the killers to raise their weapons, and were about to bring them down and stab each of the companions and finish them off simultaneously. When that moment came, Hank sat up and yelled, "Now!"

Carl, Stewart and Laurie went into action at Hank's command, and as the killers stopped in shock to see their drugged prey coming to their feet, eyes wide with anger, jaws tight with determination, the four men realized the tables had turned against them.

It happened so fast, and later, no one would be able to remember exactly what happened when and in what order.

One second the APC was silent, Hank's false snoring the only sound, and then the inside of the vehicle became a charnel house of blood, screams and gore as the companions lunged upward, their blades slashing at the men.

Hank's sixteen inch panga slid ten inches into the stomach of the man standing over him, then he ripped the blade to the side. When he withdrew it, the man's intestines spilled out to splash on the metal floor. The man began to scream, loud and high-pitched. Hank grabbed him by the shirt and pulled him close, then slid the bloody panga across his throat, severing the man's jugular, warm blood splashing outward to bathe Hank in crimson.

Beside Hank, Laurie attacked her killer, her small blade finding the man's thigh and slicing into his femoral artery. Hot blood shot out to splash on her arm as the man screamed and shrank to his knees. It had only been seconds but already his pants were soaked in blood and with each beat of his heart more of his life's fluid left him. He would be dead in a minute.

Stewart was lying with his sword-cane by his side, the blade exposed and ready. When Hank gave the signal, Stewart simply lifted the thin sword straight up, then stabbed his attacker in the chest, the tip of the blade slicing into the killer's heart and stopping the powerful muscle instantly. The man dropped onto Stewart who then had to fight to push the dead weight off him.

Carl almost waited too long, his attacker already coming with a hammer to crack Carl's skull in two. As Carl opened his eyes and turned to meet the killer, he turned his head to the side. The hammer only gave him a glancing blow, struck his shoulder, then the back of the seat. Carl lost his knife as his hand spasmed from the blow to his shoulder. Acting fast, he reached down and pulled his AUG pistol, shoved the muzzle into the man's chest, and squeezed the trigger three times, the sound muffled as it dug into cloth and the flesh beneath. The first 5.6 mm round went in and ricocheted off a rib, but the second went in at a slightly different angle and tore through the man's body, erupting out his back in a spray of blood. The third bullet followed the second, tearing apart more flesh. The man gasped, not saying a word, before he slumped over onto his side and lay still, a pool of blood expanding beneath him.

Hank was on his feet, his SIG-Sauer coming up to aim directly at the man standing in the rear door opening. The man's face was livid, for it was almost pitch dark inside the vehicle and he assumed the screams had been that of the companion's dying. But as Hank took a step forward and into the wan moonlight filtering in through the opening, the man let out a squeak like a mouse at the sight of the large man before him, covered in blood and gore and leveling a pistol right at him.

The man parted his lips to sound a warning, but as he did so, Hank fired, sending the round into the open mouth. The back of the man's skull blew out just above the neck, sending bone fragments into the air to pepper the other three men, who had been standing behind him, waiting for the order to start cleaning up the mess inside the APC.

Inside the APC, Carl turned on the powerful diesel engine and put on the headlights, bathing the area in front of the vehicle in white light. Like a deer caught in the headlights of an approaching semi, ten men were exposed with weapons in hand, as they crouched nearby, waiting for the order to move in if things got hairy. They were well armed, carrying everything from AR-15s to Bolt-action M-40s with synthetic stocks, as well as an assortment of shotguns and pistols.

Hank shot the three men standing at the rear of the APC, killing two and wounding the third, then he slammed the door closed and bolted it.

"Okay, people, let's show this town what they get for fucking with us." He climbed out of the roof hatch so he was exposed from the chest up, and after priming the Browning .50-cal machine gun, he swiveled it to face the front of the APC and began firing. The .50-cal burped and a man went down hard, knocked down by the ounce –and-a-half slugs that stitched him from groin to neck. The men behind him were struck by the rounds as they went through the first man and into them as they stood in shock.

Finally, they snapped out of it and the men dove for cover, while others returned fire. Hank never let up, glowing tracers lighting up the night as he swung the .50-cal left and right. Bullets punched through the gas tank of a parked car, igniting the tank and banishing the night in a golden firestorm.

There was a man lying in front of the blazing car in a pool of blood, his insides trailing back behind him, where he'd dragged himself after being eviscerated by flying debris. He was screaming at the top of his lungs, his face scorched beyond recognition, his hair gone. He might have continued screaming if a stray bullet didn't hit him in the temple, ending his pain and silencing him forever. Other men had been doused with flames from the burning wreckage and they ran shrieking off into the night, resembling human torches.

Carl put the APC into drive and it began rolling, Carl not wanting to be attacked, and knowing a moving target was harder to hit. Inside the APC, Laurie and Stewart were at the blaster ports, firing out into the night and taking down more men.

From somewhere, a siren began to wail and more people showed up, men and women, all armed to the teeth. This was the true town, a collection of coldhearts that waited to ambush anyone foolish enough to seek to befriend them. Hank sprayed the first arrivals with steel-jacketed death and the rest fell back to seek cover.

AR-15 rounds bounced off the hull, along with heavier caliber armament. Someone threw a grenade, the orb rolling to explode a few feet from the APC. Hank ducked back inside as it went off, dirt and gravel spraying the vehicle but doing little damage if any.

Laurie jumped and almost tripped over one of the corpses on the floor when something flew by her head; she didn't understand what had happened. Had a bullet penetrated the armor of the APC? It didn't seem possible. She looked down to see a bolt head on the floor at her feet. Picking it up, she looked at it curiously.

"It's called spalling," Stewart said as he took a break to reload.

"What?" Laurie asked.

"What happened to you just now. Momentum from bullets hitting us can knock lose bolt heads and pieces of hull metal around the inside of this thing."

Laurie only nodded, then went back to shooting at shadowy targets.

The steady thrumming of the Browning .50-cal filled the night as bullet after bullet tore into men, women and buildings. Carl drove out of the parking lot and deeper into town, while the APC took gunfire from all sides. A bearded man came charging out of the tavern, along with five others and Marshall, who made sure to stay in the rear and thus be safer.

Hank swiveled the Fifty and sprayed the bearded man with steel death, brass casings flying off to roll over the roof. Five rounds got the man in the chest, spun him around, and sent him to the ground in a spray of red mist. Right behind him, a second man felt the impact of the Fifty's slugs directly in the face, which disappeared in a glorious spray of bone and brain matter, the shards peppering the other men in line like shrapnel.

From the side, a red-headed man with a few days worth of growth on his face ran up holding a grenade. Hank didn't see the man in time, and if not for Laurie, who shot the man in the leg and caused him to trip, things might have gone much differently than what happened next.

When he fell, the grenade landed under him. The man let go of the handle and three seconds later he and the grenade exploded, sending body parts and gore to the four corners of the town.

"Get them, you idiots!" Marshall screamed from the rear. "They're just one car! Surround them and advance!" Hank sent a spray of rounds over Marshall's head and the man ducked down, bleating like a terrified goat. Behind him, the front of the tavern was riddled with bullets, the glass window shattering, terrified screams coming from within.

From the center of town, a blonde-haired woman popped up from behind a parked car, holding a lit Molotov made from an old wine bottle. She never got the chance to throw it. Just as she popped up, Stewart spotted her, the burning wick like a spotlight in the night. He stuck his HK submachine gun muzzle through the blaster port and fired, moving the muzzle up and down and from side to side. There was no way to aim, only send the bullets in the general direction.

Most of the bullets missed the woman, but one didn't. It hit the wine bottle in her hand, shattering it and igniting the liquid within. As she was coated with fire, the bullet continued through the bottle and into her chest, striking her heart. She barely felt the pain of the flames as she fell onto her back, stone cold dead. Her flesh began to bubble, and the odor of cooking flesh permeated the air.

As the APC rolled deeper into town, from above, a rain of hissing objects dropped towards the vehicle. Looking up, Hank couldn't make out what the objects were in the dark. Then one landed on the roof of the APC beside him and he saw it was a pipe bomb, the wick still hissing. Reaching out, he grabbed and threw it in one smooth gesture. Though it looked like a casual gesture, Hank's heart was pumping so fast he thought it would explode out of his chest. The pipe bomb went flying off into the night to land twenty feet from the APC, where it exploded, doing no harm and leaving a long gash in the pavement.

Hank tried to shift the .50-cal so it would fire up at the rooftops, but the angle was bad and he only managed to chew up the moldings a foot below the roof edge. Still, it had the desired effect and the townspeople backed off.

"Jesus, the entire fucking town is trying to kill us!" he screamed and stopped firing for a few seconds, wanting to let the

Fifty cool for a few moments. The .50-cal was the only reason the companions hadn't been surrounded and trapped.

A jeep came screaming around the corner at the far intersection, three men inside it. Two in the front and a man in a police uniform in the rear, holding an M-19 grenade launcher. Hank began firing but the jeep driver was good and he swerved back and forth, none of the rounds doing serious damage to the jeep. One round did find a home in the passenger's head, the skull exploding outward. The other men ignored the death of their comrade and barreled forward.

"Carl, little help!" Hank yelled as he tried to stop the jeep. Despite the rocking jeep, the man with the grenade launcher was about to fire.

Carl saw this too and he did the only thing he could. He gunned the engine, the APC surging forward. As the grenade popped from the launcher to soar into the air, the APC shot forward, the steel tracks churning up the asphalt. The grenade went well over Hank's head and exploded in the middle of the street behind the APC. Carl wasn't stopping however, and he used the APC for what it was built for. As the jeep tried to swerve out of the way, Carl drove head-on into it, catching the jeep in the side and sending it skidding but not rolling over. The APC didn't stop and the steel tracks began biting into the jeep as the armored carrier drove onto it and the shrieking men trapped inside.

The sound of crunching metal filled the interior of the APC as the armored carrier drove over the jeep and came down on the other side, leaving behind it a trail of dark blood, twisted metal and viscera.

"That's one way to stop them," Stewart said as the screams from beneath the metal floor ceased, the two men crushed to a bloody pulp.

"Stewart, get up here and work the .30-cal, I need backup!" Hank yelled through the hatch.

The older man did as instructed, coming up through the second hatch, right where the Thirty had been mounted. Without waiting to be told anything else, he picked a target and began firing.

Inside the APC, Laurie ran out of bullets so she dropped her gun and grabbed one of the M-16s found in the vehicle. Popping in a clip, she began firing at anything that moved, more often than not missing as the APC jumped and bounced through town.

Most of the townspeople were either running for their lives or dead, and Hank was thinking that the battle was about over, when a low rumbling came from somewhere nearby, the surrounding buildings blocking the true source of the sound.

"What the fuck is that?" Carl asked from the driver's seat. Even through the sound of the metal tracks tearing up the ground, he could feel the new rumbling. Whatever was coming was big, much bigger than the APC.

No one replied, all too busy taking out targets.

A man wearing a policeman's uniform stood on a second floor balcony overlooking the street, a LAW rocket propped on his left shoulder as he prepared to fire down at the APC. A second before he was able to fire it, Hank raised the .50-cal and began shooting. Bullets tore up the side of the building, spraying pieces of brickwork and insulation into the air. Stitching the side of the building, the rounds made their way up to the balcony, then the man's legs and finally his chest.

Thrown back from the assault, the man fired the LAW, only he was now aiming it at a right angle. The rocket streaked off into the night to hit a building the next street over.

"That was a close one," Stewart said, seeing what Hank had managed to prevent. The LAW could have done serious damage to the APC, perhaps destroying one of the tracks.

"Tell me about it," Hank said over the thumping of the large gun as he fired into a crowd of armed people hiding behind a dumpster. The bullets chewed up the green dumpster as if it was paper, scattering the townspeople behind it.

The rumbling was getting louder and Hank found himself glancing around even more, trying to discern the origin to the sound. A bullet zipped past his head so close he heard the air shift and he swore he lost a few errant hairs from his scalp. Swinging the Fifty around where he thought the shot had come from, he sprayed the darkness with steel death.

The night wasn't as complete as before, thanks to all the fires burning here and there. Shadows flitted among the streets as people ran for their lives. Hank spotted shadows to his left and he swung the Fifty around, his finger already squeezing the trigger. Then he stopped, seeing it was a group of women and children. None held weapons, and a few women were holding babies. He let them go, not wanting to kill any innocents. He felt bad for them, caught in the middle of what must seem like yet another war, but there was nothing he could do for them. The first rule was to take care of your own family, then you could worry about others. Laurie, Carl and Stewart were his family now and he would kill everyone in the entire town if that's what it took to keep them safe.

Bullets whined through the air. Stewart swung the Thirty around and fired into an alley. He was rewarded with cries of pain and a man stumbled out into the street. His chest was covered in bloody wounds, and as the APC rolled past him, the man fell to his knees and then his face.

"Jesus, how many of them are there?" Carl yelled from inside the armored carrier. It felt like the companions had killed hundreds of people, and still the town of Arcadia kept coming at them, despite suffering staggering losses.

A pickup truck was in the middle of the street, someone having put it there to hopefully slow the APC down, but Carl simply drove over it, crushing the frame under the steel tracks of the APC. Carl whooped with laughter, enjoying the carnage and destruction. He hadn't asked for this war but by God, he would give the people of Arcadia one they would never forget.

He swung the APC around a corner at the next intersection but then he slammed the APC to a halt, his eyes wide as he stared at what was before him. Above, the Fifty and the Thirty stopped chattering as well, both Stewart and Hank seeing what Carl saw. Laurie stopped firing, too, joining Carl at the front to peer out through the blood-covered windshield.

Behind the Fifty, Hank spit a wad of phlegm to the side and simply said, "Ah shit, that's not good."

The APC sat idling in the center of the street, as all around it, buildings continued to burn. For a moment there was a lull in the combat, as if the remaining townspeople believed the fight was over.

Though not knowing this, and if he had, Hank might have agreed, at last in that initial few seconds that he stared at the lumbering behemoth before him.

At the end of the street, smoke belching from its vertical exhaust, sat a Caterpillar D9 bulldozer, the machine taken from some construction or garbage dump site. On the front of the large machine, a straight blade was attached. This blade was flat, with no curves or side wings. If used correctly, the blade would have been used for the fine grading of dirt and sand, or for flat-out moving of earth in large quantities. The metal was pitted and missing paint, and before today had seen some use. On the back of the faded yellow bulldozer was what was called a ripper, a claw-like appendage used for tearing up the ground. The Cat sat on long tracks, larger than the ones on the APC but a similar design.

As the two vehicle sat apart from one another, the bulldozer topping at forty-nine tons and the APC around twenty-one thousand pounds, it was like a scene out of the Bible between David and Goliath.

Behind the controls to the Big Cat, Marshall smiled widely, a maniacal gleam in his eyes.

"Shit, what the hell is that?" Carl asked from the driver's seat. He knew damn well what it was, and what he meant was: what was he supposed to do now?

"I think it's time to go," Laurie said by his side. "We can't fight that, it's too big." She called up to Hank, "It's too big, Hank, we need to leave!"

"And we will, but not before we take that bastard down," Hank called back. "Carl!"

"Yeah, Hank?" Carl called back.

"We're more maneuverable than that monster. We need to keep moving, use its size against it."

"Sounds like a plan." Carl squinted as he peered out the windshield. "Is that Marshall driving that thing?"

Before he received an answer, he saw another man pop up from behind the driver's cab on the Cat. The man was holding another LAW.

"Oh shit. Hank, Stewart, get down here now!" Carl yelled and gunned the throttle, turning right and driving straight into a storefront, just as the man fired the LAW. Hank and Stewart did as they were told, dropping into the APC and slamming the hatches closed.

The missile streaked through the air, right on the trail of the APC, but the armored carrier was already inside the store, and as debris fell around it, the LAW only struck the framework on the outside of the store, exploding in a massive fireball that rolled through the building. People screamed as they were roasted alive, a few crushed under the steel tracks of the APC.

When the initial blast was over, Carl backed up and onto the street.

"I'm going back up, the rest of you stay in here," Hank said. "Carl, get us moving towards that 'dozer, but don't get too close."

"Will do."

Climbing back up, Hank had to be careful what he touched, as the outside of the APC was still hot from the searing flames, a few places still burning as hot debris covered the roof of the armored carrier. Wrapping his hands around the Fifty, he ignored the heat and prepared to fire, but first made sure it was still in working order. Other than covered in dust, it seemed to be fine—which was fortunate for him.

Carl gunned the accelerator, the tracks digging into the ground and propelling the APC forward quickly. As the vehicle got closer to the Cat, Hank began firing, peppering the bulldozer with round after round. Marshall laughed and raised the front blade and used it as a shield as he began to roll forward as well.

Hank sent everything he had at the bulldozer but he couldn't get past the massive steel shield. Finally, the Browning .50-cal cycled dry and that was it for Hank's best offensive weapon. Cursing, he dropped back into the APC, slamming the hatch closed as dust and dirt rained down inside from what had been on the edge of the opening.

As the bulldozer came barreling down the street, Carl looked to Hank for where to go.

Hank leaned over Carl's shoulder, pointing at another building with a glass facade. "There, go in there," he ordered. "He won't follow."

Carl swerved and drove into the building, the bulldozer right behind the APC.

But just like Hank figured, the Cat didn't follow. Instead, it turned and drove to the next street over.

"Why didn't he follow?" Laurie asked as she peered out a blaster port.

"He's too heavy; he'd fall right through the floor if there was a basement," Hank explained.

Carl drove through the building, smashing into support posts and furniture, pushing it aside as if it was made of paper. Seconds later, he erupted out another storefront and onto the next street, glass and debris flying off the hull to land in the road.

Swinging around, Carl rolled up the street only to come face to face with the bulldozer again. "Shit," he spit.

"It's my turn now," Stewart said and went topside to use the .30-cal. He had to step over one of the corpses on the floor, though he still stepped in congealing blood.

"Okay," Carl said. "I'll try to keep some distance between us and Marshall."

Stewart opened the hatch and popped up, pushing aside debris still on the roof. The .30-cal was okay and he began firing immediately, sending bullet after bullet at the Caterpillar. One round ricocheted around the blade and hit the man that had been hiding behind the operator's cab. He fell to the ground with a large hole in his chest, directly in front of the left side track. If Marshall knew where the man had fallen, it was unknown, but as Carl began to drive down the street backwards, and Stewart began chattering the Thirty, Marshall rolled forward.

The track went over the wounded man and he screamed in utter agony as he was slowly pulverized from the legs to his chest and then his head. By the time the tracks ran over his chest, though, the man was long dead. His head popped off his shoulders from the pressure of being crushed, just like a tube of toothpaste when it's rolled to get the last of it.

"Dead end," Carl said as the APC slammed to a stop at the end of the street. The dead bodies on the floor slid together into a pile. There had been no time to dump them.

"Bullshit, just go through it," Hank said as he peered into the side mirror that miraculously was still welded to the hull. The road was indeed a dead end, a large cement wall sealing off the thoroughfare of the small side street. There was a small opening for pedestrians only.

"No can do," Carl rebutted. "That wall looks pretty damn thick and we don't know what's waiting for us on the other side. It's too risky. This isn't a tank, you now, though it's as close to one as we may ever get."

Hank only gave it a moment's thought, as there was no time for more. "Fine, then go forward and act like you're going right and at the last second go left. We're faster than that thing; you should be able to get by it easily."

"Okay, here goes. Hold on, everyone." Carl gunned the throttle and the APC began to roll forward, at the same time, the bulldozer doing the same, the Cat's large tracks tearing up the asphalt.

Carl managed to get the APC up to thirty mph before he began to let the vehicle slide to the right. He'd heard one time that people that were right-handed would have a natural inclination to lean to the right, whether it was to take a turn or pick a direction. He hoped Marshall thought that too as the two metal machines bore down on each other.

At the last second, just before they would have collided, Carl swung the APC to the left. He almost made it, but as he sped past the Cat's straight blade, the corner managed to catch the right track on the APC. There was a loud tearing of metal as the blade caught the metal track, and for a brief second, the APC slowed, then it was free again and roaring past the bulldozer.

In the cab of the Cat, Marshall acted fast and swung the ripper around as the armored carrier zoomed by him. The ripper struck the APC in the center of its right side, sending it skidding to the left and into a building. Bricks rained down onto the roof of the armored carrier and only Carl wasn't thrown from his seat.

Stewart was knocked from his perch to fall back inside the vehicle. Dazed, the companions lay on the steel floor, shaking their heads as they tried to get up. Carl was slightly dazed to, after striking his head on the dashboard. As he shook his head to clear it, the rumbling of the Cat's tracks grew louder.

As his vision cleared, he looked to the left out the small side window to see the bulldozer coming right for him. The engine had stalled upon the crash and now Carl fought to get the diesel going again. The engine cranked over but wouldn't catch and he swallowed the knot that had formed in his throat as he thought about what that bulldozer would do to the APC when both vehicles collided.

The Caterpillar was twice the size of the APC, and with so much more weight, it could drive over the armored personnel carrier and crush it as easily as an eighteen wheeler over a soda can.

Cursing the engine under his breath, Carl continued working at the ignition and finally it came to life with a throaty roar. Accelerating immediately, he broke free of the building and drove off into the street, the straight blade of the bulldozer missing the rear end of the APC by inches.

Even over the din of the APC's diesel and the 474 hp motor of the Cat, Carl heard Marshall's frustrated yell upon missing his target.

Carl glanced over his shoulder to see Hank standing there. The grizzled warrior was holding his forehead, from where he'd whacked it on the floor.

"This cat and mouse shit needs to stop, Carl," Hank growled. "Listen, I have an idea, but it's tricky."

Carl was fighting the steering, the APC wanting to pull to the left. The right track was damaged and the vehicle was now a bitch to control. The odor of burnt oil filtered into the APC and the engine was making a loud banging sound as well. There was no way of knowing how long it would last until it finally blew.

"Tell me. It's not like we have a lot of choices here," Carl said.

"You need to make Marshall follow us, just close enough that he thinks he'll catch us. Then we need to find a building with a basement."

"A basement? Why?"

"Doesn't matter now, just do what I said." Hank turned and went to the hatch leading to the .30-cal. "I'll make sure to keep him focused on us." Before Carl could ask for more information, Hank was up and into the hatch opening, the Thirty before him.

Swinging the machine gun around, he fired off a few shots at the bulldozer but Marshall brought the steel blade up to protect him. But he had to lower it or he couldn't see where he was going.

He only lowered it enough to see over it, however, so only an inch or so was all he needed to raise it to protect him. Hank stopped firing, and after a few seconds, the blade went down slightly.

Hank raised both hands to Marshall and flipped the man off, then took his left hand and slammed it into his right arm at the elbow.

The universal sign language was clear to Marshall.

Fuck you.

Cursing, Marshall gunned the engine and the Cat lunged forward, the tracks digging into the ground like the hooves of a manic bull. Carl fought to keep the APC straight as he drove down the street and turned onto another. Townspeople fired at the APC but for the most part the battle with the people of Arcadia was over. Evidently, the worst of the townsfolk had either been killed or driven away, and only a few remained behind to take up the fight.

The bulldozer kept pace with the APC, sometimes even rear-ending it and causing the armored carrier to jump and swerve, but Carl always managed to gain control. They were four streets over from where they'd begun the chase when Hank spotted what he believed was the perfect building. He fired off a few more rounds at the bulldozer to make sure Marshall was still going to chase them and then he dropped back into the APC, slamming and dogging the hatch behind him.

"There, Carl, that's the one, go in there," Hank said as he pointed at a steak joint three buildings down.

"How do you know that place has a cellar?" Stewart asked. He'd heard Hank tell Carl the plan before.

"I don't, but most restaurants do. They need a place for all the shit needed to run a restaurant, and they use the basement for storage, too. There's gotta be one in there." He patted Carl on the shoulder. "Do it, go right in, full speed, and don't stop or we might fall through the floor. Just keep going right out the back."

Carl looked hesitant but did as he was instructed. "Okay, here goes nothin'."

When the restaurant was only a few feet away, Carl swung the APC around and went straight in, the bulldozer right behind the APC.

Crashing through the glass front, the APC charged in, tearing up walls, crushing tables and chairs and sending the chandeliers flying in all directions. A large bull's head was mounted to a wall and it dropped to the floor to be crushed under the metal tracks.

Furious that the companions were getting away, Marshall threw caution to the wind and followed them into the restaurant, the straight blade pushing the debris aside as if it was made of marshmallow fluff. He was fuming, his eyes wide in rage. These people had destroyed his town. Why couldn't they simply have died like the rest that had come to Arcadia? Why were these people so damn special? Well, he would make sure they died in the end, only their deaths would be harder than any other travelers to come to his town.

Driving into the restaurant, the tracks tore into drywall and insulation as the Cat followed the APC through the dining room and into the kitchen.

In front of Marshall, the APC plowed through the kitchen section with the ovens and grill, leaving behind explosions as the propane tanks used to fuel the grills erupted. Then the APC was crashing into the brick wall of the kitchen that was the back of the steak house and out into the night.

But as Marshall attempted to follow, he found that the bulldozer was suddenly tilting to the left. He gunned the engine and the tracks began to spin faster but still the Cat listed more, until with a thunderous crash, the floor gave way and the bulldozer dropped fifteen feet into the basement and beyond, directly on its left side, the weight of the machine too much for even the cement floor of the basement. Anyone watching would have been reminded of a sinking ship listing to the port side before finally sinking.

Smoke, dust and debris poured into the air, a massive cloud rolling out of the restaurant to fill the entire street. There was a gentle breeze blowing, and as the minutes passed, the cloud dispersed until only a light haze remained from the fires still burning hotly.

The APC pulled up before the destroyed restaurant after circling the block and the rear door opened and Stewart, Laurie and Hank climbed out with weapons drawn. As the engine rumbled heavily due to a bad cylinder or valve, Laurie and Stewart took up positions to guard against attack, while Hank walked over to where the bulldozer lay on its side deep within the wreckage. The SIG-Sauer was leveled in the warrior's right hand, the muzzle tracking back and forth slowly as Hank searched for a target.

The smell of spilled fuel came to his nose as he crossed the ten feet of floor before it ended in a large hole. Staring down, Hank studied the Cat. The ripper on the back had been torn off and the blade on the front was almost bent in half.

As for the operator's cab, it was caved in halfway, and inside it, still alive and pressed against the side framework, cursing, sat Marshall, his legs trapped between the bulldozer's dashboard.

When the police chief spotted Hank, he roared with rage and raised the pistol he was holding, but Hank was faster and fired one shot, hitting Marshall in the arm, the pistol falling out to disappear in the wreckage.

Crying out, Marshall bit off the outcry and began to laugh. "It's not over, you know. My people will get me out of here. And when they do, you're dead! Do you hear me? You'll fucking hang for this. You and your friends!"

Hank gave Marshall a quick smile, which was more of a smirk. "Sorry to disappoint you, Marshall, but there's no one to help you—at least not anymore. They're either dead or running for their lives. It's over, you're done."

"No, it's not over! In fact, it's only just begun!"

"Like I said, it's over." Hank used the muzzle of the SIG to point to the left of where Marshall was. Deep in the pit, fuel from a broken intake line from the Cat poured out, spreading with each passing second. As this happened, a few branching rivers began to spread out, meandering to where there were flames.

Marshall's eyes went wide as the realization of what was about to happen came to him. "I'll be waiting for you in hell!" Marshall screamed. "Then we'll have a reckoning!"

"No problem," Hank said calmly as he turned to leave, not wanting to be caught in the blast. "I've sent better men than you there already. At least you'll have company while you're waiting for me to arrive."

Marshall screamed a few more choice epitaphs as Hank climbed into the APC with Stewart and Laurie. They took a few seconds to toss out the corpses of the slain killers from earlier that night and then slammed the door closed.

"Okay, Carl, I think we're through with this town," Hank said. "Let's get the hell out of here."

"Sounds good to me," Carl agreed as he began to drive away towards the gate they had used to enter the town.

Behind the APC, the restaurant erupted in a massive conflagration, as not only did the fuel tank on the bulldozer explode, but propane tanks in the surrounding buildings ignited as well. By the time the armored carrier reached the gate, the flames consuming the buildings had doubled. In the streets, people ran to and fro, some with water buckets in hand but none paid the APC any attention.

When the APC approached the gate, the men on the wall and guardhouses were long gone and no one shot at the APC. Carl never slowed down, but rammed the gate and kept on going, the bad track on the carrier fighting him the entire time.

But then a few rounds did ricochet off the hull just as the APC crashed through the gate, some brave souls still not accepting defeat, but the bullets did no damage. Carl maneuvered through the boulders and then the armored carrier was free and moving away from the town.

When a half mile was between the APC and the town, Carl stopped and turned off the engine and everyone climbed out to finally rest and breathe some clean air for a while.

Though the hatches had been opened to air out the APC while it drove, all the spilled blood within it continued to stink up the inside. But once they had a chance, and if they felt it worthwhile, they could use dry grass and dirt taken from the shoulder of the road to sop up the blood and clean the interior.

Carl stretched his arms and legs, moaning softly as he moved in front of the headlights, which had been left on so they could see. It felt like he'd been in that driver's seat for ages. Leaving the lights on was taking a chance they'd be seen but they only planned on stopping for a few minutes and the chance that anyone was around was small.

The four warriors stood side by side and looked back at the horizon, where the flames could still be seen. More than half the town was nothing but rubble and the other half was on fire, and no doubt would burn to the ground, probably taking the rubble half with it as well.

Carl took off his Yankees cap and wiped his brow. "We don't have much fuel left, Hank, we burned a shitload of it in that fight."

"How much do we have left?" Hank asked.

Carl shrugged. "Hell if I know. Maybe another twenty miles if we're lucky, maybe less."

Hank put his arm around Laurie and hugged her as he rested his other hand on the butt of his SIG-Sauer. "Then we'll go till we run out of gas and then it's back to walking."

"The APC takes diesel, Hank," Stewart corrected him.

"Whatever," was Hank's reply.

Laurie was having second thoughts now that they were safe. "Do you think what we did was right?" Laurie asked. "I mean, once we knew it was safe to leave, we could have simply left. We didn't need to destroy the entire town, despite what they tried to do. Surely killing all that attacked us would have been enough retaliation."

Stewart nodded as he listened. "Perhaps, Laurie, but what we did was justice, isn't it? Before the bombs, if you killed someone you were punished. Those people were evil and we served them justice for their crimes. A long overdue one, I might add."

"Justice, huh?" Carl added. "To me it sounds like it was just plain old revenge. You try to kill me so I'll kill you. An eye for an eye. Just like in the bible."

"Justice or revenge, it's really the same damn thing when you come right down to it," Hank said. "Either way, it doesn't matter anymore. Now, the only justice or revenge is what a man sees fit. There's no higher power to tell us what to do anymore, no governments."

"There's always God," Stewart said.

Hank laughed. "God huh? Well, Stu, you can believe what you want, but if there really is a God, he's one hell of an asshole for letting us blow ourselves up."

"Some would say it's all in His plan," Stewart said. "Even blowing ourselves up."

Hank began to grow angry and he turned to Stewart with fire in his eyes. "Oh please, that's some horseshit and you know it. All God is, is an excuse for people not to have to take responsibility for their actions. Something bad happens and they say it was God's will, or they say it's all in 'his' plan. It's all bullshit, Stu and I would think someone as smart as you would get that, especially after all the evil shit we've seen."

Stu didn't reply, seeing how emotional Hank was. "I'm going back inside," he said. "I'll wait for the rest of you." He walked away, his back stiff as he climbed into the APC.

"You were pretty harsh there, weren't you, Hank?" Carl asked.

Hank sighed and the fire dulled in his eyes. "Yeah, I probably was. I didn't mean to snap at him like that. Guess I'm still wired from our fight. I'll tell him sorry later once we're moving again."

Carl went to inspect the broken track, not that there was anything he could do to fix it. He wasn't looking forward to driving the rest of the way till they ran out of diesel, the APC threatening to roll over every second of the way.

"It's not your fault, lover," Laurie said. "Religion is a sensitive subject at the best of times and right now is not the best of times."

He kissed her and calmed down further. "Yeah, I know." Hank was quiet for a full minute and then asked, "What about you? What do you believe in?"

She gave him a sly smile. "Me? Why, I believe in you, Stewart and Carl, and my gun. That's what I believe in; the rest is irrelevant, isn't it?"

"It's times like this that I know why I love you so much," he said as he wrapped his arms around her.

She laughed. "Really? Only these times? I guess I'll have to try harder the next time we're alone and have a bedroll under us." She pushed herself against him and he felt himself growing hard immediately.

"Hey, lovebirds," Carl called from one of the open hatches on the roof, only his head exposed. "How 'bout you save that shit for later, it's never good standing out here in the dark in the middle of a road."

They kissed one more time and returned to the APC. Carl fired up the engine and with it rattling from somewhere deep within the engine, the armored carrier began to move once more.

Behind the APC, in the west, the sky glowed orange and red, and in the east, the first patches of dawn were appearing. It had been a long night and the day would no doubt be longer. But once more, the four warriors had survived to fight another day, and they would continue to do so for as long as they breathed.

END GAME

The dirt road seemed to go on forever, stretching off into the horizon like a brown snake. On this road, Hank, Laurie, Carl and Stewart trod in the middle, their heads down, their backs hunched and their feet aching.

A day and a half ago they had been riding in style, after finding an armored personnel carrier, an APC, almost a week ago. The vehicle had been loaded with M-16's and ammunition, as well as grenades of all types, but almost all of the stores had been traded for more diesel fuel when they had passed through a small enclave that had diesel but nothing to use it with. Still, the town managers hadn't let it go cheaply.

With a full tank, the four companions had continued on in their travels, until finally running out of fuel in the middle of nowhere and no way to refuel. With nothing else to do, they packed up what they could, drove the APC into a stand of trees with the last drops of fuel, and hoped one day to return to it with more diesel.

None of them truly believed that would happen. Even if they did, the APC was on its last legs. With a bad track and an engine that was on its way out, it was only a matter of time before the vehicle broke down and stayed that way forever.

"Man, I miss the APC," Carl said as he slugged along on the side of the road after drifting away a few feet from the group. "That machine was damn good to us."

"I completely agree with you, Carl," Stewart said. "We were riding around like kings. Nothing could touch us."

Laurie let out a slight chuckle. "True, but we were also a target for every damn cutthroat and coldheart that spotted us."

"They would have tried to take us either way, Laurie," Hank said. "The APC was just the icing on the cake."

Laurie didn't reply, though she knew what Hank meant. Everyone was fair game nowadays it seemed, and murder was just par for the course if you had no morals. It was an easy way to get some food for your belly or ammunition for your gun. The fact that people were slaughtered mercilessly as a result didn't fit into the equation.

Laurie said something in reply to Hank but the grizzled warrior didn't hear her, having drifted off, thinking back to the last time the companions were attacked before the APC had finally run out of fuel.

It had been late in the day, and the companions were about to leave Kansas and cross over into Nebraska as they drove down Route 80. The state line was so close that they passed a sign proclaiming: **Nebraska…the good life. Home of Arbor Day**.

On both sides of them, rolling fields of corn, wheat and soybean floated past the open blaster ports to let in the cool breeze. It was as if the bombs had never fallen.

Carl was in the driver's seat again, as he usually was. He'd become the defacto driver and he enjoyed it immensely. No one argued; they were glad one of them wanted the job. The only time Carl didn't drive was when he needed a break or to eat.

While Hank and Stewart played cards to pass the time, Laurie was filing her nails. Just because the world had ended didn't mean she couldn't take care of herself.

The APC rattled loudly, thanks to the bad right track, which had been damaged in the fight with the Caterpillar bulldozer back in Arcadia. Add the rattling track to that of the rumbling diesel—what Carl guessed was a bad cylinder—and it was so loud inside the APC that no one could talk or be heard without screaming at the top of their lungs.

The engine changed in pitch and the rumbling began to wan. Hank looked up to see Carl was slowing down. Getting up, he joined Carl in front, both men peering through the scratched and pitted slit that made up the front windshield.

"Something wrong?" Hank asked as he looked outside.

"Yeah," Carl replied, "we got ourselves a roadblock. Saw it as soon as I got over the rise."

The APC was on the top of an incline in the road and the roadblock was easy to see. "Shit, that's not gonna be anything good," Hank said, studying the blocked road. Fifty feet ahead, seven or eight cars had been pushed together so that they resembled one giant lump of twisted metal. The wrecks filled the road so that there was no way around them.

"What do you want to do?" Carl asked.

Hank's brow creased as he gave that exact question some thought.

"We could always turn around," Carl suggested.

"We could do that," Hank agreed. "And it's possible we would if we were in a car or a regular truck." He looked at Carl as he said this, seeing if the other man would pick up on his wording.

Carl did almost immediately. "But we're not in a regular car or truck, are we?"

Hank smiled. "No, we're not. We're in an armored personnel carrier." He patted Carl's shoulder. "What do you say we give whoever's down there a greeting they'll never forget?"

"Let's do it. I've been itching to run some shit over again," Carl said.

Stewart and Laurie joined Hank and Carl, both having heard the entire conversation. "So we're going in?" Stewart said.

"You okay with that?" Hank asked Stewart and when the older man nodded, Hank looked at Laurie, his eyes asking the same question.

She smiled. "Let's go. If we can take out a few more coldhearts and make the world just a little bit cleaner, I say okay with that."

"Good, then get ready for a fight, 'cause there's no way that pile of cars was put there by accident," Hank stated.

The companions got to work, preparing for battle, while Hank studied the roadblock with a pair of binoculars. He scanned the wrecked cars for almost two minutes straight before he spotted a shaggy human head moving behind a bumper. It was a small bit of movement, but it was enough to draw his eyes. There were raiders down there—or worse. Some raiders were lazy and would simply block the road with debris and beset anyone who drove up, taking down the wayward travelers before they knew what hit them.

Most people didn't travel, but picked a spot of dirt and struggled to eke out a living, so if they did go out on the road, a roadblock like the one now would usually catch people off guard. But the companions traveled constantly, so they'd seen the same trick more than once, so were ready for what would come next.

"I see one hiding behind one of the wrecks on the right side," Hank stated. "If there's one there's sure to be more." He nudged Carl. "Go 'head and start rolling."

Carl began to drive, the tracks leaving marks in the asphalt. As the APC approached the roadblock, Hank spotted more movement, counting at least six individual bodies. "Christ, they must think we're idiots," Hank said. "I can see them plain as day." He frowned. "They don't seem that scared of us. That doesn't make any sense. We're in an armored carrier after all."

"Maybe they're just stupid and think they can take us?" Carl surmised. The APC was within fifty feet of the roadblock when Carl slowed and stopped, the engine idling roughly. He'd already picked a weak spot in the center of the wrecked cars for when Hank told him to break through. In the spot, there was a two foot hole separating two cars and there was nothing behind them. The APC could punch through there easily.

At a blaster port, Stewart peered out into the austere landscape surrounding the roadblock on both sides. Something wasn't right, he could feel it. He agreed with Hank. The raiders had to be pretty damn cocky to try and take an armored vehicle like the APC. Either that or they had an ace up their sleeves.

Suddenly, Stewart's eyes went wide as he considered this and he turned to face the front of the APC, yelling, "Hank, we need to leave here, now?"

Hank glanced over his shoulder, unsure why Stewart was so upset. "Why? We're perfectly safe in here. It's not like they can…"

Before he could finished his sentence, two battered pickup trucks came roaring and bouncing out of hidden dips to the left and right sides of the APC, catching the armored carrier in a crossfire. Both pickups had three man crews. Two were in the front cab and one was on the back. The men on the rear of the pickups both stood behind mounted Maremont M-60 lightweight machine guns, the weapons already firing the 105-round ammunition at the APC with the help of autofeeds.

"Shit, they've got heavy firepower!" Hank yelled. "Carl, evasive maneuvers, now!"

Carl gunned the engine and shot forward as more raiders popped up from behind the roadblock and began firing. The men and a few women carried a multitude of weapons, from M-16s to AKs to shotguns and deer rifles. These bullets bounced harmlessly off the APC's hull but that couldn't be said for the M-60 rounds. Being a heavier caliber, the rounds striking the armored hull made it sound like the end of the world was happening all over again. Bolt heads exploded from the walls as spalling came into full effect. The bolt heads ricocheted around the interior like bullets themselves and the companions had to duck and wait them out or risk being hit.

Carl struck the roadblock dead center, sending cars skidding across the road to then flip over. Three raiders didn't move fast enough and were trapped under the cars, crushed to death as the vehicles rolled over them.

The APC got hung up for a brief second and a pickup truck with no front end began to be dragged behind the armored carrier, its rear bumper caught in the damaged right track. Carl now had to fight the drag and the bad track, the APC threatening to roll over.

Meanwhile, the two pickups with M-60s were attacking in full force, their large rounds taking chunks out of the armored hull of the APC.

"I don't know how much more of this we can take!" Carl yelled as he fought to control the APC. "If one of those rounds hits something vulnerable like the tracks, it's all over for us!" His Yankees ball cap fell off and he ignored it, not having the time to pick it up.

"Just keep her steady a little longer," Hank ordered. "I'll take care of our two friends."

Taking two Wily Peters with him, Hank climbed up into one of the two roof hatches, the one with the .30 caliber machine gun. There was a Browning .50-cal as well, but that had been out of ammunition since leaving the town of Arcadia.

As he popped his head out of the hatch, he had to duck down immediately as rounds peppered the hull a few feet from him. Cursing, he waited a few seconds, popped up again, pulled the pin on one of the grenades, and waited for the right time to use it.

That time came seconds later when one of the pickups came screeching around the APC, the driver zooming past, planning on spinning around and coming back head-on so that the gunner could take some shots at the front grille and slim windshield.

But the pickup got a little too close and Hank used this to his advantage. As the pickup zipped by, he tossed the grenade into its rear bed. The white phosphorous grenade burst as soon as it landed in the bed, directly behind the gunner. A starfish of smoke and incandescent metal consumed the gunner and the M-60, the rounds beginning to cook off a few seconds later. Some of the exploding rounds went into the front cab, killing both the driver and passenger. With the rear bed a rolling ball of flame, the pickup skidded off the road to hit a dip and flip end over end. One of the tires—now burning—flew off to land and roll across the tall grass lining the road, setting it aflame. Whiter hot debris spun in all directions, creating a wildfire that would burn for quite some time as there had been no rain for more than a week.

With only one pickup truck to deal with now, Hank took hold of the .30 caliber machine gun and began sending steel death at the gunner of the M-60.

Both vehicles were side by side as each one fought for dominance. Hank felt bullets zip by his head and displace the air. One clipped him in the shoulder. Ignoring the flash of pain, he focused on stitching the pickup from front quarter fender to the driver's door, and then up to the gunner.

Unknown to Hank, the gunner was doing the exact same thing, tracking rounds along the APC as he zeroed in on Hank. It was a race of the two men to kill the other, and just before the M-60 linked up directly with Hank's chest, Hank leveled the muzzle of the Thirty directly at the gunner and fired, his finger pressed firmly on the trigger, brass casings flying off in all directions.

A split second before a 105 round slung would have found Hank, the gunner suddenly was blown off the rear bed with half his chest resembling ground hamburger. The driver, who had taken a bullet to the side as the round went through the door, spit blood and lost control a moment later. The pickup truck's engine roared as it hit a depression in the ground and then flipped over, the passenger flying through the windshield to land in a limp pile of arms and legs twenty feet from the truck.

The APC slowed and Carl began to swivel it in a circle as Hank continued to fire at the few raiders remaining. Bodies were stitched from groin to head, and in a matter of seconds, there was no one left alive.

Hank let go of the trigger of the Thirty, the barrel glowing red hot from so much use. He could feel the heat the muzzle was giving off and he had a feeling if he hadn't stopped, it would have misfired at any second.

Other than the crackling of the flames from the burning pickup, the road was silent. Hank spun in all directions, looking for another target, but there were none. Only bodies strewn across the road and in the tall grass. When he was satisfied all the raiders were dead, he dropped down into the APC to check on the others. "Everyone okay?"

"Fine here," Stewart said.

"Me too," Laurie added and then saw Hank's shoulder. "Oh, Hank, you're hurt."

"It's just a scratch, I was barely nicked."

"Well, let me see it anyway." She grabbed the first aid kit mounted on the wall of the APC, and pulled off his shirt to inspect the wound. It was bleeding a lot but when she wiped the blood away, she saw the wound wasn't serious; thank God. She quickly cleaned and sterilized the wound and bandaged it with gauze and tape.

As Hank shrugged back into his shirt, he smiled at her. "Thanks, baby, that's a lot better."

She merely nodded. It had only taken a minute, the wound being so minor. "You were lucky."

"Hey, Hank," Carl called from the driver's seat. "Looks like we got a live one out there."

Hank joined Carl and he pointed out the windshield to show Hank what he'd spotted. At first, Hank didn't see anything in the grass, but as he continued looking, he saw that the passenger of the second pickup that had gone through the windshield wasn't dead and was now trying to crawl away.

"You guys stay here," Hank said and pointed at the crawling man. "Looks like we got a survivor. I want to have a little chat with him." He went to the rear door, opened it, and climbed out.

"I'm going with you," Laurie said as she prepared to leave the APC.

"No, baby, you stay here, I got this. Just keep an eye out through one of the blaster ports and make sure there's no one else we need to worry about."

"I'll go up on the roof and watch from there," Stewart said and went to the hatch leading to the .30-cal.

"Good idea," Hank agreed. As he turned to close the rear door, he glanced at the metal, seeing the new pockmarks from the bullet strikes. His inner voice told him they had been lucky this time. The two armed pickup trucks had been a formidable enemy and things could have easily gone bad. It was good fortune the raiders hadn't had an LAWS or ground to air missiles. Seemed outlandish, but National Guard and military bases were up for grabs nowadays from looters.

Carrying his Heckler and Koch G-12 automatic rifle, Hank scanned all around him again. Off to the right, the wildfire was spreading and he began walking to where he'd seen the man crawling. He could see the man when he was closer, the tall grass hiding the raider's location. Wary that the raider might still be a threat, Hank went wide, skirting the fire and coming at the raider from behind. There would be no reason for the man to think he had to watch his six as there was nothing out there but grassland. Still, Hank wasn't taking chances and he kept low as he picked up the drag trail the man left as he crawled through the grass. Droplets of blood stained the crushed grass and a blind man could have followed the trail. Twenty-five feet away, the trail ended with the raider lying prone. The man was on his stomach, his face in the grass.

Hank crept up to him, the HK G-12 leveled in case the man was playing possum.

Kicking out with a foot, Hank pushed the raider's left leg and was rewarded with a grunt of pain but nothing else.

Seeing no movement, Hank used his foot to push the man onto his back.

The raider looked to be in his forties with a scruff of a beard and bushy eyebrows. He had a head wound from going through the windshield of the pickup. It didn't look serious, but it had dazed him. Hank figured the man probably had a few broken ribs, too. His left arm was limp at his side, no doubt broken.

Checking for a weapon, Hank found none and relaxed a little more. He turned and waved to the APC, giving the all clear sign. Stewart waved back from behind the Thirty.

There was a water canteen on the raider's hip. Hank took it and splashed water on the man, reviving him slightly. The raider sputtered and spit red-tinged water, thanks to biting his inner cheek during the crash. He blinked slowly and looked up at Hank, who was nothing but a tall broad figure with the sun directly behind him.

"Who the fuck are you?" the man whispered, his voice cracking.

"I'm the guy who is about to put a bullet in your head," Hank said flatly.

The man swallowed and spit again as his eyes grew clearer. "Were you in that rolling tank me and my men just tried to take down?"

Hank only nodded.

"Looks like I bit off more than I could chew this time, huh."

"Seems that way," Hank said and leveled the G-12 rifle at the man's head. "Well, it's been nice but it's time to die."

"No wait, don't shoot me. I've got info, real top secret shit. I'll tell you if you let me live."

Hank was already squeezing the trigger as the raider talked but he hesitated at the last second. Easing up slightly, he cocked his head to the side. "Go on, I'm listening."

Spitting blood, the man licked his lips. "You gotta promise you'll let me live. Please, I don't want to die. You can't shoot me."

"I'm not agreeing to anything before knowing what you think is worth your life."

"But if it's good, you won't kill me?" There was a glimmer of hope in the man's eyes now, as his mind raced with thoughts of surviving this debacle. If he lived, he could easily gather more men, and within a week he'd be right back to killing and raping. It would be like this setback had never happened.

Hank decided he had nothing to lose and slowly nodded. "Go on."

"But you won't kill me right? Promise me."

Hank sighed. "Fine, I promise I won't kill you, now spill it, what do you know that's worth a trade on your life?"

The man slowly reached into his pocket under Hank's watchful eye and pulled out a map covered in his own blood. "I took this off of a National Guard guy a few months back."

"I think you're wasting my time here. Goodbye." Hank leveled the rifle at the man's head.

"No wait! It's a map to one of them government installations, an underground bunker? The guy and his squad were supposed to be part of a government convoy when the bombs began to fall but it never happened, so the squad were selling themselves out as mercenaries. We took down the squad in a raid and he was the only one left alive."

Hank stopped now, looking at the man in a new light. He'd heard stories since after the bombs fell about underground government bunkers filled with caches of food, weapons and military vehicles. The installations had been built back during the Cold War and were stocked with what the government believed would be needed after a nuclear war. When the people living inside it finally crawled out of the bunker, they would have all the resources they needed to begin rebuilding the country. Of course, Hank had never met anyone who had really seen one and it had become more of a fairytale to the survivors of the nukescape, something to dream about while lying around a campfire with your belly growling from lack of food. Still, if it was really true, there would be a fortune in supplies, all waiting to be taken.

"How do I know the map's real? It's probably a fake," Hank said. "I think you're full of shit and this conversation's over."

"No, I'm telling the truth!" He spit more blood. "I tortured the guardsman for three days before he died from the wounds I inflicted. Trust me, no man could take the pain I gave him and not tell me what I wanted to hear."

"He could have lied, told you what you wanted to hear." Hank ripped the map from the raider's hand and glanced at it quickly. It was a road map, like a million he'd seen before the world ended, only this one had a spot marked in Nebraska in the middle of nowhere. On the bottom were seven numbers, but he didn't give them a second thought; coordinates maybe, or a phone number?

"If this place is so real, why haven't you gone there to check it out? Why are you still here?"

"I was going, but I wanted to pick this area clean before I left." He flashed his blood-stained teeth at Hank. "There's easy pickings around here, you know."

"Oh yeah? Then how do you explain me and my friends?" Hank growled.

"Ah, yeah, you guys were the fly in the ointment." He sat up slightly, wincing in pain. "So, are we good?"

Hank gave the man the slightest bit of a shrug. "No, we're not." He squeezed the trigger without even the slightest bit of warning of his action, the 4.7mm round hitting the raider directly between the eyes from no more than three feet away. The back of the man's head exploded outward to paint the grass scarlet. The head snapped back and bounced off the ground as the man's feet began to kick up and down. Hank detected the odor of feces and urine and glanced down to see that the raider's bowels had let go upon death.

Hank glanced up at the sky and away from the corpse, letting out the breath he'd been holding. He felt no guilt for breaking his word. The raider was the lowest form of human life. He was a parasite, a plague far worse than even the bombs that had laid waste to the Earth. That man would have killed anyone he wanted to and would have never given it a moment's thought. He was the worst kind of shit.

When people should be banding together to work for a common cause, this man was out there raping, killing and pillaging.

Hank was a man of honor, but would a man give a promise to a rabbit not to eat it if he was starving? Would a man tell a tree he would promise not to cut it down and use it for firewood if he was freezing? Of course not, for those things were not equal to a man when it came to honor.

So to Hank, the raider was so far beneath him that he felt nothing for breaking his word. You had to respect the person you gave a promise to, otherwise it meant nothing.

Turning away from the body, he began walking back to the APC, the blood-covered map still clutched tightly in his hand.

"Hank, are you listening to me?" Laurie asked, grabbing his arm and shaking him gently.

Blinking, Hank was pulled from his reverie of the encounter with the raiders and back to the present. He cursed inwardly, knowing he'd made a grave mistake by drifting off. In the new world, to drop your guard for even a second could prove fatal.

"Sorry, I was thinking of something. What did you say?" Hank asked.

"I said if we're gonna get to that bunker we'll need wheels."

Hank grunted at Laurie's statement. She was right. If it was real, they would never make it the Nebraska bunker if they had to walk. When Hank had killed the leader of the raiders and returned to the APC, he'd filled the others in on what the man had said and about the map. They had all agreed it was worth a try to see if they could find the bunker. But that was when they had an APC and were driving; now they were on foot and the miles between them and their destination seemed like half a world away.

"Well, hell, Laurie," Hank said with a slight grin. "Let me bend over and pull a car out of my ass."

"Ha ha, you're so funny. Stop ignoring the problem, we need a vehicle."

"And we'll find one. Carl, you still have those grenades, right?"

Carl nodded. "Of course I do, where would they be if I didn't?"

When they'd abandoned the APC, Carl had taken all the grenades in the small armory. The plan was to try and trade them for a vehicle at the next town they came to, if there was one within walking distance of course.

"See, Laurie?" Hank said. "Carl's got the grenades; they're worth more than gold nowadays. We can buy a ride with those. We'll be fine."

She simply harrumphed and crossed her arms over her full breasts. Stewart had been walking in the lead and now he slowed and raised his right hand, the signal for the others to stop. "There's a building up ahead."

The others joined him and gazed down the road. Hank pulled out his binoculars and studied the building. It was small, one-story with a pitched roof. It reminded him of a barn. He continued to scan it and then saw a newspaper dispenser, two soda vending machines and an old plexiglass and aluminum telephone booth, complete with swiveling door that slid inward.

"I think it's a small rest stop," Hank said. "Looks deserted. But still, get sharp and pay attention. Spread out till we reach it. Stewart, you and Carl take the lead and I'll be right behind you. Laurie, you take the rear this time."

Everyone nodded and they spread out so as not to make an easy target for a sniper or even if a grenade was tossed at them as they drew closer. Leapfrogging down the road, they were soon only fifty feet away and still there was no sign of life.

Picking up a fist-sized rock, Hank signaled the others to stay put and he crept up closer. Taking cover behind an old sign telling about the sights nearby, he threw the rock at the structure. It soared through the air and struck the side of the building, then dropped to the ground. If anything was inside, it would most certainly be startled by the loud noise.

But nothing stirred and after a full three minutes, Hank was fairly confident the building was indeed deserted. He waved the others to him and waited till they were by his side.

"We going inside?" Carl asked.

Hank considered it and then changed his mind. "No, not this time. The last time we went into a place like this we were attacked."

"But nothing's shown itself," Laurie said.

"True, but we haven't been walking that long, we don't need a rest yet."

"We could check the place out anyway, see what's inside?" Carl suggested.

"Why?" Hank asked. "There's nothing we need. What? You think there's a stash of food and water in there? Maybe rows upon rows of freshly oiled guns and clips as high as your head?"

"Well no, of course not. It's obvious this place has been picked over already." Carl said as he gestured to the main door hanging off its hinges and the broken windows, the glass littering the sidewalk to reflect the sun.

"Right, so we don't need to go in. I just wanted to make sure there was no one inside that was going to try and pick us off as we passed by. Doesn't seem that way, so let's keep moving."

It's possible if any of them had been truly tired they may have protested to go inside but they all felt fresh and reluctantly agreed. Walking side by side a few feet apart once more to make a harder target, they began moving again.

As they passed by the rest stop, Laurie took in the building and objects around it. "Don't see many of those nowadays, even before the bombs," she said, studying the phone booth. The plexiglass was opaque from being sandblasted by the wind and dirt, and from sun exposure from so many years outside.

As the companions passed it, they saw that there was a large rat inside chewing on the phone cord. Carl raised his Mini-Uzi, wanting to kill the foul rodent but Hank stopped him with his hand held up.

"Why not?" Carl asked with annoyance in his voice.

"Because it's a waste of ammunition and the shots will be heard if anyone's in the area. Besides, what are you gonna do? Kill every rat you see?"

Carl thought back to the time they had been forced to seek shelter in a cave, only to find it filled with mutant rats the size of dogs. He felt a shiver run down his spine at the memory. "Yeah, actually, I was."

"Leave it alone, Carl, it's not worth it."

Stewart gestured with his sword-cane as the rat disappeared inside the building. "It seems the discussion is mute anyway. The rodent's gotten away."

"There's plenty more where that one came from," Carl said as he slung the Mini-Uzi over his shoulder again.

"Unfortunately," Stewart added with a smile.

They walked in silence for a while, each enjoying the day and the feeling of being alive. The sky was clear of clouds for a change and the sun was bright, though the blue was still gone to be replaced by the burnt orange of the new world. Whether the blue would ever return was anyone's guess and not worth the energy to contemplate. Why worry about things far beyond your control?

At midday they took a break in a field forty feet off the road. It was a pleasant glade with felled trees they could sit on while they ate, drank and rested.

Hank glanced at his radiation badge and saw that it had slowly begun to creep into the yellow. "You guys see your badges?"

Carl was the first to speak. "Yeah, but it's nothing to worry about yet, right?"

Hank nodded. "So far. A missile strike must have happened a few miles from here. Either that or the winds are blowing it in from somewhere."

"What do we do if it gets worse?" Laurie asked.

Hank shrugged as he drank from his canteen. "Without protection we'll have to go back and find a way around this zone."

"Shit," Carl said. "My feet are beginning to hurt as it is. I'd hate to think we've been walking for days for nothing."

"For now we'll keep an eye on it. Hopefully it's a false alarm. For now it's nothing more than background radiation. We're fine," Hank said.

When the bombs had fallen, particles of dust had been sucked up into the clouds that formed from the ground bursts, the dust soon rendered radioactive. Unstable elements inside the miniscule particles then began to decay constantly, releasing ionized radiation in three separate forms: alpha and beta particles and gamma rays. The alpha particles didn't do much harm to humans unless it was breathed or swallowed. Beta particles were simple electrons, and other than causing burns if they came in contact with the skin, were about as dangerous as the alphas. But the gamma particles were the worst and caused the most damage to human cells. Even radiation suits could do little to stop gamma particles from causing harm.

But with two years since the bombs fell, the radiation levels had dropped significantly in many areas not close to the blast zones, but still, there was always a chance of exposure due to the high rad count in the atmosphere and the acid rains. How the Earth would heal would be anyone's guess and only time would tell the tale.

The companions finished eating and they walked back to the road and continued their journey. Hank studied the map as he walked, knowing the others were watching the surrounding area carefully and had his back. According to the map, there was a small town seven miles away. He had no way of knowing if the town still existed but at least it was someplace to set their minds to. With luck, the town might even have vehicular transportation or horses the companions could trade for.

He quickly filled the others in, who all agreed it was worth the chance. And the best news was they could be there before nightfall if they kept up the pace they'd been taking.

Putting the map away, Hank let out a sigh, smiled, and slowed to let Laurie catch up to him, from where she was trailing last in the group.

"Why are you smiling?" Laurie asked when she joined him.

He shrugged his broad shoulders. "No reason, just happy to be alive, with you, here, now. Life may be rough but it's still life."

"Oh, you're a big softy sometimes, you know that?" she leaned over, stretched on her tip-toes, and kissed him, then she had to back away as they were still walking.

"Shhh, don't tell Carl or I'll never hear the end of it," he joked.

She chuckled. "You're secret's safe with me."

The rural land around them sprawled out far and wide and only the dirt road they traveled marred the vista. Off in the distance, a roof could be seen of a farmhouse.

The day was more than half over when they followed a bend in the road to see the way was partially blocked by kudzu and a tumbling mass of rose bushes, the bright red flowers standing out against the otherwise green surroundings. Perhaps a pickup truck full of roses had come this way years ago and one of the plants had fallen off the rear bed, only to take root on the shoulder of the road, or perhaps they had always grown wild here. Either way, it was an unexpected sight.

"Oh, how beautiful," Laurie said, her eyes going wide at the magnificent tableau. In a world filled with death and destruction, to see such beauty blossoming was a welcome image.

Fifty paces ahead of the companions, coming from behind a copse of particularly dense bushes, more than a dozen radiation lepers suddenly appeared. It happened quickly; one second the road was clear, then it was full of burned and scarred humans.

"Shit," Hank hissed and swung his HK G-12 rifle around as he made sure the others had fanned out on the road.

The mutants stared at the four warriors, as if surprised to see them, too, and for a moment no one moved. Hank used the time to size up his enemy.

One of the radiation lepers was pregnant, the belly round and full, looking as if the woman would give birth at any second. Her breasts were swollen and full, and she was naked other than a loincloth. Her entire body was covered in blisters, some having popped to ooze a clear liquid down her ravaged flesh. She had no fingernails, her hands cracked and bleeding. It would be a miracle if her baby was born alive and even then it was doubtful it would live past the first few hours.

The rest of the group fared no better, with sores and pustules covering their bodies. Most wore rags but a few had on more intact clothing. One even wore a filthy University of Nebraska sweatshirt. Most were barefoot but a few wore sandals or blood-covered sneakers and one was naked but wore a pair of black leather shoes, the laces missing, the tongues hanging over the front like a dog dying from thirst.

Though a few held crossbows, there wasn't a firearm among them, but all carried melee weapons of some kind, whether it was a wooden club, a thick stick, baseball bat, claw hammer or a crowbar. The one with the crowbar swung it back and forth and Hank saw clots of dried blood and what looked like brain matter on the tip of the weapon.

The two groups stared at one another silently for the breath of five heartbeats.

Then Carl opened fire with his Mini-Uzi, not needing to be told what had to be done. As soon as Carl squeezed the trigger, the rest of the companions joined in. After all, it wasn't like any of them were going to stop and question Carl on why he had taken the lead without discussing it with the others. All four warriors knew there was only one result to coming upon a group of scavenging radiation lepers.

Three of the mutants holding crossbows raised them to shoot but a barrage of hot lead took them down before any could get off a single shot. Two were killed instantly, and the other was hit in the throat. The burned man dropped his crossbow and placed both hands around his throat to staunch the flow of blood, but it did little, and scarlet fluid pumped through his fingers. He went to his knees before falling face first onto the road, a small cloud of dust erupting as he landed.

Hank fired a tri-burst at the first ones in line, taking them down in a spray of blood. The pregnant woman charged him, waving a butchers knife and he shot her, stopping her cold. He stitched her from belly to neck. He felt no regret in taking her down.

She was the enemy, pure and simple. Two 4.7mm rounds finally struck her neck and nearly severed her head from her shoulders.

She slumped to the ground, dead, as a pool of blood spread out beneath her. Her belly was a gaping mass of blood and tissue and a tiny hand could be seen jutting from one of the bullet holes.

"Grenade!" Carl yelled as he pulled the pin on a dual-purpose grenade and threw it. A second later, there was a bright flash in the midst of the mutants and then they were screaming and running as body parts flew off in all directions. Unfortunately, most of the rad-lepers ran straight at the companions.

Stewart sprayed the crowd as well. A man on a crutch tried to hobble at him and Stewart stitched the man's stomach, spilling his intestines into the dirt.

The man howled in pain and desperately began trying to push the greasy coils back inside him, then went to his knees with his slimy innards sliding out of his hands. An instant later a stray bullet hit him in the chest and destroyed his heart. He fell over, dead and out of pain.

Hank took down another assailant as the woman ran at him, shooting her legs out from under her and then adding one more to her head.

The next attacker he took down was already wounded and off balance from gunfire one of the other companions and he finished the man off with a shot to the heart, killing the man almost instantly.

Laurie moved closer to Hank and slowly picked her targets with her .22, each one a head shot. Her heart was beating fast and she forced herself to slow her breathing and stay calm.

A small man with a beard and only one arm ran at her from the left and she shot him in the face, directly through his right eye. Already in motion, he ran past Laurie to tumble onto the grass on the shoulder of the road, his legs still moving though his brain was already shutting down.

A maniacal scream filled with anger and hate broke through the din of battle from behind and Hank glanced over his shoulder to see at least another dozen radiation lepers running up the road. This wasn't good; the companions would soon be caught in a vice that they may not be able to escape from.

"Carl, behind us, another grenade!" Hank ordered as he spun around and leveled the G-12 automatic rifle and fired, the burst of the caseless ammunition sending two mutants to the ground with their insides spilling out before them.

Carl threw another dual-purpose grenade, this time to the rear, and it exploded with the familiar starfish cloud of white dense smoke. It didn't do much damage to the attacking horde but it did slow and scatter them slightly; a few were wounded and only one was killed.

This group carried firearms and bullets began to zip by the companions' heads. Hank realized the chance of being overwhelmed was too high; the time to retreat before all four of them were slaughtered was now or never.

"Everyone, with me, this way!" he yelled, his comrades following immediately. The others understood what Hank saw and knew they were in big trouble.

Dashing into the tall wheat lining the road fifteen paces in, the four warriors ran for their lives, only pausing to shoot over their shoulders to try and slow the trailing mutants.

The hunt was on, and they were the prey.

It was a desperate chase, one that lasted all afternoon and into the night. A rainstorm came and it was only luck that it wasn't acid rain, though it did have the faint taint of sulfur.

Hank, Carl and Laurie were able to keep moving at a good pace, but Stewart was having a hard time due to his age. Once they had made it through the wheat field, they charged into a wooded area lining the field.

Hank used his panga to slash at the underbrush as they made their way through the forest. Every now and then, they would all stop and wait, doing their best to control their breathing so they could hear if they were still being followed.

Stewart was grateful for these rests, and he gulped in air as he leaned against trees or sat on moss-covered logs. His complexion was pale from pushing himself so hard.

The screams of rage and anger were enough to tell the group that they hadn't lost their pursuers just yet, that the mutant horde was still following them.

So they ran some more, and every fifteen minutes they stopped and listened, and by the time they stopped for the eighth time, the screams began to fade slightly, resembling the droning of car engines as they zipped by on a busy highway.

But they were still there, still following, like bloodhounds. One of the radiation lepers must have been a hunter or a tracker before the bombs fell, and Hank had no doubt the companions were making a trail easy to follow by anyone with tracking skills. Sooner or later, the warriors would have to turn and face their pursuers, and knowing that, Hank wanted to make sure when the time came, he and the others had the advantage.

"You need to go on without me," Stewart gasped as he tried to regain his composure. His chest heaved with the exertion, his face flush, his skin covered in sweat. "I'm too old for this shit. I can't keep up with you. Go, I have my guns. I can defend myself if it comes to it?"

"Forget it, Stewart," Hank snapped. "Don't even talk like that. Maybe if you were mortally wounded I'd consider it but you're fine. So, we all get away or none of us do. You know that, so you can shove that heroic movie shit and don't bring it up again." Hank got Laurie and Carl's attention from a few feet away. "You two help Stewart. This isn't gonna end unless we stop and fight. Let's keep moving, but now while we move, we keep our eye out for a good place to make our stand."

Carl and Laurie went to Stewart, and though the older man protested a little, he didn't put up much of a fight. And why would he? Of course he didn't want to be left behind, but he also didn't want to cause the others to be caught because of his weaknesses.

He wrapped his arms around Laurie and Carl's shoulders for support, and with Hank slashing the brush once more, they melted into the undergrowth, the shrieks of the horde taunting them from afar but getting ever closer.

Hank found the perfect place to make their stand thirty minutes later.

The area was on a slight incline so the companions had high ground, and the trees were so dense there was only one clear way through the thick trunks, the forest closing in to make a natural channel. The mutants would have no choice but to use it when they reached this spot.

"This is it. This is where we make our stand and fight," Hank said as he studied the trees to see where the best place to lay in wait would be. He pointed to Laurie and Stewart. "Laurie, take him further up the hill and wait for us, Carl and I will take care of our followers."

"But, Hank, I want to stay and fi…" she began but was cut off.

"No, Laurie, your .22 wouldn't matter much here. This is a 'spray and pray' situation. So take Stewart and get to a place where you can cover us if we can't stop them and have to retreat."

"No, I want to…" She protested some more but Hank went to her, raised his hand to her cheek and cupped her face.

"Please, Laurie," he said softly. "I'm counting on you to help Stewart." His soft tone took her off guard and she paused, then nodded in ascent. "Fine, but you better be right behind us."

He smiled. "I will. Just let me and Carl take a few minutes to clean up these woods."

She kissed him once. It was quick but passionate. Then she went to Stewart, helped him up from the ground where he was resting, and the two moved off. Stewart simply waved, too tired to talk if he didn't have to.

Hank waited a full minute until their footfalls could barely be heard before he turned to Carl, who had been studying the ground to see if there was any other way it could be used to his advantage.

"Well?" Hank asked.

Carl grinned, a knowing smile that said he had something up his sleeve. "I think I have another way to level the playing field."

Hank nodded in approval. "Then let's get to work, we don't have much time."

While the two men waited for the radiation lepers to arrive, Hank inwardly hoped that they never came. Good fortune would be that the horde had lost the trail and had gone off in another direction.

Unfortunately, his hope was dashed with each passing minute. Second by second, the howls of the horde grew louder and there was no doubt they had the companions' trail.

Hank was on the left side of the trail and Carl the right, both ten feet from the channel in the trees, each man hidden behind a large trunk with peeling bark. Above in the trees, sparrows flitted from branch to branch and locusts could be heard from not too far off. It was almost tranquil in the middle of the forest, Hank thought. As if the world was still intact.

But that picturesque scene was shattered a moment later when the first mutant appeared.

The first one through the channel of trees was a man of American Indian heritage, which explained the tracking skills. The man was wearing a *Warriors* jersey stained with blood and pus. Hank shot the man so that the bullet hit him right in the middle of the two *R*'s in the logo of the shirt. The man was punched back to fall into the others following, and just like Hank had planned, the body created a stopgap that the rest of the mutants had to remove before advancing.

Hank squeezed the trigger of the G-12 right into the thickest part of bodies, and three more mutants were killed, creating an even worse blockage. Across from him, Carl did the same, his Mini-Uzi on full auto. More screaming people were taken down by the combined firepower of the two warrior's guns, making it so that nothing could get through without going over the pile of bloody corpses.

But a second later, the bodies were pulled away to be pushed onto the path, then the mutants continued the assault.

A woman with no hair and a drooping face, as if her flesh was made of wax, was the leader of the pack. She climbed over the corpses and was once more on the path up the hill, a half dozen more behind her. She managed to make it five feet easily, but then her left bare foot struck a finger-thick branch that had been connected to another branch, that in turn was pressing on another.

Three seconds after she disturbed the branches, the grenade that had been tenuously being held in check was knocked loose, the entire path becoming filled with blue-white smoke when the Willy Peter was ignited, bathing the woman and the ones behind her in white phosphorous. As their skin burned, they went down screaming.

Carl had one more present for the horde. Pulling another grenade from his pack, he pulled the pin on an M-26 high velocity frag grenade and tossed it underhand into the squirming, burning bodies. The grenade had a fifteen meter kill radius, so inside the channel of trees, it was even more devastating.

Another explosion shook the forest as the grenade decimated the horde—what was left of it anyway. Mutilated bodies were thrown into the air to bounce off the trees, leaving a dark smear of blood on the trunks before sliding to the ground. Their numbers were all but gone, and if they weren't insane they would have retreated by now. Hank and Carl stepped out into the path and walked down it side by side, firing until their clips went dry, then they covered each other while they popped out a spent clip and slid in a new one to continue the killing.

It was over in seconds, and as the two men ceased firing, they stared at the carnage of torn and brutalized bodies, arms and legs tangled within one another, severed heads with eyes open wide, mouths gaping in death, severed body parts without owners.

A few of the radiation lepers weren't totally dead, but only wounded, and Carl and Hank went through them, shooting the wounded in their heads. They had learned from past experience that even a wounded mutant was dangerous.

A few escaped the battle and their screaming shrieking could be heard as they ran through the forest. They were left alone. As long as they were going the other way, it was fine with Hank and Carl.

Satisfied the mutants were either dead or retreating, Hank grunted in satisfaction and patted Carl on the arm. "Let's get back to the others," he said, before turning and making his way through the bullet-ridden bodies as he walked back up the path.

Carl gazed off into the woods, his eyes scanning the surrounding area, and when pleased it was truly empty, he turned and followed Hank.

Upon joining Laurie and Stewart, Carl and Hank quickly filled them in on the battle, then the group began moving again, not wanting to take any chances. Between the gunshots and the grenades, any scavengers or raiders would no doubt come to investigate; if not to attack than to pick over what was left.

They walked for two more hours, and now that their gait had slowed, Stewart was doing better and was able to keep up easily. The land had been gradually becoming steeper, and when they finally reached the top, it was revealed that the group had been traveling in a valley.

Hank was the first to reach the top, and when he was there, he scanned downward. He smiled widely, the others making their way to the top to see what he was so jovial about.

"My word, will you look at that," Stewart said upon joining Hank and gazing down at the land below.

Nestled within the trees was a small long cabin. The chimney wasn't smoking, nor did the cabin look as if it was being maintained. There was a pickup truck parked beside it on the west side. It was covered in leaves and fallen branches and didn't look like it had moved in quite a while.

"What do you think?" Carl asked.

"We check it out," Hank said, the smile still on his face. Finally, some good fortune had come their way. "But stay sharp. For all we know there's a sniper on us right now." He pulled his binoculars and studied the two curtained windows, one on each side of the single wooden door. The curtains hung loose and didn't so much as flutter as he watched them. "It seems deserted, though."

"Then there's only one way to find out for sure," Laurie said and began walking down the hill, directly towards the cabin.

"Laurie, wait, get back here," Hank hissed. "Dammit, that woman is gonna get herself killed."

"Shouldn't we follow her?" Stewart asked.

"In a second. If there is a sniper on us, following her isn't gonna do us any good. She made her decision, now we have to wait." He hated saying it but it was the truth. He could only pray her foolishness wouldn't get her killed.

Laurie made her way to the cabin, sticking close to the trees as she moved from trunk to trunk. Her eyes studied the cabin, the windows especially, but she saw nothing that would signify the structure was inhabited. When she reached the last tree before a small clearing in front of the cabin, she counted to three and dashed to the door, then put her back to the wall beside it so that her body was only inches from the doorframe. With a brief wave back up the hill to Hank and the others, she leaned over, and with only her arm before the door, knocked twice, then pulled it back quickly in case someone shot through the door.

There was no response.

She counted to ten and knocked again, then waited for another count of five. When there was still no reply, she slowly turned the doorknob and was pleased when the door opened easily. Made sense. There was really no point in locking a door in the middle of nowhere.

Using her foot, she pushed the door open on squeaky hinges, and then ever so carefully, she peered into the gloom of the cabin. It took a second for her eyes to adjust and when they did, she saw a sparse, one-room cabin with a bed in the corner, a table and four chairs and a wooden frame couch with thin pads to sit on, plus a small kitchen.

There was a fireplace as well, cut wood piled beside it, ready to go.

As her eyes took in the room, she saw a lump in the bed. "Hello, is anyone home?" she called but the lump didn't move.

Confident it was safe as it would ever be, she walked into the cabin, and with gun in hand, went to the bed.

Slowly pulling down the blanket, she gasped and covered her nose, then left. By the time she had reached the door and was about to step out, Hank, Carl and Stewart had made their way to her and were just about to enter the cabin.

"Well?" Hank asked, the displeasure on his face for her rashness clear to her. "Is it empty?"

"Sort of," she replied, and when Hank looked at her in confusion, she waved him and the others inside. "It'll be easier if I just show you."

The four companions gathered around the bed, gazing down at the desiccated corpse of an old man. There were no signs of violence on the body. It was as if the man had laid down to rest one night and had passed away peacefully.

From the state of the body, it had been there for months, perhaps even a year. At a certain point, it was hard to detect the passage of time on a dried husk of a corpse unless a coroner happened to be around.

"I wonder who he was," Carl said softly, in deference to the dead.

"Doesn't matter. He's dead and we're not." Hank patted Carl and Stewart on the back. "Can you guys take the mattress with the body still on it outside?"

Carl nodded. "Sure, but I got it, Hank, let Stewart rest."

"My thanks, Carl, it's much appreciated." Stewart went and sat in one of the kitchen chairs.

Carl grabbed the mattress by the bottom end and gently pulled it off the wooden frame, then dragged it across the floor and outside. It wasn't heavy. The mattress was thin and the body was basically a skeleton with dried flesh.

Stewart picked up a black leather wallet that was on the table with a set of keys. Blowing the dust off it, he opened it, and pulled out a driver's license and studied it. "It says here that Robert Forester was seventy-nine this May. He lived in Omaha."

"The guy was old," Laurie said. "Hmm, I wonder..." She trailed off.

"Wonder what?" Hank asked.

She shrugged. "Well, there was no sign of a bullet or knife wound on the body, right?"

Hank nodded.

"Well, what if the guy came up here when the bombs fell to hole up and then simply died of a heart attack or something months later after arriving?"

"Sure, it's possible," Hank greed. "Huh, just think, the whole world is dying and you escape, only to meet your maker the natural way a year later. Guess when it's your time, it's your time, no matter what the rest of the world's doing."

"Amen, Hank," Stewart added. "When God calls you home you have to go."

Hank gave Stewart a hard glare, ready to put a stop to him if he began talking about God. Lately, Stewart had been more philosophical than before and it was beginning to rub Hank the wrong way. But Stewart didn't continue so Hank let it go.

"Hey, guys," Carl said when he returned from outside. "That pickup truck might still run and out back behind this cabin is a small shed with a generator. Electrical wires are running right to the back of the cabin." He went to the rear wall and ran his fingers along it, searching between the cracks in the wood where plaster had been added to seal the wall. "Ah, here they are. The wires come in right here." He followed them to a wall socket, which then split up into two more. "We may have power if we want it."

Hank shook his head. "No, it's not worth the chance the genny gets heard. Sound travels in the woods. Leave it alone. But once it gets dark we can build a fire in the fireplace. The darkness will hide the smoke."

Laurie walked into the small kitchen area and opened a few cabinets. "Hey, there's food in here." She began taking out boxes of dry food but the second she did, the contents began spilling out of holes in the boxes. "Shit," she said and tossed the box on the butcher block counter. Peering into the cabinet, she spotted mouse droppings. "Looks like field mice got into the dry stuff." She reached into the cabinet again and this time pulled out a can, then a few more. "But they didn't touch the canned stuff."

The paper on the cans had been chewed at but the cans themselves were intact.

"Huh," Carl said as he ran his finger over the table's surface and came back with a coating of dust on his finger. "It looks like no one's been here at all for a long time."

"Sure," Hank added. "This cabin's in the middle of nowhere — literally. It was only dumb luck that we stumbled on it." He clapped his hands and got everyone's attention. "Okay, we stay here tonight and maybe even longer. It's been a while since we had a place we could relax a little. But there's still a lot to do before we can rest for the night. Carl, take those keys on the table and check out that pickup truck. If you can get it running, we won't have to walk out of here when we leave. Laurie, search everything in here and see what you can salvage, then put it all on the table so we can go through it together. Stewart, I want you to stay here with Laurie and help her out."

"What about you, lover?" Laurie asked.

"I'm gonna recce the area and make sure we're truly alone out here, and I want to erase our tracks leading up to this place as much as I can." He smiled. "It looks like we found a home to put our feet up for a while, folks."

They stayed for five days, resting and recuperating, and headed out the morning of the sixth day. Longer wasn't an option as by then, the food found in the cabin was gone and the area had sparse game for hunting, nor was fresh water nearby.

For dinner on the second night, they ate kudzu taken from around the cabin where it grew wild. Carl fried it up with vegetable oil and seasoned it with salt, pepper and oregano, the only seasoning found in the cupboards. He'd used a cast iron skillet found in one of the cabinets.

"Not bad," Hank had said, the others agreeing. "Tastes like dandelion leaves."

"I didn't even know you could eat this stuff," Stewart said. "Where on earth did you ever find out this plant was edible?"

Carl had shrugged. "Read it somewhere I suppose."

As something new, the group didn't mind eating at first, but after eating it for lunch and dinner for two more days straight, it soon lost its appeal.

Besides, they were becoming restless. They were used to being on the move, traveling, and to simply sit each day in a cabin with nothing to do grated on their nerves.

Hank especially was impatient to move on. He'd cleaned and oiled his weapons so many times he could now do it blindfolded. His panga had never been as sharp as it was now. Near the fireplace, there was enough firewood to last five years, maybe more. Hank had found himself cutting wood each morning, wanting to exercise and pass the time.

He'd also go off on recces of the area more than was needed, mostly alone but sometimes with Laurie. The few times he went with Laurie were the most enjoyable. They would skirt the perimeter of the cabin, and when they knew they were entirely alone, would lay their clothes on the ground after shucking them and make love passionately as the crickets and cicadas sounded around them. But despite this, the longing to move on overrode those pleasures for Hank, and Laurie felt the same way.

A few old paperbacks had been in the cabin and Stewart read most of the time, sitting on the couch with his feet up. Carl was busy, too. He'd gone through the pickup truck from top to bottom and it was now running. He was lucky that everything he'd needed had been within his reach. The battery had been drained from sitting for two years but a battery charger that plugged into a standard wall outlet had been in the rear bed under a tarp along with a toolbox and other mechanical odds and ends such as starter fluid and carburetor cleaner.

After getting the generator in the shed running, he used the charger to bring the battery back to life and once the engine was running, he'd charged the battery that way. When the generator had been running, everyone but Carl had been on full alert, walking the perimeter around the cabin to make sure no one was around to hear it.

There was a downside, too. The gas tank in the pickup only had a quarter tank of gas, though before they left, Carl drained the generator and managed to add another half gallon to their reserves.

On the morning of the sixth day they ate a quick breakfast and gathered their belongings to leave. Carl, Laurie and Stewart got into the cab of the pickup and Hank climbed into the rear bed. Carl was driving and he started the engine, then let it run for a few seconds until it evened out.

"It's still a shame we don't have more gas in the tank," Carl said as he put the transmission into drive.

"The old guy probably didn't have time to fill her up when he ran from the city," Laurie mused.

"Yeah, probably," Carl agreed. He leaned his head out the window slightly. "You okay back there, Hank?"

"All set, let's go already," Hank said, slapping the side of the truck with his hand. "Get us back to a road we can see on a map and from there we'll make our way to that government bunker." He paused. "That is, if it really exists." It had been a popular topic of discussion while at the cabin and in the end, there could be no resolution, as until they arrived at the location marked on the map, it was all conjecture. But they all agreed it was worth a shot. To find a cache of weapons and food and all kinds of items that could be sold and bartered with...why, the companions could set up their own fiefdom or simply buy one. It was too good to pass up, even if there was a slim chance it was true.

Carl stepped on the gas pedal and the pickup began to roll down the small driveway, and upon reaching its end, Carl had to force the pickup through some overgrown bushes that had been planted to disguise the driveway. From the dirt road it connected to, the driveway was almost entirely invisible. The dead man at the cabin must have planted them when he'd first arrived to hide the cabin from trespassers.

Turning onto the dirt road, the trees were encroaching so far into the road that it was barely wide enough to fit the pickup, and even then the branches brushed against the sides of the vehicle.

The companions left the cabin and the forest behind.

They drove for over two hours before coming to Route 70 and Hank was able to get their bearings and figure out where they were. From there it was simple to follow the map to where the bunker was located.

For a change, the trip was uneventful and the companions only came upon another group of people one time.

Walking in the middle of the road, a group of ten refugees moved to the shoulder to let the pickup truck pass. The group was a mix of men, women and a few children. Three of the adults pulled small carts piled high with what were probably their only belongings. Carl drove slow, his left hand on the steering wheel, his right holding his AUG pistol. Laurie and Stewart also had their weapons ready, though they kept them on their lap where the refugees couldn't see them. In the rear bed, Hank held his G-12 with the muzzle pointed at the sky, but he was ready to level it at a threat if it appeared.

As the pickup rode passed the ten travelers, all the companions could see the hollow eyes, the downtrodden looks cast their way. The entire group was basically wearing rags. The men were carrying firearms, mostly deer rifles and shotguns. They kept them pointed at the ground, though their eyes were alert for danger.

The people watched the pickup warily as it passed them by and Hank locked eyes with one of the men, a burly fellow with dark black hair and a thick beard and mustache. The man nodded at Hank curtly, and in that gesture, volumes were spoken. Hank nodded in reply, then the pickup was past and Hank watched the people recede.

"It's supposed to be around here," Hank said as he stood in the tall grass while holding the open map, the others standing behind him, the pickup fifty yards to the north on a path that could never be considered a road, and even a bike path would have been pushing it. There was no way to actually count, but there had to be a hundred acres of absolutely nothing going off in all directions, rolling hills interspaced with tracks of flat land. They did see a few signs stating that the property was owned by some company none of the group had ever heard of and there were **No Trespassing** signs, too, but there was nothing that said the land was owned by the government.

"I doubt it would simply be out in the open," Stewart said. "It's probably camouflaged somehow."

"Yeah, that's true," Hank agreed. "Okay, guys, everyone split up and check the area, then come back in two hours."

"Two hours isn't much to check all this land, Hank," Carl said.

"I know, but it's a start. If we don't find anything, we'll broaden the search," Hank said.

"Should we go in pairs?" Laurie asked.

Hank shook his head. "There's nothing around here that should be dangerous and it'll take even longer." He gestured to the large field they were in, interspersed with hills of green grass. There wasn't even the hint of human encroachment. "But if you see anything at all that might be dangerous, fire off a shot and we'll all come running."

They each picked a direction and moved off, searching the land for signs of the bunker. It would have helped if they had an idea what they were looking for, but of course, that would have been too easy. A few times Hank checked the map again but it was no help. Once the companions had reached where the X was on the map, the rest was up to them.

They began their search, walking the acres of land, then returning to the pickup truck exhausted and tired hours later. When they met at the pickup late in the afternoon, they rested and ate, then went out again and only stopped when night fell. They made camp there that night, but didn't light a fire, concerned it would be spotted, as the land was so flat in most places. They posted a watch and rotated it so that each of them got a few hours sleep in the bed of the pickup. The next morning they ate quickly and headed out again, crisscrossing the land like surveyors from the old world.

They did this for the entire day. Hank was alone at the west end of the acreage and he was sitting so that his back was pressed against a hill that was about thirty feet tall. The hills were scattered everywhere, and he assumed they were once giant piles of dirt that had been slowly taken over by grass and foliage until becoming small hills. He was ready to call it quits. Obviously the raider that had given him the map had been lying, so desperate to save his life that he would have said anything if he thought Hank might have spared him.

Hank looked at the map one more time, then squeezed it into a ball and shoved it into his pocket. He decided he would walk around the hill and see what was on the other side, and knowing there would only be more grassland, he would then circle around and head back, meet up with the others, and tell them it was time to move on and forget about this pipedream he'd put into their heads.

Getting up with a soft moan from the constant exertion, he slowly strolled around the hill, his eyes always searching for signs of danger.

It was as he was passing the far side of the hill that he stopped cold, and walked closer to it. Where the other sides had been covered with grass and weeds, this side was a flat wall. He went right up to it and tapped it with his knuckles, and was rewarded with a dull thud that said the wall was made of thick metal. He couldn't believe it, he'd found it. He took a few steps back, then some more until he was twenty feet away from the hill and he could entirely take it in. He could barely tell the door was there and he *knew* it was there. Hidden in the grassy hillside was a large metal door painted brown and green to make it blend into the surrounding countryside from a distance. He went closer again and began inspecting the door, then the sides of it. He spent another half hour searching, using his panga to prod the soil until he finally hit something solid on the right side.

Whatever he'd found was about chest height. Scratching at the soil, he was surprised to find a metal box about seven inches in width and length embedded in solid concrete. After clearing it of dirt, he found a latch on the side, and after unlatching it, he opened the metal cover to find a standard numeral keypad hidden within, the numbers back-lit with light so they could be seen in the dark.

Closing the cover, he decided he'd done enough without the others. He climbed on top of the hill and used a dozen twigs and sticks to make a marker so he could find the same hill again easily, then he slid back down on his butt and took off at a ground-eating jog back to the others. He had more than two miles to cover if not more, but he now found he had energy to spare. He couldn't wait to tell the others.

"We could try and blow the door," Carl suggested as he and the other companions stood before the camouflaged door. Behind them, parked as close to the hill as possible, was the pickup truck. There was a trail of crushed grass and tire marks leading to the hill but it couldn't be helped. It had been a hell of a ride, the pickup bouncing into hidden ruts and sometimes threatening to become bogged down in patches of mud. The land might have looked relatively flat but that was when a person was walking. Being in a pickup truck and not a four wheel drive SUV, well, that was entirely different. But eventually they made it to the hill, and it had taken a lot less time than if they had walked.

"That's your answer to everything, Carl," Hank said sarcastically.

"What? Are you crazy?" Stewart asked Carl. "This door must be five inches thick if not more." He banged on it to prove his point, the dull thump coming back.

"Okay, then we could blow the keypad and try to hotwire the thing open," Carl suggested.

Hank shook his head. "I highly doubt the wiring to a government bunker is the same as hotwiring an old Buick, Carl." He pressed a random assortment of numbers on the keypad, as if he would somehow find the correct sequence and the door would magically open. When he pressed the 'enter' button, the keypad let out an annoying sound, then returned to normal. "I think we have to face facts. We found the bunker but without the access code it was all for nothing."

"So what now?" Laurie asked. "We just leave? Knowing there's probably all kinds of stuff we could use in there?"

Hank shrugged. "I don't know what else there is to do."

"I do, we could blow the door," Carl said again. He pulled put a block of C-4 he'd been saving. "This should do the trick."

Hank bit his lip as he eyed the C-4. He looked at Stewart. "He may have a point, Stewart. It's worth a shot."

"If you want to try it then fine, but I know it won't work," Stewart said. "This is solid metal with a heavy steel frame. No doubt the entire hill is reinforced cement many feet thick and the grass is only a covering. But if you want to try, I won't protest."

"Okay then, Carl, let's do this," Hank said. "Everyone in the pickup and we'll move a good distance away to watch. Carl, put five minutes on the detonator. I don't want to take any chances." He gestured to the C-4. "Use the whole block on the seams. We'll only get one shot at this; might as well make it count."

"Gothcha," Carl said and got to work.

A few minutes later he was finished, the C-4 now lining the seams of the door on the left and right sides from the ground to head height. He set the detonator, ran to the pickup, and hopped into the rear bed with the others.

In the driver's seat, Hank drove the pickup around to the far side of the hill, then stopped and got out of the cab to wait, the others climbing out of the rear bed to stand with him.

The minutes ticked by and finally there was a massive explosion, and smoke billowed up from the far side of the hill from where the companions were. It was so powerful the ground shook as the shockwave rolled out over the land.

Hank waited a full thirty seconds and then everyone climbed into the rear bed and he drove the pickup back to the metal door.

"Shit, will you look at that," Carl said, scratching his head as he took off his baseball cap.

The smoke cloud mixed with dust was almost cleared, and as the companions admired Carl's handiwork, they each stared in amazement as the result of an entire block of C-4.

"See, I told you it wouldn't work, though I must admit, I wished to be proved wrong in this particular situation," Stewart said as he studied the hill and door. The metal door was perfectly fine, only some scratches and scorch marks on the paint to even show there had been an explosion. The dirt and grass that covered the sides of the hill near the doorframe hadn't fared as well and now there were many places where the white of concrete could be seen. The concrete was also unmarred, other than scorch marks.

"Shit, I was positive that it would've worked," Carl said, disgusted.

"So that's it, right? We're done here?" Laurie asked, the disappointment in her voice prevalent to all.

Stewart walked over to the door again. The ground was now churned up ten feet before it and he had to step carefully. He opened the keypad cover again to stare at the pad. It had been unharmed from the explosion as it was recessed into the wall of the hill and the blast had gone nowhere near it. Stewart studied the pad as he rubbed his chin in deep thought.

The others joined him a few seconds later and Hank patted the older man's shoulder. "Come on, old friend, it's time to get going. This was a bust, though I hate to admit it."

"Maybe not," Stewart said. "Hank, do you still have the map you showed us before?"

Hank reached into his pocket and pulled out the balled-up crushed map. He tossed the paper ball to Stewart, who caught it easily. The older man opened it and smoothed it out on the door.

The metal was slightly warm to the touch but not hot. It was so thick even the heat of the explosion couldn't penetrate it.

"These numbers," Stewart said, pointing to the bottom of the map. "Did you by chance try and input them into the keypad?"

"No, why?" Hank asked, and then his eyes went wide when Stewart's suggestion became clear. "Oh shit, you don think…"

"Why not? The Guardsmen the raider tortured must have known the numerical sequence and he give it to the raider under torture." He turned around to face the keypad after reading the numbers again, then began to type them in. "Let's see if my hunch is correct?"

As he typed in the last numeral and pressed the 'enter' button, the keypad let out a high-pitched siren and then the door began to rumble, dirt and debris from the hill raining down on the companions. They all jumped back and watched in awe as the giant metal door slowly began to move downward to recede into the ground. It hesitated for one brief second, which was thanks to one side of the frame being slightly knocked off plumb from the explosion, but then the door squealed past that section and continued moving downward.

As it did, Hank was able to see the thickness of the door and he was amazed to see it was nearly a foot thick. Stewart had been right. There was no way conventional weapons would ever blow that door open.

There was a loud rumbling of hydraulic gears as the door finally settled into the ground and a waft of stale air came out of what basically looked like a large cavern.

Hank was the first one to walk up to the entrance and look inside to see total darkness. He leaned in cautiously over the threshold but nothing happened. Then he glanced back at the others, shrugged, and took one step over the threshold. As soon as he did, fluorescent lights came on along both sides of what he could now see was a long tunnel—motion sensors were hidden at the door-frames, he figured. The ground slanted sharply down, the ramp then curving to the right so there was no way to see what was around the bend. In many ways it reminded him of a parking garage ramp.

The others joined him to peer into the tunnel.

"Well, the door's open. What's next?" Laurie asked.

"That's simple, isn't it?" Hank said. "We either go in and check it out or stay put here and never know what's down there."

"Then I say we go inside," Laurie said.

"Perhaps we should wait a bit," Stewart suggested as he studied the large tunnel. He didn't know why, but a chill went down his back to see the empty tunnel leading into the unknown. It reminded him of Dante's Inferno, where the ramp would lead into the bowels of Hell itself.

Suddenly, the roar of engines sounded from behind them and the four warriors spun around to see an assortment of seven vehicles coming right for them at high speed. Each vehicle was loaded with men. Two were pickup trucks with M-60s mounted to their rear beds with gunners holding on. As soon as the first gunner felt he was in range, he immediately began firing, sending a stream of death directly at the companions.

"Shit!" Hank yelled as bullets ricocheted all around the group, some entering the tunnel to hit the far wall. "That explosion alerted people we were here." He leveled his G-12 and returned fire, but there was nowhere to go for cover except into the tunnel and he wasn't ready to commit to that just yet. A second later, the pickup truck the companions had arrived in was struck with a barrage of gunfire and the gas tank was hit. Though there wasn't much fuel left in the gas tank, it was still more than enough to ignite the fuel and the vehicle erupted into a ball of flame, pushing the companions back into the tunnel. With the fiery wreck now partially concealing them from the attacking raiders, the companions used this to their advantage and poured on the firepower, taking down a few men as the vehicles zipped by the opening.

One vehicle—a jeep—filled to overflowing with men, drove right at the tunnel opening, the men screaming and whooping as they fired their weapons. Hank stitched the grille and then shifted his aim to the right front tire. When the jeep was less than twenty-five feet away, and before it would have barreled right into the tunnel, the tire blew and the rim hit a rut in the ground. The jeep was stopped cold and the back end flipped over to bring it down on its top, crushing the men within. The screams of battle changed to one of pain as the crushed men tried to free themselves. Laurie fired one shot into the now exposed gas tank on the undercarriage of the jeep and it erupted into a blazing fireball, cooking the men trapped within. The screams stopped soon enough.

"We can't hold them back forever!" Carl yelled. "Sooner or later they're gonna get in here!"

"I agree," Stewart said. "These men got here quick. They must have been watching this bunker and waiting for government envoys or someone like us to get it open. They want this as bad as we do."

"So what do we do?" Laurie asked and shot a man in the head as a pickup truck zipped by. The man had been in the rear bed, holding the ammo belt to the M-60. His head snapped back and he fell off the vehicle to land in the grass. Another jeep was right behind the pickup and it rolled over the fallen man, breaking the back of the now twice dead man.

Hank knew exactly what they had to do, though it made his gut flip-flop. They had to get the bunker door closed. It would seal them inside, but it would also stop the raiders from getting in. The companions only had so much ammunition and the raiders could easily keep them pinned down while they went back for reinforcements, or if they came at the companions all at once, there was no way they could be stopped from getting inside. So far, the raiders had been cautious and weren't risking a full-on blitz, and though Hank was hesitant, he knew there was no choice. "We need to get this door closed, and right fucking now!" He sent a spray of bullets at a car with pieces from five different models holding it together. The side of the car was stitched from front to rear bumper but it suffered no further damage.

"I'm on it," Stewart said and he ran to the other side of the tunnel—the same side the keypad was located on the outside. He was guessing but he'd guessed right and there was another key-pad there, too. From memory he typed in the same number that was used on the outside pad and pressed the 'enter' button. At first nothing happened, and he was about call out to Hank that it didn't look like the door would be closing any time soon when the ground beneath his feet began to rumble and then, ever so slowly, as an alarm sounded and red lights in the ceiling flashed, the door began to rise. The raiders, seeing this, renewed their efforts and began to drive directly at the closing door.

"We have to hold them off for a few more seconds!" Hank yelled and sprayed the radiator of an old Ford pickup. Steam erupted from the engine but the truck kept coming.

Carl fired at a red SUV that had no roof, the lack of one allow-ing the men inside to stand up and shoot easier. Carl sprayed the car, hitting three of the men inside it, but the driver ducked down and avoided being hit, though the already cracked windshield became a mesh of fractures.

The door was closing far too slowly for Hank's liking but it wasn't like he could do anything about it. He emptied the clip on his G-12, and he let it hang from its strap and drew his SIG-Sauer. He shot the driver of the SUV when the man's head popped back up to see where he was going and the vehicle began to swerve.

Only it swerved into another jeep coming at the tunnel and bounced off it and righted itself, all without a driver. The SUV was coming right for the tunnel entrance, though out of control. Inside it, the surviving men had no idea their driver was dead as they continued shooting, or the danger they were in.

"Shit, this is gonna be close!" Hank yelled as the door slowly inched up, each second of waiting torture to watch. If he thought it would have helped, he would have run to the door and began using his own weight to force it up faster.

When the door was four feet off the ground, the companions all backed away from it, staying close to the walls of the tunnel but knowing they needed to get away from the opening. When the door was six feet up, the sound of crashing, rending metal came from the other side as well as screams of pain as the SUV drove head-on into the door at full speed. Smoke and fire rose up to be seen in the opening above the door as it inexorably crept upward. A second later, the second vehicle struck the door. One of them had exploded on impact from a ruptured fuel line. In the shrinking opening as the door still rumbled closed, a severed head came flying into the tunnel, droplets of blood spraying out in all directions. It landed and rolled down the ramp, around the bend, and was lost from sight.

On the ramp itself, the line of sunlight was slowly becoming smaller as the door ponderously moved up into its frame. Then, finally, with a loud thud, it seated into the roof, and the cessation of all sound and light was cut off from the outside. It was as if Hank had gone deaf, and he was wondering if it was true when Carl let out a loud yell of happiness and the others began to laugh, relieved they were safe for the moment.

"Damn it, Hank, that was too close for my liking," Carl said and Hank had to agree that the man was right. If the door hadn't closed, it would have been all over for them. Even if they had tried to run down the ramp, the raiding party could have easily followed and taken them down, as there was no place to seek cover. Their escape was one for the record books, he had to admit.

"So, we're inside the bunker, as amazing as that seems," Laurie said. "I know I keep saying this, but what next?"

Hank went over and hugged her, then gave her a kiss on the forehead. "You're just saying what we've all been thinking, baby. And to answer you, we follow this ramp down and see where it goes. But we need to stay sharp, we don't know what's down there." He pointed to a small camera mounted to the wall near the ceiling. "There's more than only that one. Look, they're every ten feet or so. We don't know if someone's watching us right now."

"Then let's go say hi," Carl said and raised his pistol. "I want to thank them for helping us out just now." He meant it sarcastically and the others nodded in agreement.

Hank took the lead, and while hugging the tunnel wall, they slowly crept down the ramp to see what was below. When they came upon the severed head, Carl kicked it again, and watched it roll further down the ramp.

Hank frowned at his actions but Carl only flashed him a smile.

As the companions' footsteps faded away, at the top of the bunker door, a long digital panel lit up. Numbers blinked to life and began counting down. Years, days, months, weeks, hours, minutes and seconds were clearly displayed.

The counter began at one hundred years.

The companions walked for ten minutes until coming to the next level. On the wall was a large number one. Crossing a wide-open space that had thick, round stone pillars for supporting the level above, they came to a simple steel door the size of a front door to a suburban home.

"What do you think?" Hank asked the others.

"What's to think? We have to go inside," Laurie said, the others agreeing with her.

"Okay, me first, and if it's safe, you guys follow me." Hank pressed the center bar on the door and it opened easily, then carefully peering inside and satisfied it was empty, he pushed open the door and charged in, then stayed low. The lights flicked on as he did this and he went from darkness to bright light so fast he couldn't see. It was a tense few seconds as his eyes adjusted, and if an enemy had been there waiting, he would have been vulnerable. When his vision was clear he saw he was in a long hallway devoid of any wall fixtures, only the ceiling lights marring the starkness. Returning to the doorway, he told the others to enter.

Once more they moved down the hallway until coming to an elevator. Hank looked at the others, who nodded, and he pressed the call button. There was the sound of hydraulics and cables and a half minute later the elevator opened with a soft ding.

All four warriors had their weapons leveled at the elevator, and when it was seen to be empty, they actually felt a little foolish. It was becoming apparent there was no one else in the massive bunker.

Stepping into the elevator, they found there were five floors, and not knowing what each floor was for, Hank simply pressed the button for four. The doors closed and they dropped down smoothly.

When the doors slid open and they exited, they found out that four was the motor pool.

"Holy shit, will you look at that?" Carl gasped as he stared at the two rows of shiny new black Humvees. Each one had a brand new M-60 mounted to its roof, and an opening in the roof where the gunner would be positioned.

They were armored too, and had large thick tires that looked puncture proof. The exhaust pipes were vertical, so that the Humvees could go through water without the risk of stalling.

The companions went in pairs of two to investigate, finding condensed fuel and a full service bay with every tool imaginable. It was something neither of them thought they would ever see again.

"It looks like when we leave here it's gonna be in style," Hank said to Laurie as he rubbed the fender of a Humvee. The machine looked brand new, not so much as a scratch on the dark paint. "Jesus, we're set for life with all of this."

"Hank, come over here, you'll want to see this," Stewart called from the other side of the large room. "Have the others come, too."

A few minutes later, everyone was gathered around Stewart, who was standing in front of a map of the facility, which was behind plexiglass and mounted to the wall.

"According to this map," Stewart said, "We're on level four as you already know, which is the mechanics bay and motor pool. Five is for the nuke generator that runs this place. Level three is the armory and research laboratories. Two is for the sleeping quarters, a gym, a cafeteria, a large media room and for laundry, and Level one is for offices, conference rooms and communications."

"I want to see the armory," Carl said excitedly.

"We should see about the cafeteria first," Laurie added.

"What about communications?" Stewart asked. "Surely we might be able to contact someone in the military. Maybe it's not all gone after all."

"Whoa, everyone slow down for a second," Hank said with his hands in the air, palms out. "We'll check everything. But first we need to make sure we're absolutely alone here. For all we know, we'll enter somewhere and have a squadron of soldiers with M-16s staring us down."

"Sorry, Hank, you're right," Carl said. "That's true. I guess I got a little carried away."

"No need to apologize," Hank replied. "I feel the same way. So let's go check out the other levels first and then we'll see what to do afterward."

"Hank, I have a suggestion," Stewart said. "Why don't we split up into two groups. Even if there were people here, surely groups of two over four won't matter very much. And we can cover more ground."

Hank considered it and then nodded. "Sounds good."

Carl's eyes lit up. "Hey, I have a better idea. You guys stay right here, I'll be right back." Before anyone could say anything, he ran off to one of the bays, and returned a few minutes later with something in his hands. "I saw these earlier. Two-way radios and they're fully charged. They were in their slots to be charged and it kept their battery level up all this time, like a trickle charger I guess. We can stay in contact in case of trouble." He handed one to each of them. "Go to channel seven so we're all on the same frequency."

Everyone did and then tested the radios. They worked fine.

"Okay," Hank said when they were done. "We might as well start looking now." He gave each of them a floor, and when everyone knew where they were going, they all went to the elevator and got in.

Hank and Laurie were together and Carl and Stewart were the second team. Hank pressed the appropriate buttons and the elevator moved up to the next floor. Carl and Stewart got off on level three and with a wave, the doors closed.

Hank pressed the button for level two and the elevator began to move again, and when the doors opened, Hank glanced at Laurie and with her ascent, they stepped out to investigate.

Two hours later, the companions were gathered at the motor pool again as it was familiar territory for all of them. There was a small office off the first bay and it was there that they sat and talked about what they'd found as they searched the complex.

Mounted on the far wall of the motor pool, in a place where it could be seen easily, was a long rectangular box with red digital numbers on it. No one paid it any attention, as there was no need to; nor did they know what it was for.

"Well, the good news is the armory is fully stocked," Carl said and Stewart nodded. "There's ammo for every gun you can think of and a few I'd never even heard of before today. There's crates of grenades of all types and get this, even two crates of LAWs. Shit, I even found a flamethrower." He paused. "One thing I thought was weird is that there's no dust on anything."

"I think I know the reason for that," Stewart said. "I believe this complex has air purifiers that constantly filter the air of airborne particles, and due to this, there is no dust. It's probably all tied in to the heating and air conditioning system."

"Makes sense, I suppose," Carl agreed.

Stewart smiled in reply, glad he was of help. "Well, while Carl checked out the armory, I went to the laboratories," Stewart explained. "It was about what you'd expect to find in labs, but there was one room that was truly massive with over a hundred adult size contraptions that sort of looked like tanning beds. I read a little from one of the notebooks I found on a desk and it says that the things are hibernation chambers."

"You mean like what happened to Walt Disney? They say he was cryogenically frozen somewhere," Carl said, though he was being sarcastic.

"Well, I suppose that's the same principle," Stewart replied, not picking up on the sarcasm. "But from what I read, these chambers are more like stasis chambers that slow down your body to the point you barely age at all. There's nothing that has to do with being frozen."

"What are they all for?" Laurie asked, curious.

Hank shrugged. "No way of knowing why they were there. Maybe they didn't have enough supplies for everyone when they arrived and some were going to be put in stasis."

"Yes, Hank, that was my assumption, too," Stewart said.

"Makes sense," Carl agreed. "But then, where is everyone? It's like they set this place up and never got here."

"I think that's exactly what happened," Hank said. "When the bombs fell, it must have happened so fast that no one in the government that was supposed to come here ever made it." He sighed. "And we have some bad news." He looked at Laurie to go ahead and say what they'd found when searching together.

She turned to Carl and Stewart, her face grim. "There's no food in the cafeteria, I mean nothing. Not even a cracker. The vending machines were never stocked either. There's running water so we have that and can shower and drink it, but there's nothing to eat."

Carl and Stewart both looked at each other and then the others.

"So you mean the only food we have is what we brought in with us?" Carl asked.

Hank nodded. "I'm afraid so, and that's not much either. Laurie was carrying her pack with her as you know but the rest of our stuff was still in the pickup truck when it exploded, so we don't have much."

Carl crossed his arms. "Then we'll just have to leave sooner than we planned. We can load up one of the Humvees with as much guns and ammo as we can carry and then head out. If those raiders are still out there, they're in for a fucking big surprise."

"I have to say you're right on that one," Hank agreed. "But we don't have to rush, there's plenty of water to drink and Laurie has enough food for a few days if we ration it."

She grinned. "You're all lucky I was the one carrying the beef jerky."

"In one of the labs, I found a few cabinets full of vitamins and stimulants to keep us going, too," Stewart added. "Though I won't look forward to later, after we stop and have to come down off the high of taking them."

"Still, it'll keep us going before we starve. Remember, once we leave here we'll still have to find food first thing, and there wasn't much out there before."

"I have a feeling in a day or two I'm going to be dreaming about eating more of Carl's fried kudzu," Stewart said with a slight grin.

"Ha, I knew you liked it, you old fart," Carl laughed. "Well, we haven't searched every nook and cranny of this place yet. Maybe we'll find a box of cookies hiding somewhere."

Hank stood up. "Okay, Carl and Stewart, you get busy down here preparing one of the Humvees and later we can all go to the armory together and take what we want, but right now I'm gonna take Laurie with me to level one and see if there's anything there worth taking."

"Okay," Carl said and Stewart agreed.

"Oh, and guys," Hank said as he was about to leave with Laurie.

"Yeah?" Carl asked.

"The showers even have hot water so when we're done for to-day, we can all take long hot showers."

"I for one am going to be thinking of that for the rest of the day," Stewart said with a wide smile. "These old bones could use a water massage."

"I know what you mean," Hank said. "At least we have that to look forward to."

The elevator doors opened on level one and Hank and Laurie stepped out into a long corridor with their guns leading the way. Once more there was no one to greet them. It was unsettling the way the entire bunker was empty.

"Where should we go first?" she asked.

Hank shrugged. "Pick a door and we'll use it," he said simply. She did and they entered an office with the standard amount of furniture and a picture of the President of the United States on the far wall.

"Check the desk and I'll check the file cabinets," Hank said.

Laurie did so but there was nothing of use. Hank pulled out files by the handfuls and dropped them on the floor. Nothing of value was found unless he needed kindling to start a fire.

"Let's try another one," he said and they left.

In the next office they found nothing either and the same was said for the following five more. In the sixth one, Laurie opened a drawer and found a handful of old, stale candy bars that were as hard as a rock but still edible. Hank found a bottle of scotch in the bottom drawer of a file cabinet. It wasn't much but it was better than what they had before.

When they finished searching as many offices as they thought was necessary, they went to the communications room. Panels had lights flickering on them but the gear was far too complicated for either Hank or Laurie to decipher. There was a large rectangular panel over the main screen with red digital numbers; some were counting down but he didn't pay them much attention. It was just more flickering lights to him.

As they left the room, he felt a little silly. What was he thinking? That there would be something like a ham radio that he would pick up a microphone, press a button and talk into it? It didn't matter anyway; there was no one to talk to outside. He did find a computer printout of the United States that had circles of where other bunkers were supposed to be. This he folded and put into his pocket. It might come in handy if they were in trouble and near one of them, that is if they could find it as they were all probably hidden. But if those bunkers had no food supplies either, they would only be good for safety, not long term survival.

"Come on, let's go back to the others and see how they're doing. Then we can eat and relax for the remainder of the day," Hank said. "We'll take tomorrow to rest up and search some more, and then on the following morning we'll roll out and leave this place behind."

"We'll be fine, Hank," Laurie said. "And just think; if we need a place to hole up and are in the area, we can always come back here. We just need to make sure to bring our own food."

"Yeah, that's true. I have to tell you, it's sure gonna be nice to sleep tonight and know we don't have to post a watch."

"I know, right? This is about the safest place we'll probably ever be," she said.

When Hank and Laurie returned to Carl and Stewart in the motor pool, they were pleased to see that the two men had been busy.

"And all we need is to get whatever guns and ammo we want to bring with us and we're all set to go," Carl explained as he patted the Humvee he had pulled out of the line and parked near the elevator. "I made plenty of room in the rear to stuff lots of gear."

"The tank is topped off and there are two extra cans of condensed fuel in the back," Stewart said. "We can go a long way with what we have." He was practically beaming.

"That sounds great," Hank said. "Laurie found some old candy bars and look what I found." He held up the bottle of scotch, and when Carl smiled, he handed it to him. "For you two for the hard work you've done."

"Thanks, Hank, really, but don't you want to share it?"

"Nah, while you and Stewart are enjoying that, me and Laurie are gonna take some alone time."

"You boys don't mind, do you?" Laurie asked with a wink.

Carl blushed and Stewart looked at his feet. "No, of course not, you two deserve some private time."

"Good, so what say we go see where we're gonna sleep tonight, then we can wash our clothes in the laundry room, eat, shower and call it a night," Hank said. "Oh, and when me and Laurie were checking out the sleeping quarters we found lockers full of brand new BDUs still sealed in plastic; underwear and socks, too."

"Fantastic, I could use a new pair of underwear and the holes in my socks have holes in them," Carl said.

"Well, I for one have been going commando for far too long. It will be good to wear the appropriate undergarments for a change," Stewart added.

"Too much information, Stewart," Hank laughed and Carl looked like he was about to throw up.

The four warriors went to the elevator together, and as the doors slid open, they stepped inside.

"Carl, where are the keys to the Humvee?" Hank asked.

"In the ignition," Carl replied. "Why, do you think I should hold onto them? I doubt if anyone's gonna jack our ride down here."

"Yeah, good point. No, they're fine where they are. I was just curious."

The doors closed on the elevator and it began to rise.

It was a few hours later and the companions had all eaten lightly—but had consumed enough water to fill a swimming pool to make up for their lack of food—and had made a temporary home in one of the sleeping quarters.

Each section was set up like a large hospital ward with one door leading to the hallway, and in the back were showers for that section. There was another exit leading to fire stairs off the showers. There were also three washers and dryers in a small room off the showers, so the group didn't have to wash their clothes in the larger, industrial machines in the main laundry room. They decided to only wash their jackets. They kept those as they were a part of them, as well as their footwear, but everything else would be tossed and replaced with new BDUs. Laurie hated to get rid of her leather outfit, but it was sweat-soaked and filthy and even she accepted that it was time for a change. At least she still had her boots with the silver plating on the tips.

Carl and Stewart had gone first into the shower room and the two had spent over forty minutes bathing in the hot water in separate stalls. Somewhere in the bunker there had to be a massive water heater, for no matter how long they bathed, the hot water never lost its temperature.

Both men walked into the main room looking like prunes. Stewart's white hair was plastered to his head and it made everyone laugh. He wrapped a towel around his head and joined in.

Hank and Laurie were sitting on one of the beds, waiting for the other two men to finish bathing. They could have gone to another room entirely but they wanted to stay together, especially when doing something like showering, which left a person highly vulnerable to attack. So it was better to shower in pairs and know your friends had your back.

As Carl and Stewart approached Hank and Laurie, Carl winked at Hank. "It's all yours, Hank, we left you some hot water, too."

"Thanks, Carl you're all right," Hank smiled.

Carl patted Stewart's arm. "Come on, old timer, I found a deck of cards in the motor pool and we have that bottle of scotch Hank found. What do you say to a game of poker?"

"I prefer blackjack," Stewart said flatly.

Carl chuckled. "Fine, blackjack it is." He glanced at Hank. "We'll be at the other end of the room, near the door, if you or Laurie needs us."

"Okay, sounds good. But I doubt we're gonna need you for a while." Hank stood up and Laurie joined him.

Carl nodded knowingly, and was more than a little envious. Hank was going to spend time with Laurie, a beautiful blonde, while he was stuck with Stewart. With Stewart prattling in Carl's ear about the odds of blackjack, the two men walked away.

"You ready for that shower?" Hank asked Laurie as he held her close.

"You have no idea," she breathed heavily and kissed him passionately on the mouth. Arm and arm, they walked into the already steam-filled shower room and began to undress.

The water spray felt incredible to Hank, as it massaged his sore body and relaxed him. Putting his face under the spray, he closed his eyes and rubbed his cheeks with his palms. He needed a shave but didn't care right now. He could feel the exhaustion melting away with each drop of water that hit him. He felt the stress of always being in danger fade to a distant memory.

There was no soap to use but the water was more than doing the job of getting him clean, as it sluiced down his muscular body.

As he turned to let the spray hit his shoulders, he winced slightly when the water struck the bullet wound he'd received at the roadblock. Reaching up, he touched it gingerly, but was pleased to see it wasn't inflamed. He'd always been a fast healer.

Opening his mouth, he let the water trickle in and he swallowed some of it. He wasn't very thirsty though, after drinking what must have been two gallons of tap water at dinner to make up for their low food stores. He was just glad that the bunker had fresh water, if not, the companions' situation might have been far worse than it was now. At least they could rest for a few days before heading back out into the harsh world.

He was pulled from his reverie when a pair of soft, shapely arms wrapped themselves around him and he felt the press of perfect breasts against his back.

"What are you thinking about, lover?" Laurie asked from behind him, her voice husky with arousal.

Hank could feel her hard nipples pressing into his back. "Nothing important," he replied then leaned back into her some more. Her hands roamed over his chest, then slid down to his muscled abdomen. He was already aroused himself, his member standing at attention the second he felt her press up against him.

With the water cascading over them, she slowly let her hands slide down until one hand cupped his balls and the other began to stroke his shaft. He moaned with pleasure, his eyes closed.

"Easy, baby," he breathed heavily. "It's been a while. This grenade is gonna go off pretty damn quick."

"That's okay," she said and stepped around Hank so she was before him. "Let's get this one out of the way so the next one will last a while." She grinned. "I plan on enjoying this to the fullest." She went to her knees and slowly took the head of his member into her mouth, her hands wrapped around the shaft. Hank felt his knees go weak from the sensation. For just one moment, there was no world outside, only the exquisite pleasure he was experiencing.

Slowly at first, and then faster, Laurie began to move her head up and down, taking his member in as far as she could. He could feel the tip of his dick hitting the back of her throat and he felt himself building and knew he wasn't going to hold off for much longer. Her lips wrapped around him, sucking him hard, taking almost all of him deep into her mouth, and with a grunt and a moan, he felt himself release into her waiting mouth.

Laurie didn't stop, her head going even faster as he thrust his hips forward. She cradled his balls and began to slow down, then she pulled back, his member popping out of her mouth. She rubbed her lips and cheek against his dick as his seed slid from her mouth to fall to the tiles where the water took it to the drain.

He leaned over and pulled her up and nibbled her neck as she moaned in pleasure.

"Now it's your turn, baby," he whispered and pushed her against the wall of the shower. He went to his knees and kissed her stomach, then slid his tongue lower until he was only an inch from her sex. With the water rolling down her beautiful breasts, he shoved his tongue deep inside her, then pulled back and sucked on her clit, which caused her to giggle in ecstasy. He looked up and saw that her head was thrown back, her eyes closed, her lips parted slightly as she enjoyed his tongue. Her wet blonde hair was flattened onto her skull and it draped over her shoulders, her nipples rock hard.

Closing his own eyes, Hank let his tongue explore her, relishing the taste of her as the water washed away it each time his tongue touched her. His hands slid up her flat stomach to cup each breast and he pinched her nipples, his head moving back and forth to go as deep as his tongue possibly could.

Then he felt her legs tense and his head became trapped within her thighs like it was within a steel vice. For just a few moments he couldn't breathe as Laurie cried out in a powerful orgasm, shaking slightly. When it passed, she released his head and he pulled back, sucking in air and coughing. She knelt down and kissed him passionately, unaware of the smothering she had given him. He wasn't going to tell her.

While his tongue had been deep within her with, his dick had been slowly coming back to life for round two, and by the time she'd orgasmed, he was rock hard once more.

Taking her in his arms, he laid her down on the tiles, and as he lifted her legs up into the air, he placed his arms on each side of her and positioned himself between her legs.

"Give it to me, lover. I want to feel you inside me," she whispered and raised her head up and kissed him, her tongue sliding between his teeth to dance with his tongue. He did as asked and pushed forward, sliding his member deep within her, feeling the exquisite sensation as she squeezed him tight and held him close.

Together, the two began to move with one another, a rhythm they knew well, and as the water fell across Hank's back and then onto her, two souls became one.

Time faded away as they grunted and groaned in pleasure, then finally Hank could hold back no more and he erupted inside her, filling her with his seed once more. Laurie bucked her hips and arced her back as an orgasm even stronger than the last one rocked her body. When it passed, she went limp and he slid off her to lay beside her, one arm draped over his body to cup one firm breast.

"That was incredible," she breathed.

"Glad you're pleased," he said.

"Oh don't worry, lover, if I'm ever not, you'll be the first to know." She smiled and he laughed.

She turned onto her side and looked at him, her hand caressing his cheek, then sliding to the bullet wound on his shoulder. "Does it hurt?"

"No, it's fine, barely a scratch."

"You were lucky….again. One day your luck is gonna run out."

"Maybe, but that day isn't today so let's not talk about it." He leaned forward and kissed her, their tongues dancing back and forth, then he sat up. "I'm gonna be a prune if I stay in this shower any longer."

"Then let's get out. I think I'm nice and clean." She flashed him a knowing smile. "Inside and out I might add."

He turned off the water and dried off, then padded into the section with beds. At the far end of the room in a bed each, near the door that led out to the rest of the level, Stewart and Carl were already sleeping, the bottle of scotch empty, the lights in the ceiling turned off. There were small red bulbs still on at the junction of the wall and ceiling though. The door leading out had been barricaded with three beds and a chair. Hank nodded approval at that. They had discussed that earlier. Instead of posting a guard this night, which seemed unnecessary, they had decided to barricade the door. The door in the back that went to the fire stairs could only be opened from the inside so there was no threat there.

Hank and Laurie pushed two beds together and climbed under the sheets, another thing found in the lockers, along with blankets.

The temperature inside the bunker was a comfortable seventy degrees though and only sheets were needed.

As Laurie curled up next to Hank with her back to him, naked and clean, he kissed the back of her neck softly, then began to explore her body with his free hand, his rough palm caressing her breasts before sliding down over her flat stomach to gently rub the velvety softness between her thighs. Now that they were out of the water and dry, her body felt even better, the hot water not a distraction.

Before he realized it, he found he was erect once more.

"Again?" she breathed when she felt him pushing gently against her buttocks.

"If you're up to it," he whispered in reply.

"Lover, I'm always up for it." She pushed her butt harder towards his member and lifted her leg slightly so he had access, then with them spooning, he slid into her, and this time they made slow, passionate love, where there was no rush and only the others' happiness was the concern. When he orgasmed, he had to bury his face in the pillow or risk alerting Carl and Stewart to what was going on at the other end of the room. When he felt the sensation fade and he slowly slid out of her, she sighed and turned her head so she could see him. "I love you," she said and kissed him once more, then she rolled over and was asleep in seconds.

Hank laid his head down on the pillow, her hair caressing his face. "Me too, baby. Me too." With the love of his life held tightly in his arms, he drifted off to sleep.

The following day was spent exploring the bunker some more. Unfortunately not much else was found, and now there was no question that the companions were totally alone inside the underground complex. Stewart kept busy by poking around the research labs, reading notes and manuals. Laurie and Hank made love many times that day as they snuck off to be alone. Carl spent most of his time in the armory, and after picking the choicest weapons and ammunition to take, he'd gathered it all into a neat pile so that the group could bring it down to the motor pool and load into the Humvee. But that chore only took a few hours and the rest of the day was for leisure.

One thing they did often was shower, relishing the hot water, something none of them thought they would be able to enjoy this much again. A few towns they'd come across might have showers, but it was usually because of a water tower or something similar on the roof of the building and then the water was never warm let alone hot, but usually freezing cold.

When the second morning finally came and they were loaded up in the Humvee and ready to move out, they were sad to leave, but their grumbling stomachs made it that much easier to move on. The bunker would have been paradise if the food stores had been in the cafeteria freezer, walk-ins and dry food lockers.

But with no food there really was no other option but to depart. Now in brand new BDUs and all their weapons gleaming with fresh oil and carrying plenty of ammunition for their weapons, they felt ready to take on the world once more.

"Okay, Carl, fire her up and let's get going," Hank said from the back of the Humvee, the others all in agreement. Carl did as he was told. The powerful eight cylinder engine started on the first try. Putting the vehicle in gear, Carl headed for the ramp that would lead them up to the massive steel door and the outside world.

"You think those guys are still out there?" Carl asked while following the ramp heading upward.

"If there are, they're in for a big surprise," Hank replied while patting the M-60 mounted to the roof of the Humvee.

"If I was them I'd stay out there for a few days easy, maybe even a week," Stewart said.

"How do you think they know about the bunker?" Laurie asked.

Hank shrugged then winced slightly. Now that his shoulder wound was healing, shrugging wasn't something he should do. "They probably found the hidden door by accident and figured it had to be for something valuable. Then they made sure to keep an eye on it in case someone showed up. We got lucky they didn't arrive before we'd got the door open."

No one replied to that, knowing what might have happened. Though most people were still good, there were many that weren't ruled by morality and such ideas as right or wrong, good and evil, were irrelevant. All they worried about was taking what they wanted. Of course, the world had been like that even before the bombs fell but now, there were even less people to stop those tyrants than before.

The Humvee followed a bend in the ramp, and then the headlights were illuminating the large outer door. Above the door, the digital display was still counting down but once more, none of the companions noticed it, all too focused on leaving.

"Stewart, why don't you do the honors of opening the door, seems you did it before," Hank said.

"Gladly," Stewart said. "Just keep the car door open. As soon as that door starts to go down, I want to be inside here with you. If there are people out there, it's going to get hairy."

"Will do," Hank said, knowing what he meant. No matter how many people and vehicles were waiting for them outside, they had no choice but to leave. To stay meant starvation, and if they had to fight to get through a blockade, then so be it.

"Okay, people, it's time to get hard. Battle stations and all that shit." Hank climbed up through the opening in the roof and readied the M-60. If there was even a hint of people outside, he planned on shooting first and then running like hell.

Stewart climbed out and walked over to the keypad, the numerical sequence memorized. It wasn't hard and he'd always been good with numbers. He'd never saved any phone numbers to his cell phone back when such things mattered. Any number he used often he quickly committed to memory. It was the same with passwords for his computer. Stewart had been a man not afraid of change and had embraced the computer revolution when he was first exposed to it. In the Humvee, Carl revved the engine, as he prepared for the coming battle that was sure to be waiting for the group. Swallowing hard, Stewart typed in the sequence and pressed the 'enter' button, then turned and ran back to the Humvee, jumping inside as the door slammed closed behind him thanks to Laurie. Nothing happened and the four warriors waited, assuming there was some sort of delay.

"What the fuck, Stewart?" Carl said finally, aggravated.

"I don't know, maybe I didn't enter the correct code. Let me try again." Stewart opened the door of the Humvee and got out, then walked back to the keypad. He took a second to make sure he had the right sequence, then typed it in and pressed the 'enter' button again, then once more dashed back to the Humvee.

The door still remained closed.

"I don't understand," Stewart said. "Hank, give me that map again, please. I want to double check the numbers on the bottom."

Hank handed him the folded map and Stewart opened it and read the numbers, his lips moving as he did. "I did type in the proper sequence."

"Then why isn't the fucking door opening?" Carl demanded, his hands gripping the steering wheel tightly, his knuckles white.

That was when Hank really got a look at the digital display for the first time. He'd seen it when first getting into position at the

M-60 but he hadn't really cared. The bunker had numbers all over the place and when he thought back, he remembered seeing the same display in a few other places, such as the communications room and on the wall in the motor pool.

"Hey, guys, what do you make of that sign above the door? The one with all the numbers?"

Carl leaned forward so he could see up through the windshield. "Oh yeah, there was one of those in the motor pool. I wondered what they were for."

"And there was one in the communications room, too. Remember Hank?" Laurie asked.

Stewart had a look also, and when he did, he frowned deeply. He got out of the Humvee and walked to the keypad. He typed in the sequence again but this time he didn't move, which seemed odd to the others.

When nothing happened, the door remaining closed, he typed the code in yet again, then one more time. Taking a step back, he put his hands on his hips and gazed up at the digital display.

He recognized the numbers and what they meant easily now, for with the display and the door not opening, it all made sense to him.

He could feel the others' eyes staring at his back, and with his head held low, he turned around to face them, raising his head to make eye contact with his comrades. Hank was easy to see, as he was perched behind the M-60, and Carl and Laurie could be seen thanks to the dome light of the Humvee, the door still open.

"Guys," Stewart said, his voice filled with trepidation. "We're not going anywhere. We're trapped in here for the next hundred years."

At first, no one said a word, each trying to take in what Stewart had said and knowing deep down he was telling the truth.

Carl leaned his head out the driver's window and said, "No way, that's bullshit. What the fuck are you talking about?"

Stewart walked over to the Humvee and sat on the frame inside the open door. He was perfectly relaxed. And why wouldn't he be? No one was getting into the bunker, they were perfectly safe. But nor were they getting out.

"Okay, well the way I figure it, and keep in mind this is all conjecture on my part, is that when this complex was set up, it was for government personnel and their families to come to when World War 3 began. The plan was probably for them to hole up here until the radiation level was safe enough for them to venture back outside and start to rebuild the country. The scientists probably expected the war to be much worse than the one we experienced two years ago and so they set this place up with a timer on the only exit and programmed it for a hundred years. Until then, this door won't open. Think of it like a bank vault on a timer."

"So according to you, we're stuck here for a hundred years?" Hank said, amazed.

Stewart nodded. "Yes, somehow when we entered here we must have triggered the countdown. But there is a rather morbid bright side to all of this."

"And that is?" Hank asked.

"Well, from our last check we have a couple days worth of food left and that's if we mostly live on water. So we'll be dead long before we have to worry about being trapped in here long term."

"Shit, Stewart, you're a ray of sunshine, aren't you," Carl spit.

"Don't blame the messenger, Carl, I'm in the same boat you are," Stewart rebutted.

"Wait, why don't we blow the door open?" Carl suggested. "We've got a shitload of grenades. Hell we could even use the LAWS."

"No way, Carl," Hank said. "I'll give you two reasons. "The first is after the C-4 did nothing when we tried it outside, I doubt some grenades or LAWS will do much better in here. And the second is we might end up caving the whole damn tunnel on our heads."

"Shit, yeah, that's a good point. I didn't think of that," Carl said, dejected.

Everyone was silent for a few minutes as they tried to take it all in, but finally Hank slapped the roof of the Humvee and said, "Okay, Carl, take us back down to the motor pool. There's no reason for us to keep sitting here. Once we're there, we can try to come up with some way of getting out of here. There's got to be an escape hatch, air vent or something we can use to escape this place."

"Okay, that's not a bad idea," Carl said.

Stewart got in and he spun the Humvee around and began to drive back down the ramp. Hank dropped into a seat as there was no reason to stay with the M-60.

"You really think we're trapped in here?" Laurie asked Hank, the concern on her face apparent.

Hank took her hand and squeezed it. "Hey, relax, it'll be fine, you'll see. We've gotten out of worse scrapes than this before."

She smiled wanly, hoping he was right, though deep down she wasn't so sure.

The next day was spent trying to find another way out of the bunker, anything from some kind of emergency shaft to some back door not on any schematic. They came up empty every time. Any airshafts were not shafts so much as large pipes that ran deep into the ground. From there who knows where they went. And the pipes were far too small for anyone to be able to fit inside them. The bunker was entirely self-contained, with air that was scrubbed of carbon dioxide and then re-circulated. The same went for the water, which any grey water was purified and then sent back into the fresh water supply.

It was always possible there was still a way out, but after two days with the bare minimum of food, though plenty of water, they were already becoming weaker. Even with all the water they could drink, sooner or later their bodies would begin to waste away.

By the third day, with all their food supplies gone but a few crumbs and only living on water, it became even worse and tempers began to flare as everyone grew agitated over their situation. Stewart had been passing out vitamins and stimulants but it did little to help their moods or give them added energy.

Ever so slowly, the four warriors were coming to the realization that they may just end up starving to death in the bunker, the massive complex becoming nothing more than a glorified tomb for their bodies that would probably never be opened again.

It was a chilling thought. On the fourth day, Carl, Hank and Laurie were too tired to do much more than lay on their chosen beds in the sleeping quarters and sleep all the time. Only Stewart wasn't around. None of the others knew where he went but for hours at a time he would disappear. Frankly, none of them cared, each lost in their own thoughts about their mortality.

On the fifth day—which was the second day without actual solid food—with all of them barely able to stay awake as their bodies grew weak, Stewart called a meeting on level three, in one of the research labs.

Everyone stumbled into the large lab room that Stewart led them to after rousing them from their sleep.

"What's the reason for us being here, Stewart?" Hank asked. "I just want to go to sleep."

"Yeah, me too," Carl said and Laurie simply nodded. She was leaning against Hank with her eyes partially closed. All their stomachs were full of water but they were still weak.

"Please follow me in here. I think I found a solution to our very serious problem," Stewart said and led the other three into another room that was huge. Hank's eyes went wide as did the others as they took in the giant room. Half the size of an aircraft hanger, both sides of it were lined with circular chambers that resembled tanning beds. Hank remembered what Stewart had said about what he'd found when they first arrived and knew right off what they were for.

"These are the hibernation chambers you told us about," Hank said. For as far as the eye could see, each chamber had a panel on its front, small lights blinking on and off. He walked over to the closest one and laid a hand on it. The metal felt cool to the touch.

"Why are we here, Stewart?" Carl demanded in a weary tone. "What's this all about?"

Stewart went to the chamber Hank was touching and opened it, the hiss of hydraulics filling the air as the door popped open. Inside it was a smooth surface, with the exception of the bottom, which had a thin white mattress pad. Hank guessed it was for someone to lay on. The chamber was also slanted slightly so a person wasn't totally horizontal when laying in it. The more Hank looked at all the chambers, the more he thought he'd walked into a science fiction movie.

"We're here," Stewart said, "because since I found out we're trapped in this bunker with no food, I decided while you guys tried to find a way out, I would concentrate on one more closer to home."

Hank's face twisted up in annoyance. "Speak English, Stewart, I swear, you talk more like a damn scientist every day."

"The hibernation chambers, Hank. The *chambers*. We can go into them and sleep until the bunker door opens again."

"What? Are you fucking insane?" Carl yelled. "That's in a hundred goddamn years!"

"No, all of you listen to me, please. I've been studying the manual to these things, and they're basically automated. There's only a few instructions to input into the master computer, such as the weight of the person in each chamber, and I've already done it. I've assigned these four chambers to us. All we have to do is get inside and close the door. As soon the locking mechanism is engaged, the stasis process will begin. We'll sleep for a hundred years, and when we wake up, the timer on the complex door will have counted down and the lock will have disengaged. Then we can leave here."

Hank went to a swiveling chair on wheels before a desk and sat down. It was a lot to take in on top of everything else. Deep inside, he'd begun making his peace that he was going to die down here and his only regret was that Laurie was going to die, too. But they both agreed though it sucked, at least they were together. But now… a chance to live. There really wasn't much to think about.

"Fine, let's do it, let's get into those damn things," Hank said.

"What?" Carl yelled, waving his hands in the air. "Am I the only sane one around here? I think lack of food is making you all nuts. We don't know anything about these things. For all we know, we'll only be unconscious and then waste away in them till we're dead."

"Is that any worse than what's going to happen to us soon?" Laurie asked as she walked over and sat on Hank's lap. "I agree with Hank, at least this way we have a chance to live."

"Oh what a shock, the two lovers are on the same side of the argument. What a surprise." Carl crossed his arms over his chest and frowned. "No, it's fucking crazy, I won't do it."

"Then you'll be all alone here for the time you have left, I'm afraid, Carl," Stewart said. "Because it looks like the three of us are going for the long sleep."

Carl pouted as he looked at each of his comrades' faces, then the hibernation chambers with their blinking lights and sci-fi look. No one said a word, knowing Carl needed to make his own decision, but finally Carl's shoulders sagged and he dropped his head. "Fine, I'm with you guys."

"So when do we do this?" Hank asked.

"No time like the present, Hank," Stewart said.

"But our weapons are back in the sleeping quarters, we should go get them," Hank said as he stood up.

Stewart waved his hand before him, dismissing the idea. "Why, Hank? If this complex is breached while we sleep, our guns aren't going to do us much good. I'm afraid we'd be sitting targets. Leave them where they are. They'll be there when we wake up."

"You mean *if* we wake up," Carl said, defiant to the end.

"Yes, well, I suppose there is that," Stewart contested, not wanting to argue any more about it.

"Okay, then just give me a second," Carl said and hobbled out of the room. "I'll be right back," he called over his shoulder.

The others talked some more and Stewart pointed out this and that of interest about the chambers, and a few minutes later, Carl returned.

"Where'd you go?" Hank asked.

"To take a piss. All this damn water I've been drinking, I have to piss every ten minutes. I figure if I gotta go, I better do it now as it's gonna be a long time before I can go to the bathroom again."

"Huh, good point," Hank agreed, but both he and Laurie had gone before the meeting so they were all set.

Stewart gently took Carl's arm and led him over to one of the chambers he'd gotten ready earlier just for him. "Here, Carl, why don't you go first as you're being the most difficult. Don't be scared. From everything I've read it's perfectly safe."

Carl let himself be lead though he was becoming more hesitant again. "Wait, I have questions. Do you think I'll dream?"

Stewart shook his head. "Sorry, I have no idea on that one. Let's hope we do. I know I do."

Carl was placed in the chamber and his eyes were wide, like a cornered animal. Hank and Laurie walked over and stood before him. Hank shook Carl's hand. "Don't worry, buddy, you'll be fine, and we'll all be right behind you."

"You better, Hank, I swear, this better not be some kind of elaborate practical joke."

Hank grinned. "If only that were true."

"Goodnight, Carl," Stewart said and pressed a button to close the chamber. As the door closed, Stewart said, "When the gas starts to fill the chamber just breath deeply. Count to ten while you do this. And get comfortable quickly. If you put your hands on your chest, that's where they're going to be for a hundred years."

Carl nodded, too scared to talk now as the chamber door sealed with a hiss. There was a small window where Carl's face was, and as his pupils darted back and fourth, the gas was released and within seconds his eyelids slowly closed and he was still. Stewart checked a few dials and was pleased with the result.

"There, he's sleeping like a baby," Stewart said. "He's in perfect stasis. All right, you two are next and I'll be last."

"Okay, just give us a second," Hank said.

"Of course, take what time you need." Stewart turned his attention to Carl's chamber and studied the panel which monitored everything from Carl's slowed heartbeat to his blood pressure. The body was slowed to the point that the heart only beat once every ten minutes — a miracle of modern science. Stewart didn't bother telling the others all this as it wouldn't have helped him convince them to use the chambers.

"Are you sure about this?" Laurie asked Hank as they stood a few feet from Stewart to talk privately.

He pulled her close and kissed her softly. "No, I'm not sure, but what choice do we have? Stewart's right, this is our only chance at survival."

"I wish we could sleep together. I'd like that. A hundred years with you beside me would be heaven," she said and nuzzled his chin with her nose. He kissed her forehead and cradled her face in his large hands. Her skin was so soft, like the rest of her. "Yeah, I'd like that, too." They hugged each other and Hank didn't want to let her go but one glance at Stewart's face told him it was time. The older man had a point about just doing this and getting it over with. Like tearing off a band aid, the quicker it began the quicker it was over. Hank walked Laurie to the chamber Stewart pointed to and Laurie climbed in.

"See you on the other side," she said with a wan smile.

"You bet," Hank said as the chamber closed. He watched her face as the gas began to fill the chamber. Her eyes darted back and forth like Carl's had and then her gaze locked on him. "I love you," she mouthed before her eyelids closed and she was still. She looked so peaceful, like Sleeping Beauty, and he longed to kiss her one more time.

Hank touched the glass over her face, "I love you too, baby."

"Next," Stewart said and Hank went to the chamber beside Laurie's.

"You know, Stewart, if this doesn't work, I swear I'll kill you," Hank joked though there was a touch of menace to his voice. He stepped into the chamber.

"Duly noted, Hank. Okay, you know what to do. As soon as you're all set, I'll be right behind you in my own chamber. I set up mine so I can press the button to close my chamber door and there's a slight delay so I can get inside."

Hank nodded that he understood. He was doing his best to stay strong but he was becoming nervous despite his iron will.

"See you soon," Stewart said with a smile and closed the chamber door. Hank didn't reply; there was no need. The door sealed with a hiss and gas began to fill the chamber. Hank breathed in deeply and immediately began feeling sleepy. His last waking thoughts were of Laurie. Stewart made sure the chamber was functioning properly before going to his own chamber. He paused to take off his shirt, then draped it over a chair. He was still wearing a t-shirt with his pants and decided to leave them on, despite the fact he disliked sleeping with his clothes on; he figured hibernation would be no different. He did slide off his boots and he placed them on the floor before his chamber. He left his socks on; he didn't want his feet getting cold during the long sleep.

Stewart pressed the button to close the chamber, then went around and climbed in, the door closing a little faster than he'd thought but it was still enough time to let him get in. As the door sealed with the hiss he'd already grown accustom to, the gas filled his chamber and with a slight smile on his face as to his ingenuity, he drifted off to sleep.

The lights on the chamber blinked diligently on the chambers as the four warriors of the apocalypse slept. With no motion detected in the complex, the lights began to turn off, one level at a time, one room at a time.

Soon, the entire bunker was in total darkness, and if there had been anyone there to listen, only the soft sounds of the automated heating and air conditioning systems could be detected.

Like the four hibernating humans within its walls, the bunker slept once more.

ZOMBIES, MONSTERS, CREATURES OF THE NIGHT

OPEN CASKET PRESS

OPEN CASKET PRESS.COM

THE NEW NAME IN HORROR

UNDEAD PRESS

UNDEADPRESS.COM

CLAN OF THE BIGFOOT
ANTHONY GIANGREGORIO

www.ingramcontent.com/pod-product-compliance
Lightning Source LLC
Chambersburg PA
CBHW060945120726

47910CB00002B/494